THE
MOST
Dangerous
THING

THE
MOST
Dangerous
THING

Laura Lippman

wm

WILLIAM MORROW
An Imprint of HarperCollins*Publishers*

This book is a work of fiction. References to real people, events, establishments, organizations, or locales are intended only to provide a sense of authenticity, and are used fictitiously. All other characters, and all incidents and dialogue, are drawn from the author's imagination and are not to be construed as real.

HarperCollins books may be purchased for educational, business, or sales promotional use. For information please write: Special Markets Department, HarperCollins Publishers, 10 East 53rd Street, New York, NY 10022.

FIRST EDITION

Designed by Jamie Lynn Kerner

Library of Congress Cataloging-in-Publication Data has been applied for.

ISBN 978-0-06-170651-6

11 12 13 14 15   OV/RRD   10 9 8 7 6 5 4 3 2 1

For Georgia Rae Simon

Alas for maiden, alas for Judge,
For rich repiner and household drudge!
God pity them both! and pity us all,
Who vainly the dreams of youth recall.

—JOHN GREENLEAF WHITTIER, "MAUD MULLER"

GO-GO

They throw him out when he falls off the barstool. Although it wasn't a fall, exactly, he only stumbled a bit coming back from the bathroom and lurched against the bar, yet they said he had to leave because he was drunk. He finds that hilarious. He's too drunk to be in a bar. He makes a joke about a fall from grace. At least, he thinks he does. Maybe the joke was one of those things that stays in his head, for his personal amusement. For a long time, for fucking forever, Gordon's mind has been split by a thick, dark line, a line that divides and defines his life as well. What stays in, what is allowed out. But when he drinks, the line gets a little fuzzy.

Which might be why he drinks. Drank. Drinks. No, drank. He's done. Again. One night, one slip. He didn't even enjoy it that much.

"You driving?" the bartender asks, piloting him to the door, his arm firm yet kind around Gordon's waist.

"No, I live nearby," he says. One lie, one truth. He does live in the area, but not so near that he hasn't driven here in his father's old Buick, good old Shitty Shitty Bang Bang they called it. Well, not this Buick, but the Buick before, or the Buick before that. The old man always drove Buicks, and they were always, always, crap cars, but he kept buying them. That was Timothy Halloran Sr., loyal to the end, even to the crap of the crap of the crap.

Gordon stumbles and the bartender keeps him steady. He realizes he doesn't want the bartender to let go of him. The contact feels good. Shit, did he say *that* out loud? He's not a faggot. "I'm not a faggot," he says. It's just been so long since his wife slipped her hand into the crook of his elbow, so long since his daughters put their sticky little hands around his neck and whispered their sticky little words into his ears, the list of the things they wanted that Mommy wouldn't let them have, but maybe Daddy would see it differently? The bartender's embrace ends abruptly, now that Gordon is out the door. "I love you, man!" he says, for a joke. Only maybe he didn't. Or maybe it isn't funny. At any rate, no one's laughing and Gordon "Go-Go" Halloran always leaves 'em laughing.

He sits on the curb. He really did intend to go to a meeting tonight. It all came down to one turn. If he had gone left—but instead he went straight. Ha! He literally went straight and look where that had gotten him.

It isn't his fault. He wants to be sober. He strung together two years this time, chastened by the incident at his younger daughter's first birthday party. And he managed to stay sober even after Lori kicked him out last month. But the fact is, he has been faking it for months, stalling out where he always stalls out on the twelve steps, undermined by all that poking, poking, poking, that insistence on truth, on coming clean. Making *amends*. Sobriety—real sobriety, as opposed to the collection of sober days Gordon sometimes manages to put together—wants too much from him. Sobriety is trying to breach the line in his head. But Gordon needs that division. Take it away and he'll fall apart, sausage with no casing, crumbling into the frying pan.

Sausage. He'd like some sausage. Is there still an IHOP up on Route 40?

Saturday morning. Sausage and pancakes, his mother never sitting down as she kept flipping and frying, frying and flipping, loving how they all ate, Gordon and his brothers and his father, stoking them like machines. Come Saturday morning, I'm going away. Hey, hey, hey, it's Fat Albert!

When he moved back home six weeks ago, he asked his mother to make him some pancakes and she'd said, "Bisquick's in the cabinet." She thought he was drinking or whoring again, assumed that was why Lori had thrown him out. It was easier to let her think that. Then it turned out it was easier to *be* that, to surrender to drink and bad habits.

When it comes down to it, drunk and sober are just two sides of the same coin, and no matter how you flip it, you are still your fucked-up own self. It sure didn't help that his current AA group meets in his old parish school, now a Korean church. It's too weird, sitting on the metal chairs in an old classroom. Drink and the line gets fuzzy. Get sober and the line comes back into sharp relief, but then everyone starts attacking the line, says he has to let it go, break it down. *Take down the line, Mr. Gorbachev.* Boy, he's all over the place tonight, tripping down memory lane in every sense of the word. Funny, he has a nice memory associated with Reagan, but it feels like he was really young at the time. How old was he when Reagan made that Berlin Wall speech? Sixteen? Seventeen? Still in high school and already a fuck-up.

But to hear everyone tell it, he has always been a fuck-up, came into the world a fuck-up, is going to leave as a fuck-up. Then again, whoever followed Sean was destined to be a disappointment. Sean-the-Perfect. You would think that with three kids in the family, the two imperfect brothers would find a bond, gang up on that prissy middle fuck. But Tim has always taken Sean's side. Everyone gangs up against Go-Go, the nickname Gordon can't quite shake even at age forty. *Go, Go-Go. Go, Go-Go. Go, Go-Go.* That's what the others had chanted when he did his dance, a wild, spastic thing, steel guitar twanging. *Go, Go-Go. Go, Go-Go. Go, Go-Go. GoGoGoGoGoGo.*

Give Sean this: He's the one person who consistently uses Go-Go's full name. Gordon, not even Gordy. Maybe that's because he needs two full syllables to cram all the disappointment in. Actually, he needs four. "Jesus, Gordon, how many times can you move back home?" Or: "Jesus, Gordon, Lori is the best thing that ever happened to you and you've got kids now." Jesus, Gordon. Jesus, Gordon. Maybe he should have been Gee-Go instead of Go-Go.

He thinks about standing up but doesn't, although he could if he wanted to. He isn't that drunk. The beer and the shot hit him fast, after almost two years of sobriety. He was doing so good. He thought he had figured out a way to be in AA while respecting the line. They don't need to know *everything,* he reasoned. No one needs to know everything. There would be a way to tell the story that would allow him to make it through all twelve steps, finally, without breaching any loyalties, without breaking that long-ago promise, without hurting anyone.

He gets up, walks down the once-familiar avenue. As kids, they had been forbidden to ride their bikes on the busy street that essentially bounded their neighborhood, which should have made it impossible to find their way to this little business district, tempting to them because of its pizza parlor and the bakery and the High's Dairy Store. And there was a craft store with an unlikely name, a place owned by the family whose daughters had disappeared. He was little then, not even five, but he remembered a chill had gone through the neighborhood for a while, that all the parents had become strict and supervigilant.

Then they stopped. It was too hard, he guesses, being in their kids' shit all the time and the children slipped back into their free, unfettered ways. Nowadays . . . he doesn't even have the energy to finish the cliché in his head. He thinks of Lori, standing guard at the kitchen window of their "starter" home, a town house that cost $350,000 and to which he is now barred entry. Is that fair? Is anything fair? Sean is still perfect and even Tim does a good imitation of goodness, Mr. State's Attorney, with his three beautiful daughters and his plumpish wife, who was never that hot to begin with, yet Gordon can tell they still genuinely like each other. He's not sure he ever really liked Lori and he has a hunch Sean's in the same boat with his wife, Vivian, who's as frostily perfect as Sean. Tim and Sean, still married to their first wives, such good boys, forever and ever. Hey, he got an annulment, he's technically in the clear. Besides, fuck the church! Where was the church when he needed it? And now it's Korean Catholic, whatever the fuck that is, probably Kool-Aid and dog on a cracker for communion.

Where was he? Where is he? On Gwynn Oak Avenue, thinking about how Sean, of all people, had figured out that if they rolled their bikes across the bridge to Purnell Drive, they could technically obey the rule never to ride their bikes on Forest Park Avenue and still manage to get over to Woodlawn, where the shops are. Or was it Mickey who had figured it out? Mickey was the one who lived above Purnell Drive, after all. She would have known the route, too. Even when they were kids, Mickey had been smart that way. She should have become the lawyer, not Tim. She was the real brains.

He walks for ten, twenty, thirty minutes, willing his head to clear. He walks down to the stream, where there once were swans and ducks, then to the public park, the site of an amusement park that closed before Go-Go was old enough to go there. It survived integration, his father always said, but it couldn't beat back Hurricane Agnes. Still, one roller coaster remained standing for years, long enough for Go-Go to feel thwarted, denied. Sean and Tim claimed to have gone many, many times, but they weren't that much older. Sean would have been seven or eight when the park closed. Maybe they had lied? It makes Gordon feel better, catching perfect Sean in a potential lie.

Soon enough, the hypothetical becomes real to him, and he has worked up a nice fury. He gets out his cell phone and punches his brother's name on his contact list, ready to fight with him. But his hands aren't steady and he fumbles the phone as Sean's voice comes on, cool and reserved. The phone ends up on the ground, where the black turtle shape is hard to find in the dark. As Go-Go crawls around on his hands and knees, he hears Sean's voice, disgust evident. "Gordon? Gordon? Jesus, Gordon—"

I shoulda been Gee-Go. Does he say that out loud? His hand closes over the cell phone, but Sean has hung up. Okay, it isn't exactly the first time he has drunk-dialed his brother. But he's had a good run of sobriety, so Sean shouldn't have been all pissy and judgmental. Sean has no way of knowing he took a drink. No, Sean expects him to fail. That's unfair. And what kind of brother is that, anyway, expecting—rooting—for his younger sibling to fail? But that's Sean's dirty little secret. His perfection is relative, dependent upon the fuck-ups of Go-Go and Tim, and Tim isn't giving him much breathing room these days. In another family, Sean wouldn't even be all that. In another family, Sean might be the problem child, the loser. Especially if he had been treated like a loser from jump, the way Gordon was. They set him up. Of course he did whatever he was asked. He was just a little boy. Any little boy would have done what he did. Right?

His head clearer, he walks to the convenience store, buys a cup of scorched coffee, and drinks it in his car, his father's old Buick, the last iteration of Shitty Shitty Bang Bang, which has survived his father by almost fifteen years now. He is less than two miles from his mother's house. He has to make exactly four turns—two lefts, two rights. There are—he counts—one, two, three lights? The first one is there, right in front of him, complicated because there are actually five points at this intersection—five points, like a star. He sees Mickey making the drawing in the dirt, the stick slashing down and up, across and down, then up.

He makes it through, heads up the long steep hill. *I think I can I think I can I think I can.* Past the cemetery, through the second light. Almost home. Almost home. Only it isn't his home.

At the next light, he turns right instead of left. *Go, Go-Go, Go, Go-Go. Go, Go-Go.* Climbs the freeway entrance ramp just before the Strawberry Hill apartments. Mickey's family had moved here right before high school and Mickey's mother was hot. Sean and Tim swore they saw her sunbathing topless once, but they probably lied about that, too. Roller coasters, topless girls—they lied about everything.

Gordon heads west on the highway, then makes a U-turn before the Beltway cloverleaf, aiming his car back home along the infamous highway that ends, stops dead. As teenagers, they treated this two-mile stretch as their own little drag strip, but now the secret is out and others race here. He wonders how fast his father's old Buick can go. Ninety, one hundred? *Go, Go-Go. Go, Go-Go. Go-Go.* The steel guitar twangs in his ears, in his memory, sharp and awful. Guy could not play for shit, much as he loved that damn stupid guitar. *Go, Go-Go. Go, Go-Go. Go, Go-Go.* He is dancing, wild and free, his little arms moving so quickly it's almost like he's lashing himself, self-flagellation, and everyone loves him and everyone is laughing and everyone loves him and everyone is laughing and he is splashing through the stream, heedless of the poisonous water, no matter what Gwen's father says about tetanus and lockjaw, desperate to get away, to escape what he's done. *Go, Go-Go. Go, Go-Go.*

By the time he hits the Jersey wall, even the needle on the old Buick's speedometer has abandoned him.

US

CHAPTER ONE

*Clement Robison's house is wildly impractical for almost anyone, but espe-*cially so for an eighty-eight-year-old man living alone, even if he happens to be the one who designed it. Forty years ago, when Clem began the drawings for his dream house, he could not imagine being eighty-eight. Who can? Eighty-eight is hard to imagine even at eighty-seven. His youngest daughter, now forty-five, summoned home—or so she's telling everyone—by her father's accident, doesn't really believe she'll ever be as old as he is. Oh, she expects, hopes, to enjoy the genetic advantage of his longevity. But the number itself, eighty-eight, is like some monstrous old coat discovered in the hall closet, scratchy and smelling of mothballs. *Who left this here? Is this yours? Not mine! I've never seen it before.*

The Robison house was modern once and people still describe

it that way, although its appliances and fixtures are frozen like the clocks in a fairy tale, set circa 1985, the last remodel. A mix of milled stone, lumber and glass, it nestles into the side of the hill on a stone base, a door leading into the aboveground basement, but the family custom was to use that door only in the most inclement weather, and Clem is not one to break long-standing habits. He has continued to mount the long stone staircase, which creates the illusion that one is climbing a natural path up the hillside. The steps are charming, but there is something off about them. Too low or too high, they fool the foot, and over the years almost everyone in the family has taken a tumble or near-tumble down. Gwen's turn came when she was thirteen, rushing outside and neglecting to consider that the sheen on the steps might be ice, not mere moisture. She traveled the entire flight on her butt, boom, boom, boom, her friends laughing at the bottom. At thirteen, the end result was a bruised coccyx and ego, nothing more.

Her father, coming outside to get the paper on a cool but dry March morning, missed a step, tumbled almost to the street and broke his left hip.

"Do you know how many people die within a year of breaking a hip?" Gwen asks her father, still in University Hospital.

"Gwen, I taught geriatric medicine for years. I think I'm up on the facts. *Most* people don't die."

"But a lot do. Almost a third."

"Still, most don't. And I'm in good health otherwise. I just have to be disciplined about recovery and therapy."

"Miller and Fee want you to sell the house, move into assisted living."

"*That* again. And you?"

"I'm holding them off. For now. I told them I would assess your situation."

They smile at each other, coconspirators. Gwen believes herself to be her father's favorite, although he would never say

such a thing. His denials are sincere when her much older siblings, Miller and Fiona, bring up the contentious matter. "I was
just more available when Gwen was little," their father says. "Less
career obsessed." "Daddy doesn't have favorites," Gwen says. But
she knows the seven-year gap between Fiona and Gwen is not
enough to explain their father's clear preference for her. There
is her remarkable resemblance to their mother, dead for almost
twenty-five years. And there is the bond of the house and the
neighborhood, Dickeyville, which Gwen and her father love more
fiercely than anyone else in the family. As a child, she used to take
long walks with him in the hills behind the house, never letting on
that she traveled farther and deeper into them when she was with
her friends. Miller and Fee, living thousands of miles away, have
been trying to get their father out of the house for years, decades,
ever since their mother's death. Gwen, who remains in Baltimore,
has done whatever she can to allow her father to stay in the family
home. Should the day come that he really can't live there, it has
always been their unspoken understanding that Gwen will take
over the house for her own family.

"How are things at home?" her father asks.

It's an open question, applicable to the physical status of her
house and a much larger, if vaguer problem. Gwen chooses to address the physical.

"Not great. The county came out and pushed the ruins of the
retaining wall back on our property, but says it's our job to rebuild
it. And even when we do, it won't necessarily address our foundation issues. The ground could shift again."

"Why—never mind."

"Why did we buy out there when our inspector warned us of
this very problem? I ask myself that every day. For me, I think it
was because Relay reminded me of Dickeyville. Isolated, yet not. A
little slice of country so close to the city, the idiosyncratic houses.
And for Karl, it was all about convenience—the commuter train

station within walking distance, BWI and Amtrak ten minutes away. Go figure—for once, my dreamy nostalgia and his pragmatism aligned and the result is utter disaster. There's probably a lesson to be learned there."

"The lesson," her father says, "is that you have a five-year-old daughter."

"Don't worry," Gwen says, pretending not to understand. "We've figured out how to make it work once you come home. I'm going to get up at six A.M. and drive over there, do the breakfast and getting-her-off-to-school thing. And I'll reverse it at day's end, be there for dinner and bedtime. But I'm going to spend the nights at your house, so we don't have to have a nighttime aide."

"Gwen, I can easily afford—"

"It's not about affording. And it's just for a few weeks. Anyone can tolerate anything for a few weeks." Months, years, her mind amends. It is amazing what one can tolerate, what she has tolerated. "Also, it's not the worst thing in the world, making Karl curtail his travel, to learn that he's part of a household, not a guest star who jets in and out as it suits him."

"He is who he is, Gwen. You went into this with eyes wide open. I told you all about cardiac surgeons. And Karl was already a star. It's not like this sneaked up on you. Not like the chicken."

"What?"

"The chicken. That's why I fell. There was a chicken on the steps, trying to peck at my ankles, and all I wanted to do was avoid stepping on it. I twisted my ankle and went over."

Gwen tries not to show how alarming she finds this. *A chicken?* There haven't been chickens in their neighborhood, ever. Except for—but those birds were far away and far in the past. No, that couldn't be. Her father must have imagined the chicken. But if her father was imagining chickens, what else was breaking down inside his mind? She would almost prefer there was a chicken. Maybe there was. The past few years have seen a flurry of stories about animals showing up in places where they shouldn't be—wildcats in suburbs, a deer crashing through the window of a dental practice, and, come to think of it, a chicken in one of the New York boroughs. And Dickeyville is the kind of place that has always attracted crunchy granola types. It is easy to imagine some earnest, incompetent locavore trying to raise chickens only to have them escape from his ineptly constructed coop. Gwen will ask around when she goes by the house this afternoon, to begin preparing for her father's return.

The Robison house is isolated, even by Dickeyville's standards, which in turn feels cut off from much of Baltimore. It is officially the last house on Wetheredsville Road, only a few feet from where the Jersey wall now blocks the street, marking the start of a "nature trail" that one can follow all the way to downtown. The blocked street means Gwen can't use the old shortcut, through what is properly called a park, but which she and her childhood friends always referred to as the woods. Their term was more accurate. Leakin Park is a forest, vast and dense, difficult to navigate. Gwen and her friends covered more of it than almost anyone, and even they missed large swaths.

Traffic is surprisingly heavy, the journey longer than antici-pated, giving the lie to her blithe words about dashing back and forth between here and the house in Relay. Still, the chance to move to Dickeyville, even temporarily, is providential. Maryland law requires a separation of at least one year to file for an uncon-tested divorce. She learned this during her first divorce, a sad bit of knowledge she had never planned to use again. Does anyone plan to divorce twice? Then again, after that first failed marriage, the fact is always there, incontrovertible. You're not going to go the distance with one person, your chance at perfection is lost.

For someone like Gwen, who is professionally perfect—she edits a city magazine that instructs others how to have the perfect house, children, wardrobe—this is particularly irksome.

Yet even if she can manage to extend her time in her father's house for a year, it won't be enough. It is the spouse who *stays* who can file after one year, on the grounds of abandonment. As the spouse who is leaving, Gwen will have to wait two years if Karl doesn't agree, and he has made it clear that he won't, ever. She can't spend that much time away from Annabelle, but nor can she afford her own place in their current school district. They aren't upside down in their mortgage, but they have virtually no equity, and home equity loans are hard to get now, anyway. Karl has lots of money, but, again, he isn't going to use it to let her leave him. And if she spends even a single night back in the Relay house, the clock resets on the separation. Maybe Annabelle will move into the Dickeyville house and they can keep this information from the school?

But the Dickeyville house will be chaotic, once her father returns. A geriatric specialist should have designed a home that would be friendlier to old age, but his house is downright hostile to the idea. There is the first level, the stonewalled basement, with the laundry room and various systems. Then the large glass-and-timber first floor, built to take advantage of the site, but with only a powder room. Yet the top two floors, with its full baths, have narrow halls and tight corners. Their father, appalled at the spiraling costs and delays, skimped on his dream house's bedrooms. She will have to set him up in the first-floor "great room," where he will have nice views and space in which to move, if no bath. But then her father will dominate the first floor, and privacy will be found only in the cramped, dark bedrooms above. And how will he bathe? Besides, Annabelle would be lonely, as Gwen once was, and she won't even have the freedom to roam the woods. What was considered safe in Gwen's childhood is unthinkable for Annabelle's.

Her head hurts. It's all too complicated. *Dial it back,* as she tells her writers when they are in over their heads on a story. Concentrate on one thing, one task. Get to the house, make sure it's clean, do laundry, call a nursing service, let the nursing service figure out the best place for her father to convalesce.

Once there, she finds three newspapers in yellow wrappers, several catalogs, but almost no real mail. Her father doesn't recycle—on principle, he believes it's a ruse, an empty, feel-good gesture—so she tosses everything, leaving only the bills on the kitchen counter. The kitchen is small, another victim of the house's cost overruns, but her mother made it a marvel of efficiency. The light at this time of the day, year, is breathtaking, gold and rose streaks above the hill. Even with the old appliances, the yellowing Formica counters and white metal cabinets, it is a warm, welcoming room.

Gwen goes upstairs. Everything is in order, there is no evidence of a man in decline. Widowed at sixty-three, her father quickly learned to take excellent care of himself. His closet and drawers are neater than Gwen's, there is an admirable lack of clutter. A single page from the *Times,* dated the day before his fall, is on his nightstand—the Wednesday crossword puzzle, filled out in ink, without a single error. The puzzle, the tidy house, it all indicates he's of sound mind and should back up his version of events. So why does she keep thinking of it that way, as a *version*? She's still troubled about that chicken.

Glancing out the narrow casement window toward the street, Gwen sees a black-haired man walking two dogs as black as his hair. She knows him instantly by the part in his hair, impossibly straight and perfect, visible even from this distance.

"Sean," Gwen calls out through the window. Seconds later,

she is running heedlessly down the stone steps that undid her father.

"Gwennie," he says. Then: "I'm sorry. Old habits. *Gwen.*"

"What are you doing here?"

"Well—my brother, of course."

"Tim? Or Go-Go?"

"Gordon," he says. Perhaps Sean has sworn off nicknames. Funny, Gwen liked hearing Gwennie, even if it always carries the reminder that she was once fat. Gwennie the Whale. She was only fat until age thirteen. They say people are forever fat inside, but Gwen's not. Inside, she's the sylph she became. If anything, she has trouble remembering that she's growing older, that she can no longer rely on being the prettiest girl in the room.

"What's the incorrigible Go-Go—excuse me, *Gordon*—done now?"

Sean looks offended, then confused. "I'm sorry, I assumed you knew."

"My father fell three days ago, broke his hip. I don't know much of anything."

"Three days ago?"

"In the morning. Coming down the steps to fetch his paper."

"Three days ago—that's when Go-Go . . ." His voice catches. Sean is the middle brother, the handsomest, the smartest, the best all-around. Gwen's mother used to say that Tim was the practice son, Sean the platonic ideal, and Go-Go a bridge too far. Gwen's mother could be cutting in her observations, yet there was no real meanness in her. And her voice was so delicate, her manner so light, that no one took offense.

"What, Sean?"

"He crashed his car into the concrete barrier where the highway ends. Probably going eighty, ninety miles per hour. We think the accelerator got stuck, or he miscalculated where it ended. I mean, we've all played with our speedometers up there."

Yes, when they were teenagers, learning to drive. But Go-Go was—she calculates, subtracting four, no, five years from her age—forty, much too old to be testing his car's power.

"He's—"

"Dead, Gwen. At the scene, instantly."

"I'm so sorry, Sean."

Go-Go, dead. Although she has seen him periodically over the years, he remained forever eight or nine in her mind, wild and uninhibited. The risk taker in the group, although it was possible that Go-Go simply didn't understand the concept of danger, didn't know he was taking risks. She flashes back to an image of him on this very street, dashing across the road in pursuit of a ball, indifferent to the large truck bearing down on him, the others screaming for him to stop.

"Thank you."

"How's your mom holding up?" She remembers that Mr. Halloran died years ago, although she didn't go to the funeral, just wrote proper notes to the boys and their mother. It was a busy time in her life, as she recalls.

"Not well. I came home for the funeral—I live in St. Petersburg now."

"Russia?"

A tight smile. "Florida."

Gwen tries not to make a face. Not because of Florida, but because the Sean she remembers would have been in Russia, a dashing foreign correspondent or diplomat. He's still pretty dashing. Close up, she can see a few flecks of white in his hair, but the very dignity that bordered on priggish in a teenage boy suits him now. He has finally grown into his gravitas.

"I feel awful that I didn't know. When is the funeral?"

"Tomorrow. Visitation is tonight."

Gwen calculates, even as she knows she must find a way to attend both. She will have to ask for another half day at work, make arrangements for Annabelle tonight. There is already so much to be done. But this is Go-Go—and Sean, her first boyfriend, even if she seldom thinks of him in that context. Gwen is not the kind of woman who thinks longingly of her past, who tracks down old boyfriends on the Internet. The Hallorans, along with Mickey Wyckoff, are more like the old foundations and footings they sometimes found in the woods, abandoned and overgrown, impossible to reclaim. They had been a tight-knit group of five for a summer or two, but it couldn't be sustained. Such coed groups didn't last long, probably. Funny, it has never occurred to Gwen until now that she and Mickey could disengage thoroughly from the group, but the Halloran brothers had to remain a set, mismatched as they were. Crass Tim, Serious Sean, Wild Go-Go.

"I'll be there." She considers placing a hand on Sean's forearm, but worries it will seem flirtatious. Instead, she strokes the dogs, who are old, with grizzled jowls and labored breathing, so ancient and tired that they don't object to this long interlude in the middle of their walk. Yet old as they obviously are, they can't be more than, what? Fifteen? Sixteen? Which is still older than her marriage to Karl.

"Mom will appreciate that," Sean says and heads back up the hill. She knows the route, knows the house at which he will arrive after going up Wetheredsville, then turning left on "New" Pickwick, a street of what once seemed like modern houses, small and symmetrical relative to the shambling antiquities for which Dickeyville was known, following it to the shortest street in the neighborhood, Sekots, just four houses. The Halloran house always smelled of strong foods—onions, cabbage, hamburger— and it was always a mess. Sometimes the chaos could be comforting; no child need worry about disturbing or breaking anything in such a household. It could be terrifying, too, though, a place where the adults yelled horrible things at one another and Mrs. Halloran was often heard sobbing, off in the distance. The boys never seemed to notice, and even Mickey was nonchalant about it. But the Halloran house scared Gwen, and she made sure their activities centered on her house or the woods beyond.

Go-Go, dead. The only surprise was that she was surprised at all.

Most thought he was called Go-Go because it was a bastardization of Gordon, but it really derived from his manic nature, evident from toddlerhood, his insistence on following his brothers wherever they went. "I go-go," he would say, as if the second syllable, the repetition, would clinch the argument. "I go-go." And he did. He ran into walls, splashed into the polluted waters of the stream, jumped from branches and balconies. Once Go-Go spent much of an afternoon running head-on into an old mattress they had found in the woods, laughing all the while.

Now he has run head-on into the barrier at the end of the highway. Gwen can't help wondering if he was drunk. Although she hasn't seen the Halloran boys for years, she knows, the way that everyone knows things in Dickeyville, that Go-Go has a problem. It is implied, if never stated outright, in the lost jobs, the broken first marriage, the rocky second one, the fact that he returns to the roost for open-ended stays.

Then again, who is she to judge Go-Go? Isn't she pulling the same trick, running home, a two-time loser in matrimony, taking comfort in a parent's unconditional love? Mr. Halloran may have been hard as nails, but Mrs. Halloran, when she wasn't screaming at her sons and wondering why they had been born, spoiled them to the best of her ability, especially Go-Go. And while most people will assume Gwen is nothing more than a devoted daughter, some will see through her. Her brother and sister, certainly. And Karl.

That is, Karl would see through her if it ever occurred to him to look, really look at her. But if Karl looked at her that way, they wouldn't be in this fix. At least that's how she likes to see it.

Summer 1976

Chapter Two

"I hate it here," Fee said. *"It's boring."*

"There's no place to go," Miller said. "There's nothing to do."

"Only boring people are bored," their father said.

"Or maybe only boring people don't realize how bored they are," Fee said. "They are so boring that it never occurs to them to do anything."

"Gwen likes it here," their father said.

"Well, *Gwen.*" Fee sniffed. "She's a child."

"Of course I'm a child," Gwen said mildly. "I'm ten."

"The thing is," Miller pressed on, intent on making his case, "there are plenty of kids for Gwen to play with—that Mickey girl, those brothers—"

"We do NOT play with the Halloran boys. They're too wild," Gwen put in.

Gwen spoke the truth, at the time. In the summer of our nation's bicentennial, the five of us were not friends yet and the Hallorans were considered wild. We were two and three—the two girls, Gwen and Mickey, the three brothers, Tim, Sean, and Go-Go. We would not come together as a group until the following spring. But we were all aware of each other. Mickey was a familiar little figure in Dickeyville, a terrifying tomboy assumed to be a loner by choice, a child who wanted to be outdoors no matter how fierce the weather. The Halloran boys were known as hellions, primarily because of Go-Go. Besides, in the summer, they went down to the ocean, then to camp.

And Gwen's family, the Robisons, were famous in Dickeyville because they had been trying to build their new house for almost seven years, stopped twice by injunction because of the neighborhood's historic status. Strangely, Dr. Robison did not resent the neighborhood's resistance to his house. This was his dream house and he would suffer anything to get it. He had bought the lot a decade earlier, around the time Gwen was born, after stumbling across Dickeyville while trying to get to the Forest Park golf course. First he had been told that the lot wasn't suitable for building, that its pitch would make it impossible. He refused to accept this and finally found an architect who said it could be done, although at great expense. Then the neighborhood had decided to fight it, although Dickeyville had its share of postwar nondescript houses. The Hallorans lived in one, in fact, but did not feel themselves hypocrites for joining the opposition. The Robison house— new, modern—signified *something*, even if no one was quite sure what. Change, hypocrisy, a challenge to traditional values. Yet nine years after the lot was purchased, five years after ground was broken, the house had asserted itself into being, through the sheer force of Dr. Robison's will.

This apparently came as something of a surprise to Mrs. Robison and the two older children, twenty-year-old Miller and seventeen-year-old Fee. And although Miller had to endure only summers there, and although Fee had only a year of high school left and she was continuing at Park, the same private school Gwennie attended, they were bitter. Mrs. Robison was not bitter, not exactly, but we all sensed *something* in her attitude. How to put it? There was a quality of withholding. In her beautiful, hippieish clothes, she moved through the world with her head down and arms crossed, as if to say to Dickeyville: *I will not love you, I will not.* Inevitably, all the fathers and even some of their sons were a little bit in love with Tally Robison, mistaking her coolness to her surroundings as a coolness toward them, which never fails to provoke a man. Gwen never doubted her mother's love, however, which was mildly infuriating to the rest of us, who sometimes wondered if our mothers were altogether pleased by our existence. Mickey's mom, the boys' mom—they tended toward moments of frustration. Doris Halloran, in particular, had a way of asking "Why were you born?" as if she didn't really know, or as if she was debating the church's doctrine on abortion. Not that abortion was legal even when the youngest of the Halloran boys, Go-Go, was conceived. But we still had the impression that Mrs. Halloran would have appreciated having a choice.

But we didn't care what the grown-ups thought, or even Gwennie's older brother and sister, impressive as they were, with their driver's licenses and studied indifference to us. In our imaginations, we lived in a world without grown-ups most of the day. We all had the same rules, more or less. Don't ride your bikes on Forest Park Avenue (busy, blind curves), be on time for dinner, and stay out of the creek. We found a way around the first rule, had no problem with the second, and figured the third didn't matter if our tetanus shots were current. We never went into the creek on purpose, but we ended up in it a lot by accident.

Gwen and Mickey met by the creek that bicentennial summer. Mickey was lying belly-down on the bank, near a culvert where crawfish were sometimes found, poking the murky water with a long stick.

"I'm Gwen," Gwen said shyly to the wiry little back and frowsy black hair.

"You live in that big house, at the end of the road. Are your parents rich?" Mickey replied, eyes fixed on the brown water.

"I don't think so." Gwen considered the evidence. Their house was grand, at least on the lower floors. The bedrooms felt a little stingy. Fee and Miller had a car, but they had to share it, and it was an old Volvo. Her parents went to New York once a year to go to the theater and shop for Christmas gifts. Did this make them rich?

"What does your father do?"

"He's a doctor."

"So you're rich," Mickey said, eyes never leaving the water. Did crawfish really live there? Gwen could not imagine it. But Mickey insisted they were there and that, furthermore, she was going to take them home and eat them. If she caught any. She had a net at the ready, but it didn't look up to the job. It was tiny, the kind of thing used in tropical aquariums. Even one small crawfish would test its capacity.

"He's the kind of doctor who teaches."

"My dad owns the service station, up the hill. Well, he's not really my dad, but my stepdad. He's good-looking. He looks like Tom Selleck."

"That's cool. Him owning the service station."

"No, it's not. Because when I want a soda or a snowball or something from the pharmacy next door, I can't go there because someone from the station will rat me out. And there's nowhere else to go. There used to be a store here in the neighborhood, where they sold penny candy, but they stopped. Do you have treats at your house?"

"What?"

"Treats. Ice cream and cookies and candy and soda? I suppose not, your father being a doctor."

"Oh, no, we have—treats. My mother goes grocery shopping

once a week, and each one can choose whatever snacks we want. But that's it, for the week. If you eat it all up right away, you have to wait until the next week." Gwen did not add that she had learned all sorts of ways of making treats last. She nibbled 5th Avenue candy bars, plucking off the solitary almond, then slowly removing the chocolate with teeth and tongue, leaving behind an unsheathed bar of peanut butter. She ate peanut M&M's by cracking the chocolate shell, removing the peanuts, then placing the peanuts in a bowl, to be gobbled in a handful. She was proud of these maneuvers but aware that others considered them gross. Besides, she was pudgy and desperate to pretend candy was not particularly interesting to her, that her condition was glandular.

Mickey sat up. "Would you get circus peanuts sometimes?"

"Peanuts?"

"Circus peanuts. The big fluffy ones. Kind of like Peeps, only not so sticky."

"Sure."

The next Friday, on her mother's weekly shopping trip, Gwen put a bag of the orange peanuts into the cart. "Really?" her mother asked. "You hate marshmallow." Gwen nodded. The next day, she took the treats to Mickey. Over the course of the summer, she brought Mickey Smarties, candy buttons, Pixy Stixs. Necco Wafers. Now and Laters. Gwen's mother figured it out within a week or so, but she didn't care. In fact, she complimented Gwen on her selflessness. But it didn't feel selfless to Gwen, more like a necessary tribute. Mickey was valuable. Mickey knew things. You couldn't have access to all she knew without making some sort of contribution.

Mickey had been roaming the wooded hills around Dick-eyville since the age of eight, when she persuaded her mother to let her walk home from the public elementary school on the other side of the hill. She acted as if she owned every inch of it, and we didn't contradict her. We never got lost when we let Mickey lead the way, while the rest of us could get turned around quite easily.

Yet Mickey was the only one of us who didn't live in Dickeyville. Her family lived above it, in the town houses called Purnell Village, on the other side of Forest Park Avenue. Most children would not have been allowed to cross that street, much less walk to school alone, but Mickey had permission. Or said she did. Mickey was not always the most reliable person when it came to herself. Her stepfather, for example, was not her stepfather and did not own the gas station. He managed it. He did, however, look a little like Tom Selleck.

Caught in a lie or a contradiction by the rest of us, Mickey would shrug, as if the misstatements that flowed from her were incidental, a slip of the tongue, like mixing up facts you knew perfectly well. And because Mickey was beautiful, despite her wild bush of hair and grubby clothes, we came to believe that was one of the perks of beauty, the freedom to lie and not be called on it. Who wanted to fight with someone as pretty as Mickey? She was prettier still for not being able to do much about her appearance. She wore jeans and T-shirts, often the same ones two days running, and her hair was never quite brushed. Sometimes, Gwen's mother would say, "Let's play beauty parlor," and Gwen understood it was an excuse to pull a brush through Mickey's matted hair, which would shine and gleam under her mother's care. Later, when we became a group, a unit, the boys wished they could have Mrs. Robison pull a brush through their hair, short as it was. Not that they ever said anything. Well, maybe Go-Go did. Go-Go never understood that there were things he shouldn't want, desires he shouldn't express. He would watch Tally Robison work on Mickey's hair, his tongue poking out the corner of his mouth as it often did, as if he thought something tasty might fall from the sky at any moment and he didn't want to miss it. Sometimes Go-Go would try to climb Tally Robison, would literally start to shimmy up her body, trying to force her to unfold those thin arms and hold him.

But that was yet to come. That first summer, 1976, there was only Gwen and Mickey, Mickey and Gwen, best friends along with everything that being best friends entailed, all the wonder and closeness, all the pain and resentment. We didn't have the term BFFs back then, and even if we had, it wouldn't have been accurate. Mickey and Gwen fell well short of forever. But that summer, it felt like forever.

Tally Robison died in Gwen's senior year of college. She had been too ill to see her daughter accept a prize for her college journalism, too ill to tell her daughter that the gorgeous college sweetheart to whom she would soon become engaged was *too* gorgeous. Gwen kept assuming Mickey would get in touch. Whatever had happened, all those years ago, did not change the fact that her mother had been good to Mickey, kind and generous. Certainly, Mickey must know of Tally's death, must have heard from someone, even if her family had long ago left the town houses of Purnell Village, which had become exceedingly rough, even as Dickeyville continued to be its placid, sui generis self. Gwen was just shy of her twenty-second birthday, much too young to lose a parent, especially a parent as lovely as her mother had been. But we were all young then, unaccustomed to death and its rituals, how important the smallest gestures were. Only Sean—forever Sean-the-Perfect—wrote a note, and it was a little stiff, almost grudging, as if he felt that Gwen's mother had died in order to force him to contact her daughter.

Five years later, the two former best friends met face-to-face on a plane. Gwen was in first class, upgraded on her husband's miles. Mickey was the flight attendant. Still beautiful, but there was a hardness to her now, a sense that the real person was layers and layers down.

"Mickey," Gwen said brightly when offered a beverage before takeoff. A blank stare. "Mickey. It's Gwen. Gwen Robison."

Mickey continued to stare blankly. No, she stared through her, which is quite different. "It's McKey now."

"Mick Kay?"

"Think of it this way—I dropped the *i*, capitalized the *K*. McKey."

"Legally?" A bizarre response, but Gwen couldn't think of anything else to say.

"You always were a stickler for rules," Mickey—McKey—said. "Can I get you anything?"

The other passengers, businessmen accustomed to life in first class, were growing impatient with this trip down memory lane. They wanted their drinks, their hot nuts, whatever small treats their status entailed. But Gwen couldn't let her old friend go.

"It's been so long. I hate that we lost touch. In fact, I thought I might hear from you when my mom died. She died, did you know that? Five years ago, from bladder cancer."

"I heard, but not right away. I'm sorry." The words had all the intimacy of *champagne or orange juice?*

"You heard from—" Foolish to extend the conversation, and what did it matter how McKey had learned?

"From Sean."

"You're in touch?" She couldn't decide if what she felt was jealousy or—stickler for the rules she was—a sense of betrayal. They weren't supposed to be friends anymore. That was the price they paid for the horrible thing that had happened.

"Sometimes. He sends Christmas cards."

"He told you about my mom in a Christmas card?" Not challenging Mickey—McKey—but honestly astonished, confused.

"Look, I'll come back and chat later in the flight, okay?"

She didn't.

CHAPTER THREE

Gwen was spared funerals as a child and accepted this practice, as she accepted so many of her parents' practices, as the inarguably right thing to do. Certainly, it has not occurred to her to bring Annabelle to Go-Go's visitation, and she is shocked to see how many young children are here. More disturbing, they are gathered around the open casket, inspecting Go-Go with a respectful but palpable excitement. *A dead person! This is what a dead person looks like!* In the face of their bravery, how can Gwen not come forward and look as well?

A dead person this may well be, but it is not the boy she remembers and not only because he is thirty years older than the Go-Go who lives in her memory. This person is too still, his features too composed. Go-Go was never still.

"Gwen." Doris Halloran holds her hands tightly, peers into her face, as if nearsighted. "Pretty little Gwen. You look wonderful."

She does? She doesn't feel as if she looks wonderful. True, she is thin. She has no appetite as of late. But she is pretty sure that the lack of food has made her face gaunt, her hair dull and dry. Then again, maybe it's all relative. She looks better than Go-Go, for example. And better than Mrs. Halloran, whose face is white and puffy in a way that cannot be explained by mere grieving. Her eyes are like little raisins deep in an uncooked loaf, her mouth ringed by wrinkles.

"I'm sorry for your loss, Mrs. Halloran. My father would be here, but he broke his hip. I'm staying with him while he recuperates."

"What happened?"

"Slipped on those steps. They've always been a hazard."

Mrs. Halloran does not let go of Gwen's hands. Pressing, squeezing. It is a little painful, while Mrs. Halloran's breath—it isn't bad, exactly, but old, reminiscent of mothballs and dimly lit rooms.

"So many accidents," she murmurs.

"Yes. It's a shame about Go—" Gwen stops herself, remembering Sean's reaction to his brother's nickname. "Gordon."

"Oh." She seems jolted. "Yes, I suppose that was an accident, too." *Supposes?* Gwen assumed that Doris Halloran, always the super Catholic, wouldn't even contemplate the possibility of suicide. Doris lets go of Gwen's hand abruptly, so abruptly that her body registers the end of the pain as a deepening of the sensation. It's as if phantom hands still gripped hers, squeezing, intent on hurting her.

"I know it's a cliché," Gwen says, "but it throws the world out of whack when a parent loses a child, at any age."

"Well, I lost a few, you know." She lowers her voice. "Miscarriages. Three. Actually four, although that one was so early it barely counted."

Gwen probably did know this in the vague, indifferent way that children intuit things about the grown-ups in their lives, but this revelation suddenly connects a series of mysterious events—Mrs. Halloran "sleeping" a lot, Mr. Halloran yelling at the boys for making noise, a grandmother who came for a visit that wasn't at all like the grandparent visits Gwen knew. (No meals out, no trips to the toy store.)

"Do you have children. Gwen?"

"Yes, a little girl. Annabelle. She's five."

"I'm sorry," she says.

"Sorry?" Did she think it was a shame to have girls? Or does she know that Annabelle is not Gwen's biological child? The senior Hallorans were never open-minded people, they would probably call her daughter a Chink or something worse. Gwen's color rose, she is on the verge of saying that Mrs. Halloran hasn't done so well herself, that only one of her boys is worth anything. But where are Sean and, come to think of it, Tim?

Doris is suddenly contrite. "I didn't mean—I'm taking something. The doctor gave me pills. And I feel like things get mixed up, my sentences come out in the wrong order or I say what people say to me. No, it's good you have a little girl. I'm happy for you. But daughters are hard. Secretive. I was sad I didn't have one, but then happy. Then again, daughters stay with you. Sons leave. Does that make sense?"

"Yes." No.

Mrs. Halloran grabs her hands again. "I'll see you tomorrow, right?"

"At the funeral? Of course."

"And at the house, after. Not everyone is invited, but we want you there. You're like family, even if it's been years. It's funny, I s'pose you come back to see your father all the time, yet I never see you. Even when Gordon moved back home, you didn't come visit him. Why didn't you visit him?"

So many reasons. *Because he was an angry drunk most of the times. And when he wasn't angry, he was pathetic, self-pitying.* But the main reason was the one that divided them long ago: it was simply too painful to be around each other. They couldn't talk about it, and they couldn't not talk about it, so they stayed away from each other.

"When Sean moved away, I lost touch. Mickey Wyckoff, too. And my father keeps to himself."

"Yes, he always did."

He did? Gwen remembers her father as gregarious. But, perhaps, a little snobbish about the Hallorans. That's why the night of the hurricane had been unusual, all the parents together in the Robisons' house, drinking and laughing late into a weekday night.

"Don't be a stranger now," Mrs. Halloran says suddenly, full of fake merriment. "We'll be seeing lots of each other. Right?" The question feels unusually earnest—and a little threatening.

"Absolutely."

Sean and Tim finally appear, explaining that they have been speaking with the priest about tomorrow's service. Sean takes his mother by the shoulders, gently, and begins guiding her to other well-wishers, making Gwen feel as if she is in the wrong somehow, that she has monopolized the grieving mother when it was Doris who insisted on prolonging their contact.

Tim gives her a half smile. "Sorry."

It seems to be the word of the evening. "No need. I think it's a miracle she's standing upright."

"Sean said your dad had an accident?"

"Yes. As I told your mother, that seems to be the theme of the week."

Tim's face is blank. It's funny, how he looks so much like Sean, yet still isn't handsome. Everything is a bit fuzzier in Tim's face.

Rougher, coarser, indistinct. It's like a face drawn by a child, the features slashed in. Plus, he's allowed himself to get plump.

"Go-Go's death wasn't an accident, Gwen. He drove right into the Jersey wall at over a hundred miles per hour."

"Sean said—"

"Oh, Sean. He's proper now, careful about what he says. Professional liability since he moved to public relations. He can't stop spinning things. No, Go-Go aimed his car straight at the barricades at the end of the highway. Probably drunk, so it's hard to know his intent, but he clearly didn't try to steer away. We're waiting for the toxicology reports. Well, *we're* not waiting for them. The insurance company is, because they're keen to deny his kids the life insurance if they can. I can't figure out if we should root for drunk and claim he wasn't capable of forming suicidal intent or pray for sober and say the accelerator got stuck."

"I thought he was in a sober phase."

"He was, best I can tell, right up to last Tuesday night. Went to meetings every week, seemed to be making progress. We only have Mom's word for it and she forgave him everything, covered for him whenever possible, but he had been clean for almost two years. He left to go to a meeting, in fact, about seven P.M. Next thing Mom knew, it was two A.M. and the cops were at her door. They had gone to Lori's first, because that was the address on his license."

"Lori?"

"His ex, although I guess technically they were just separated. The second ex, the one with the kids." Tim points to two blondes, tiny things. These girls are not inspecting the dead man in the casket but keeping their distance, clinging to their mother. Even in their sadness, all three are gorgeous. "Only decent thing he ever did for her and those kids was taking out that policy and now he might have screwed that up. All he had to do was hit the brakes, leave some skid marks, but no—"

"Shut up, Tim," Sean says, joining them.

"It's just Gwen."

The words are at once warm and vaguely insulting, conferring a privilege while making it sound as if Gwen is a person of no consequence.

"Gordon did not commit suicide."

"Look, we're not going to rat him out to the church, keep him from being buried in consecrated ground. And I'm not going to break Mom's heart. But among the three of us, can't we at least drop the bullshit?"

"He was drunk. He called me an hour before, wasn't making any sense."

"Probably."

"If he was drunk, then he didn't know what he was doing. He was drag racing, like in the old days, and he miscalculated."

"OK, but—we lived here all our lives. We all learned to drive on that patch of dead-end highway. Drunk or asleep or dead, he couldn't have forgotten that there were barricades, that it ended."

"Let it go, Tim."

"Speaking of drinking—anyone want to?"

They end up at the Point, once a reliably sleazy dive on Franklintown Road. To their horror, it has been yuppified. Live music on the weekends, a decent wine list. The bar food is traditional but prepared with care. It isn't the kind of experience Gwen—or most Baltimoreans with money, or even the city's pseudohipsters—are inclined to seek out on Franklintown Road, although Gwen realizes she might find it a handy retreat as long as she's staying in her father's house.

The boys drink Rolling Rock on tap, while she has a microbrew.

"Raison D'Être." Tim pronounces the name of her beer with great disdain. Ray-zohn Det-ruh. "Faggot beer."

Sean winces at his un-PC brother, but Tim isn't shamed: "Any beer with a French name has to suck."

"It's very good," Gwen says. "And it's made in Delaware. Taste it."

Tim refuses, but Sean is polite enough to try it and say nice things, although he clearly doesn't care for it.

"You are such a fucking yuppie," Tim says. A new insult, but in the same vein of all the insults heaped on her when they were children. Gwennie the Whale. Gwen the Goody Two-shoes. Yet Gwen was never as proper as Sean. She wonders if Tim knows that.

She responds, because Tim wants her to and his brother is dead, so she owes him a little good-humored argument. "That term is incredibly dated to the point of being meaningless. When did it come into vogue? The eighties? And who isn't an urban professional among the three of us? Young we're clearly not."

"But you work at that stupid magazine—"

"I *edit* it, yes."

"And it's all about what to buy and what to eat and what to wear."

"We do a lot of substantive journalism. More than ever, given how the *Beacon-Light* has been gutted. I'd love to commission an article on the trial you've got going, Mr. State's Attorney. We also still make money. You know why? Because we are business friendly, which kept our advertising stable when the economy bottomed out. And we don't give all our content away."

"Best doctors. Best restaurants. Best neighborhoods. Best of the best. Why not—best places to pick up hookers? Hey—why not best hookers? That's news I could use."

"I didn't know you had to pay for it, Tim."

"I don't. I *prefer* to pay for it."

"He's kidding," Sean puts in, ever the PR man, worried that Gwen is going to run off and write a headline: ASSISTANT STATE'S ATTORNEY PREFERS HOOKERS. "Tim's so straight he doesn't even drive over the speed limit. And he's still stupid-in-love with Arlene."

It's funny, how quickly they revert to their roles—their roles as they first were, when they functioned as a group with no relationships within the relationships. The only thing different about their interaction is the alcohol. And that they are three, instead of five. They can never be five—the starfish, as Mickey called it—again. Gwen realizes she always hoped they might be, if only for a night, that they would come together once more and confront all the little ragged pieces of their shared story. Other than her father and her siblings, no one in her life knew her as a child. No one has any sense of the totality of who she is. Not even Karl, and certainly not Annabelle. Not her current staff and not her former colleagues from her newspaper days, scattered throughout the city. The Gwen that most people know is the adult Gwen. She wants to be among people who know her. She yearns for her mother, who made her feel special even when she clearly was not, who trusted her to morph into a swan. She even misses Mickey.

That is, she misses Mickey until the next morning when *McKey*, swathed in black from head to foot, enters the church moments before the funeral service begins and takes a seat in the Hallorans' pew, as if she's a part of the family. McKey even reaches around Sean to pat Doris Halloran's shoulder, then leaves her arm around Sean for several seconds.

It's easy to miss some people, Gwen thinks, *until they actually show up.*

Autumn 1977–Spring 1978

CHAPTER FOUR

It was Mickey who decided we should be a group, that the duo of Mickey and Gwen should be joined to the trio of the Halloran brothers. Before, we were two and three. Five together was stronger than two and three. Our country's own Department of Defense, Sean later pointed out, was contained within the Pentagon, so it must be the strongest thing possible.

But our coalition began as a dispute, an argument over territory. Although the Hallorans lived on Sekots, at the far end of the neighborhood, they often used a vacant lot at the end of Gwen's street as their makeshift kickball field. The squarish mound of grass was just large enough to approximate an infield, but the lack of an outfield was problematic, dangerous even. A strong kick—and all the Halloran boys were powerful—inevitably sent the ball into the street or skittering across the foundation of a long-abandoned springhouse on the other side. And while Wetheredsville Road—oh, how Gwen complained about having to learn to spell her street name—was not heavily trafficked even then, the mill was still open and enormous trucks rumbled past several times a day.

Mickey, who cared nothing for the field but liked to cut through it to reach the stream, decided the Halloran boys were presumptuous. The lot was not theirs to annex, she argued. *Not yours, either,* Tim argued back. *You don't even live in the village.* Mickey countered that Gwen, as the resident of the last house on Wetheredsville Road, should have the right to use the lot, or not use the lot, as she saw fit. The boys should have to pay Gwen to use the field, Mickey insisted.

"Or"—and this was clearly where she had been heading all along—"let us play, too."

It was fall. The promise, the glow of back-to-school had already faded. Gwen's denim binder was full of torn papers, and she could never find her little box of reinforcements. At St. Lawrence, Go-Go had already been given multiple detentions, and Sean was bored by the writing assignments, which never allowed him to show his range. Tim was getting by at Cardinal Gibbons, but getting by was Tim's particular genius. A letter had already been sent home to Mickey's mother, noting that she was not working up to her potential. That is, the letter was sent, but it never arrived. Mickey stuffed it under a rock in the hills behind the Robisons' house, where she arrived every day and waited for Gwen. When Gwen got off the private bus that took her to her door, she found Mickey in the kitchen, eating cookies and drinking one of her mother's diet sodas. Gwen wasn't allowed to have diet soda, but Mickey was, because she was a guest. Years later, when her mother was dying of bladder cancer, Gwen couldn't help thinking of all those diet sodas. She knew science was not on her side, but the notion still persisted. She tricked Annabelle into thinking sparkling water was a treat, making it in a penguin-shaped canister from Williams-Sonoma that produced wonderful belching noises, sometimes adding juice and slices of lemon to give it something extra. But it was all parental sorcery, and Gwen knew that Annabelle would see through the ruse eventually, start asking for soda, or god help her, putting Equal in her cocoa.

When they were indoors, Gwen set the agenda, teaching Mickey how to play the elaborate make-believe games that were the cornerstone of Gwen's de facto only-child status. Miller and Fee were both gone now. But the girls spent as little time as possible indoors. Mickey was restless. Mickey liked action, she wanted to move. She wasn't a particularly good athlete, as would become evident when the girls joined the Halloran boys' kickball game. Mickey was wildly uncoordinated at almost any organized sport. Yet, stalking through the woods, climbing over and under fallen branches, jumping rocks across the stream—no one was more graceful or strong. Mickey could even do chin-ups, something no other girl of our acquaintance could do. She said she had won the Presidential Medal for Fitness, although she never remembered to show it to Gwen on those rare occasions Gwen was allowed to go to Mickey's house.

The day that Mickey decided to crash the kickball game was early November, the first fair day after a week of lashing rains. The hills and fields were muddy, and Gwen's mother, sighing, reminded her to come in through the basement, *please*? And leave her boots down there? *Please*? Mickey didn't even have boots, but she said her mother didn't mind if her tennis shoes were caked with mud. "You just have to let it dry and then it brushes off as easy as anything," she told Gwen.

But despite the break in the rain, Mickey didn't want to roam the hills today, looking for places they could claim as their own. Instead, she led Gwen up the road and across the street, to the vacant field where the Halloran boys were playing kickball.

"We want to play," Mickey said to Sean.

"No thanks," he said. "It works best with three."

Tim was less polite. "Go screw yourselves."

Gwen sucked in her breath. That was a curse, or as good as. Go-Go was delighted, repeating it over and over. "Go screw yourself, go screw yourself."

Mickey was not easily intimidated. She put her hands on her hips and stared Sean down. "This lot doesn't belong to you."

"Doesn't belong to you, either."

"It belongs to her, though." Pointing at Gwen. "To her family. They bought a whole bunch of land when they built their house."

"No way," Sean said. We all knew—except gullible Go-Go— that it was an outrageous lie.

"Go look it up," Mickey said.

"Where?"

"Downtown."

"Get out of here," Tim said.

Go-Go was running in circles. "Go screw yourself, go screw yourself, go screw yourself."

Sean took Mickey's measure. "You any good?"

"What does it matter? It will be a better game with five than with three. We'll play two-on-two, with a permanent pitcher."

Gwen assumed she would be the permanent pitcher. She was. She rolled the ball across the plate, first to Sean, then to Tim, then to Go-Go, finally Mickey. Tim's ball came back at her, hard, right to her midsection, and it clearly wasn't accidental. Gwen clamped her lips tight to keep from crying.

But it was a better game, just as Mickey had said. She and Tim faced off against Sean and Go-Go. Gwen was supposed to get a turn at some point, but she didn't, not that day, and not often in the days ahead. The game evolved into something more like football or rugby or dodgeball, with complicated rules about tackling and catching. We became attuned to the noises of the street, the sound of approaching cars and trucks, and learned to time the action of the game around the traffic. We fought sometimes, went home early, yet came back together the next day, or the day after if there was rain. We suspended the games during the heart of the winter, but started playing again long before spring. The Halloran boys were baffling to the girls. Sometimes they presented as a unified front, sometimes it was every man for himself, and, most often, it was two against one, with Go-Go, the baby, the odd one out. And Go-Go was easy for the girls to gang up on as well, so it was just as often four on one. Every group needs its goat, and Go-Go was the inevitable choice in ours.

We were having a four-on-one day in late April, a cranky, frustrating day in which all the gains of spring seemed to have been lost. The sky was gray, the air had a real chill in it, and the things that had budded and bloomed over the past month looked miserable. Daffodils and tulips bent their heads, beaten down. On the way to the field, Go-Go jumped on one of Tally Robison's flowerbeds with both feet, irritating the rest of us, who understood our freedom came at a price. If we gave adults any reason to complain about us, we knew we would lose privileges.

But Go-Go became only more intolerable when we tried to explain to him why he shouldn't jump on flowers. He pinched the girls, he pulled at their clothes, he flailed at his brothers. Finally, in frustration, Mickey threw the red rubber ball over his head, into the street. Later, she said it wasn't on purpose, which would fit with her general incompetence on the playing field, yet it had seemed deliberate to the rest of us, an exaggerated, high, arching throw that would have soared over anyone's head, but especially over little Go-Go's. There's no doubt that she said: "Go get it, you moron."

Which Go-Go did, despite the rumbling noise that we all knew to heed. He dashed into the road after the bouncing ball just as one of the huge mill trucks came around the curve, going much too fast, but we all knew the mill trucks went too fast and it was our responsibility to be careful. The rest of us watched, frozen, mesmerized. We were going to see someone die. We

watched the truck bearing down on the boy and the ball, saw the
ball disappear under its wheels, heard terrible noises—honking,
brakes squealing. But Go-Go seemed to change the rules of physics, accelerating so that he reached the other side of the road just
before the truck passed by. We were amazed to see him, upright
and laughing, after the long truck had passed.

Tim was the first to speak.

"Screw you, Go-Go," he said. "The ball is ruined." But his tone
was admiring, almost reverential, his voice shaking.

The ball had been split by the truck's wheels. We looked at
the flattened red mass. "That could be Go-Go's head," Gwen said.
We all nodded. He could be like one of the squirrels we saw in the
road, a red smear with hair sticking out of it. We weren't to touch
the squirrels, or any other roadkill, lest we risk rabies.

Sean ran across the road and grabbed his brother by the arm,
shaking him violently, angrily.

"Don't ever do that again."

"But Mickey said—"

"Mickey's not the boss of you."

"No one's the boss of me," he countered, pushing out his lower lip.

Without a ball, kickball was over. We couldn't get a new ball
unless we told a grown-up what had happened, and no one thought
that was a good idea. And, although it was hard to envision on such a
cold, gray April day, summer was coming, and not even our odd brand
of kickball/dodgeball/rugby could fill those longer, emptier days. We
needed a new game. Mickey suggested an explorer's club. Sean and
Tim said it was babyish, yet the next day we all ended up following her
deeper and deeper into the woods, marveling at the things we found.
Abandoned campsites, downed trees. Beer cans, garbage. "Teenagers
did this," Go-Go would say solemnly, as if Tim and Sean were not
already teenagers, Mickey and Gwen both about to turn thirteen that
autumn. Teenagers were fearsome creatures to Go-Go.

And then we met the man who lived in the woods.

Chapter Five

"What's the point of this charade?" Karl asks Gwen the morning after
Go-Go's funeral as she arrives with only minutes to spare before
Annabelle awakens and comes down to breakfast.

The question catches her short, her mind snagging on his
choice of word, *charade*. What, exactly, is a charade? Where is the
pretense? She puzzles through this as she sets breakfast in motion.
She isn't pretending to Annabelle that she spends the nights here.
Her daughter knows that Gwen is staying at her grandfather's
house while he heals, but that she still wants to be here for meals,
bedtime, and off-to-school. The charade, to use Karl's word, is
pretending that the household will return to normal after her father's situation has been normalized.

*Charade. The mothers had played charades that night, first with
their husbands, then alone after the men left. How innocent they had*

seemed in the candlelit living room, making the familiar, exaggerated gestures. Paging through a book, running a movie camera, flipping channels. She and Sean had watched them from the steps, feeling more akin to them than they did to the others by that point. They—well, she—honestly believed that they would get married, that they would one day be a couple among other couples, laughing and clowning. They—again, maybe just she—had been preternaturally attracted to adulthood, eager for it, in a way that Tim, Mickey, and Go-Go weren't. They were the normal ones, trying to grow up, be typical teenagers.

"I'm not sure what you mean," she says, trying to be careful with Karl's feelings but also her words. She doesn't want to be drawn into making promises she can't keep. But his eyes are sad and hurt. He clearly wants to ask other, softer, more vulnerable questions. *Why did she leave? Doesn't she love him? Doesn't she want to be with him?* But these are not the kind of questions that Karl will ask out loud because Karl does not know the answers and Karl never admits he doesn't have answers. "That's a surgeon's personality," her father, Karl's onetime professor, told Gwen early in their courtship. "He's used to being in charge, having authority." Like most people in love, she ignored any observation that didn't serve her vision of her romance.

"Aren't you running late? Go save lives," she says now, not meaning to be cruel, only factual. But Karl takes offense.

"It's not—" he begins, then stops because Annabelle has entered the kitchen, frowning at the morning, slow and cranky, quite unlike both of them. Gwen is a morning person, while Karl, like many hyperachievers, permits himself no more than four or five hours of sleep.

Annabelle, by contrast, is a night owl who fights bedtime and treats morning as a personal offense. Another reason for Gwen to be here for bedtime every night. Karl would never have the patience to cajole Annabelle through her nighttime routine. There are circles under Annabelle's eyes, bigger and darker than usual.

Gwen wonders if Karl knows that Annabelle sometimes creeps down to the kitchen with the earbuds from her little MP3 player and then watches the television on the counter, standing all the while. Once Gwen found her with her chin resting on the counter, asleep on her feet, while an infomercial touted the miracle of mineral makeup. She wonders at the secrets of her daughter's DNA. Were her parents night owls? How had they coped? Given the remote orphanage where Annabelle spent the first eleven months of her life, her parents were almost certainly farmers. Did they frown at sunrise, did they stay up late, despite knowing the price they would pay come morning? Did they abandon their daughter to strike out for the city, find a life that suited them better?

"Good morning, sweet pea."

"Peas are not sweet," she says. Then: "Can I have pancakes?"

"We're a little pressed for time. But we can have them this weekend. I thought you could come over to Poppa's, have a sleepover?"

"You should check with me—" Karl begins, but Annabelle is already lighting up. "Can I have the princess room?"

"Of course," Gwen says. The princess room is nothing more than Gwen's childhood room, virtually untouched since she left for college. If her mother had lived—but her mother did not live.

"You didn't ask me," Karl says in a low voice after she sends Annabelle back upstairs to put on real pants. She was trying to coast by with her pajama bottoms. Plaid, they would have fooled her father. This is another reason why Gwen has to come by every morning; Annabelle gets too much by Karl. Their daughter is the one person impervious to his surgical authority and expectations.

But for all the reasons Gwen can list for being here every morning and evening, none really matters. She's here because she cannot bear being away from her daughter. Yet she has chosen to be away from her daughter. No, she doesn't understand it herself.

"I know we have no formal arrangement—" Karl continues.

"Yet."

"But you didn't ask me if you could have Annabelle this weekend."

"I don't have to," Gwen says, putting bread in the toaster, getting out the cinnamon sugar that Annabelle likes. It comes in a plastic yellow sifter shaped like a bear, a relic of Gwen's childhood. Her own did not survive, but she bought this one at an antique store, laughing at herself for paying seven dollars for a piece of plastic that used to cost less than two—and was filled with cinnamon sugar.

"If you are serious about this—"

"I am serious. Serious as a heart attack, as they say in your world. But then, my world doesn't have metaphors or similes about what matters because, as you so often remind me, nothing matters in my world."

"I never—"

"Always," she says. She is aware that she is interrupting him, aware that she is enjoying it a little too much. "You *always* let me know how trivial my life is. Not in words. Through your lack of words, your lack of questions, your inability to feign interest. By your silence, you let me know every day that what I do and who I am is of absolutely no interest to you."

Annabelle has returned and is standing in the doorway, regarding them. She is bright, exceptionally bright, although no child could be expected to compete with the brainiac powers of Karl Flores. Still, she is probably aware of more than they want her to be. Gwen hopes those dark circles aren't from lying awake, worrying. When she first started out testing the idea of leaving Karl, trying it on in front of her friends, as she might have asked them about a particularly bold fashion choice or luxury purchase, the litany of questions had been consistent: *Did he cheat? Is he abusive? Is he an addict? Has he lied to you about important things?* When Gwen said no, everyone said: "You should stay together for Annabelle's sake." Karl said the same thing. No one understands that she could leave for Annabelle's sake. She likes to think her mother would have, if she had lived. But if her mother had lived, would Gwen have chosen the men she has chosen? Certainly, she never would have married Stephen. Ironically, her mother's death probably drove her into that doomed, ridiculous marriage.

"You'll be late, Daddy," Annabelle says. Ah, she wants to defuse the bomb, ticking away, separate them now so they might choose to be together later. So that Gwen might choose. Karl has made it clear that he has no desire to divorce her. But not because he loves her, only because he can't stand to lose at anything.

"Will the film crew be there today?" Gwen asks, taking in her husband's suit, one of his nicest, and the bright blue shirt that flatters his dark complexion.

"Only for—I'm not sure what you call them. No interviews, but walking, sitting in meetings. Establishing shots? Something like that. I wish I hadn't said yes."

Under her breath: "But you always do."

"What?"

"Never mind." She turns back to the task of fixing Annabelle's breakfast, as if it requires great concentration to butter toast and sprinkle it with cinnamon and sugar, pour a glass of juice. But it works. When she looks up, he's gone.

Friends have pointed out to Gwen that it is hypocritical of her to complain about the constant media demands on her husband, given that she was a journalist who met him on assignment. She knew of him, of course. Dr. Karl Flores had been famous for a long time, more than fifteen years, when they met. He became famous for performing heart surgery on infants, working with tiny instruments of his own design, precious things that appeared to be plundered from a doll's hospital.

Plenty of surgeons do what Karl does, with just as good results. But few have Karl's charisma, and no matter how the world changes, some aspect of his life always seems to be in sync with the zeitgeist. Gwen met him when he was in handsome-surgeon mode. Never married, he was the subject of much gossip. But the ordinary truth was that he worked too much and had no taste for a playboy lifestyle because it would have undercut his good-guy image, which he enjoyed mightily. His self-knowledge on this topic was his saving grace. "I like the attention," he told Gwen on their third interview, which somehow mutated into their first date, upending her professional life when she failed to reveal this fact to her bosses before her article ran. "Not because I'm egotistical but because I can use it."

"Oh, you use your powers for good," she said, laughing.

"Yes," he said, laughing yet earnest. On the first night they spent together—which happened to be the next night—they watched a movie on cable, a wonderfully campy affair in which a doctor, asked during a deposition if he had a god complex, replied: "I am God." Oh, how they laughed.

Oh, how true it was.

Karl is a surgeon. Karl is handsome. Karl goes to third world countries on his "vacations" and makes miracles. Five years ago, as the subject of immigration heated up, Karl revealed that he had entered the country illegally as a child, obtaining citizenship status under the Reagan-sanctioned amnesty of 1986. He testified before Congress. He wrote op-eds for the *New York Times,* although with considerable help from Gwen, who made his language less pedantic and high-handed. Karl may not have a god complex, exactly, but he has a touch of Zeus in him, flinging his words like thunderbolts. He wrote a memoir, this time with the help of a not-so-ghostly ghost. The memoir led to a cable television show, and while it wasn't a huge hit, it scored solidly in the ratings, renewed year after year. Every journalist who wrote about the show seemed obligated to include the detail that it was the rare case where a Hollywood actor wasn't quite as good-looking as the real person he portrayed.

Seven years ago, when they started the process that would bring

Annabelle into their household, Gwen thought, hoped, prayed that a child would change the balance in their lives, that their professional selves would recede somewhat. She was right, and yet she was wrong. Karl adores Annabelle, despite initially resisting Gwen's choice of China. Why not his native Guatemala? (Gwen claimed she feared that country's bureaucracy, but the truth was she couldn't bear to have a daughter who would be like Karl, but not her.) What about Zimbabwe, where he had performed yet another surgery? He wanted to find the child that needed them most, he wanted to save someone. But Gwen understood that a child would save her. If they had a child, at least one person would find her essential.

"How was the freel?" Annabelle asks, mouth full of toast.

"The what?"

"You said you were going"—she swallows—"to a funeral yesterday. For your friend."

"Oh. It was very sad. It's always sad when people die. But I saw some old friends."

"Your best friends?" Annabelle is entranced with the idea of best friends. Since entering kindergarten this year, she has had no fewer than five. She tries them on like hats. She has a heartless quality. Nature or nuture? Gwen or Karl?

"Yes, I guess so." Does Gwen really want to affirm Annabelle's belief that best friends are interchangeable, disposable, that they come and go like trends? "We were best friends until high school, when we went to different schools." True, but a lie. She was suggesting to Annabelle that the different schools changed the nature of their relationship. But Gwen and Mickey had never attended the same school, and their friendship was irrevocably broken before they started high school.

"Who's your best friend now?" Annabelle asks her mother.

"Miss Margery, I suppose," Gwen says, although she considers all her female friends equally close. Which is to say—not very. But Margery is the one she would call if there were major trouble.

She's the one she called the night she decided she wanted a trial separation from Karl.

"Did he cheat on you?" Margery asked. Everyone starts there. Everyone expects it. He's too damn handsome. Gwen's looks are holding up well, and Karl is ten years older, yet it's clear that everyone thinks she's competing above her weight class.

"No, not really."

"Not really?"

"A woman's after him, but he really doesn't get it. I mean, he has no clue. He's pretty naive that way."

"How do you know, then?"

"He's so naive that he showed me her e-mails because he thinks they're funny. He's, like, 'She's such a good writer. You should hire her, give her a column.' I had to explain to Karl that women don't write funny, flirtatious e-mails about being newly single to their old boyfriends in order to get the attention of their editor wives."

"Someone from high school?"

"College."

"Had they seen each other recently? At a reunion? Did he e-mail her first?"

"No. And no. Margery, that's not the point."

"What, then?"

What, then. She toys with the story in her head. It still hurts, thinking about it, but she knows others would find her overly sensitive. Babyish, even.

It was last month. Karl came home from one of his full, full days. The White House had called. Not the president himself, but *still*. And now there was going to be this documentary, serious stuff, made by an Oscar winner. Two hours of Karl's life, his real life, not the cotton-candy version on the cable network, with all the fake romances and intrigue thrown in. Gwen listened, happy for him, happy for their life. Gwen never had a problem being happy for Karl. Annabelle put out place mats in the renovated kitchen alcove, where they preferred to dine. It's a lovely house. A lovely house is practically obligatory when one is the editor of a consumer service magazine, but that doesn't make obtaining and maintaining one any easier. Their life, at that moment, looked like the kinds of lives in Gwen's magazine. The house and the magazine had just come through a year of turmoil but were relatively solid now. (It was two weeks before the retaining wall gave way and the basement filled with mud.)

As they ate dessert—homemade apple pie with a cheddar crust, made by Gwen—she started to tell Karl about her problems with a fairly big story, something a little tougher than the magazine usually did. She had a showdown with the publisher, the money guy, and had persuaded him to see things her way, although he wouldn't let her make it the cover story. Still, it would run as written. It would make news.

"I met with the publisher about the Figueroa story today," she began.

He nodded absently, pulled out his BlackBerry, and began scrolling through his messages as he left the room. Annabelle, who had started to clear the table, didn't notice.

And that was the problem.

I can't do this to her, Gwen thought. *I can't let my daughter grow up in a household where Daddy matters, but Mommy doesn't, where only one person's day matters. She'll make bad decisions, she'll choose the wrong men. Just like I did. Twice. Once. Twice.*

Back in the kitchen, which looks quite perfect, although now there's a pervasive dank smell from the basement problems, she still feels the same way. Everyone keeps telling her she has to stay for Annabelle's sake. If she were to tell them why she left Karl, would anyone agree that it was *for* Annabelle's sake? Probably not. Besides, it's not the whole truth. But it's part of the truth, a big part.

Then again, parsing out the truth—deciding what needed to be told and what could be held back—wasn't that the beginning of the end for Gwen, Mickey, and the Halloran brothers?

Summer 1978

Chapter Six

Sean—of course—found the fact in a book, and although he could never find it again, that didn't make it not so: our own Leakin Park was one of the largest parks within a city's limits, 1,200 acres or so when combined with Gwynns Falls Park. We loved telling that fact to out-of-town guests, who always countered: *What about Central Park?* But Sean had an answer for that, too: Central Park was a paltry 843 acres. Still, our visitors—cousins and the like—were seldom impressed. To them, it was just a bunch of trees and hills. Even if we took them to the tamed part that had tennis courts and ball fields and a little train and the wonderfully spooky chapel on the old Crimea estate, they remained bored. But that was the thing about our park, as we thought of it: It required day-in, day-out commitment to find its treasures. It was a place that rewarded persistence and stillness. In the summer of 1978, we pushed farther and farther into the park every day, Mickey at the lead, and each day brought a discovery. A branch of the stream, with tiny minnows and frogs and snapping turtles. Bright blue flowers in places so shadowy that it was a miracle they bloomed at all.

Sometimes the park turned on us, reminded us of its power and immensity. We blustered into mud as deep as quicksand, came home with burrs in our hair, rips in our clothes, scratches on our faces. On such days, our exasperated mothers would threaten us with day camp or chores or house arrest. But they never followed through. Mickey's mother worked, and Gwen's mother had one hobby after another, and Mrs. Halloran did whatever she did. Cleaning, she said, but either she was bad at it or the Halloran boys were too much for her because their house was never really tidy. Clean, perhaps, but messy. By the summer of 1977, when Go-Go was seven, she was reduced to buying underwear in various sizes and leaving them on a sideboard in the upstairs hall. It was up to the boys to find pairs that fit.

Anyway, the primary rule, in those days before cell phones, was that we had to stay within shouting distance of Gwen's house. But what was shouting distance? How far could sound carry? Whose lung power dictated the range? We would sometimes tell Go-Go to let the rest of us walk ahead for five minutes or so, then bellow. We could always hear Go-Go, so we kept going. And, yes, we understood that we were cheating, that Go-Go's shouts did not expand the farther we walked, but we were prepared to plead ignorance of this bit of physics if ever confronted. The fact is, our parents didn't want to look too closely at how we spent our days because then they would have to be responsible for us. And, as noted, Mickey's mother worked late and slept later, Mrs. Halloran did whatever she did, and Tally Robison threw pots, scribbled on legal pads, and, eventually, stared trancelike at blank canvases in her little studio, frozen with doubt. It could take her days to apply a single stroke of color, and her paintings were never really finished, not that anyone could tell. Tally Robison painted the kind of pictures that made people like Mr. Halloran say: "My kids could do better than that. Even Go-Go."

But one overcast day, we walked so far that some of us began to wonder how we could ever get back by dinnertime. It was one of those gray-green days that feels deliciously poignant after so much summery perfection. Rain threatened, but it was an empty threat. The air was moist, heavy, yet not unpleasant. We walked for what felt like hours. Gwen struggled at the end of the line. She was the least athletic of us and fat to boot. *Over hill, over dale,* she sang in a soft whisper, and the rest of us picked up her song, although we all found it mystifying. We weren't clear on what *dales* were, much less the *"case-ons"* that kept rolling along. Gwen must have learned the song from her father, who was old, in his fifties already. We sang absentmindedly, glad for the sound of our voices. If we had taken time to contemplate how queer this was, we would have stopped. But not even Tim, sixteen at the time, uttered his favorite insult: *This is so gay.* We just kept marching and singing, singing and marching.

Over hill, over dale . . . Mickey was in front, but it was the Halloran boys who began to piece together the landscape, who saw the connections. "That's Suicide Hill," they said, shocking Gwen, because our favorite sledding spot was far enough that we drove there as a special treat. It was not particularly dangerous, just very long and straight. We crossed the road and walked along the stream. No one said anything, but we could all tell that everyone felt relieved at finding a recognizable landmark. We weren't lost, after all. No one would have to cry uncle, admit to being worried about how far we had gone. Mickey began to walk faster, as if she knew where she was headed, running up and over a small hill, then disappearing from view.

"Hey," she called back to the rest of us. "Do you know about this?"

"This" was a house, a log cabin set back in a thicket of trees. If it were in a book, it would have been charming, the kind of primitive dwelling that makes girls want to play dress-up and pretend they are living in the olden days. But this place—it was dirty. And it smelled. Not of woodsmoke and apples, but of, well—it had a bathroom smell, very strong. Go-Go held his nose, and the rest of us wanted to do the same.

"It's the outhouse," Sean said. "This place has no indoor plumbing."

"Does someone live here?" Gwen asked.

"Not now," Sean said. Always confident, always the one with the answers. Not even Tim contradicted him back then. "Maybe once, but you wouldn't be allowed to live like this now. There are rules about how you have to live, zoning and things. You have to have a bathroom."

"Then how do you explain the chickens?" Mickey asked. "And the laundry on the line?"

There was an assortment of clothes, men's shirts and jeans, drying on a coarse piece of rope, and three unusually calm chickens bopping toward us with herky-jerky movements. We were used to the aggressive geese that guarded the Gwynns Falls, so most of us stepped back. But Mickey was already at the threshold of the house, peering in.

"Mickey," Gwen called, trying to get her to stop. But now Sean was beside her, then Tim, then Go-Go. Gwen had to step up.

Although the day was not bright, we still needed time for our eyes to adjust once inside. It was a simple room. Something—burlap—had been tacked over the windows, which accounted for the dimness. There was a chair, a small plastic tub that held dishes. A rickety pair of cabinets hung crookedly on the back wall and there was a makeshift counter—it looked like something you'd find on a church altar—piled with boxes and canisters. The cabin wasn't neat, but some sort of order was at work. Someone was taking care of it, in a fashion. The only really messy thing in the room was a pile of rags left on a cot. These smelled, too, not like the outhouse, but of something dank and strong.

"Who lives here?" Go-Go asked in a hoarse, awed whisper.

"No one lives here," Sean said. Sean didn't like to be wrong. "Hunters use it, maybe, but you couldn't live here."

"Hunters?" Gwen asked. "In Leakin Park? Is that legal?"

"No, but that doesn't stop some people."

Go-Go, with his magpie eyes, had spotted something glinting. "Look," he said, darting toward the cot with the pile of rags, no longer perturbed by the smell. "A guitar."

As he crouched down to drag the guitar from beneath the cot, a hand shot out from the pile of rags and grabbed Go-Go firmly by the wrist.

"Don't," the rags said.

CHAPTER SEVEN

*Sean still needs a moment to register where he is when he awakens, al-*though he has been staying at his mother's house for almost a week now. *Not. Home.* This is his first conscious thought the morning after Go-Go's funeral. He's not at home, and home is St. Petersburg. He's clear on that much. The first clue is the light. It is different from his bedroom in Florida, especially this time of year. He loves the light in Florida. It's one of the few things he loves. The light, winter, and the lack of state income taxes. But this room is dark, depressing, although he's glad for the darkness this morning. His head is so heavy, his mouth and throat feel as if they are coated with sand. Not a hangover, exactly, if only because Sean believes he never gets hangovers. Allergies, perhaps. He thought he had outgrown them, but maybe he's just not allergic to stuff in Florida.

So: Baltimore. So: a dark room, although it's beginning to brighten around him. The light is gray, watery, the sheets a little grainy beneath him, as if someone has been eating here, as if these are the crumbs of crumbs of crumbs. Go-Go ate in bed, among other things. Go-Go still fouled the sheets when he was nine or ten. Their mother made excuses for him, said it was a medical condition. But the medical condition vanished when Go-Go was given the single room that, by all rights, should have been Tim's, then Sean's when Tim left for college. It was a narrow, dark room, not particularly desirable except for its solitary state. Besides, Tim and Sean enjoyed rooming together, talking late into the night. Go-Go, always terrified of being left out, ended up more left out than ever.

Sean's in a double bed, but that's right. The twin beds in his room were replaced by a double bed when his mother decided the room needed to be at least nominally welcoming to her sons and their wives.

Only this bed *moves*. Sways and rolls beneath him.

But maybe that's okay, too? At home, he has a memory foam mattress, bought because his wife, Vivian, is a light sleeper, so the movement is merely relative to what he's used to. His mother is not someone to splurge on a mattress that was used, at most, five or six nights a year, because Tim never sleeps over, and Sean is lucky to make it home for Christmas. And when Go-Go returned home, he always chose his old room, dark and sunless and unimproved as it was.

The bed moves again, an actual roll. Sean sits up, puts his palm against the mattress. Warm to the touch, it pulses.

"A water bed?" he asks wonderingly, waiting to awaken from yet another banal dream. Sean has the dullest dreams of anyone he knows, assuming other people tell the truth.

"I know," replies a woman's voice, with a little throb of Baltimore in it. *Aye knoah*. "I'm such a cliché. The swinging flight attendant and her water bed."

Mickey—McKey—is standing across the room, her back to him as she fashions her long dark hair into some kind of upsweep. She is wearing a navy dress, and even in the pale light of what Sean realizes now is very early morning, it looks a little cheap and too tailored for McKey. Funny, she lived in jeans and overalls when they were kids—she was defiantly not a girly-girl, not like Gwen—but she was, well, sexy, even when she was eleven. Sean, two years older, felt guilty for noticing that and felt angry when Tim actually articulated the same thoughts, lying in their twin beds. "I saw Mickey's underwear yesterday. That's why I let her lead the way—when she's going up the hill and wearing those old cutoffs, you can see right up them. She's got a bangin' body."

She still does. The tailored dress—her uniform, duh—can't hide that, but it doesn't take advantage of it, either. McKey should have been a flight attendant back in the day when they were called stewardesses, when being a Pan Am or TWA air hostess was basically one step away from being a beauty pageant contestant. As a child, she always seemed slightly out of place—in her boyish clothes, in her friendship with Gwen, in her chaotic household, a thousand times crazier than his. Yet the undercurrents in her house never seemed to touch Mickey, whereas the relatively mild disorder of the Halloran household resonated within Go-Go. He was like a tuning fork, vibrating from the tiniest bit of tension, while Mickey could be still and composed in the middle of a hurricane. Literally, come to think of it.

When Go-Go was in his twenties and going through the twelve steps for the first time, he came to the making-amends part and ended up twisting it, demanding that his parents apologize to him for the handful of spankings he had been given, all quite justified in Sean's view. Go-Go also cited the time his mother had tied him to the laundry pole because she had to go to the grocery store and Go-Go threw a tantrum and refused to get in the car. Yes, it had been primitive, inexcusable, but their parents were throwbacks, raising their children as they had been raised. They had been younger than most of their peers, Doris only twenty-two when Tim was born. And while they were native Baltimoreans, going back two generations, they could have been right off the boat in a lot of ways. The Hallorans seemed perpetually baffled by the world at large and always—what were the phrases they used? *At the end of my rope. This is the last straw.* When they counted to ten, they started at nine. Angry, angry people, although his mother prefers not to remember that now.

So many memories clamoring for his attention. But not one of them can change the fact that he is in McKey's bed, his head throbbing, and she's getting dressed.

"Where—"

"My apartment in Riverside, south of Federal Hill," McKey says. "Close to the highway—hear it?—but also only ten minutes from the airport. Not really within walking distance of the restaurants and bars, except for Rub, the barbecue place across the street. That's where we went last night."

She's toying with him. If McKey were a cat, she would spend hours batting her prey between her front paws, she would tease other animals to death. Sean takes inventory. He is shirtless, but he has his jeans on, boxers beneath. Surely—

"I took your keys away from you," she says. "You were way too drunk to drive. Tim was long gone, and Gwen didn't come out with us. Said she had to get up early to drive over to her house, have breakfast with her daughter, that she was already guilt-ridden about missing her bedtime. That story doesn't quite hang together, does it? Her moving back home, I mean. They've got the money to provide her old man with all the care he needs. I thought about being a nurse. For about three seconds. It wasn't the gross stuff that changed my mind. As you know, nothing really grosses me out."

Sean nods carefully, not wanting to move his head too much. His headache is worse than he realized. It feels like a blister, like something he yearns to pop, but shouldn't. Mickey is right, she never shied away from things that other girls, even some boys, found disgusting. She would touch anything they found and with her fingers yet, not stand back, prodding with a stick. Except for snapping turtles. On those she used a stick.

"But all that, well, *caring*. It's exhausting, being all about another person. That's why I'm not married, although I tried it. A flight attendant—those expectations I can meet. A drink, a blanket, a meal when I work first class. Maybe a little bit of attention when some guy gets on all pumped about himself, needs to find a way to brag while pretending he's not. It's funny, it's never the really famous or successful people who hold forth about themselves. I haven't had that many celebrities on my flights—I fly mainly Baltimore to Detroit, sometimes Minneapolis and sometimes I'm on a route that continues to Seattle—but I've had some famous people on board and they really do NOT want to be hassled. They want to be recognized, sure, but that's enough. No, it's usually some salesman who's just made, I don't know, whatever milestone his industry uses, some big sale or award, who needs to impress upon me just how very, very successful he is."

Sean doesn't recall McKey talking this much. Maybe that is another change, part of the transformation from Mickey to McKey. One of the nicest things about Mickey was that she used words for concrete, tangible purposes. *Let's go here. Let's do this.* She had been like a boy that way. A boy with a bangin' body.

"We didn't have sex," she says, turning back from the mirror, fiddling with her scarf.

There's the girl he remembers. Direct and blunt.

"You were wasted. I had to drape your arm over my shoulder to get you here. You didn't even drink that much, not that I noticed, but you were fucked-up. And suddenly, really fast. If Tim had seen the way you were headed, I don't think he would have left when he did."

Sean feels as if he remembers the evening, which isn't quite the same as remembering it. There was barbecue, quite decent, and he was drinking beer. He switched to Jameson at some point, but he didn't pound shots or anything. He didn't drink that much, but he probably hadn't been eating regularly. Funerals were like weddings that way. Family members barely got a bite down, they were so busy consoling the people whose ostensible job was to console them.

Of course, the guest of honor at a funeral never eats at all.

McKey sits on the water bed, which shivers beneath them, exacting a toll on his aching head.

"I wanted to," she says. "But you're married. Happily, Gwen told me. *Warned* me. Maybe that's true, but I think she wants you for herself."

"I am," he says, his voice weak, croaky. "Happily married. I've never—"

"Of course you haven't. You're the good one. You'll always be the good one, Sean."

If he is so good, then why is he thinking about what it would be like to take that uniform off McKey?

"It's my fault, how drunk you got," she says matter-of-factly, patting his cheek. "I wasn't thinking of you, only myself, what I needed to tell you. Of course it was upsetting. I kept talking and talking, and you kept drinking because I wasn't letting you get a word in edgewise."

He has no idea what she is referring to. His blankness must be transparent because she then says: "You don't remember? Maybe it's for the best. We'll talk about it later. Or maybe not. I'm sure it was hard. And it violated everything AA is about. Still, I thought you should know, and we ended up alone together in a bar."

"In a bar." But she just mentioned AA. Something's not hanging together.

"They know me there," she says. "I drink club soda with a splash of tonic and lime. It looks like a gin and tonic and it keeps people from being so damn *pained* around me. There are different ways to be sober, you know. Some of us learn to navigate the other world, the one where people drink. Go-Go was the opposite. When he went into a bar, all he saw, all he thought about, was drinking. There was no other reality for him. He shouldn't have tested himself that way. I wasn't there, but I can figure out what happened, Sean. I *know*." No trace of the arch Baltimore accent this time. "I don't care what anyone says. Go-Go didn't kill himself. He got drunk. He crashed. End of story. No matter what the toxicology report says. It would take very little alcohol to fuck him up."

She glances at the clock on the wall. It is charming, yet generic, the kind of thing Sean's wife despises. His wife's entire life centers on not having anything that anyone else has. She buys into the idea that there is one perfect everything, all the way down to the light plates. The problem is, Vivian's process is so time-intensive that it never ends. Every time she "finishes" one room, another room is begging to be redecorated, having gone out of style or spawned low-end imitators, which means she is no longer one of a kind.

"Gotta go," McKey says. "Just push the button on the lock, don't worry about the dead bolt. I don't. Another perk of this location. It's pretty safe."

She kisses him on his cheek and leaves, sending the water bed lurching again. After a few minutes, Sean manages to heave himself out of it without actually heaving, gathering up his shirt and socks, folded neatly in a chair, locating his shoes, oxfords that someone—well, OK, McKey—has untied and removed, finding his jacket and overcoat in the closet. She wanted to sleep with him. He can't help feeling good about that.

Only what did she tell him about Go-Go, exactly? Something about Go-Go and AA, why it wasn't working for him. Why can't he remember? Is it possible he simply doesn't want to remember? Sean has always been very good about forgetting inconvenient things.

Summer 1978

Chapter Eight

"Don't touch my guitar, little boy."

The voice was as grimy as the hand, low and guttural and flecked with debris, but matter-of-fact, not particularly harsh or threatening. Although we had all yelped when the hand shot out—even Tim and Sean, although they later denied it—we felt strangely calm. Except, perhaps, Go-Go, who writhed in the hand's grip but could not free himself. Go-Go was terrified.

The man sat up, releasing Go-Go, although Go-Go continued to twist and turn as if held by invisible hands. The man was not really grimy, we saw, but extremely dark-skinned, black as ink, although with large patches of pink-white skin. His forehead, the area around his right eye, his right cheek, and chin were all ghostly, without pigmentation. Later, we managed to find a way to ask Gwen's father about this without revealing why we were asking. He explained that a person with this skin condition wasn't a burn victim, as some of us thought, or diseased in any way. But before that explanation was offered, we speculated at length on his appearance. Leprosy, Sean said. A horrible accident, Gwen said. Burned himself up smoking in bed, Tim said. Go-Go said he was a monster, and Mickey said he was just born that way, and she was closest to right.

"What are you children doing in my house?" the man asked us, although the word sounded like *chillrun* in his mouth. We would come to understand that his words were as soft and mushy as the food required by his rotting teeth, which made his breath fearsome. He didn't seem angry. He didn't even seem particularly curious. And, unlike most adults who asked that question, he apparently wanted an answer, a real one. He wasn't quizzing us as a pretext for scolding us, or setting us up, testing to see if we would lie to him. He honestly thought we might have a good reason for being there.

"We didn't know it was anyone's house," Mickey said.

"We didn't know it was anyone's house," Sean repeated, a little louder. Sean had a way of saying what someone else had already said, yet making the words his own.

"You knew it was *somebody's*," the man said. His voice was mild, though. "Laundry on the line. Chickens. Didn't you see my chickens?"

He made a clucking sound, and the chickens crossed the threshold, almost as if in a parade. They gave us a wide berth, cutting as large a circle as possible in the small house. He picked up the one in the front, stroking it and cooing to it as if it were something much more cuddly, a kitten or a puppy.

"Do you eat them?" Go-Go asked, and the rest of us wanted to shush him. But the man didn't seem to mind Go-Go's question. He didn't seem to mind Go-Go, which was unusual in an adult. Go-Go got on grown-ups' nerves quickly, very quickly.

"Sure," he said. "What else is chickens for?"

"Eggs," Tim said.

"That's true," the man said. "And I eat eggs, too. But I got to make do with what I have. My garden, my chickens, things that folks bring me."

"What do you do when the cold weather comes?" Mickey asked, bold as ever.

"Build a fire in the stove. Put an extra blanket on the bed. Keep the door shut."

"And the chickens?"

He had grown tired of the conversation, or tired of us. He bent down and pulled the guitar out from under the bed. We were kids then, all adults were old to us, but Chicken George, as we would come to call him, was especially confounding. You could have told us he was fifty, not that much older than Tim is now, or you could have told us ninety, and we wouldn't have argued. He was *old,* someone who had seen a lot and knew a lot.

He began to play the guitar and sing. His voice was awful and he didn't know the words to whatever song he was trying to play, so there were a lot of uh-huhs and moans. If Mick Jagger had been standing there, he probably would have been in ecstasy at this raw display of old-fashioned blues playing and singing, but we were callow kids. We listened to Billy Joel. Some of us still do, even if we don't admit it.

"It is customary," he said when he finished, "to reward a man if you like his song."

He held out his palm, which was amazingly pink, pink as the pads on a newborn kitten's feet. It was creased and craggy, a hard-working hand, yet rosy pink. We stared at his hand, not gleaning what he wanted. Sean, at last, put a quarter in it, and the man actually bit the coin. But then he smiled, letting us know he was in on the joke, that he knew biting a coin was something people did with gold pieces in a movie, not with a quarter from Sean's pocket.

"Well, I guess you weren't expecting a show, so that's okay that you don't have more," he said. "Tell me your names."

Mickey took the lead.

"I'm Leia," she said.

"Han," said Sean, always quick.

"Luke," said Tim.

"Carrie," said Gwen, who couldn't think of another girl's name from *Star Wars*, clearly begrudging Mickey's decision to crown herself as the princess.

"Go-Go," said Go-Go, not getting it. Even if he had, he probably would have said R2-D2 or Obi-Wan. It was funny about Go-Go. He lied. He lied a lot, trying to avoid punishment for his various misdeeds. But he was bad at it. He couldn't tell a lie to save his life. And his honesty often came out at just the wrong time.

"Where y'all live?"

"Franklintown Road," Mickey said. There probably weren't four or five houses along Franklintown, but it was nearby and a credible place for us to be from. If we mentioned Dickeyville, we would give ourselves away. Should the man ever come up that way, determined to find the five children who had come into his house and tried to take his guitar—not that we would have taken it, but that's probably what he thought—he would find us all too easily. All he would have to say is: blond girl, brunette girl, three boys with their hair cut way short, and everyone would say, Oh, the Halloran boys, fat Gwen, and that dark-haired girl they play with.

"And you came all the way down here. Huh. You going to come visit me again?"

It sounded more like a request than a question. Why would we come here again? What was the point of visiting this strange old man, who smelled bad and couldn't sing?

"Sure," said Sean, our spokesman.

"I need some canned goods," he said. "Beans, soup. And I wouldn't mind some new shirts. I like them flannel shirts, but I need T-shirts, too."

"Sure."

Why not agree? We were never going to return here. It was a far walk, something to do on a summer's day when you had all the time in the world. Come Labor Day and school, we wouldn't have the time. What was the harm in promising that Leia, Han, Luke, Carrie, and Go-Go would return?

We were back within the week, with all the things he requested.

We called him Chicken George, after the character in *Roots*, which had aired the previous year. He never seemed to remember our names, nor notice when we slipped and used our real ones. He asked almost nothing of us, beyond the canned goods and old shirts we pulled from our parents' homes, and each visit was the same: he would play his guitar, singing in his caterwauling style, and Go-Go would dance his dance, flinging his body around as only he could. It shouldn't have been fun and yet it was, if only because it was a secret among the five of us. There was no one else in Chicken George's life, no one else who knew of him or cared about him. He was ours, a new toy.

And, in time, we treated him as all children treat their toys—with increasing carelessness and indifference.

Chapter Nine

*For four years, Gwen has lobbied for the right to telecommute, only to re-*ceive the most infuriating argument in the world from her boss: she wouldn't like it. As if she were a child who didn't know what she wants. But then, Gwen has always hated pronouncements about her character, anyone else's attempt to define her. She tolerates this tendency, just barely, from loved ones, although Karl's observations about her these days are hurtful. But she cannot stand it when anyone else attempts to sum her up. She would hate to be profiled in her own magazine, which allots a few breezy sentences, equal parts biography, description, and idiosyncrasy, to summing up someone's entire character. Besides, her request should be considered on its merits, not on her publisher's belief that he knows better than she what she wants.

But in caring for her father, Gwen has quickly discovered her publisher is right: she's not built for telecommuting. Not that she ever wanted to work from home every day. Her work life involves too many meetings and lunches and functions for that to be feasible. But she thought everyone would thrive if she were allowed to work at home one day a week, shutting herself away with her reporters' copy, free from the interruptions of the workplace. In her father's house, she has discovered there are even more distractions away from the office than there, and she can't even blame her father, a stoic patient, almost to a fault. He never asks for anything from her and can barely force himself to seek the day aide's help.

Gwen keeps cooking, for instance, rationalizing that she is trying to find dishes that are gentle, yet not insulting to her father's palate. Homemade puddings and soft-boiled eggs in delicate sauces, milk shakes and smoothies. She has tackled the rather messy job of dusting his books, a task he used to do every year but has clearly ignored for at least a decade now.

And then there is her mother's closet.

Gwen was a senior in college when her mother died. Back then, she was still very much the family baby, still young enough to be allowed the privilege of falling apart while Miller and Fee, proper adults, stepped in and helped her bewildered father make arrangements, short- and long-term. Tally Robison's end was at once shockingly fast and excruciatingly slow, six weeks from diagnosis to death. It was agreed that Gwen should stay in school, up at Barnard, until the semester ended or she was summoned home. She submitted her final paper on an eerily balmy December day, then returned to her apartment to find the message light blinking on her machine, something that had once heralded only joy, usually in the form of a new conquest: *Come home now.* It didn't occur to her to spring for the Metroliner, as the fast train was known then, and the old NortheastDirect wheezed its way down to Baltimore, indifferent to her urgency. By the time she arrived at University Hospital, her mother was dead.

"She was out of it the past two days. She wouldn't have known you," Fee said, meaning to comfort her. Or did she? To this day, Gwen can't help wondering. With her dark hair and eyes, Fee looks exactly like Clem and Miller, which is a kind way of saying she is plain. Although not what anyone would call butch, she always disdained Gwen's girly-girly ways, her flirtatious style of wheedling. She probably resented the way that Gwen was raised practically as an only child, not to mention the duties thrust upon Fee as Gwen's primary babysitter, starting at the much too young age of eleven. That was when Tally started going to the ceramics studio in Mount Washington, or was it the weavers' collective in Clarksville?

Gwen feels bad now, looking back, at how she acted. It was as if her mother's death had happened only to her. And, maybe a little bit, to her father. But not to Miller and Fee. Her brother and sister, edging toward thirty, seemed old to her. They had jobs, spouses, children. Well, Miller had all three, and Fee was living with the woman she would one day marry. It was part of the natural order for them to experience death. But not Gwen. She moped around the house through Christmas break, of help to no one, unaware that there was any help to be provided, that death required anything besides mourning. Then she went back to school and wrote a lot of poetry in between her journalism assignments, never stopping to consider that Miller and Fee had lost their mother, too. She did think a lot about how Mickey failed to come by over the holidays, which functioned as an open-ended mourning period. No Mickey, although she had remained in the area when her mother moved to Florida. The senior Hallorans made a dutiful visit. Mrs. Halloran brought crab dip, which Gwen's father wasn't sure was safe to eat.

That was almost twenty-five years ago. A quarter of a century, and now Gwen is approaching the half-century mark, only five years out. She realizes some of her mother's things must still be in the house. True, the jewelry was divided between the sisters long ago, not that Fee has much use for Tally's jewelry, although she insisted on taking a coral squash blossom ring that Gwen coveted. Other things have been boxed up, donated to thrift stores. But the closet is still quite full, and Gwen keeps returning to it, losing hours in it. Each dress has a memory. Some even hold on to Tally's signature perfume, Shalimar.

So Gwen is sorting through her mother's clothes, putting aside items for Annabelle's dress-up chest and appropriating some more timeless things for herself—cashmere sweaters, a fabulous wool cape—when the doorbell rings. She shouts to her father's aide that she will answer it and runs down the stairs to throw open the door.

"Mrs. Halloran!"

She looks awful, understandably. Puffy, sleepless, possibly unwashed. But she carries a dish in her hands. More crab dip?

"You didn't have to do this," Gwen says. "I should be doing this for you."

"Oh, it helped take my mind off things." She looks around, as if in search of something.

"Would you like a cup of tea?" Gwen asks. "My father is napping, but if he wakes up, he'll be happy to visit with us."

"Tea would be nice."

Gwen takes the plate to the kitchen and peels back the aluminum foil. They are store-bought cookies, she recognizes them from the wake. And not even good store-bought cookies. How had throwing these leftovers on a plate helped to distract Mrs. Halloran from anything? Gwen doesn't want to be unkind, but there is something *hostile* about these cookies. She struggles with the etiquette of the moment. What would be ruder: putting them out with the tea or leaving them in the kitchen? Gwen arranges them on an elaborate pink-patterned plate, then washes Mrs. Halloran's white plastic one while the tea brews. She assumed Mrs.

Halloran would follow her into the kitchen, but from the sound of things, she is moving around the living room, probably wondering at the disarray of Clem's books, still in stacks on the floor. Gwen hopes she doesn't bother her father, asleep in the sunroom at the rear of the house.

They have tea in the dining room, at the heavy Swedish modern table that was out of style almost as soon as Tally bought it. Now it's finally *vintage*.

"So," Mrs. Halloran says, "I guess the young people had quite a night of it."

"The young people?" Gwen is honestly confused, assumes that Mrs. Halloran is referring to Tim's daughters, three steely-eyed beauties who give the impression of having said something devastating about someone else in the room. Go-Go's children are little more than babies, and Sean's son did not make the trip from Florida. Neither did his wife, come to think of it. There was something about a commitment on his son's part, something he couldn't get out of without ruining it for others—a big game, a performance?—and Sean's wife stayed behind with him.

"You and the boys," Mrs. Halloran clarifies. "And that Mickey."

"Thanks for calling me young," Gwen says. "But I didn't go out. I had to check on my daughter. Even though I'm staying here, I drive home to put her to bed each night."

So don't gossip about me, Doris Halloran. Of course Mrs. Halloran would be within her rights to speculate about Gwen's marriage. But she can't *know* based on the information available to her, so she would be gossiping.

"I just assumed you were all together," Mrs. Halloran says. "He said you were all out late, talking about old times, and he didn't think he should drive, so he stayed over at Tim's."

"Sean always was the sensible one," Gwen says.

"Yes, he's a good boy." Doris Halloran sips her tea, takes one of the cookies, but holds it in her hand, as if she can't remember what it is. "All my boys are good boys."

Gwen notes the present tense in her voice. It is a lie twice-over. Go-Go is no longer anything, and he was never good, everyone knows that. Not bad, but not good. The statement is like this plate of stale, off-brand cookies. Baffling, challenging, passive-aggressive. She decides to agree. "Yes."

"You know—" Mrs. Halloran says, then pauses significantly, and Gwen realizes she *doesn't* know, that she has no idea what Mrs. Halloran is going to say next and that's actually unusual in life. Even when she told Karl she was leaving him, he wasn't particularly surprised. "You know, I called Tim's wife this morning."

"Is everything okay?"

"There was a pair of gloves, I thought it belonged to one of the girls. Pink ones. Tim said they might be Lisa's. The funny thing is that Arlene didn't mention that Sean had stayed over."

Gwen feels she's being taunted, but she's not sure how or why. The only thing she knows is that she wasn't with the boys last night. But maybe that's what Mrs. Halloran is trying to find out? The old loyalties kick in, as automatic and destructive as ever.

"Maybe she assumed that he had called you."

"Why would she assume that?"

"Because Sean has always been the conscientious one, of all of us. He always does the right thing."

This, apparently, is what Mrs. Halloran has come to hear, or close enough. She finishes her tea and leaves, taking with her the washed plate, her little Trojan horse of an offering.

Gwen goes into the sunroom, now the sickroom. Her father's awake, alert, staring into space. It's the aide who sleeps, dozing in her chair, her head bent at a painful angle.

"Poor Doris," he says in a whisper, careful not to wake the woman who is supposed to be caring for him. So he knows Mrs.

Halloran came to call, probably heard their entire conversation but didn't ask to join them. "I do feel awful that I couldn't go to the funeral."

"That's okay, Dad. I was there. I represented for our family."

"It's unnatural," he says. "To outlive one's child."

Gwen knows he's right, she said as much at the wake. But there's a part of her that finds it surprising that Go-Go made it to forty. She sees him in her memories, scurrying along high, flimsy branches near power lines, taking his sled down slopes far scarier than so-called Suicide Hill. There was never any joy in his risk taking, come to think of it. He wanted to fall, to be shocked, to hit a tree. Go-Go has been reaching for things and running into things as long as she's known him. Could a little boy have a death wish? If so, did Go-Go always have it, or was it something that came later?

"There are no good deaths," Gwen says, just to say something.

"Oh, no," her father says, adamant. "There are some. You haven't known any, yet. But I'm planning on one."

"Don't talk that way."

Her father smiles. "You look so like your mother. You should keep that."

Gwen glances down. She hasn't registered the fact that she's wearing one of her mother's old cashmere cardigans, truly old, one she must have worn as a teenager, embroidered with pearls and sequins. When the doorbell rang, she was in too much of a hurry to take it off. Now she feels guilty, as if she's been caught rummaging through things that are rightfully her father's, not hers, waiting for the good death he has just promised her.

"I didn't mean—I never realized there was so much of her stuff left, and I thought I might organize it."

"You should go home, Gwen."

"I'll leave in a little bit. No use fighting the traffic."

"I mean to stay."

"No."

"Nothing's perfect," her father says. "Nobody's perfect."

"Karl is. Haven't you heard? Haven't you seen his television alter ego, solving everyone's problems?"

Her father sighs.

"You told me not to marry him."

"I told you what it would be like to be married to a surgeon. That's not the same thing. Now there's a child. Think of her."

"Maybe I am thinking of her."

"When we were young, your mother and I—well, not young exactly, I was never young with her, but younger—and you were the only one left at home, there were so many divorces all of a sudden, so many parents who thought their children couldn't be happy unless they, the parents, were happy. I'm afraid that's simply not true."

"You had a great marriage, Dad. It's not fair to lecture others on marriage, when you had such a good one."

Her father doesn't answer right away. "I see your point of view," he says, forever fair and evenhanded. Later, she will parse these words. Not: *you're right.* But: *I see your point of view.* Was he trying to suggest that his marriage, like hers, might have looked better to those outside it than those in it? But, no, that's impossible. Everyone knows that the Robisons loved each other madly.

Autumn 1978–Winter 1979

CHAPTER TEN

We would have quickly grown tired of Chicken George except for one thing: he turned out to be mysterious. At least, that's the way we saw it: He cultivated mystery, excited our curiosity. He was vague in the face of all questions, no matter how benign. How he had come to live in this house, when he had learned the guitar. How old he was. (Go-Go asked the last one. The rest of us knew better than to ask a grown-up's age.) He avoided all questions and had few of his own, other than: "What did you bring me?" Still, it would have been better, harsh as it sounds, if we had stopped visiting him. It's nice to think so, at any rate, because if we had tired of him, then things might have gone differently. And this is a story about things we wished had gone differently. Aren't all stories?

Anyway, Chicken George had a way of disappearing. The first time, it was November, and we assumed it was weather-related.

The wind had started to kick up, the pleasant tang of October had given way to a steady dank cold. Weather was more reliable then. This is not memory, but hard scientific fact. The weather of our childhood was part of an unusually temperate time on our planet, with fewer extreme variations. The things we have seen in recent years—the events of just the past year, with almost a hundred inches of snow in Baltimore and floods, not to mention volcanoes and earthquakes, birds falling from the skies—might well be connected to climate change, the wear and tear that humans wreak on a planet. We are not here to argue science. But weather was more predictable then, and when it turned cold, it stayed cold, so cold the pond froze for days, even weeks of ice-skating. It made sense that Chicken George would disappear during such weather. Not that one could tell, by the look of the cabin, that anything had changed. It was as we had first found it, complete with the chickens in the yard and clothing on the line. Go-Go was the one who thought to look for his guitar. That was missing, too.

"What about the chickens?" Gwen asked.

"What about them?" countered Tim.

"They'll die out here. Animals will eat them."

"So what? Chicken George was going to eat them, too. What's the difference?"

"But Chicken George would have been more humane."

Tim laughed. "You think so, Gwen? You think that snapping an animal's neck is that much more humane than being snatched up in the jaws of a dog or a fox? Dead is dead."

Go-Go liked that. "Dead is dead," he raved. "Dead is dead!" He began throwing rocks at the chickens, then running among them, scattering them. But those chickens were tough. They spread out, giving Go-Go room, but they didn't disperse.

Mickey and Sean had been quiet throughout, systematically looking through George's things, trying to find clues. Mickey, although uninterested in school, had a talent for deduction. Gwen's father, noticing how she examined facts and reached conclusions, had tried to interest her in the works of Arthur Conan Doyle, but she had no patience for Sherlock Holmes. Or Nancy Drew, or Trixie Belden, or books in general. She was disdainful of people who read but not in a defensive, anti-intellectual way. She thought reading was a ruse, a completely wasteful activity. If Mickey were the kind of person who trafficked in similes or metaphors, she might have compared reading to rules such as not swimming an hour after a meal, or never going out of the house with wet hair. Instead, she just didn't read and was baffled by those who did. She didn't like television much, either. Mickey plain didn't like sitting still. She wanted to make things happen. She wanted to see if she could jump from mossy stone to mossy stone without falling. She wanted to poke snapping turtles with sticks, and if one snapped, well, that was the point. She would have liked to live like Chicken George—in a cabin, accountable only to herself, although preferably with indoor plumbing.

"He's gone," she said and then it was real. Chicken George was gone. Sean picked up her words, repeated them. "He's gone."

We were sad. No one cried. Tim, Sean, and Mickey never cried, and Gwen and Go-Go had learned to follow their example. But we were all disappointed, and surprised at how disappointed we were. We had brought a bag of canned goods that day, plucked mainly from the Robisons' kitchen, as Tally Robison was the least likely to notice anything missing, although once there was an amazing rage when she didn't find the artichoke hearts she was sure she had in the pantry. Inventories were tighter, more closely monitored, in the other households. Sean, though, sometimes bought a few things out of his allowance, and he had added a can of deviled ham and ready-to-eat baked beans to the sack that Gwen carried. Now he took them out and placed them on Chicken George's shelves.

"They'll just get stolen," Tim said.

But everyone understood what Sean was doing. He was acting as if Chicken George was okay, as if he would return. And soon, much sooner than we expected, he did. It was a raw February day, with plenty of winter left to go, when Mickey saw, or said she saw, a plume of smoke rising from his house. We trooped over there, our feet sticking in the muddy paths, which had been snow-covered only a week or so earlier.

When we arrived, Chicken George was inside his cabin. It wasn't warm, exactly, but it was tolerable, a wispy heat emanating from the old woodstove. He wore multiple layers of clothes and fingerless gloves.

"Where you been?" he asked, as if we were the ones who disappeared. "What did you bring me?"

Chapter Eleven

When the man in 17F rings his call button and announces he is pretty sure he has thrown his dentures into one of the trash bags by accident, McKey need only to glance at her less-senior colleague.

"I don't see why—" Wendy begins.

"Seniority has its privileges," she says. McKey has no idea if seniority applies in this situation, but she isn't about to go scrabbling through the trash because some geezer can't keep track of his own teeth. It isn't her problem. She has a full set of teeth.

"Seniority is a terrible way to determine who does what," Wendy grumbles.

"Yeah, that's what everybody says when they don't have it."

McKey has been with the same airline fifteen years now and has lineholder status, which means she usually knows her schedule a month in advance. Wendy is still a reserve, being plugged into the schedule where she fits. Maybe she'd be a better sport about working her way up if she weren't also McKey's age, possibly older. She looks older, that's for sure. The airlines hire lots of over-forty attendants these days, women reentering the workforce as nests empty or husbands decamp. The airlines probably think that mothers and wives are well suited to waiting on a group of people who regress to childhood—and a surly, drunken childhood at that—the minute they board an airplane. McKey isn't so sure. She's neither wife nor mother, yet she is good at this, has been from the start.

Oh, she was briefly married in her twenties. But it was hard to count that as a marriage, even a starter marriage. They married out of inertia. Inertia and the desire to have a party. They were twenty-eight, long enough out of college and close enough to thirty to feel a little desperate about the numbing sameness of day-to-day life. In the back of McKey's mind, she entertained the idea, even as she was planning the wedding, that it was better to marry before thirty and later divorce than to hit thirty without ever having been married.

But, mainly, she wanted a party, something to break up the tedium. The marriage worked for a while and then it didn't, like a cheap car. They parted with relative ease, given that they didn't own their house and their possessions had never really mingled. It was shocking to realize how few things they had acquired jointly. A mattress, some of the kitchen goods. If it hadn't been for the wedding, complete with registry, there would have been almost nothing to split. They pretended generosity toward each other, when the fact was that neither one wanted to pack up all that shit. A waffle maker that made heart-shaped waffles. A George Foreman grill. A rice maker! *A goddamn rice maker.* McKey realized she had made a very human error, filling out those registries. She thought she was going to change, that in acquiring a rice maker and a waffle iron, she might become the kind of person who made rice and heart-shaped waffles. She knows herself better now, what she can do and what she can't. She even likes herself. Perhaps more than she should, but she's all she has.

Her mother used to warn her—indirectly, then directly—that life was hell for an attractive woman once she ceased to be attractive. McKey isn't buying it. For one thing, she isn't like her mother, relying on men to support her. Besides, her looks are holding up surprisingly well. Not smoking, keeping her weight constant, avoiding the sun—it all adds up. She looks good. Not good for her age. She plain looks good. Every male who boards her flight checks her out, a particular triumph in this polyester getup. Men will always look at her, she has decided, and it isn't conceited to recognize this fact and even exploit it. Did anyone ever say that someone was conceited about money, another commodity to which some people were born?

And she is clear on this: her beauty is a commodity. She uses it to get what she wants or needs. She is not cruel with it, not anymore. She does not wield it like a weapon. She uses it. So what? Everyone uses what they have in this world.

Take Gwen. She isn't as pretty as McKey, but she has this saucer-eyed, you're-so-wonderful thing going on, which boys ate up sideways with a spoon when they were kids. To give her credit, she seemed to come by it naturally, and she didn't use it only on boys. She cast those looks on her parents, on McKey when they first met, eventually on Sean, although never on Tim, not really, and definitely not on Go-Go. The youngest Halloran always made Gwen a little nervous, although perhaps that was her parents, talking through her, especially Tally Robison. Everyone thought Gwen's mom was so saintly, especially after she died. A well-timed death could make a saint out of anyone, as McKey would have reminded the others if they were in touch. But McKey, then Mickey, saw Tally Robison differently. Oh, yes, she was kind to Mickey, sitting down with her in the kitchen in the afternoon, waiting for Gwen to return from school, feeding Mickey the treats that Gwen had chosen for her. But Mickey quickly realized that Mrs. Robison was being kind, and there is no real kindness in obvious magnanimity. Oh, wasn't she the bighearted grand lady, dispensing candy and cookies and Hi-C to the poor little girl who lived in Purnell Village, with her waitress mother and her not-quite-stepfather. Wasn't she enlightened? Wasn't she democratic?

But if an eleven-year-old girl could figure that out, imagine what the rest of the world intuited. They saw Mickey being pitied, that was what, which wasn't fair at all. Mickey's mother might have been a little on the trashy side, but she was pretty steady for a divorced woman who needed a man around. And Rick, the stepfather of record for most of those years, was a good guy. Too good for her mother. He was sincerely kind to Mickey, not fake kind, and when baby Joey arrived, he did what he could to keep her from feeling left out. If anything, he went out of his way to make her feel even more like his daughter. Even after he left, he stayed in touch.

Then, when Mickey was going on nineteen and Rick long gone, an attorney had contacted her. "About custody," he said, and at first Mickey had this crazy feeling that Rick wanted to adopt her all these years later, make official the status he had sworn was hers all along. Rick had done okay for himself, maybe there was some money coming to her.

It turned out that Rick had hired the attorney because Rita was now saying that Joey wasn't his and he was trying to figure out if he could recoup the child support he had been paying her. Legally, the case was kind of interesting, sort of like the Solomon story in the Bible, only instead of offering up a baby that would be sliced in half, it was an all-or-nothing decision about the relationship between Rick and Joey. Rick could have a court establish he was no longer Joey's father and stop paying child support, although he would have a hell of a time getting back what he had paid in. But if he did that, he would have to abandon the relationship, too. It was real fucked-up stuff. Rick, of course, did the right thing. He decided he didn't care what the blood test said. He was Joey's father and he would continue to be, even if that meant paying support to a kid that he seldom got to see. Her scheming skank of a mother really played that poor guy.

Scheming skank of a mother? Have those words really run through McKey's head as she gathers newspapers and trash from the passengers who were sentient enough not to throw their teeth into the bag? She's being unfair. Her mother wasn't a schemer, wasn't skanky. Well, maybe a little skanky. She had been sleeping with Rick and Joey's father at the same time. But she made a genuine mistake about Joey's paternity, and it was harder to test for those things then. Besides, that mistake kept Rick in the fold until McKey went to high school, and she was glad for that. He was a good man. He protected her. He believed her, always.

She catches a man coming out of the lavatory, the smell of smoke clearly on him. She pulls him aside. He looks so furtive and guilty that she doesn't have the resolve to write him up, but she explains to him in an urgent, intimate whisper that she's doing him a favor, that he could be flagged in the reservation system if she reported the infraction as required.

His furtive look switches to flirtatious. Great, now he thinks she's hot for him because she cut him a break, when it was merely her generosity toward her mother overflowing into the world. She goes back to the galley, tells a surprised Wendy that she will take over denture duty, which is still under way, if Wendy will help her keep her distance from Mr. Not-So-Smoking-Hot.

The thing is, she felt kindly toward her outlaw smoker because his face reminded her of Sean's this morning. Not in its particulars, but in the emotions. She had planned to keep Sean in suspense about the night before, but he looked so guilty that she couldn't bear to goad him. She thought, hoped, it might happen, but even as she was piloting him up the stairs, she realized he would be no good to her. A shame. She always had a crush on him. She was surprised, in fact, when he chose Gwen to be his girlfriend, because she assumed he was hers for the taking should she decide she wanted him. She always chalked his relationship with Gwen up to the circumstances, which had been so very *Picture for a Sunday Afternoon*. Sean, carrying Gwen in his arms. Heck, the summer before he couldn't have made it three steps holding her, given how much she once weighed. Gwen clinging to his chest, crying, dazed, that pretty little trickle of blood on her forehead. Who could compete with that? Mickey thought she could, but she was wrong. For a few months there, they acted like they were married, or were going to be. It was nauseating.

Yet Sean and Gwen didn't even make it to Christmas of that year as a couple. And Mickey was *glad*. She wonders how Gwen feels, seeing him now. Childhood sweethearts seem to hold a lot of power over people. McKey's forever hearing of this friend or coworker who has rediscovered someone at a reunion or on the Internet and ends up running off with them. McKey finds that baffling. Who would want to be with the person who remembered you as you once were? She has cut her ties with almost everyone who knew Mickey and she can imagine a day when McKey morphs into yet another persona, shedding her current set of acquaintances and coworkers.

Still, she wishes she had found a way to sleep with Sean, drunk as he was. Just the once. She bets she's better than Gwen, despite Gwen's success rate at landing impressive husbands. Of course, the first one turned out to be a faggot, and McKey has a feeling that even Dr. Wonderful, who put in a brief appearance at the reception after the funeral, isn't quite the prize he seems. They never are. Sean, however—Sean tempts her, if only because he belongs to someone else. The thing she can't work out is whether she wants to steal him from his wife or from Gwen.

Summer 1979

CHAPTER TWELVE

In the spring of the year she would turn fourteen, Gwen did a very odd thing: she asked her parents to take her to visit a classmate, Chloe, who had been stricken with mononucleosis. That was not the weird part, although the two were more friendly than friends, but their school was small enough that Gwen's parents did not question her suddenly fervent desire to visit this particular girl. No, the weird part was when Gwen, after spending a polite twenty minutes chatting with Chloe and catching her up on class gossip, asked to use her bathroom and then stuck Chloe's toothbrush in her mouth, praying that there were still germs on it and she, too, would get mono. We all found out, too, because Gwen told Mickey and Mickey told Tim, who told Sean and Go-Go.

It was an article of faith at the time that mono was a good way to get skinny. We all knew some girl who had lost weight that way. Chloe was already skinny, but another girl at the Park School had caught the so-called kissing disease and appeared six weeks later, suddenly slender, her eyes now huge in her face, cheekbones and collarbones sharp. Gwen was desperate for a similar transformation, but her parents refused to let her diet. That is—they would not let her try Scarsdale, very trendy at the time, or any of the strict, rigid diets that approached religions, with their arbitrary lists of things allowed and things forbidden. The Robisons were happy to make healthy meals for her, to substitute fruit for dessert, to fill the refrigerator with cut-up carrots and celery and hummus, quite avant-garde at the time. Go-Go took a mouthful once and spat it out on the refrigerator door. But Gwen was not allowed to diet. Her mother said that Gwen would come into her height, and the pounds would fall away. Miller and Fiona had gone through similar transformations. Gwen, however, did not believe Tally Robison. She was desperate for her own cure, and Chloe's toothbrush was her best bet.

Yet mono never did come for Gwen. Instead, things happened as her mother had prophesied. She added three inches to her height in three months, and what had been an extra fifteen pounds became just right. Her mother let her buy new clothes, dropping her off at the mall with an allowance and no rules. Gwen bought gauzy, "ethnic" things, long and floaty. She clearly thought she looked a little bit like Stevie Nicks, and she wasn't entirely wrong. She would have looked more like her if her mother had let her get a perm, but that was another one of those odd lines that Tally drew. She, with her long, straight hair, couldn't bear the idea of her daughter having a curly mane.

The rest of us never commented on the change, no matter how Gwen preened and waited for the compliments she believed she deserved. Oh, we noted her clothes, but only to mention how impractical they were. "Those blouses will get caught on tree branches," Mickey said. Tim said he could see her underwear through the thin material of the skirt. Sean told her that she was going to slow us down in her stupid new sandals—that's exactly what he called them, stupid new sandals.

Only Go-Go reached a dirty hand toward her draped arm, eager to feel the material, and she let him. He rubbed it between forefinger and thumb, curious. "Kind of scratchy," he said. Then: "Can boys wear shirts like that?" How Tim and Sean hooted at him, but Go-Go, for once, was not the naif. Lots of boys, other boys, were wearing clothes very much like Gwen's that summer. Even Mickey's stepfather, Rick, wore a linen shirt that made us think of medieval days, peasants toiling the land. It was off-white, with a slit that showed lots of his dark chest hair. And Rick wasn't someone that the Halloran boys could mock. He knew how to fix engines, he had a motorcycle. He really did look like Tom Selleck.

It was the Halloran boys who were out of step with the times, with their short hair and plain white T-shirts. Their summer clothes were what they used to wear to summer camp, but there was no summer camp for them this year. Something had happened. Mr. Halloran had lost his job, which wasn't new. Mr. Halloran was rather famous for losing jobs. He had a temper, he liked to tell the boss what was what, as he said, and that usually ended up with him leaving. It was a bit of a chicken-or-the-egg question whether Mr. Halloran was asked to leave his jobs because he told the boss what was what, or whether he sensed the end was near and decided he had nothing to lose by making such a speech. He had lost enough jobs so that he kept his workplace possessions to a minimum. The difference, in the summer of 1979, was that he was having trouble finding a new one. We didn't talk about it and we didn't know why we didn't talk about it. Over time, there would be more and more subjects like that, things we didn't talk about, for reasons we couldn't identify. Gwen's new appearance. Mr. Halloran's job situation. How good-looking Rick was. Go-Go's increasing craziness, the things he was rumored to do to cats and small animals. But that came later, when we hardly spoke to each other at all.

Gwen and Sean, falling in love, then out. We *never* spoke of that. They held it close, like a secret, but the kind of secret that you were dying for others to ask you about. The rest of us refused to acknowledge it.

Perhaps we should have spoken about that because that was what killed us, as an us. We couldn't be we anymore, not in the face of that impenetrable twosome. We had been a we, and our mathematics teachers, different as they were—the nuns and priests of St. Lawrence and Cardinal Gibbons, the beaten-down old crone at Mickey's public school, the love-is-all hippie type at Park—agreed that a subset of a group could not be greater than the group itself. Venn diagrams proved it. Yet Gwen and Sean were. They formed a group within the group, and it swamped us like a wave, we couldn't escape it. All because of the damn clothes, which were the result of Gwen getting thin, which we still trace back to Chloe's toothbrush, even if it didn't give Gwen mono, as she had hoped. It began with the toothbrush, with moon-faced Gwen sneaking into some girl's bathroom sucking on her red-handled Oral-B. Some girls aren't very good at being pretty. There, it's been said. Gwen became very pretty, very fast, and she didn't know how to handle it. She was as destructive as Go-Go, running through the woods with a pointed stick or tossing rocks in the air, heedless of where they might land. But everyone knew to get out of Go-Go's way when he was acting crazy. Gwen tore through us with no warning.

It was late July, that point on the calendar where summer has gotten a little old, boring. After two days of heavy rains, the stream was wide and fast in places. Emboldened by our friendship with

Chicken George, we had been pushing deeper and deeper into the woods each day, taking sack lunches prepared by Mrs. Robison or Mrs. Halloran. We found what appeared to be a broken concrete dam, most of it submerged in the rushing brown stream, but with a few jagged pieces above the waterline. Tim insisted on crossing there. Mickey scrambled behind him, sure-footed as ever in anything that wasn't an athletic contest.

Go-Go went next, forever indifferent to the water, no matter how many times we had been told it was polluted and deadly, and his very indifference somehow kept him safe. Sean waited for Gwen to go. She clearly didn't want to cross, but it was too late to argue against Tim's plan, and she would have been shamed if she didn't try. She lost her footing on her second or third step, and although she righted herself, the sleeve of her filmy, flimsy blouse caught on something in the water. If she had pulled back sharply, she would have been fine, but she didn't want to tear the blouse. She reached down, determined to gently extract the material from whatever had snagged it—and that was when she fell into the water. The horrible, murky water, which we had been told countless times could kill us, the water whose merest contact required tetanus boosters.

She didn't come up.

In water that brown, it would have been impossible to see blood, but Go-Go pointed, screaming in that way he had, so we couldn't tell if he was happy or scared. "Blood! Blood!" Gwen bobbed to the surface, floated, like the Lily Maid of Astolat. Not that we knew the poem, but Gwen had read *Anne of Green Gables,* in which Anne has to be rescued after attempting to re-create the maiden's fate. We knew a lot of stuff in that secondhand, watered-down way, through cartoons and books and television shows. Which, perhaps, is a way of saying we knew nothing.

Those of us who had crossed to the other bank froze, but Sean plunged into the water. Gwen's body kept moving away from him, almost as if it were a game. *Catch me if you can.* The others ran down the bank, shouting contradictory instructions. "Shut up," Sean shouted through gritted teeth. "Shut up." He was wading, the water up to his waist, reaching for her, but she kept slipping from his grasp. Gwen might have eluded him forever, but a stick saved her this time, catching her skirt just long enough to give Sean time to catch up to her. He gathered her up in his arms and carried her to shore, then began giving her mouth-to-mouth, which he had learned in swimming classes at the camp the Hallorans could no longer afford.

"She'll be brain damaged," Mickey said. "She was unconscious too long, she took in too much water."

"Shut up," Tim said.

Go-Go jumped up and down, chanting: "Out goes the bad air, in goes the good air." That's how it worked in cartoons. We had all seen it ourselves on the old *Captain Chesapeake* show. In cartoons, the characters pushed on each other's stomachs with great force and manipulated their arms.

In cartoons, the people always woke up. Gwen was not waking up.

But after what seemed an eternity, she coughed, spitting up a little water before vomiting a violent brackish stream. Sean sat back on his haunches, but he ended up catching some of it on his ankles.

"Are you OK?"

Tim stood over her. "How many fingers am I holding up?"

Sean swatted at his leg. "Don't be stupid."

"Three," Gwen said. "What happened?"

"You fell," Sean said. "You hit your head, you almost drowned."

"Drowned!" Go-Go said.

She lifted a hand to her head, but there was no cut, there had been no blood, no matter what Go-Go thought he saw. "I feel a bump," she said. Sean's fingers followed hers, probing tenderly. It was hard not to notice that the gauzy shirt, the source of all this trouble, was transparent and clinging now, her bra visible. Gwen crossed her arms over her chest.

"The important thing," Mickey said, "is to figure out what to tell the grown-ups."

"What do you mean?"

"Gwen's soaked, her shirt is torn. Her mother will see that and demand an explanation. They'll know we had to go pretty far downstream to get to a place where the water runs this fast and deep, and we'll be in trouble."

"No one said we couldn't," said Tim, the master of the loophole, the king of technicalities.

"Mickey's right," Sean said. "No one said specifically we couldn't go this far, but we never ask, because we know they'll say no, and if they find out where we were, they'll make rules against it. We have to get Gwen as dry as possible. When did you have your last tetanus shot?"

"Last summer, after I cut myself on that rusty fence."

Sean said: "It's been at least a few years for me. How long do the shots last?"

We didn't know. We knew the horrors of lockjaw, though. Gwen's father had covered that for us in great detail.

"I don't have any cuts, though," Sean said. "And I didn't swallow any water. I'll be okay."

We thought at the time that Sean was taking one for the team, that he was willing to forgo the tetanus shot if it meant that we could continue to roam the park with no boundaries placed on us.

But Sean's only concern was Gwen. He was making this heroic gesture for her because she had been unconscious during his true heroism and unable to appreciate it. Or had she been? Some of us wondered.

"Chicken George," Mickey said. "He'll help us, and he won't ask any questions."

"There's no shower there," Gwen said. "And I don't want to wear his dirty clothes."

"Trust me," Mickey said.

We made our way back through the woods, to Chicken George's house. He wasn't surprised to see us. He was never surprised to see us. Although our comings and goings appeared random to us and therefore unpredictable, Chicken George seemed attuned to our movements the way he was attuned to his chickens, the seasons, the park. He was never caught off guard. He examined Gwen carefully, with those strange hands, so pink on one side, so dark on the other. He produced a Goody comb, still in its plastic wrapper, and worked it carefully through her wet, matted hair. He gave her a sheet from the line, so she knew it was clean and fresh, told her to go inside and change out of her wet clothes, wrap herself in the sheet as if it were a toga, and bring her clothes out. He actually said *toga,* and we were surprised he knew the word.

"To-ga, to-ga," Go-Go began to chant. We had not seen the movie *Animal House.* We were too young. But it had filtered down into the culture, and we knew the set pieces, some of the lines. It was soon to be the era of trickle-down economics, but if you asked us, we would have said that adulthood, too, was a process of trickling down, that we picked up the scraps of adult life as surely as we went behind our parents at their dinner parties and stole sips from their glasses, bites from their plates. We shook cigarettes free from open packets, took tiny swigs from the bottles in the liquor cabinet. They knew, they had to know, because we know now everything our children do, no matter how sly they think they are. The difference is that our parents approved. They preferred for us to tiptoe into adulthood through these tiny subterfuges. It's not a rationalization, but a truth: they encouraged us to lie, to keep things from them, to protect them from what we knew. It started small. The forays into the park. Our friendship with Chicken George. Gwen's near-drowning, the time the truck almost crushed Go-Go. It started small, and then it got so large, so fast, that it swept us all away.

But the real problem was that Gwen and Sean fell in love. As five, we were mighty, the points on a star. Remember learning how to draw a star? When you are little, it seems impossible, out of reach. You draw lopsided, lumpy things. Then one day, someone shows you the secret. Mickey taught it to Go-Go: one line slashing down, a second shooting up in a diagonal. Straight across, diagonal down, diagonal up. A mere five lines, but when you have finished, there are six shapes within the one: five triangles clustered around a pentagon. Yes, there are even more, you can add and subtract lines, creating more shapes. But if you are true to the integrity of the lines you have drawn, there are five triangles and a pentagon. The pentagon was what grounded us, a magnetic field that held us together. Some might say the pentagon was Chicken George, but it was our talent for secrecy, our sense of ourselves as a single community. Once we five joined, truly joined, it was never boys against girls, or Hallorans against the other two families. No, it was Sean and Gwen who destroyed us. Two of our triangles cut themselves off and ran away together, and we were never whole again. Never.

Less than a week after Chicken George gave Gwen a sheet and dried her clothes by his fire, he disappeared again. And this time, he seemed to be *gone* gone—his cupboards bare, the line empty of wash, the chickens pecking at our ankles in a newfound desperation, but we had no feed to give them. You couldn't say the place was clean. It would never be clean. But it was neat, emptied out. Even Chicken George knew that an era had ended. The five of us stopped going to his cabin.

But Gwen and Sean still went. All summer long, they slipped away to that cabin, never dreaming that anyone was watching them.

Chapter Thirteen

"*And he—*" *Giggle.*

The sentence and the giggle ends before Tim comes through the swinging door into the kitchen and confronts three sets of round, blue eyes. Round with innocence, which, he's pretty sure, is fake. But also round with cold, if such a thing were possible, like the mass-manufactured ice found at buffets. His daughters have taken to regarding him with round, cold eyes these days, as if by widening them they could empty them of all hints, all clues to their existence and inner thoughts. However, he is pretty sure that their thoughts run something like this: *boys boys boys boys shoes boys.* And maybe, although he hopes not, *partying,* although he is unclear if partying is simply a by-product, a place to wear shoes and find boys, or if the partying is the destination, the boys and shoes the vehicles. Even the littlest one, only eight, is in on the act. They are three of a kind, thick as thieves. Identical blue eyes, long blond hair, worn straight and parted down the middle, heart-shaped and heartbreaking faces.

"Good morning," he says. He knows better—now—than to ask about the interrupted, overheard comment. He knows not to ask anything. Move along, nothing to see here. His daughters remind him of the salamanders he and his brother hunted at the old springhouse. Salmon pink with tiny spots, they were easy enough to see in the clear, rushing water. But to grab one—almost impossible. Only Go-Go had been quick enough, and even he could never hold on to the little buggers. Tim can observe his daughters, but he can't hold them, not anymore.

"Can I have the car today?" asks the oldest, Michelle. "I have to go to Mary's."

"I was going to play golf." He is careful not to say no immediately, to offer the reason before the rejection. The mere sound of that syllable, *no,* seems to drive his daughters insane, triggering horrible pouting rages. Instead he tries to let them work their way toward *no* through inference. If he has a golf date, it stands to reason he will need the car for a good chunk of the day. Certainly his daughters can figure that out.

"Can't one of your friends take you?" Michelle counters.

He wants to say the same thing back to her. But, no—be Joe Friday. Just the facts, ma'am: "My tee time is at eleven A.M."

"I don't need the car until one," Michelle says.

"And she could drop me at the movies, then pick me up on the way home," says Lisa, the middle girl. He waits to see if the baby, Karen, is going to throw herself on the pile, a little pyramid of daughters he will then be forced to knock over with his unfathomable cruelty, his desire to use his own car on his day off. How could he? He is the meanest daddy in the whole wide world. Until recently, he would have given them the car, found another way. He used to believe that if he said yes to all the easy things, the girls would be grateful and well behaved.

Then he saw the much-too-old-for-her boy—twenty, twenty-one?—dropping Michelle off on a Saturday morning, when she was supposedly returning from a sleepover at Mary's. *Who was that?* he asked, struggling to keep his voice casual. *Oh, Mary's older brother. He was nice enough to bring me home early when I said I didn't feel good. The smell of pancakes made me want to vomit.*

He and Arlene waited until all the girls were out of the house, then tossed Michelle's room. They found the birth control pills beneath a pile of bras, filmy insubstantial things that didn't look up to the task of harnessing his daughter's frighteningly developed breasts. But neither he nor Arlene was sure what to do next. Obviously, they couldn't take the pills because Michelle would probably stop using them, possibly fulfill her unspoken ambition to be picked for MTV's *Teen Moms*. Yet if they confronted her, what would they say? *You can't have sex? You can't use birth control? You can have sex and use birth control, but we have to be part of the decision?* Tim doesn't want any part of his daughter's sex life. He wants his daughter not to have a sex life. Is that so much to ask?

They were still trying to figure out what to do about Michelle when the mother of Lisa's best friend called. They had discovered a joint in her daughter's room, and the daughter said it was Lisa's, that she let her hide her "stash" there. The two sets of parents talked to the girls alone, then together. They played good cop, bad cop. They threatened, cajoled. And those two little teenyboppers turned out to be tougher than the most hardened career criminals that Tim could imagine. And Tim, as an assistant state's attorney in Baltimore County, knows from hardened career criminals. He blames *Law & Order*. Everybody is too fucking savvy these days. When he tried to tell the girls that he could send the joint to the crime lab and figure out which one of them had smoked it, Lisa's friend, Dani, said blandly, "There's a huge backup. Plus, our DNA isn't on file, and I'm not letting you swab my cheek unless you get a court order."

He decided to believe his own daughter. Why would a non-drug user let someone stash drugs in her home, especially a hard little number like this Dani, a fleshy, unattractive girl who has trouble written all over her? That gut on her was probably the result of pot-inspired munchies. It was a weird thing, maybe a trick of memory, but teenage girls these days seemed fatter to Tim. Either really fat or a little too slender, his daughters falling in the second camp. It kills him, when he does the laundry, to see how tiny their clothes are, and not just the baby's, as they secretly still think of Karen. The tiny underwear, which wouldn't hold one of Arlene's ass cheeks even in her college days, the little T-shirts, the narrow blue jeans. Anyway, this Dani is bad news. The two sets of parents decided to keep the girls apart for a while, see what transpired. The other parents got custody of the joint. Tim wondered if they had smoked it. They looked a little unsavory, those parents.

Michelle having sex. Lisa maybe smoking pot, or friends with a stoner. He wonders what Karen has up her sleeve. Only eight, one of those drunken mistakes that married couples make on their anniversary nights, she should be Daddy's little angel, years away from breaking his heart. But with Michelle and Lisa as her role models, she is clearly ready to raise some hell as soon as she figures out how. Just last week, he caught her playing a kissing game with a neighborhood boy. Only kissing, not doctor, but *still*. He wishes, not for the first time, that St. Lawrence was still open for business, that he could send his girls to a school where the nuns knew how to terrify children into behaving. But the problem isn't that his old parish school has closed. There are, after all, other parish schools, although fewer of them each year, thanks to the financial troubles that never end for the archdiocese. No, he needs his girls to go to his school in the past. Circa 1950 might work.

"Girls have always had sex," Arlene said when he confided his retro fantasy. "The difference is that they used to get pregnant and ruin their lives."

"Really? Where were all those girls when I was seventeen?"

Arlene laughed, punched his arm, assuming he was joking. But Tim was a virgin at seventeen, which wasn't unheard of in 1979, although kind of a torture when you thought your younger brother was getting it.

The summer Sean and Gwen started going together, Tim had been obsessed with their sex life. It was weird, given that she was not quite fourteen and Sean was fifteen, but his imagination had been inflamed by the possibility they were doing it. He decided they must be doing it because Sean never wanted to talk to him about it. He tried to follow them when they escaped to the woods in the afternoons and weekends, even agreed to drive them to the mall and attend the same matinees, in hopes of seeing what they did with—and to—each other. But they mainly watched the movie, attempting no intimacy greater than sharing popcorn.

Once, however, he stumbled on them by accident, down in his family's basement, a room marooned somewhere between its utilitarian origins and his mother's dream of a rec room. The dream basically began and ended with a plaid sofa, carted down there after his mother bought a new living room set. Tim had been in the walk-in pantry, searching the metal shelves for an air pump when he heard them come in. He stilled himself, waiting to see— or at least hear—what they did alone. He hadn't done it himself yet and he was dying to see someone do it, even if it was Sean and Gwen. He waited for what felt like ten, fifteen minutes, listening to their whispered giggles, then the long silences. "Oh," Gwen kept saying in a soft breathy exhale. "Oh." They had to be doing it. He allowed himself to creep up to the door, crouching so he would be eye level with the old sofa. To his disappointment, they were sitting side by side, kissing very softly, lightly. His brother took his time. No, his brother wasn't even trying to make a move. Although he had his hands inside Gwen's shirt, he wasn't trying to go any further. To Tim's amazement, it was Gwen who seemed to be moving things forward. She pulled away from Sean, but it was to lift her top. Wow, she was pretty built for her age. Tim raised his head slightly to get a better view and his elbow struck something on the shelves by the door. It wasn't a big noise, but it was enough.

"What was that?" Gwen asked. "Your mom?"

"She's not home," Sean said, but he was helping Gwen back into her shirt, buttoning it, leading her out of the basement. He seemed almost relieved by the interruption.

That night, as they were drifting to sleep, Sean said suddenly: "Tim, were you in the basement today?"

"What?" He felt like there was an appropriate level of surprise in his tone. Surprise, but nonchalance. He shouldn't be shocked by the question, or indignant in his innocence. If he hadn't been there, if he had no context, he would find the question odd, nothing more.

"Were you in the basement this afternoon?"

"I went down there to get the bicycle pump. My tires were flat. I think Go-Go's been riding my bike. Have you seen him?"

"No." He could tell Sean was frustrated. But he couldn't follow up without tipping his hand. "Where was Go-Go today, anyway?"

"He was with that new friend, Billy or something. He goes to his house."

"So Go-Go wasn't around this afternoon?"

"I don't think so." Tim smiled in the dark. If Go-Go had been lurking in the basement, he would have made far more noise, probably jumped on Sean and Gwen, tried to join in the *game* they were playing. Go-Go knew how babies were made, technically, but he didn't think it had anything to do with him. It was just something stupid that parents did.

As they fell asleep, Tim was pretty sure that Sean was whacking off. Lord knows, he was, and thinking about Gwen, although he felt a little pervy about it. Only thirteen, and his brother's girlfriend. If he were to confess such things—and he never did—he wondered what the priest would find more egregious, the girl's age or the covetousness. Not to mention all the impure thoughts backed up behind his desire for his brother's girlfriend. The thing was, he didn't want Gwen, not really. Mickey, maybe, but there was something about Mickey that scared him a little. He wanted a girlfriend. He had one at camp, last summer, and it was frustrating when they didn't get to go back because he was pretty sure that he and Anne would have worked their way up to all sorts of things. Then his dad had to go and lose his job, and Tim lost his chance to get laid.

Tim was a virgin until senior prom, when his date seemed to assume that giving it up was virtually required, and he did nothing to disabuse her of that notion. But she wasn't special. He met Arlene freshman year of college, however, and she was. Pretty and bubbly and in love with him, and he still can't quite get over that fact.

When their girls arrived, Michelle and Lisa practically on top of each other, then Karen after a long pause, almost everyone made the same two observations. One: they were spaced out just like the Halloran boys, with only twelve months between the first two and then six years, a daddy-got-lucky baby. Then everyone added: "But girls are easier." Really? *Really?* He looks at the three girls clustered together on the padded banquette in their breakfast nook and has to wonder. Sure, Go-Go broke their mother's heart, driving into that Jersey wall, almost assuredly drunk after another failed attempt at sobriety. Go-Go had broken her heart over and over. With the first divorce and then the separation, which had led to the estrangement from her two grandbabies. Six grandchildren and only one boy, and of course it would be Sean who produced the much-beloved grandson, another chip-off-the-oh-so-wonderful block. When the families gather—rare, because Sean's wife and her family have a stranglehold on Sean, and the distance is not insignificant—Duncan appears to be every bit as perfect as Sean, a dark and contained little soldier among his fluffy blond cousins. When they were younger, Tim's girls had fussed over Duncan, but now Michelle and Lisa say he is stuck-up and boring. "Yeah, he makes his parents proud, with his straight A's and cross-country running and jazz band, what a dipshit," Tim wants to say. He doesn't, though.

Aware of his daughters' glares—even the little one is eye-fucking him and he hasn't done shit to ruin her day—he hoists his golf bag over his shoulder and heads out to his car. *His* car, goddammit. He is entitled to take his car to the golf course on his day off, to have a little relaxation after working hard all week to buy their shoes and their criminally tiny T-shirts and whatever else they want. Isn't he? But already he is thinking about dinner, concocting a plan that will make things up to them, assuming they will even deign to spend the evening with him and Arlene. Did he shut his parents out at that age? Of course he did. But his parents wanted to be shut out, whereas Arlene and Tim flutter around their children, courting them, wooing them. In some ways, he is still a hopeless seventeen-year-old, trying to win the approving glance of a teenage girl, no matter how fleeting.

Maybe pizza will win him some points. From the good place, which he thinks is Fortunato's. He better check with Arlene, though. Fortunato's was the good pizza place last month, but things change so quickly.

September 5, 1979

CHAPTER FOURTEEN

Gwen was the only one of us queer enough—that's what we called it then, sorry if it offends—to look forward to the first day of school. Perhaps Sean did, too, but he had the good sense not to say as much. Tim, in his Tim-like way, accepted school as a fact of life. Couldn't get out of it, so why waste energy complaining. Then again, he wasn't about to celebrate the fact, either. Let Gwen and Sean grade-grub. Tim had carved out a groove for himself as a B student, the path of least resistance, as he saw it. To be an A student would have required more work, to slide down to C's would risk his father's ire. That was Tim's particular genius at the time, getting by. Doing just enough, but never too much.

Poor Go-Go had no genius, except for destruction, with a sub-specialty in self-destruction. He was miserable in school, and if there was some root cause that might have been treated—attention deficit, dyslexia—the nuns of that particular time and that particular school weren't inclined to investigate or address it. Go-Go was told he was lazy, incorrigible, bad. Work harder, try harder, think harder, his teachers lectured him, and he would see results. He was almost grateful for the reprieve of Mass, boring as it was. Go-Go could fake his way through an hour of Mass.

As for Mickey—she hated school because she hated being indoors. Ironic, one might think, given her later choice to spend her working life inside a long narrow tube, but Mickey would argue that she never felt freer than she did on a plane, thousands of feet above the ground, hurtling through the air. Free, if she chose, to disappear into a new city, to start life over again in Chicago or Seattle or Dallas. Not that she ever did, but the opportunity was there. She could grab her wheeled suitcase and disappear.

So: Gwen was the only one who cared that summer, in 1979, when Hurricane David began moving up the coast over Labor Day weekend, threatening the first day of school. Well before it reached us, David was a monstrous storm, destined for the history books, killing more than two thousand people in the Dominican Republic. But all Gwen cared about was the possibility that she would be denied her triumphant return to school. Triumphant because she had a boyfriend now, one that almost any of her classmates would envy. Good-looking, a grade ahead of her—a high school freshman yet. She had a photo of Sean in her new wallet, ready to go. In a photo, Sean was perfect. Did this imply he was not perfect in the flesh? As the first day of school drew closer, did Gwen start to notice the things about Sean that her private-school friends would find uncool? His politics, for example, inherited from his father, were conservative. The way he dressed, almost as if he wore a uniform even when not in school. Plus, his family didn't have money, which everyone at Gwen's school professed not to care about, but—everyone at Gwen's school had money.

Yet, no, that can't be. Gwen could not have had any doubts

about Sean because that foils the before-and-after symmetry of
our story, in which everything was perfect until the moment it
wasn't. Gwen and Sean were still in their honeymoon period,
although perhaps understandably with some trepidation about
whether this was a flimsy summer romance or something stur-
dier. Tim and Sean, good soldiers, marched off to the first day of
school at Cardinal Gibbons. Gwen, giddy with reinvention, rode
in her father's car to Park School. For the second year in a row,
Go-Go was alone at St. Lawrence, where Sean, and even Tim, left
behind long, long, long shadows that the nuns kept holding up to
him, like some Punch-and-Judy silhouette on the wall, a play in
which Go-Go was always the butt of all the jokes. Mickey stood
on Forest Park Avenue, waiting for the bus to junior high, furious
and forlorn.

The first day of school came and went, without incident.
But just as a change in barometric pressure anticipates a hurricane's impending arrival, things were changing, even if we didn't
acknowledge it. Tim, advised by his father at breakfast that he
would need a scholarship if he planned to attend school beyond
community college, came home and cracked the books. Sean
and Gwen raced through their homework so they could be alone.
Mickey and Go-Go were left to their own devices. The last month
of summer had been like this, too, with Sean and Gwen isolating
themselves from us. But their continued desire to be just two instead of five was somehow more striking, now that a new season
had arrived. The first day of school established what we had long
suspected: the five of us, as five, as a star, as a constellation, were
over.

Hurricane David moved up the coast. It was not as destructive as feared, not in the United States. Five dead in Florida, which
was as remote to us as the Dominican Republic. As was Savannah
and the Carolinas and even Virginia and suburban Washington,
D.C., and western Maryland. It was only when the rains started

in Baltimore on September 5, the *second* day of school, that we cared about Hurricane David. Yes, we were young, but this is how people are: we care about what affects us. Two thousand Dominicans, five Floridians—we could not muster true worry in the abstract. But when the rain started that afternoon and there were disturbing reports that the creek might rise and cross the road, as it had during Agnes, Mickey's mother called Tally Robison and asked her to send her home.

"Mickey?" Tally said. "Mickey's not here."

Sean was. He was lying on top of Gwen in her bedroom, the pretense of homework abandoned. They had all their clothes on—Tally Robison was within earshot, after all, and the door was ajar, house rule—but they were dizzy and amazed at the things that could be accomplished through their clothes. At Tally's polite knock, Sean jumped back with so much force he almost hit the opposite wall. But they had their clothes on. No one could prove anything.

Tally, who had come up the stairs on swift, stockinged feet, took in the scene—the rumpled bedspread, the mussed hair, the high color in Gwen's and Sean's faces—without comment. She told them that Mickey was missing and her mother was worried, asked if they might know where she was.

"There's one place—," Gwen began.

"We'll go," Sean said quickly. "It's just over the hill."

He called Tim at the Hallorans' house, who arrived with slickers and high-beam flashlights. Like Gwen and Sean, he did not invoke Chicken George's name. Why didn't anyone say his name? Did we really believe that we would get in trouble if our parents found out we had formed a friendship with the odd man who lived, off and on, in the woods? What was our transgression?

That we had traveled so far from home in our walks there, or that we had stolen from our families' pantries at his instigation? That Sean and Gwen had then used the cabin to do whatever they did? Or was it something less rational, a desire to have a secret for the sake of the secret? Chicken George belonged to us. He had been missing for many weeks at this point and we believed we would never see him again. Still, we did not speak of him, not then. Tim, Sean, and Gwen walked, calling Mickey's name, the flashlights strafing in the growing gloom. The rain had started, heavy and thick. Hurricane rain.

When they crested a hill, still about a half-mile from Chicken George's, they saw Mickey and Go-Go running toward them, breathless.

"What happened?" Tim asked. "What's going on?"

Neither one answered.

"What happened?" Tim repeated.

"Something bad," Go-Go said.

Mickey tried to keep going, but Tim caught her by the arm. "Show us." She paused, and it seemed she was considering whether she could outrun Tim. She probably could, but she didn't try. Mickey was crying—and Mickey never cried. Shrugging off Tim's hand, she turned around and led us back down the hill, to the stream, which was growing in width and speed. Chicken George was there, lying on his back, his precious steel guitar nearby.

"He went nuts on us," Mickey said. "He found us in the cabin, playing his guitar—"

"You know you're not supposed to touch it," Tim said. "And what where you doing over there, on a day like today?"

"He's been gone so long this time," Mickey said. "I didn't think he was coming back. We were going to save the guitar from the weather."

"The guitar wasn't there," Sean pointed out. "He took his

guitar when he disappeared, the way he always does. And if you wanted to save it, why did you carry it out without the case, into this rain?"

"We didn't," Mickey said. "Chicken George did. He went nuts, when he found us there. It was like he didn't know us, had never known us. He cursed us, he said terrible things. He called us—he called us robbers, although we only meant to surprise him. That's when he grabbed the guitar from Go-Go and started to chase us. He went nuts."

Sean looked at Go-Go.

"He went nuts," Go-Go said.

"And then he fell, lost his footing. It wasn't our fault. He thought we were robbing him, but we only meant to help."

"Mickey pushed him," Go-Go said in a small voice.

She whirled on him. "Go-Go."

He backed away, but he didn't change his story. "You did. You pushed him."

Sean—of course it would be Sean—knelt next to Chicken George, pressing a finger on his throat. "He's alive. We have to call someone, figure out a way to get an ambulance crew in here."

"But he'll say we were robbing him," Mickey said. She grabbed Sean, came close to hitting him. "He'll get us in trouble. Don't you understand? It doesn't matter that he's crazy. People will believe him, take his side."

"Mickey—" Sean took her wrists, surprisingly gentle, unafraid of her aggression, the fingernails that raked his cheek.

"Look, I didn't want to tell you this, but—it's not about the guitar. That's not what happened. I decided to go check on the place. It's been empty so long now. I—I had a feeling. So I got off the bus from school and went straight there. It's not like Gwen cared if I came to her house."

It was clear she wanted Sean and Gwen to feel guilty, that she wanted them to confront what they had done to her, to us.

"And?"

"Go-Go was already here, and Chicken George. He was touching him."

"Go-Go was touching Chicken George?"

"Chicken George was touching Go-Go."

Tim and Sean looked at their brother. He didn't exactly nod, only shrugged helplessly, as if he didn't have the vocabulary to speak of what had happened. Then said: "But Mickey pushed him."

"Go-Go!"

"You did. He tried to grab you and you pushed him. That's when he fell."

"He was trying to hit me. Because of you, because of what I knew." Mickey was yelling at Go-Go as if everything was his fault. He hung his head. "I pushed him to keep him from hitting me."

"We still can't leave him here, without telling anyone," Sean said. "Even if he did that. We have to tell our parents."

"Can't we go back and call 911 anonymously?"

"There's no way to explain to them how to get here. There's no road—and the street may already be impassable. If we hike back to the Robisons', though, our dads might be able to carry him out of the woods. And Gwen's father is a doctor. He can help him."

"Help him," Mickey said. "He's a child molester. He's been waiting all this time to get Go-Go alone and he finally did."

There was an accusation there, for all of us. But mainly for Sean and Gwen. Go-Go wouldn't have been alone in the woods if it weren't for Sean and Gwen, if we were still a we. That was how Chicken George got to him.

"It's the right thing to do," said Sean, who still wanted to be a doctor then, having not yet been defeated by organic chemistry.

"What do we tell our parents?"

"The truth." Sean paused. "Why is the guitar there?"

"He tried to hit us with it," Mickey said.

"The truth," Sean said again.

"That is the truth."

He looked to Go-Go. After a second, he nodded. "He was trying to hit Mickey with it. He called her terrible names. He wanted to kill her. We didn't take it."

We made our way back to Gwen's house as quickly as possible. To our surprise, all the adults were there—Dr. and Mrs. Robison, the Hallorans, Mickey's mom and not-quite-stepdad, along with her baby brother.

"It's an impromptu hurricane party," Tally Robison said. "Your parents came here to wait for you all to return, and now people are worried it's going to be like Agnes, with water rushing down the road. In which case, we'll be stuck." She seemed jolly about it. There were wineglasses out, the fathers had beers. Tally Robison liked parties and she tried to create them out of the flimsiest of pretexts. Still, we were struck by our parents' naïveté, their assumption that we would all return safely. Didn't they know, or had they forgotten: things could go wrong, so quickly.

Tim and Sean took their father aside and spoke to him. Certain things were not said, by unspoken agreement among all of us. We did not mention that we had a long-standing relationship with the man who was lying in the creek. We did not say that Mickey had pushed him. The story was only that Mickey had found him touching Go-Go and he had chased them both, then slipped and fell.

"Touching? What do you mean by touching?"

"Just—*touching*," Sean said, for he didn't know, and he didn't want to know.

Mr. Halloran then left the house with Dr. Robison and Rick, Mickey's sort-of-stepdad. The boys wanted to go with them, fearful that the grown-ups could not find their way, but Mr. Halloran was adamant that they stay behind. They were gone for about an hour, but it seemed much longer. It seemed like days had passed before we saw the beams of their high-powered flashlights at the top of the hill. They came in through the basement door, and Tally Robison brought them towels and fresh T-shirts, then mugs of coffee with whiskey in them. She still wanted her party. She and the other women had played charades, and she wanted the men to join in.

"Where's the—man?" Mickey asked.

"He was gone," Dr. Robison said.

"Gone? Are you sure you went to the right place?"

"I mean—he didn't make it. There was nothing we could do. I'll call the police, but—you see, when he slipped, he fell and hit his head. He lost a lot of blood, and by the time we got there—" He shook his head. "We made our way down to the road, hoping to flag someone down, but there's no one out there because of the storm. Our part of the road is clear, but there's flooding farther down and up on Forest Park."

"The phones are out," Tally said.

"We'll call in the morning, then," Dr. Robison said. "We can't leave him there."

"Why not?" Mr. Halloran said, bolting his beer.

In the wake of the hurricane and the damage to the neighborhood, the police did not come for several days. We never knew exactly what Dr. Robison told them. We were not even sure if Chicken George's body was found, or if it ended up being washed away as the stream gained in power. It rained very hard that night, and the streets did flood, as predicted, but they were empty by morning and everyone made their way home.

A week later, we went back to his house, perhaps the last thing we ever did as a group. It was empty, but then—it had been empty before.

"Do you think he had a funeral?" Go-Go asked.

"Who cares?" Mickey said. "He was a bad person. Not you, Go-Go. Chicken George."

It was the right thing to say. Yet why did it sound as if Mickey was saying the exact opposite? In telling Go-Go that he was not a bad person, wasn't she suggesting that some might think he was, that everything was his fault?

"What if he's still alive," Go-Go said. "What if he never really died?"

"It's not like a horror film," Sean assured his brother. "He died. He most definitely died. Dr. Robison said so."

Chicken George died. From his head injury, according to Gwen's father, but it was hard not to wonder about the water rushing around him, growing in power, carrying him and his guitar—where, exactly? Where did the stream end up? In the harbor, at a treatment plant? We knew the stream so well, understood its moods and shifts, its dangers, but we didn't know its ultimate destination. We knew only the part we saw.

Chicken George died. Our group, already splintering, died with him. Sean quickly became unsatisfactory to Gwen, and he didn't seem particularly brokenhearted when she invited another boy to the Homecoming dance in October, her way of telling Sean that things were over. Tim worked even harder for those elusive A's, determined to get a scholarship. Mickey's mother broke up with Rick and moved across the county line—not even two miles, to the Strawberry Hill apartment, but far enough away that we never saw Mickey, now in a new school, hanging out with new friends. Go-Go got caught shoplifting at the Windsor Hills pharmacy. Go-Go got caught setting a small fire. Go-Go put a stray cat in an old insulated milk box, but maybe that was just a rumor. At any rate, with each incident, people sighed and said: "Oh, that Go-Go." We never spoke of Chicken George again, and perhaps some of us even managed never to think about him, although that's harder to imagine.

Tally Robison died—cancer at age forty-nine. Tim Senior died, a heart attack while sitting in his recliner, watching the 1996 play-off between the Orioles and the Yankees. Mickey's mother met another man, someone older, and followed him to Florida. It was sad, but natural, the way things happen. It was life.

Then Gwen's father fell down the steps. Tripping, he said, on a chicken. And Go-Go drove his car into the concrete barrier at the foot of the highway. The highway that, had it been completed, would have cut straight through the park and the land where Chicken George once lived. Could the highway have saved Go-Go? Could anything save Go-Go? Could we have saved Go-Go?

Thirty-two years later, we are still trying to figure that out.

THEM

Autumn 1979

Chapter Fifteen

Tally Robison has made a private game of cooking dinner out of whatever is at hand. She doesn't plan the week's meals in advance. That would be cheating. She flies down the aisles of the Giant every Saturday morning, picking up things on a whim, never using a list. The rest of the week, she stays at her easel as late as possible, channeling a character in a fairy tale, an enchanted princess who shifts shape every evening. *Sunset is coming! The dark forces are gathering.* Once the light is gone, she will be transformed into an everyday wife and mother, making dinner and small talk.

This strict separation between her daytime and evening lives is entirely her choice. Neither Clem nor Gwen challenges the hours she devotes to painting, much less suggests she is neglectful of them in any way. Tally is the one who has decided that her artistic self must be banished with the dying of the light. Clem and Gwen wouldn't mind if Tally threw buckets of Kentucky Fried Chicken on the table, or fell back on Chinese takeout. They wouldn't notice if she remained in her painting clothes or allowed a few romantic spatters to linger on her hands. But she minds. She notices. There has to be a clean break between her two lives, no overlap. That way, she is wild to get back to her work in the morning.

Even so, it's hard to let go of her daytime life, now that the days are short. The inevitable consequence is that she tests time, working feverishly to the last possible moment, showers as quickly as possible, then descends to the kitchen to face the challenge of assembling that night's meal.

Today, it is barely five-thirty when she enters the kitchen and sets to work on a quiche recipe out of the *Moosewood Cookbook*. Tally's vegetarian aspirations are another secret, a new regime launched with no fanfare just after Labor Day and the big storm, when the lights went out for several hours and she decided she didn't trust any of the meat in the house. September is a better time for new beginnings than January 1, when she is usually so depressed she can barely haul herself out of bed. No fanfare, no resolutions, no grand pronouncements, yet September's changes stick. Now, two months later, neither Clem nor Gwen has picked up on the fact that Tally prepares red meat only once or twice a month and that the evening meal is altogether meatless every other night. Do they notice anything she does? But who would register the lack of steak and pot roast when there is quiche with homemade crust, pizza from scratch, red beans and rice, Moroccan stew with couscous? Besides, food isn't important to them. Clem is one of those odd people who eats mainly for fuel, although he has a yen for greasy fast foods. Gwen, untrusting of her newfound slenderness, evaluates every mouthful based only on what it might do to her figure.

Where is Gwen? Tally stands still, listens to the house, catches the buzz of a radio or television coming from Gwen's room. She is supposed to check in with Tally upon arrival home, but that is Clem's rule, and Tally doesn't bother to enforce it now that Gwen is alone behind her closed door. Tally doesn't want to be disturbed while in her studio, and Gwen understands that. She's a considerate girl. She is Tally's favorite child, a sentiment she would freely profess if it didn't horrify others. She believes all mothers have favorites. Hers did, and it wasn't Tally. Miller is a stolid, dutiful lump, Clem without a sense of humor. And Fee, lacking any talent for introspection, is an utter bore. How did Tally have such dull children?

Two months ago, *Where is Gwen?* was a much more freighted question because Gwen would have been with Sean, and the two of them were clearly working their way toward serious mischief. Clem professed to be unconcerned, called it puppy love, said Gwen was too young to get into trouble. Tally considered that an interesting bit of denial for a man whose own bride had been a mere eighteen to his thirty-two on their wedding day. But Clem's naïveté turned out to be justified. The romance with Sean was fleeting. Now Gwen is seeing other boys, determined not to be tied down. She's all about quantity now, flitting from one to another. Tally approves, for the most part. Her only worry is that Gwen will meet a boy who ignores her and mistake his lack of interest for love.

Tally zips through the crust, thanks to the Cuisinart she received last Mother's Day, at her request, grates the cheese, slices the mushrooms, marveling—no false modesty for her, thank you—at her dexterity and speed. A tidy person, she cleans up as she goes, which is all to Gwen's benefit, as it's Gwen's job to clear the table and load the dishwasher at dinner's end, not that Gwen notices, much less thanks her. *I am a good mother. I am a good wife. I take good care of my family.* It is the very same theme embodied by a new perfume commercial, the one that uses the old blues song, although the woman in the ad also makes money for her household. Tally might not bring home the bacon, but she is creating beautiful, beautiful things in her makeshift studio. And the new project—

Her litany of self-congratulation stalls when she opens the refrigerator and discovers that she has only one egg. Good at improvisation Tally may be, but not even she can make a quiche with one egg. She has forgotten that Gwen is going through a phase where she exists on hard-boiled eggs, eating them for breakfast and lunch. Stupid fad diet. Tally will have to drive to the little grocery store at the top of the hill, an errand that quashes her spirits. She has lost at her own game. Plus, she hates the gloomy makeshift grocery at the top of the hill, which seems to exist only to remind her how far she is from everything, how her husband has chosen a place that is the worst of all worlds—in the city, yet as remote as any suburb, with nothing within walking distance, and no sidewalks on which to walk, anyway. She wants to move to Paris.

She wants to move to Paris. It's a stupid thought, petulant and impossible. Such a notion should flit across her mind and disappear in the minute it takes to grab her purse and car keys, yet it lingers, stubborn and defiant. *Get out,* she tells the thought, as if it were a neighbor's dog that has wandered into her house. *I have a wonderful life. I love my husband, and he adores me. I have terrific kids and I was young when I had them. I won't even be fifty when Gwen goes off to college. I'm already doing what I want to do, what I was meant to do. Nothing is holding me back.*

I want to move to Paris.

She turns on the car radio, hoping to drown out her own thoughts. "Those Were the Days." An oldie, at least a decade past its prime. Clem clearly drove her car at some point in the past few days.

What Tally actually wants is a do-over, to move to Paris at age eighteen, to return to a time when she had such choices. The problem is, she is forever destined to make the same choice, because the facts never change: she was eighteen, accepted at Wellesley, having a wonderfully secret affair with a thirty-two-year-old man, her father's colleague and her uncle's best friend.

And she believed she was pregnant, although she never told Clem that. If she *had* to get married—and she thought she did—at least the groom could believe it was pure love. Besides, she wasn't an artist then, she wouldn't have dreamed of Paris, or even New York. She thought her choices were Clem or Wellesley. If she had found a way to get rid of the baby, it just would have been Wellesley and then another, possibly lesser, version of Clem four years later. Girls of her time and class were not programmed to bring home the bacon. Her dilemma—the eternal human dilemma—is that she wants a chance to revisit her choices with full knowledge of the future. But there's a reason that there's no game show where they throw a car, a washer-dryer, and a goat onstage and ask you to select forthrightly among them. Where's the drama in that? Where's the suspense? The only possible surprise would be the one-in-a-million person who picks the goat, on the grounds that he doesn't drive and already has a serviceable washer-dryer.

If Tally ever had three wishes, she expended them long ago, on the most mundane things. Everyone has wishes—and everyone squanders them. The fairy tales got that right. Magic exists only to screw with you. Eggs, for example. She wished for eggs not five minutes ago, and while most people think a wish should produce the desired thing at that instant, in a puff of smoke, who's to say that her wish isn't being granted as she drives to the store, money in her purse? Somewhere on the planet, in this very city perhaps, a person is wishing for eggs right now and can't have them. So Tally wishes for Paris and somewhere else right now—in Logan Airport, the airport of her youth—a beautiful young woman is waiting to board an Air France flight, a rucksack at her feet, her future wider and broader than the ocean she's about to cross. Whatever you want at any moment, someone else is getting it. Whatever you have, someone else is longing for. In the time it takes her to work this out, Tally has driven the mile to the store, parked, gone in, and grabbed a carton of eggs, checking the expiration date. She can't begin to list all the stale, expired, past-their-sell-date items she has brought home from this store.

And now she is waiting in an interminable line because the store is, of course, perpetually understaffed. She tries to hold on to the serene, wise persona she discovered in the car, focusing on the back of the head in front of her. *Be in the moment. Breathe. Live. That's the secret to happiness.* Notice the pink-and-blue flowery scarf, over pink curlers, which are twisted around pinky-red hair, the material of the scarf thin enough so one can see how sparse and dull the hair is. Sad. Ugliness is sad.

The woman turns, as if she knows she's being judged.

"Oh." Tally tries to cover the rudeness of her shock, tries to make the exhalation sound more *what-a-pleasant-surprise* than *fuck-you-look-awful.* "Hi, Doris."

"Hello, Tally." Doris Halloran holds up her box of Hamburger Helper, as if Tally is a higher authority to whom she must report her nutritional decisions. "It's what they want."

"Gwen loves it, too. I guess I'm meaner than you because I never let her have it."

"That girl gets prettier every day."

Tally wants to say thank you, except she doesn't feel as if her daughter has been complimented. Doris's tone is almost accusing, as if Gwen has achieved her prettiness by guile. Custom dictates that Tally should respond with a kind comment about Doris's children, but she is stumped. She never sees the boys anymore, come to think of it. When did they stop coming around? Mickey, too, no longer visits. The candy drawer hasn't needed to be replenished in some time. Let's see—Tim, the lummox as Clem calls him, is probably the same stupid frat-boy-in-training he always was. Go-Go can't be any worse than he's been, although there are rumors linking him to the cats that have been found suffocated in the neighborhood's old insulated milk boxes. Sean, the best of the lot, is a natural-born politician. Tally doesn't consider that a compliment, but Doris might.

"That Sean," she says. "He's a charmer. All your boys have"—grasp, grasp, grasp—"such distinctive personalities."

Tally wonders if Doris is as curious as Tally is about who broke up with whom, if Doris doubts Sean's version of events the way Tally doubts Gwen's. Something happened. Her hunch is that Gwen traded up, realized there was greater cachet in a Gilman boy or a football hero.

Tally wonders if she doubts her daughter because she is aware of her own proclivity for lying. Fudging, as she prefers to think of it. Or maybe *nudging*—easing a complicated truth toward something simpler, more comprehensible. Tally never lies for advantage or gain. Her lies are no different from, say, a fresh coat of paint or wallpaper in an old house. Something pretty over something unsightly. There's never been a home that didn't eventually require updating or renovation. A life is the same way. You live inside it for a long, long time if you're lucky. Things fray, break, go out of fashion. There's no shame in bringing a life up-to-date.

She buys her eggs, wishing the store stocked fresh herbs, but one would be hard-pressed to find so much as a jar of dried oregano here. She should have her own herb garden, but the property is too shady to grow anything but ferns and a few complacent flowers. Why hadn't Clem seen that flaw in his dream lot? It's formidably dark, with trees to the east, west, and south. The northern light is good for a painter—or would have been, if Clem had been thoughtful enough to include a studio for Tally. She paints in a prefab toolshed bought at Sears, which means choosing between freezing or running a space heater in the winter, a dangerous option around her oil paints and turpentine. *I didn't think you were that serious about painting,* Clem said when she asked for her little cabin last year. He was sad; Clem hates to disappoint Tally. Clem, to his credit, did not bring up all the other things tried and abandoned. Throwing her own pots. The novel, which never got far enough along to have a title, other than *The Novel.* Macramé. Candle making. Jewelry making. Okay, so he was entitled to be dubious, especially given her decision to keep her latest project under wraps, refusing to let anyone see it until she's finished. But she is finding—what does a painter find? Writers discover their voices. Tally guesses she's on the verge of achieving her *vision* of things.

In the parking lot, she notices that Doris Halloran is still sitting in her car, hands gripping the wheel, yet she hasn't turned on the engine. Poor thing. Although she looks at least ten years older than Tally, she is actually younger, younger even than Tally's real age, about which she is always a little vague.

"So you started your family young, too," Doris Halloran said to Tally in this *very market, when the Robisons were finally settled in Dickeyville. Settled, but not exactly accepted. Hard feelings lingered about Clement Robison's dream house, the way he got around the village's strict rules on historic preservation. He argued that his house, the farthest house down Wetheredsville Road, lying beyond the mill, technically wasn't part of Dickeyville after all.*

"Too?"

"I was married at twenty, but there were two miscarriages before Tim. He's fourteen now."

That made Doris, what? Thirty-five, thirty-six? Tally wondered if it was the gray light in the little market that made Doris look so gray. If Tally had been forced to guess—thank God she hadn't guessed—she would have put the other woman's age at forty-five, a very hard and unforgiving forty-five.

"Oh, I'm older than I look," Tally said. Adding swiftly, lest she seem vain, which she was, but why advertise it: "It's the way I wear my hair that makes me look younger."

Doris nodded. "We've noticed."

To this day, Tally wonders about that "we." Doris and her husband? The royal we? All the women of Dickeyville, sitting in silent judgment on the newcomer, with her long corn-silk hair and pretty, impractical clothes, living in the modern monstrosity that no one wanted? The mid-1970s was the era of *The Stepford Wives,* and if the women of Dickeyville were not the empty-eyed automatons of the book and film, they were not as individualistic as they wanted to believe. They were merely a hipper variation of Stepford wives. Eating granola and living in a historic district didn't make you a freethinker.

Of course, Doris Halloran was and is a different kettle of fish from the other Dickeyville wives. She still wears housedresses and panty hose. Her pale red hair, on those rare occasions when it is released from its curlers, is worn in tight, unflattering waves. Yet she is younger than Tally. How can that be? Doris Halloran looks as if she has been old all her life. Had the miscarriages done that? Tally yearns to feel superior to her. Why shouldn't she? She is pretty, vibrant, smart. She paints, and not in a dilettante way. Who is Doris Halloran to be talking about Tally's hairstyle, to be judging Gwen for breaking up with Sean? Tally may claim to be older than she is, but she could shave five, ten years off her real age and be believed.

Tally has been lying about her age since she and Clem left Boston two years into their marriage. She lies about Clem's age, too. Not outright lies, but evasive bits of gentle misdirection, fudging and nudging, nudging and fudging. She nudges her husband's age down, ever so slightly, her own up, thereby narrowing the gap between them, which she finds embarrassing, although not as embarrassing as the fact that she married at eighteen and had her first child at nineteen. It isn't the math that tortures her, but the other facts that can be inferred from these bits of arithmetic. Tally Duchamp Robison did not graduate from college, maybe didn't even attend. Among her people—and Tally comes from people who are the sort of people who think of themselves as having people—this was unfathomable, shaming. Her great-great-grandmother had gone to college, her grandmother was a lawyer, her mother is an ob-gyn. OK, maybe she was brought up to bring home the bacon after all, but Betty Friedan be damned, the only rebellion available to Tally was an early, conventional marriage to an older man. It felt exciting and daring at the time. Now, in 1979, no one gets that. To the world at large, she is no different from the Doris Hallorans, marrying at twenty because there were no other options. Tally had all the options in the world when she was eighteen.

And she threw them all away because she was headstrong and shortsighted—and didn't know where to go for a pregnancy test without being found out, and didn't want to wait too long, lest others figure out her predicament.

I want to go to Paris, she thinks, waiting to turn left at the always busy intersection near the store, still overwhelmed by traffic from the Social Security Administration at this time of day. It's taking the line of cars two, three cycles to get through the light. *I want to be the person I've been pretending to be all these years.*

Tally was never foolish enough to claim to have a degree, but she drops her selected facts like bread crumbs and lets people follow them where they seem to lead. She was accepted at Wellesley. True. She married young. Again, true. Her husband was a college professor—oh no, not at her college—her uncle's best friend, from the medical school. A bit of a *scandale,* if one must know.

Still true, and is it her fault if people think she was seduced while a college freshman? People eye Clement differently after they hear these bits. With more respect, because a thirty-two-year-old man who had an affair with an eighteen-year-old was not necessarily out of line, especially if he married her in the end. Tally still remembers the gleam of *who'd a thunk it* in the eyes of their new acquaintances. Clem benefits as much as she does from this misunderstanding. Dear as he is, he is a bit of a fuddy-duddy. At a recent faculty party, someone produced a joint and Clem not only declined to try it, he also insisted they leave immediately. Geriatric specialist? Clem *is* a geriatric specialty.

But such instances of disharmony are rare. Tally is an old soul, in her opinion, older than Clem in many ways. When Gwen, their surprise baby, was born, Clem was already forty, Tally not even twenty-eight, yet it was Clem who got down on the rug with her and played without inhibition. Tally didn't have it in her. She felt ancient. She adores Gwen, who has turned out to be a most satisfactory child. But having Gwen—finally, an accident, not that she regrets it—meant postponing her next stage. What if she had started painting in her twenties? Where would she be now?

She is—what is her real age?—forty-two years old, pretending to be forty-six-ish. Clem is fifty-six, although she says early fifties when pressed. Gwen will leave for college in four years. Now throw in another four years. College-age children expect their homes to stand as shrines, as Tally learned from Miller and Fee. She will be forty-six, and Clem will be sixty, married almost thirty years. He probably won't want to take early retirement, but he'll be ready to leave teaching at sixty-five, once Gwen is out of college, she's sure of it. Then they can go to Paris. Somehow, some way. She will go to Paris before she's fifty-two.

You'll be dead at fifty-two.

The thought runs an icy finger down her spine. This is not at all like her. She is not morbid. She is not given to dark premonitions. She blames the shiver on the black cat in the window of the dry cleaners, the one holding up its paw in salute to the glories of Black Cat rubber heels. Mired here in the line of traffic waiting to turn left, she has been absentmindedly staring at the cat, whose face has a decidedly sinister cast. "Shoo," she says as she accelerates, her turn for the green light finally arriving. *Shoo.* Doris Halloran is still sitting in her car, back at the market. Tally assumes Doris is too exhausted to go home, that the interior of her car is the only place she can be alone. It's different for Tally. She has her studio, she has a vocation, she has—well, it's different for her, it just is.

Winter 1980

CHAPTER SIXTEEN

Doris gave Go-Go the spare room when he started wetting the bed last fall.
Tim Junior raised a stink, of course, and Sean took his side, but
she stood up to them, said it made sense because Go-Go has the
earlier bedtime. It was odd because bed-wetting was never Go-
Go's problem as a toddler, if only because she was too tired to
care much by the time he was born and her very nonchalance
succeeded where all her effort never had. *Wear diapers the rest of
your life if that's what you want,* she told him once, *but when you
learn how to tie your shoes, you can change your own pants.* At his own
initiative, Go-Go was completely potty-trained at age two, a feat
neither older brother could claim.

It may be his only accomplishment, Doris thinks as she gathers
up the sheets one weekday morning. No one else in the household knows about Go-Go's problem. She doesn't want his brothers

to have any more ammunition for teasing. As for his father—she can't bear to think what he will do to the boy if he finds out. So no one knows except Doris. At this point, Doris isn't sure if even Go-Go realizes he's wetting the bed up to four times a week. Why would he? She does everything possible to minimize, conceal, the problem. There is a plastic mattress pad, at no risk of being discovered, since no one else in this household would ever strip his own bed, much less wash another person's sheets. She checks Go-Go's bed every morning as soon as the house is empty, washing the sheets if necessary, often doing all the household linens for cover.

Thank goodness they have a washer-dryer in this house. For the first six years of her marriage, they lived in a brick town house without any laundry facilities and only one bathroom. It was hard, especially after Sean was born. What if she had actually given birth to all the children that she and Tim Senior had conceived? She would have eight children now. They never could have afforded that. Did God know? Was that why God took her children? And of all the children God took, why had he given her Go-Go? Didn't she deserve a sweet baby, a well-behaved little girl, someone who might take her side from time to time? She had prayed to St. Gerard for such a baby. Instead, she got Go-Go, and no one, not even his mother, could consider Go-Go an answer to a prayer. Still, for all his exhausting craziness, he was sort of sweet, too, the only one of her boys who liked to be cuddled and held. That is, he liked to be cuddled and held until his brothers teased him out of it.

Now Go-Go is all sour, no sweet. Crazy, sullen, sarcastic, more destructive than ever, at least at home. Strangely, his behavior at school seems to be getting marginally better, if not his grades. There is a new priest, Father Andrew from Boston, and he seems to think Go-Go is a good kid at heart. "High-spirited, but wasn't I the same as a boy?" he asks in his Boston accent. Doris thinks Father Andrew is very good-looking. And smart. She almost wishes he were more worried about Go-Go, which would entail meetings at the school, with Father talking to her in that wonderful voice. He is so *masculine*. He risks the little kindnesses and sentiments that Tim Senior never attempts. Once, when Doris was arriving at St. Lawrence for altar duty, she saw Go-Go's class in the yard, playing kickball. Go-Go kicked a magnificent home run, soaring, soaring, soaring over his classmates' heads and when he trotted to home plate, Father Andrew rubbed his hand across Go-Go's head, congratulating him. Later, at bedtime, Doris did the same thing. She had forgotten how soft her son's hair was, how appealing, even when in need of a wash.

"Stop it," Go-Go said. The next morning, his sheets were yellow again and she wanted to scream. She can't. She mustn't. She is all Go-Go has. Tim and Sean will be fine, especially Sean. But Go-Go needs her.

Sheets in the washing machine, she shuffles into the kitchen, but she doesn't have the energy to face the breakfast mess. Tim Senior insists on eggs and bacon every morning, and how can she deny the boys a full breakfast when their father is having one? He has been out of work since the end of the holiday season, and there was a three-month layoff before that job. He should be able to find something, though, with his experience. Maybe not at one of the big department stores—he's pretty much burned his bridges there—but at Robert Hall, Tuerkes, Hamburger's. He says he's looking, but Doris doesn't know where he goes during the days, taking their only car. "I've got a lead," he will say, and she doesn't have the nerve to ask what sort of job interview leaves a man's breath sour from cigarettes and beer. She has heard he's hanging out in Monaghan's over in Woodlawn. It's a decent place as taverns go. He isn't running around with women. She is pretty sure he isn't running around with women. Sex isn't that important to Tim. After Go-Go, there had been one more miscarriage, and Doris told Tim that she didn't think she could take it anymore, that they had to be more careful, find a way to make things work while being true to the church. The miscarriages were harder than the pregnancies. He was very sweet about it, said it was OK, his needs weren't that great.

Abandoning the kitchen, she takes a cup of lukewarm tea into the living room and turns on the television, catching the last bit of *People Are Talking*. *Exactly,* Doris thinks. People are always talking. That's why she has to be vigilant, keep the family's secrets. Go-Go doesn't wet the bed, Tim Senior isn't out of a job, they didn't start raiding the boys' college funds last summer to stay afloat. She misses the program *Dialing for Dollars,* which is off the air, killed by the state lottery. At least that's Tim's take on it. Hard to get excited about winning forty dollars, he says, when you could win thousands and you don't have to sit around waiting for a phone call. Still, she misses it. *Dialing for Dollars* was her respite when Go-Go was little. True to his name, he was always in motion, and when his brothers were at school during the day, Doris never knew any rest. However, he would settle in with a bottle of juice to watch *Dialing for Dollars* with her. Go-Go was frustrated that the host, Stu Kerr, never called them once, but Doris held no grudge. It's a big city, and Doris never wins anything, small or large. She remembers when Sean put together the fact that Kerr, beneath a wig and funny nose, was also Professor Kool on *Professor Kool's Fun Skool.* Sean was outraged. That is, he pretended to be outraged about the principle of the thing, as he saw it, but he was really embarrassed to have been fooled. Sean doesn't like to be wrong, ever. It's almost a little unnatural, the one characteristic that makes her nervous for her otherwise most golden child. Only Jesus gets to be perfect.

The phone rings. For a second, she thinks it's Stu Kerr, and she panics because she doesn't know the count and the amount, but then she remembers the show is on only in her thoughts. She rushes to the kitchen, taking inventory yet again of the sink of dishes, the cast-iron frying pan filled with bacon grease.

"Mrs. Halloran?" It is Father Andrew's lovely voice, but she doesn't want him to know she recognizes it instantly.

"This is she." She stands up a little straighter, tucks a strand of hair behind her ear. Where's the curler that held the hair? She spots it on the drainboard.

"Father Andrew up at St. Lawrence. We have a little situation with Gordon."

Doris appreciates the euphemism but knows it has to be bad for the school to call.

"He's OK," the priest says, rushing to assure her. He is so nice. "But you see, another boy brought a baseball mitt to school today, a birthday gift he wanted to show off. It went missing and we found it in Go-Go's desk."

"He isn't a thief," she says quickly. "He just likes . . . nice things."

"He was also very forthright. Didn't lie or pretend it was put there by mistake. Just said he admired it and couldn't help wanting to touch it. Still—I thought it might be effective if we spoke to him together."

Together.

"I would be right there, but we only have the one car and Mr. Halloran has it and—" She breaks down, begins to cry, which is as shaming as Go-Go's thievery. It's too much. Her son, stealing from a classmate. Her husband unavailable to her, and even if she could reach him, she would never dare ask for his help in such a situation. Tim Senior would probably take a belt to Go-Go for this offense, and Lord knows, a part of her has yearned to beat him, to scream at him, to shake him. Father Andrew being so nice—that makes it worse. The thing is, she would like nothing better than to drive to the school—after taking out her curlers, maybe a quick bath—and talk to Father Andrew. Men who give up women, as priests do, are so much easier to talk to. She can take him some cookies, store bought, and maybe he will make her tea on the little hot plate he keeps in his office. She is surprised to realize how much she has noticed in her visits there—the hot plate, the mug from Northeastern University, the photos of children, presumably his nieces and nephews, a large photo of what was clearly a family reunion in some place very green. It could be anywhere, but she wants to believe it was Ireland. They would speak to Go-Go constructively, then send him back to class, and then talk privately about what a challenge he is. Like Father Andrew, she will find positive, optimistic words. *Challenge, situation, incident.* She might even tell him about the chronic bed-wetting, ask if he has any insight into why an almost ten-year-old boy would regress this way. Father Andrew probably has all sorts of reassuring insights.

But she is stuck here because they have only one car. No other family in the neighborhood has only one car, except for that chaotic single woman across the street, the one who doesn't mow her lawn until the neighborhood association insists, tells her it's a breeding ground for rats. What are they going to do when Tim Junior gets his license? How are they going to afford the extra insurance for having teen drivers on their policy? She cries harder.

"There, there," Father Andrew says. "I can handle it alone."

"Does everyone know?" she chokes out.

"I'm afraid it was a little public for my tastes. But he was caught, he confessed, he was punished. I'll make sure that the children understand there is no point revisiting such things."

He will, somehow. Father Andrew has that kind of power. The children love him as much as their mothers do. Only the fathers don't seem to get Father Andrew's charm. The thick, dark hair, the high color in his face, the bright blue eyes, the broad shoulders. It would be unbearable if he were a regular man, because then he would have a girlfriend or a wife. But as a priest, Father Andrew is available to her.

"Maybe we should still have a meeting one day?" she asks. "About Go-Go's . . . situation."

"Sometimes, the less said, the better. Let it go. He's learned a valuable lesson."

She is torn, wanting to tell him about the sheets, the other problems, if only to prolong the conversation, yet feeling it would be a betrayal.

"About Go-Go," she starts.

"Yes?"

She can't do it. "What do you think of him? Truly."

"I think he's a boy, ma'am, with all the inherent contradictions and conflicting impulses. He wants to be good. He really does. But it's hard to be good."

This is such a generous assessment of her son that she yearns to believe it. Yet a part of her mind steps back and hisses like a goose: *You're a fool, Father. He's a bad, bad boy. He's an awful boy. And maybe he has every reason in the world to be that way, but I don't know how much longer I can keep all his secrets.*

Chapter Seventeen

Tim Halloran starts each weekday by circling job prospects in the morning paper, the *Beacon,* every red loop an exercise in positive thinking. He has never used the want ads before to find a job, managing to rely on word-of-mouth leads from friends and colleagues. But since he left the seasonal job at Goldenberg's, there is nothing. Or so people say. *Sorry, I don't know about anything. Sorry, things are god-awful tight.* Tim knows what's going on. His boss at Hutzler's was a vindictive little prick, and he's spread the word all over town that Tim has a bad temper. Bad? He simply has a temper, unlike that faggot, who liked to hold forth about film—as opposed to movies, some airy-fairy distinction that the guy insisted on—when he didn't know shit. Guy went on and on about how John Wayne had died on-screen only once, such complete and utter bullshit that Tim, who loves John Wayne, all but recited most of the titles in one breath. (*SANDS-OF-IWO-JIMA-MAN-WHO-SHOT-LIBERTY-VALANCE-THE-COWBOYS-THE-SHOOTIST*. And that was off the top of his head, not even complete.) OK, Tim's fuse is a little short, but it's never affected his work. Tim's only failure is not kissing ass. He is good at what he does, probably could have been a true mathematician instead of a bookkeeper if he had the freedom to fart around with that academic bullshit. But he was a husband at twenty-one and a father at twenty-three, which means parking the ego and providing for your dependents.

Only he isn't exactly providing now. They are running through their savings at an alarming clip. Running through? They have run through the savings and kept on going, like a car with no brakes. After the first of the year, he started dipping into the boys' college funds to keep them afloat. Luckily, the boys don't even know they have college funds, although Tim Junior seemed kind of surprised when Tim Senior told him last fall, anticipating the worst, that anything beyond community college was going to be a DIY project. For once, Tim took something seriously. His grades are decent and he even won a prize for something called moot court. He says he wants to be a lawyer. Just what the world needs, another lawyer.

Sean will be OK, that's a given. He's got a shot at the National Merit Scholarship, which would be sweet. And maybe the little one will straighten out. He's a mess, but Tim sees something of himself in Go-Go's chaos, a too-big-for-itself energy that needs only to be organized and focused. Tim was the same way before the Marines put him together. He volunteered when he was eighteen, knowing he wasn't going to get a deferment or exemption. But by volunteering, he had been free to choose the branch he wanted. The Marines suited a scrappy little bantam like Tim, who had learned to fight growing up in the Pigtown neighborhood in Southwest Baltimore. He also happened to catch a break, for once in his fucking life, got in after Korea and out before Vietnam started to escalate, then went to UB on the GI Bill. There's another option for his boys. Volunteer, then let Uncle Sam pay for tuition. What's the risk? There are no wars. Let those towelheads scream and gibber. They couldn't organize a panty raid in an underwear factory.

He glances at his wristwatch, at Doris's back at the sink, where she is moving a dishrag around with few noticeable results. A day is a hard thing to fill, especially in these gray winter months when he can't throw golf clubs in the trunk, spend the afternoon at the public Forest Park course. Doris has to know he isn't looking for work the whole day long, but she doesn't dare question him. She doesn't dare oppose him in any way. And it's not like he's ever raised a hand to her. With Doris, all it takes is getting loud, really loud, and she caves. She can't stand the sound of a raised voice. She's weak. The weakness in the boys—and there is weakness, a softness, in all of them, even Sean—that's pure Doris, her blood and her ways. He should have taken a closer look at that family of hers, picked up on the fact that her prettiness wasn't so much prettiness as frailty. Doris at eighteen was so thin and so pale she glowed, like one of those catfish in the Ozarks. He mistook that for class, breeding, when it was probably anemia and malnutrition. She can barely stand up straight these days. And that glorious, glorious red hair, which once promised to fulfill Tim's every *The Quiet Man*/John Wayne/ Maureen O'Hara dream of Ireland—it has faded to a pinky color, and you can see her scalp in spots. When he met Doris, her mother was dead and there weren't a lot of womenfolk in the family, so he didn't have anyone to study. He should have looked at the men, the most rabbity, watery, bucktoothed, swaybacked bunch of Irishmen he had ever seen in his life. But, like the song said, he only had eyes for Doris. Doris made him feel tender and protective, where other women just made him want to fuck, fast and dirty. Those aren't the kind of girls you pick to bear your children.

Then again, a milky white, pink-haired rabbit of a girl whose uterus killed as many babies as it made wasn't the best choice for motherhood, either.

He stubs out his cigarette and stalks out to the car, not bothering to say good-bye. He tells himself that he's going to Security Square Mall or maybe Westview, drop off a few applications, see that guy he knows at Gordon's Booksellers. But no one's in, not at the first couple of places, and he's at Monaghan's when it opens its doors at eleven. Not that Tim is a drunk. He can't afford to be. He nurses one beer, then two, all the way to happy hour, then asks for one more, knowing that the bartender won't charge him for the third one. The bartender, Jim, is a good guy. He understands that Tim is looking for a job, and he mentions leads here and there. He even suggested that Tim could work at Monaghan's. But he can't do it, can't squander all he has fought for—a job where you wear a shirt and tie, a desk, regular hours, benefits.

Not that he actually likes bookkeeping. But you aren't supposed to like your job. It makes him a little crazy, listening to Tim Junior and Sean talking about what they want to do. Not when they were little, still in the astronaut-firemen phase. Heck, he wished they'd go back to the firemen phase. With overtime, those guys make out like bandits. No, it was all this current talk of fulfillment, of what would be *meaningful* to them, that makes him crazy. Sean wants to be a doctor, and while Tim knows he would burst with pride if that happened, he resents it, too. Same with Tim Junior, with his half-assed dream of being a lawyer. As for Go-Go—the last vocational desire he expressed was being a garbageman. Sincere as anything. He thought it would be fun, he said, picking up other people's trash. Two kids aiming too high, one aiming too low.

He blames their mother's blood. He wonders about the children lost, what they might have been. All daughters, Doris claims, but she has no way of knowing. Tim believes a son, his real son, the boy most like him, was one of the lost children.

The bar grows dimmer as the day grows brighter. About 4 P.M., as he's getting ready to ask for his last beer, he sees a vaguely familiar woman enter the place, a real slinky piece even in her nylon waitress uniform. She feeds the cigarette machine, yanks the knob hard, curses, and slaps the side. She's overdoing it, making a spectacle of herself. She likes having everyone's eyes on her.

"Can you make good on the money I lost?" she asks Jim.

"Didn't you read the sign?"

"What sign?"

"The one plastered on the front of it that says 'Out of Order, do not use, no refunds.'" Jim's smiling, though. She's too cute to ignore.

She glances back over her shoulder. "Oh, *that* sign." It's droll, the way she says it. "I was in such a goddamn hurry to get to work I didn't even look. Can't you cut me a break?"

"Best I can do is take your name and the amount lost and the boss will fish it out for you when the repairman comes by."

"Aw, c'mon." She doesn't put much oomph into it. She might have gotten what she wanted if she had. She is a good-looking woman. Maybe that's her problem. Too proud to use charm, thinks her looks alone should carry her. Where has Tim seen her before, or is that wishful thinking? Then he remembers.

"You're—that girl's mother. Mickey. We've met."

"Have we?" She extends a hand so limp that the fingers curl like cocktail shrimp.

"Halloran. Father of Tim, Sean, and Gordon."

"Rita." She studies him. "Oh yeah, the night of the storm. Mickey went out looking for your boy—"

Is that how she remembers it? Is that all she knows? The men told the children never to speak of Go-Go's secret, not even to their mothers. Tim didn't want everyone knowing his son had been touched by that queer. A story like that could ruin a boy's life. He had to tell Doris, but he didn't tell her much. He's pretty sure that faggoty Dr. Robison has kept his mouth shut. Rita's boyfriend, Rick, shouldn't have had any problem not telling Rita. It's Mickey and Gwen that Tim wonders about, though. Do girls tell their mothers stuff? How many people know?

He says: "Funny how the kids used to be together all the time and now they're not. I guess Tim and Sean are too old to be playing with girls."

"You don't think boys and girls can play together?" Her mouth curves, not quite a smile. Something else. Something better.

"Not into high school. It's not natural. They were right to segregate kid by sexes in school. They learn more when they're apart. At least the Catholic high schools are still all-boy."

"You know what? I kinda agree." She sticks out her lower lip and blows upward, ruffling her bangs. She wears her hair in an upsweep. Not quite a beehive, but something with some height to it. It's not fashionable, but he likes it. Better than those crazy hippie curls women are wearing now. He also likes her liquid eyeliner, laid on thick.

"Where'd you go to school?"

"I'm not from here, not originally. We moved here my last year of high school and I didn't bother going anywhere." Her tone borders on rude.

"Well, I still might be interested in the answer, did you ever think of that?"

"No. People here, they only ask that so they can play 'Do you know.' I've never lived in a place where people were less interested in people not from here."

"I'm sure lots of people are interested in you," he says, trying to stick up for his hometown and flatter her at the same time.

"If by people you mean *men* and if by interested you mean want to *fuck* me, yeah, then some are."

He hates women who use that kind of language. He also has a hard-on. Which she notices, and tries not to.

"Doesn't it seem like spring's never going to come?" she asks the room in general. "I grew up in Florida. I cannot deal with these winters much longer." Softer, to him. "I got a guy. He's a good guy. You know that."

She's being kind, the most insulting thing she could ever be. And just because she has a good guy—what did she mean, "You know that"—doesn't mean she's happy with him. She would definitely fuck someone else. Just not him. Not that he asked, by the way. She shouldn't be so full of herself. Popping a boner was a reflex, nothing more. His stomach had been known to growl when he couldn't be less interested in food. Fuck her. No—*don't fuck her.* He won't even whack off to her, although he was thinking about doing that a little later.

She glances at her watch. "I'm going to be late. And now I gotta make it through a six-hour shift with no cigarettes."

He takes out his pack and offers it to her.

"Marlboros?"

"You were expecting maybe Virginia Slims?"

She laughs, selects two, as if picking chocolates from a box, as if one might be better than another. "You're a nice guy, Hank."

"Tim."

"Right."

He is a nice guy. Having a temper doesn't mean you are a bad guy, just that you were born with a shorter fuse, less tolerance for bullshit. No one blames short-legged people for not being able to walk with longer strides. How can people hold him account-able for his temper? Plus, he gets mad only when people fuck up. He always has a reason for what he does. He's not a bully. True, sometimes he yells at his kids or Doris, but he has his reasons. He's trying to explain things to them. What the light bill is every month. Why they can't have a dog or a cat. He's trying to get everyone else to join him here on Planet Earth.

"You know, maybe the adults should get together, have dinner sometime."

"The four of us, or do we have to invite the good doctor and the grand lady?"

He misunderstands this for a second, thinks she said grand-baby. "Oh, the Robisons."

She makes a face. "I don't really know him. Her—"

This is the kind of woman talk he usually disdains, pure gossip, petty hurts over who said what or wore what, the kind of bullshit that Doris brings home from the altar guild, the unending chatter about so-and-so trying to get in good with Father Whosis. But there is something intriguing about Rita's dislike of Tally Robison. Something earned.

"Just the four of us," he says, knowing he can't afford a night out until he finds work again, knowing Doris has no desire to go out, knowing he would be ashamed to be seen with her, the way she looks now. She would seem even more washed out and dried up alongside juicy, vivid Rita.

"Maybe," she says. "If that no-good daughter of mine could be trusted to watch her younger brother for even an evening."

He watches her go. She has a sweet ass, an upside-down heart in that tight skirt. He hasn't been rejected, exactly. You can't be rejected if you never enter the race. He's a married guy, their kids are friends, or were. Of course they'll never go out as couples. Too dangerous.

Over the next few weeks, it seems the most natural thing to take the back way home, along Purnell Drive, and stare up the hill at the town houses, not that he knows which one is hers. He imagines coming upon her after dark, her car broken down, needing help. Somehow they end up at the Millrace Tavern, or back at Monaghan's, and then they end up in the backseat of his Buick. His kids make fun of his love for Buicks, but they all have nice big backseats, as his sons will discover one day.

He allows himself these stories, then he goes home, where his house is a mess and his wife slumps on the sofa and there's a faint smell, something dirty. Have the boys adopted a dog or a cat against his wishes? One day he'll tear the house apart, find out what they're hiding from him. They can't be laying out for pet food, not now. He's a good guy. He deserves a break. He has given his children everything—*everything*—and they don't seem to know or care. He watches this new late show every night, the one about the hostages, counting off the days. He would have thought the whole thing would be over in a week, maybe two, but now the days are in the triple digits. Where's John Wayne when you need him? Dead of cancer, going on a year now.

John Wayne, the good old Duke, is what got Tim canned at Hutzler's last year. Tim's stupid faggot of a boss, embarrassed by being one-upped on his knowledge of movies, joked they were going to rename the Orange County airport John Wayne *Terminal*. Tim honestly doesn't remember what happened next, but his coworkers say he literally went over the desk, almost cleared it in one leap. They had to slap him in the face until he let go of that pencil dick's pencil neck.

Spring 1980

CHAPTER EIGHTEEN

*Rita sizes up the customers left in her section. Two young lovers. A middle-*aged man, alone, stretching his coffee and cigarette. Wherever he lives, he doesn't want to go there. Three kids in surgical scrubs, too tired to eat. The man will tip well. The lovers—that can go a lot of ways. They could be a new item, and he'll want to impress her. Or they could be a new item and she'll be insecure, wonder aloud if he's leaving a big tip because he thinks the waitress is cute. Most women who have put in their time waiting tables, they don't let their boyfriends or husbands get away with undertipping, while women who have never carried a tray get all huffy if they think the tip is too big. As for the young almost doctors—they'll do their best, and their best will probably be about 10 percent. They will rationalize that their tab is mostly beer, as if that made it any easier to transport to the table, that their food was only so-so, even if it did get there hot and fast, which is all Rita should be judged for. Besides, everyone knows the food at Connolly's is mediocre. It's almost a point of pride. The food sucks, yet everyone still eats here. Even the mayor comes here regular. He was in earlier this evening, with his mother. Now *he's* a good tipper, but Rita didn't have him tonight. The manager spreads him around.

Rita has been at Connolly's only five years, but she feels as if she's part of the fixtures, a piece of the original building, in place when it opened, whenever that was. Back in the 1930s? 1920s? A long time ago. Like a lot of things in Rita's life, its heyday was over long before she grabbed a piece of it. Oh, it's still crowded, still beloved, but with the development of the Inner Harbor now the big thing, the owners have been put on a month-to-month lease. A smart cookie would get out before she's forced out.

Rita is a smart cookie, but she's also a very tired cookie these days. She has enough on her plate, what with needing to find a new place to live, pronto. She can't make the rent on the town house if Rick is moving out. He's going to pay child support—Mr. Good Guy, bully for you, you're so swell—but, man, that's not the same as splitting all the living expenses. Based on what she's seen so far, she's going to be forced to take a two-bedroom, make Mickey double up with her, at least until Joey gets a little older. There's also no way she's going to be able to stay in the city school district.

Mickey seems okay about changing schools, almost eager for it. Rita had steeled herself for a big showdown, only it never happened. Mickey's an okay kid most of the time, doesn't ask for much. But when she does want something, she is ferocious in her desire for it. She argues, she screams, and, on occasion, even lashes out, trying to hit and scratch Rita. She's a hellcat. Well, she comes by that naturally, through her mother and her father, may he rest in peace. Rest in pieces. What a loser he was. Killed in jail, in the overnight lockup on something small, but he had to go pick a fight with a little guy who beat him to death before the guards could get to them. When Mickey was young, it was too complicated to say her father was dead and not say how, so Rita said he was in the wind. She planned to kill him later, in some more civilized way. "Oh, honey, I just heard—your dad died in a car accident in Whereverthehellishe." Or cancer. Something nice. But as Mickey gets older, it only grows harder for Rita to speak to her of her father's death. She's such a funny kid, always focused on who has what, very into fairness. It bugs her that Joey has a father and she doesn't.

Man, how bugged she would be if she ever finds out that Joey has two fathers, in a sense. But even Rick hasn't figured that out. At least she doesn't think he knows that part.

Rita's tables are all in lulls; she ducks outside for a cigarette. The air is nice tonight, balmy and bursting with scents, spring coming on all of a sudden, like it overslept and needs to make up time. But maybe what she's smelling is only what's left in the breeze from McCormick spices on the other side of the harbor. People are excited about the changes coming to the harbor, and Rita knows there will be opportunities—new restaurants, which will draw crowds if only because they're new. But she's skeptical. Tear down the old things, build new things, it's still Baltimore. She should have gotten out while the getting was good, headed to San Francisco or Los Angeles, maybe Dallas. Some big city, although not New York. New York never appealed to her. It's almost as bad as Baltimore. Crime, drugs. Dirty. She wants to go someplace clean, fresh, and warm, a place where the air never turns red with powder from the steel mill. Atlanta? Florida, although not Jacksonville, where she grew up. *Real* Florida, Miami or Fort Lauderdale.

But her last chance of a fresh start was sixteen years and two kids ago. She met Mickey's father, Paul, and got knocked up. Talk about wham, bam, thank you, ma'am. She couldn't afford an abortion, and even if she could, she didn't trust the guy that Paul said he knew. Then Paul had to go and get himself killed before his daughter was even born. At least she could claim they were married, pretend to respectability, not that her own father bought it. He only let her stay at home because her mother was wild for the baby. They moved out as soon as Mickey was in school and Rita got the lunch shift at Hot Shoppe Juniors. She moved on to Connolly's when Mickey turned nine. Then she met Rick. Then she met Joey's dad-to-be, not even a month later. That was a complicated time. But *fun*. She smiles, remembering, two new romances at the same time, both fulfilling in their own way. There was Rick, handsome and steady, ready to take care of her, so sweet with Mickey. Rita loved her daughter a little more, seeing her with Rick. Not that she didn't love her like crazy, but part of being a single mom was never getting to step back and take in the view. Rick made that possible.

Then there was Joey's dad, Larry. He was bad, in the best sense of the word. Drove a hot car, usually had a little toot on him, liked to have sex anywhere but a bed. He had come into the restaurant one night, sat at the bar, watching her, making sure she saw him watching her. He was waiting outside when she got off at ten, leaning against his Monte Carlo. "Need a lift home?" "I need to make a phone call first." He gave her the dime for the pay phone. She liked that. She went back inside, called Mickey. "Mommy's got to stay late," she said. "We're doing inventory." The girl was nine, there was no harm in leaving her alone. Within an hour, Larry had her bent over a picnic table in a kids' park and she was all but baying at the moon. Maybe it was the cocaine, maybe it was cheating on Rick, maybe Larry really did know some things that other men didn't. All she knew was that the sex was better than it was with Rick, and it shouldn't be. Larry wasn't even as good-looking as Rick. Bad skin, too thin. She assumed part of the reason he liked sex in odd places was because he never had to get all the way naked, he could conceal his caved-in, almost hair-less chest, his pin-thin arms and legs. Didn't matter. He was thick where it counted.

Then Rita got pregnant. She couldn't be sure who the dad was, so she figured she'd tell them both, see what each one offered, kind of like making two employers compete for her. Rick said they should get engaged, move in together. Larry said he would help her out however he could—and promptly disappeared. So that sealed it. She had the right guy, and who cared who the actual sperm donor was. Rick was solid, reliable. She could have given up working, but she was reluctant for reasons even she didn't un-derstand. She told Rick she would keep working so they could put more aside to buy a house, yet she never put anything aside, except for the tip money she hid in a little metal box in the kitchen. Rick worked days and she stayed home with the kids, keeping her evening shifts. By afternoon, she looked forward to getting out of the house, although she knew enough to complain now and then about her job. Sometimes, heading out the door, she all but did a little jig.

Then last December, Larry came into Connolly's. Sat at the bar, eyed her the whole time. Sure enough, he was waiting for her, leaning against a new car. Still thin, still pockmarked. Still sexy.

"Hey, babe," he said. "Been too long."

She had worked out what she would say if she ever saw him again. It was good, too. She was going to flash her engagement ring, say that some men knew how to treat a woman. Those plans evaporated. She still wanted him. It was even more exciting than the last time around. Now she was *really* cheating. But she was cheating with the father of her child. And there was no doubt in her mind that he was the father. Joey was almost five now, and people kept commenting on how he didn't resemble anyone in the family, except maybe Mickey a little. Only Rita knows that he looks just like his father.

She was up in the air, incapable of making a decision, wanting Larry, scared to leave Rick. It turned out not to be her decision after all. Rick caught wind of what she was doing. How, she's still not sure, but it didn't matter. They were over.

She tosses her cigarette in the water, goes back inside. She has gauged her tables well: the young lovers tip fairly, the man tips generously, the doctors-to-be can't even make 10 percent among the three of them. She tries not to watch the clock, but she's aware of it over her head, its hand creeping toward nine, sending her home.

He walks in at eight forty-five, making the bartender sigh. Rita sighs, too, only happily. She hasn't told Larry yet that Rick moved out and she has to start over. Rick is her ace in the hole. She'll be smart this time, play it right. The magazines she reads at the beauty parlor, the women she knows—you can't call them friends, but they gab sometimes—all these so-called authorities would argue that it's not smart to want this man, that he's already proven he can't be trusted. But a person can change in a few years. He came back for her. When he sees Joey, everything will fall into place.

They make love parked outside her town house. This has been their pattern since Rick moved out two weeks ago, Larry digging what he thinks is the big risk, getting caught. Larry follows her home, she runs inside, tells Mickey she's going out for a pack of cigarettes or a carton of milk, please keep the door locked and listen for Joey. Then she gets in Larry's car, which has these divine seats that go all the way flat. Tonight, the two of them are extra quick, but not in that efficient I-know-you-let's-get-it-done way. They're quick because they can't hold back. After, she smokes a cigarette, helps herself to the bottle under his front seat, laughing about nothing. God, did she and Rick ever laugh about anything? If so, she can't remember. He was always so superdutiful, and then he started getting superparanoid about her and the kids, accounting for everyone's whereabouts. Glancing back at the house, she thinks she sees the curtain twitch in the window. But Mickey knows better. Rita will snatch that girl bald-headed if she's spying on her. She pulls Larry's head to her breasts, thinks about the dinner she'll cook in her new apartment the first time she has him over. Something good, but not too fancy. Candles on the table? No candles, she decides. Very casual, maybe even take-out pizza. She has the man she wants, not the one she's supposed to want. It was trying to be good that made her bad, leading with her brain instead of her heart. If she lets herself have what she really wants, it will be easier to be good this time.

CHAPTER NINETEEN

The last student on Clem's schedule this morning is very young, very pretty—and destined for failure. These things are not related, not directly. But her youth and her beauty have protected her for much of her life, and this girl—Clem sneaks a look at his appointment calendar, Amanda something, he can't read his own handwriting, he's the ultimate doctor cliché—cannot quite believe that these attributes will not get her through medical school as well. She got in, didn't she? Besides, based on what Clem has gleaned, she was a legitimate admission, not an affirmative action reach or a legacy. She had good grades and MCATs. She is earnest and hardworking.

But she's not meant to be a doctor, not unless she chooses a field like pathology, where her ineptness with people won't matter. Oh, doctors can be cold, brusque, high-handed. Many are.

But they at least need to understand people on some level, which this girl does not. Inevitably, she wants to be a pediatrician. She thinks children *like* her. No one likes her. Clem tries to imagine a child wretched enough to deserve her "care," and his mind slides across an image of little Go-Go Halloran, which shocks him. He doesn't harbor any ill feelings toward the boy. He pities him.

"Dr. Robison?"

"Yes, Amanda?"

"What do you think I should do?"

Quit. But his instincts about people, which are excellent, tell him not to be direct with this young woman. There is something a little dangerous about Amanda. He's not going to flatter himself into thinking she would sleep with him to improve her situation, yet she clearly wants *something* from him. She almost vibrates with neediness. She is used to people volunteering to help her, figuring out what she requires even when she doesn't have a clue herself.

"We would have more options if you had come to me before you received a failing grade," he says.

"But I wasn't failing until I took the final."

"You were marginal throughout the year. You had to know you were skating by, that you were rolling the dice."

"No," she says, shaking her head. Her mannerisms are so childish. Perhaps she has confused her own immaturity with an affinity for the young.

"You could take a semester off," he says. "Come back at midyear, retake the class. Plead special circumstances."

"Such as?"

You're not very intelligent. "That's not for me to say. Amanda"— she brightens at the very sound of her name, like a dog or a small child—"tell me—why do you want to be a doctor?"

"I've always wanted to be a doctor." She is slipping into a speech, a performance. She has recited this story before, probably to much nodding approval. "When I was four, I opened a hospital for my toys. And I really fixed them—put dolls' arms back in their sockets, sewed on a teddy bear's eye."

Ah, but the toys couldn't complain.

"It's the only thing I've ever wanted to do. I can't imagine anything more rewarding than taking care of children. Especially babies, who can't tell you where they hurt or what's wrong."

"I'm not sure being a doctor is supposed to be rewarding," he says.

Amanda's eyes bug at this bit of sacrilege. She is not, upon second look, as attractive as she clearly thinks she is. Her features are not proportionate. The big eyes are a little goo-goo-googly, the mouth broad, and the heart-shaped face can't quite contain it all. She looks like a cartoon deer.

Goo-goo-googly makes Clem think of Go-Go again. Again, there is a flash of—it can only be called revulsion. But he's a little boy. Nothing was his fault. The adults have to take responsibility for what happened.

"I mean—it is, at times, very rewarding. But that's not the point, the main thing of it. We don't become doctors because of how it makes *us* feel. We become doctors because we want to care for others. What we feel and experience is secondary. We are here to serve patients."

"Your specialty is geriatrics."

"Yes?"

She is groping toward a point, although lord knows what it is. That he doesn't understand her desire to care for children? That his patients are closer to natural death and therefore less important, or simply crankier and more demanding? Why does he even bother? She probably will muddle through, end up in a pediatric practice. Chances are, she will be no worse than clumsy, the kind of doctor that children hate and everyone thinks it's just their child. There will be mistakes, but they won't be fatal. Serious, perhaps. Vulnerable to lawsuits. But she won't manage to kill anyone, and her colleagues will cover for her because that's what doctors do. Clem believes every profession covers for its incompetents. So do families. Any group, no matter how loosely affiliated, will always close ranks against the world at large.

He gives Amanda a generic pep talk, sends her on her way. He needs to review three other student files before he meets with them this afternoon, but he feels logy. If he sits here, he'll fall asleep. He will go for a walk, maybe buy a hot dog from one of the carts.

The University of Maryland sits in a forlorn, somewhat forgotten corner of southwest downtown, although the neighborhood is beginning to catch a second wind. When the highway project was halted by community opposition—and Clem was one of those who fought it, because of what it would have done to Leakin Park, its flora and fauna—the city was left with blocks of houses it had planned to demolish. These "dollar" houses in nearby Otterbein ultimately were awarded in a lottery to those who promised to renovate them and live in them for at least five years. Some of those houses will come on the market soon, although the neighborhood is far from gentrified, despite talk about Federal Hill becoming the next Georgetown. Baltimore is one of those cities that defines itself by such comparisons. The next this, the next that. Except maybe Johns Hopkins, which considers itself far above the city, apart from it. But Clem has no regrets about choosing the University of Maryland. It's a good school, too, and it doesn't have to shoulder the weight of a worldwide reputation. Renown is overrated. Plus, one becomes responsible for all of one's colleagues at such places. In the public's mind, Hopkins is Hopkins is Hopkins. He can't imagine that everyone at Hopkins is pleased with John Money right now, given his recent pro-incest comments in *Time* magazine. If Clem worked at Hopkins, he'd probably be asked about that constantly, would not be able to persuade people that a geriatric specialist has no overlap with the sex clinic.

It's a finer day than the morning had promised, and Clem decides to walk north, up Eutaw, to the pleasant chaos of Lexington Market. He won't go so far as to say that he prefers Baltimore to his hometown of Boston, but he considers it a fair trade, especially since they moved into the house on Wetheredsville Road. Boston was fine. He understood it, and it understood him. But Tally wanted to leave, so they left—and allowed her to make him the scapegoat, telling her family it was Clem who desired a change. He shields Tally often from such unpleasant situations, but it's a small price to pay for being married to her. He's a lucky man. Other men, seeing Tally next to him, have told him that over and over. Twenty-five years after the fact, he still flushes at the memory of those early days with Tally. At least she wasn't his student, although that's what everyone seems to infer.

Still, it was illicit by his standards, even a little sordid. That was part of its charm. And she had taken the lead. No one would ever believe that, and he would never say as much out loud. It's not gallant, for one thing. Perhaps the truth is seldom gallant. Eighteen-year-old Tally Duchamp seduced thirty-two-year-old Clement Robison. He had no idea why she wanted to be with him, and he is even more baffled by why she stays with him. She is a headstrong woman, capable of marrying someone merely to antagonize her parents, then staying in that marriage to prove them wrong. Tally has enormous staying power for grudges.

But she is fickle in almost all other aspects of her life. Clem has watched her flail and fail her way through a remarkable number of projects, attacking each enterprise with great energy, then dropping the new activity when the early passion dissipates. He should find it reassuring that painting seems to have taken hold, that she finally is finding a place to channel her formidable energy, especially now that Gwen is only a few years away from leaving the nest. But Tally's current obsession unnerves him. She seems to be using it to wall herself off, to escape from the family. Did he feel that way before the night of the hurricane? Or is he projecting on her the burden of his secret? If she knew what he knows, she would be within her rights to distance herself.

He wonders if Tim and Rick have broken their pledge. There is a prevailing theory that there are no secrets in marriages, not good ones. If they have confided in their mates—well, he envies them. He would love the release of telling someone, to hear someone say: *What could you have done?* Or: *I don't see that you had any choice.* The problem is, he doesn't trust Tally to say those things. Her best quality is also her worst. She's relentlessly, reluctantly honest when asked her opinion. Oh, she won't volunteer it, won't go out of her way to make someone feel bad. She tries to be tactful. But if you insist on knowing what she really thinks, you'd better be prepared to take it. Sometimes Clem isn't.

He enters the market. Noisy and chaotic on this Thursday before Memorial Day, it comes at him in a wave of aromas. Fried food, deli meats, fish, flowers. The sweet, buttery smells of Konstant Candies' peanut brittle trumps everything else. He will buy some for Gwen only—she doesn't eat candy anymore. His mood flags, thinking of his daughter, the obsession with her weight. Worse, her intense interest in boys. She used to have a lively, curious mind and now all she cares about are clothes and how many boys call her each week. It wasn't that long ago that she walked with him through the woods on weekend days, raptly absorbing his knowledge of plants and wildlife. Only two years ago, they read *A Tree Grows in Brooklyn* together, which provided a lot of opportunities for valuable discussion. Poverty, the lives of immigrants, even sex crimes. When he speaks to her now, she is very patient and kind, as if he were mildly retarded.

He decides to have a crab cake at Faidley's. And a beer. It's practically the holiday weekend.

Someone has left a copy of yesterday's *Star*, the afternoon paper, on the counter. Clem flips through it reflexively, pushing it away when he chances on an item from Chicago, something about a possible appeal in John Wayne Gacy's case. Every year, there seems to be a new unthinkable horror. Jim Jones in 1978, John Wayne Gacy last year. What will 1980 bring before it's over? And will his first name begin with a *J*?

His food arrives and he focuses on enjoying the platter, a cholesterol horror show—French fries and macaroni and cheese, the fried crab cake. He would chide a patient for eating such a lunch. But his own cholesterol is excellent, as is his blood pressure. He knows his good health is a lottery ticket, but he's proud to show patients what is possible as one ages. Yet no matter what he does, statistics show his wife is destined to be a widow at a relatively young age. That's a bum thing to do to the person you love most in the world.

Tally was adamant that she understood the actuarial odds. That she would rather have a foreshortened time with him than a longer marriage to anyone else. Still, he wonders if she will decide that it was a poor bargain, giving away her youth, only to find herself alone with much of her own life ahead of her. Say she's sixty-three when he dies, which would make him seventy-seven. That's too late for a true second chance. She'll almost definitely be a grandmother. She might be on her way to being a great-grandmother, if either Miller or Fee decides to start a family early. His money's on Miller, a bit of a throwback, short-haired and stalwart and dutiful. Miller, born in 1956, almost seemed disappointed that he had to sign up for the draft but not actually serve. Miller lives to serve. He always wants to do the right thing. In other words, he's just like his father. He has made a good marriage to a terrific girl. And that girl, like her mother-in-law before her, has persuaded Miller to abandon his hometown, only in her case she wants to be close to her family. He calls every Sunday, recounting his week. In some ways, Clem feels he knows more about Miller's life than he does about Gwen's.

Now Fee is quiet, withdrawn. She has a secret, even if she doesn't know it. Tally believes it's her sexuality, which makes Clem sad, only because he believes Fee's life will be harder for it, that she will not be comfortable in her own skin. She's in San Francisco, but she might as well be in . . . Dubuque, based on what Clem has gleaned of her life. She goes to school—she's working toward a master's in psychology—and spends her weekends biking obsessively, almost as if she's trying to get away from herself. Clem hopes she eventually finds a way to be still.

As for Gwen—sweet, pretty, eager-to-please Gwen. Whatever she does, she'll do well. So much younger than her siblings, Gwen had the best of both worlds: she was essentially raised as an only child, but by parents with plenty of field experience. Some might call her spoiled, but Clem thinks she's the opposite. Gwen is a delight. Or was.

"What if it were your child? What if it was Gwen or Mickey?" Tim Halloran asked Clem and Rick that night. To this day, Clem has to fight down the impulse to blurt out: *It wouldn't be. Gwen isn't stupid that way.* He isn't blaming the victim, Go-Go. He's castigating the Hallorans for not preparing their son for the world at large. Was it because he was a boy that his safety in the world was presumed, or because he had two older brothers who were supposed to show him the ropes? Yet Clem and Tally hadn't abdicated their responsibility to Gwen because of Miller and Fee.

"Hey, he tried to *hit* Mickey," Rick said. "He could have killed her. The kids say he kept an old shotgun in that cabin. What if he had grabbed that instead of his guitar?"

"It's not the same," Halloran shrilled, his voice high-pitched as a woman's. "It's not the same."

Halloran was right, but not in the way he believed. Clem could not bear to tell Tim that a violent physical assault on a girl would, according to the law, be judged much more harshly than the touches that the old man had bestowed on Go-Go. What would the courts have done to him? He would have gotten a year or two at the most. And what if he had denied it? How could it be proved? According to Sean, Mickey couldn't describe what she had seen in the darkness of the cabin, only that the old man had become violent when she found him alone with Go-Go. Yes, the man was old and black and indigent. The justice system would not be predisposed in his favor. But whatever sentence was meted out would never have satisfied Tim. Hell, a smart defense attorney might summon Dr. Money as an expert witness, ask him to tell the court what he had told *Time* magazine: "A childhood experience, such as being the partner of a relative or of an older person, need not necessarily affect the child adversely." But what was a child? What was a relative? Clem remembers, as he often does, the image of eighteen-year-old Tally, passing canapés in her parents' house, offering her tray to her bachelor uncle's best friend, pregnant by him not even a year later. Utterly different, of course—and yet some people wouldn't consider it so. Both situations would be covered by Dr. Money's rubric.

The discussion was moot. The man was dead at their feet. Events and possibilities swirled around them, fast as the water rushing around the man, unstoppable, implacable. Any number of things could have killed him. The fall, the blow to his head, a heart attack, drowning. What good would it do to tell anyone about the children, how the man had chased them through the woods, much less why. They agreed that Clem would place an anonymous call to 911 from a pay phone downtown, reporting a body in the woods, then check the morgue to find out when a John Doe was brought in. An autopsy would determine if it had been a heart attack, or even a stroke, brought on by exertion. No one was to blame for what happened.

But when Clem finally called the morgue on an elaborate pretext, claiming he needed to collect data on all over-fifty deaths in September for a research project, there wasn't a single John Doe who matched the description of the man in the woods. Had his body not been found? Could he have been wrong about the man's death? If so—

He pushes his plate away, incapable of finishing. He should buy something for the girls, as he thinks of Tally and Gwen. But what can he take them? Tally is proprietary about her menus and resents any unsolicited contributions. Gwen no longer eats sweets. The market's flowers are not the best, a little bedraggled and mealy-looking. He has nothing to bring them but himself, old and tired at the end of another day.

CHAPTER TWENTY

"I found my thrill," Larry sings, *"up on Strawberry Hill."*

"Strawberry *Hill* Apartments . . . for–e–ver," Rita sings back, unwrapping glasses. Lord, Mickey did a shit job packing them, and a few are chipped. Inevitably, it's her nice ones, the matched set of heavy Mexican amber from Pier One. Why couldn't the freebies from the filling station giveaways end up cracked?

But even the broken glasses can't dim Rita's mood, although she makes a mental note to find Mickey later and give her what-for.

Moving, which is supposed to be one of the most stressful events in a person's life, has brought Rita nothing but a constant, giggling joy since she signed the lease on the Strawberry Hill apartment last month. She floats through her days, her temper soft, and she rockets through her nights, shooting up, up, up on waves of sex, then falling into the best sleep she has ever known.

She can't believe Larry volunteered to move in with her, without even being asked. Being legit—sharing a bed and an apartment with Larry, if not the actual lease—is the best high she has ever known. Everything is better. Each cigarette, each drink, punching out at work. Even Joey, something of a wild child, is suddenly an angel. It's almost as if he knows who his real father is, although Rick—of course!—continues to be the superdutiful dad, coming by every other weekend and Wednesday nights. God, Rita would love to tell him the truth, just to wipe that superior look off his face, but she doesn't want to say good-bye to his checks.

Besides, Rick's visits seem to be the only thing that rouses Mickey out of her permanent sulk. Suddenly, nothing makes that girl happy. Take the school thing. She hates her current school, Rock Glen. She was excited about the transfer to a new district when Rita first told her. Then Rita told Rock Glen that Mickey has a medical condition and wouldn't be able to attend the last three weeks. She now lives too far away to walk to the bus stop, and who's going to drive her there at 7:30 A.M. every day? Not Rita. Besides, no one learns anything the last three weeks of school. You think a girl would be happy, getting a head start on summer vacation. Plus, Rita's paying Mickey to babysit during the mornings, when it would be entirely reasonable to expect her to do that for free. A dollar twenty-five an hour, five hours a day, five days a week. Heck, that's better than Rita does some nights. The girl should be delirious.

But Mickey hates the new apartment. She has to share a bedroom with Joey, at least until Rita can justify buying a sofa bed, but it's not like either kid can be in Rita's room, now that Larry is sleeping over. The new place may be smaller, but it's nicer. Clean, freshly painted. Besides, her car insurance dropped almost by half just for moving out of the city, and they are a mile closer to the shopping centers up on Route 40 and out Security Boulevard. Mickey could take the bus to any of those places, go shopping, go to the movies. But when Rita points this out, Mickey sighs and says: "I miss my woods." Her woods? Foolish girl.

Rita can't waste time worrying about Mickey. Her immediate goal is to make Larry a man, a real man. Someone who provides. Someone who doesn't deal drugs, maybe uses them from time to time, but doesn't sell.

"What is this?" Larry asks, pulling a long, lidded metal pan from a box. She needs a beat to identify it.

"A fish poacher."

"Have you ever used it?"

"No. I brought it home from work one night because I heard that was a good way to make fish, but my kids hate fish." Actually, it was Rick who hated fish, but she tries to mention him as little as possible. She wants to erase Rick from the record, pretend he never happened.

" 'Brought it home'—you mean you nicked it." Larry smiles. He likes her wicked side.

"Maybe." She gives him a sideways bump with her hip as she passes him in the small galley kitchen, then turns and bumps her rear against his crotch, moving lazily back and forth until she sees Mickey standing in the living room, watching them through the pass-through. No expression on her face, no comment, just watching. The girl sees too much. Rita wonders if Mickey has noticed her brother's marked resemblance to Larry. Thank God both Rick and Larry had dark hair and eyes. There's nothing obvious to link Larry to Joey unless one looks for the resemblance, as Rita does, repeatedly. There's a thinness at the bridge of the nose, camouflaged by Joey's chubbiness, a sameness to the ears. Yes, the ears. She knows Larry that well, inside and out.

Which means she understands it won't be easy, domesticating a man who loves her wild side. Rick was the big attraction, the thing that brought Larry back to her. Now that they aren't cheating, his interest could fall off. If she leans on him to give up dabbling in drugs, move in officially—no, he has to make those decisions on his own. Or think he's making them. So be it. She knows how to keep him happy and interested. Last week, they went to the drive-in up on Route 40 and Rita was dead tired, but she made sure to go down on him. Twice. Her hair was coated with grease and salt from his popcorn when she finally pulled her head from his lap. The people in the next car gave her a dirty look. They had a bunch of pajamaed kids with them. So what? It was an R-rated movie about two teenagers trying to lose their virginity. Those righteous parents were the creeps, bringing their kids to something like that.

She wonders if Mickey has gone all the way yet. She thinks not. She doesn't want her to, of course, although Rita was only sixteen when she did it the first time, and girls grow up faster now. Still, Mickey needs a boyfriend, someone to distract her so she wouldn't be in the apartment all the time, sneaking up on Rita and Larry. Maybe Rita should take Mickey to her doctor, get her on the pill? Or an IUD, like she uses, because she smokes. Does Mickey smoke? Does she use drugs? Rita won't let her get away with that, even if it does make her a hypocrite. Does Mickey know she uses on occasion? Used. Probably, the kid doesn't miss a trick. Look at her, standing there, staring. Who is she to judge Rita? It might look bad, leaving Rick, taking up with Larry so fast, but if only Mickey knew the whole story. Rita isn't taking a family apart, she's putting one together. The girl should be kissing her feet with gratitude.

"I'm going to go outside," Mickey says. "Look around."

"You get all your stuff unpacked?"

A pause. She's actually thinking about whether to lie to her. The thing that kills Rita is that Mickey wants Rita to see her thinking about lying. "I've done enough," she says. "For now."

"You did a shit job packing my glasses," Rita says.

"Maybe you should have packed them. I guess you were too busy."

She puts a lot of spin on *busy*. There's no doubt what she means.

"Yeah, I was busy. Busy working every night, so you can have food and clothes and a roof over your head."

"Yes," Mickey says, looking upward. "And what a roof it is."

Rita raises a hand, her temper roaring back, even as Larry says, "Ladies, ladies." Larry doesn't like conflict. She better keep it in check if she wants to keep him, not let Mickey get a rise out of her. She wonders if Mickey understands this, if she's baiting her mother to make her look bad in front of Larry.

Joey bellows from the bedroom, waking up from his nap. Rita's policy is that if he takes a nap at nursery school, he sure as hell is going to take one at home. But he never goes down without a fight.

"Go get your brother," she tells Mickey.

"I was going to—"

"Get your brother. Your stepfather and I have to—wash the sheets."

"He's not my stepfather," Mickey says, and Rita can't be sure, but she thinks Larry nods.

"Get your brother," she says.

"Half brother," Mickey says. She always has to have the last word.

As soon as Mickey leaves the room, Rita grabs the laundry basket and a random selection of clothes, doesn't even bother with detergent.

"Why do I—" Larry starts, and she gives his crotch a quick squeeze. "You'll like it," she whispers. "Doing laundry is good clean fun."

They can't lock the door as it turns out, but they close it and start out standing. No one's coming through that door unless they're determined to push 250 pounds of human aside. But Rita doesn't want to finish that way. It's too tempting for her to press herself against the rattling washer, full of someone else's clothes, Larry behind her, vibrating all over. She has to stuff her fist in her mouth to keep her pleasure to herself, and even Larry, expert at stifling his own cries, has to bite her shoulder to muffle his groans. He breaks the skin, although he doesn't draw blood. She thinks she hears someone start to open the door, only to retreat.

This is how I will keep you. She almost says it out loud. She has to be fun, spontaneous, *dirty.*

Back in the apartment, little Joey is running around naked, screaming at the top of his lungs, and Mickey's just watching him, no expression on her face.

"Nake! Nake!" he screams. "I'm nake." It's the word he used as a toddler. He knows it's funny.

"What the hell, Mickey?"

"He took his clothes off," she says with a shrug. "I can't help it if he's retarded."

"Don't call your brother retarded."

"Look at that little thing," Larry says. "No resemblance there."

Rita shoots him a look. *Shut the fuck up.* Luckily, Mickey is oblivious, for once. She's watching her brother run in circles as if she can't remember what it's like to be that young and silly. "Nake! Nake!" he cries. Rita reminds herself to be kind to Mickey, the less advantaged child, the one without a father, whereas Joey has two in a sense. Rita can tell it baffles Mickey that Rick Senior doesn't have any obligations toward her since moving out. He's kind enough to include her on some outings, but everything's tailored to Joey—tot lot, cartoons—which makes it boring as hell for Mickey. Yet Rita can't blame Rick, either. It's biology. He's taking care of what he believes to be his child. Eventually, Joey is what will bind Larry to her, far more important than hot sex in the laundry room and blow jobs at the drive-in. He just needs some time.

"Nake! Nake! I'm nake!" Joey screams.

"Retard," Mickey says under her breath, but she's smiling. They're all smiling. Rita wonders if it would be wrong to start calling Joey by his middle name, which happens to be Lawrence.

Summer 1980

CHAPTER TWENTY-ONE

Tim stands outside his house, watching the participants gather for the Fourth of July parade. He tries not to take it personally, that his one-block street, Sekots Lane, is used as a staging area for the annual parade, but he can't help feeling slighted. Sekots has always felt like an annex to the real neighborhood, some orphan street that got tacked on by mistake. Sekots dead-ends into a hill where children sledded once, but the Dickeyville Garden Club planted it aggressively, hoping to block out the view of the Wakefield Apartments above them. Seemed ridiculous at the time, all those little saplings, but trees grow, and the club's objective has been achieved. Tim remembers when those trees were smaller than his boys.

It's been years since his family was home for this parade. Even through last year, with his work life on and off, they were able to take their usual week in Ocean City. They always go to an old-fashioned rooming house that Tim's family stayed in when he was a boy. It's not fancy. In fact, it's downright crummy, but what's the point of spending dough on a place where you only come to shake sand out of your suit and hang wet towels over the railings. The location is prime, two blocks from the beach, within walking distance of the attractions along the boardwalk, where they spent almost every evening. Last summer, it broke Go-Go's heart when he just missed the height cutoff for the bumper cars. Tim pleaded, even tried to slip the attendant a fiver. Go-Go threw a tantrum, not entirely out of character for him, although it struck Tim as particularly violent and out of control. Last summer—no, Tim tells himself. It hadn't happened yet. It was only the one time. Go-Go said it was the only time he was ever in that old bastard's cabin.

No shore this summer, even though Tim is back to work. He has a gig at Tuerkes, which sells luggage and leather goods. Not doing the books, but working the floor as a sales associate. He likes it, sort of. He actually has to dress better than he did when he was working in accounting, and he enjoys the store's deep leathery smell, the company of the other guys. They're young, blow-dried. They go to discos and come in after the weekends, talking about the pussy they get, claiming a girl's drink preference tells you everything about her, whether it's a Wallbanger or a Sex on the Beach. They swear that the best girls, the classy girls, drink white wine spritzers or Bristol Cream. The women they talk about—they seem like an entirely new species to Tim. They could be imported from the moon.

The Tuerkes job felt like a demotion at first, but now Tim thinks it might be a turning point. Learn the ropes at Tuerkes, rise up, maybe start his own business. The economy is god-awful, but it won't always be. People will have money to spend again one day. The trick is figuring out what they'll want, or how to make them think they want what you're selling. He's seen customers in Tuerkes who have no more need of a $200 briefcase than a pig needs a sports car, but the briefcase represents something to them, a dream, an ambition. What will people want when the money flows again? High-end appliances? Jewelry? With men wearing it now, the market has doubled. Gadgets? Look at Hechinger, beginning to spread all over the goddamn place. Who knew that a fucking hardware store could get so big? A hammer is a hammer is a hammer.

In the meantime, Tim has no seniority and no paid vacation. Which is a better excuse for not going to the shore than 'fessing up to his kids that they pretty much have no money. Interest rates hovering at 17 percent this year, and he had to pay a penalty to cash in a CD. That hurt. He told the older boys that they had to get part-time jobs this summer, making it seem like a character-building exercise. But he can't force Go-Go to get a job and the kid's a nonstop fount of needs. Lately, he's obsessed with this video game where some yellow dot eats other yellow dots until some ghosts eat the big yellow dot. Thank god there's not an arcade within walking distance or Go-Go would spend all his days there, buying time at what Tim has figured to be about three minutes per quarter, give or take.

A month ago, Go-Go started pestering him for money for a Fourth of July costume. The kid's all excited about marching in the parade, although he's keeping his outfit a secret, says he doesn't want anyone to steal his idea. There are prizes for the best ones, penny-ante shit, but Go-Go's acting like the crown jewels are at stake. Tim said he couldn't give him money if he didn't know what it was for, and Go-Go stopped asking. Very un-Go-Go like. Also unlike him to keep a secret, but he has managed to hide his costume from everyone, even his brothers. Even now, he is still in the house, in his room, determined not to put in an appearance until the parade actually starts.

The Dickeyville Fourth of July parade is one of those things that people love about the neighborhood, but the preciousness of it is a little much for Tim. Jesus, it looks like everyone is going to march in the damn thing, who's going to be left to watch? The theme is vaguely patriotic, yet also kind of feel-good: *We are all Americans.* No shit, Sherlock. Who else celebrates the Fourth of July? Maybe the Brits are lifting a pint, glad to be rid of us, but their economy is in the crapper, too. Adherence to the theme doesn't seem to be that hard-and-fast, anyway. Tim sees a platoon of tiny little girls in old-fashioned dresses, with buggies and baby dolls. Behind them, a Cub Scout troop. Tim didn't realize there were so many little kids in the neighborhood. Judging by their ages, the Bicentennial was a big year for making babies.

As Tim looks around, he can't believe this mix of hippies and preppies are his neighbors. He doesn't fit in with either crowd. How did this happen? Was it always this way? He can't remember now why he bought the house on Sekots Lane, other than that the price was right and he wanted a place whose walls didn't connect to someone else's walls. That seemed like a big step up. He'd like to blame Doris, but she fought him about the house—after the fact, which is the only way she fights. She said the neighborhood was too isolated and that she'd rather wait until they could afford something bigger. She also asked what was the point of moving to a place full of old-fashioned stone and brick houses surrounded by wooded hillsides, only to buy a new house that backed up to an apartment complex. "Things don't break as much in a new house," he argued. That's a laugh. Things are constantly breaking in the house on Sekots Lane. There's probably not an original appliance left in the place, and he's pretty sure the hot-water heater is going down for the count.

Five minutes until the parade. It's going to be a bitch of a day, hot and steamy. It makes Tim sweat just to look at the guy dressed up as George Washington. Even the sucker doing Jimmy Carter in shirtsleeves looks hot, and the poor Reagan impersonator is wearing a suit. Tim might vote for Reagan, although he's keeping that to himself. If Teddy Kennedy can wrest the nomination away from Carter next month, then it will be different. Tim could never vote against a Kennedy. Sure, he knows about the dead girl, the secretary, and believes Kennedy was probably banging her, or planning to. So what? Those were his prerogatives. Tim doesn't begrudge him a thing. He should be president, although Tim can't imagine how many Secret Service agents it would take to keep him safe. Some nut will take a shot at him. There's always a nut somewhere, willing to take a shot.

The parade is finally under way, transforming itself from a milling, formless mass into something with shape and purpose. The fife-and-drum trio has started playing, everyone is lining up. Where's Go-Go? Tim begins to wonder if the boy understands how parades work, or if he even bothered to register, surely a prerequisite for marching and being considered for a prize. Go-Go has trouble understanding things like that, rules and regulations. His old man can sympathize.

The parade stretches out, heading down Pickwick toward the more picturesque heart of the village, wending its way toward the banks of the Gwynns Falls. Tim wonders if it's too early to have a beer. It's a holiday, isn't it? The usual rules don't apply. He goes back into the house and grabs a Schaefer. It is, as the song says, the one beer to have when you're having more than one and Tim definitely plans to have more than one today.

A young mother, one of the ones who's shadowing the buggy brigade, shoots him a dirty look. Hey, he put it in a Styrofoam koozie. No one can see the can. It's a holiday, dammit.

Then he sees Go-Go, coming out the front door. *Shit.* He's dressed as one of the U.S. Olympic hockey players. Not a bad idea, actually, for a display of patriotism. He's more on the money than those little girls with their baby carriages. But the kid has to be dying inside all that gear. Because he's not just any hockey player, he's the goalie, Jim Craig, complete with pads and face mask. Although the pants are nothing but red sweatpants with duct tape and white paper stars along the sides, the rest of the costume looks authentic. Tim wonders where Doris got the scratch for it, if she's one of those women who squirrels away money behind his back. She better not be. Shit, did Go-Go steal the stuff?

All those concerns are overshadowed by the fact that the kid is wearing actual skates. Sure, he's got rubber covers on the blades, but he's *walking in skates*. Short and rinky-dink as the Dickeyville parade is, there's no way Go-Go is going to make it to the end in that outfit, brandishing a hockey stick.

Tim goes up to him. "Great costume, buddy."

Go-Go nods his thanks, his entire being focused on what he has to do—the sweater, those skates. He's almost vibrating inside all that gear. At least he has the good sense to wear the mask up on his head.

"But, buddy, you'll never be able to walk in that getup. Even if you took off the skates—"

"I *won't*," Go-Go says. "The skates are the best part. I'm Jim Craig."

"I got that, buddy."

"I turned away thirty-six of the Soviets' thirty-nine attempts on goal."

"Yeah, in February, at Lake Placid. But it's July in Baltimore. You'll die. I mean, literally, Go-Go. You could die from the heat."

Doris comes up, wringing her hands. "You can't walk in that outfit, Go-Go. You'll get sick."

Funny, but Doris taking his side makes Tim want to find another one. He isn't going to be like her, the enemy of fun, the worrywart.

"Look," he says, "how about if I walk with you? Maybe bring some water. That way, if you get thirsty or something—"

Go-Go has been mincing forward all this time, slowly but surely, the gap between him and the parade growing larger and larger.

"You mean, like a bodyguard?"

"Sure," his father says. "Like a bodyguard. I bet Jim Craig had a bodyguard when he went home to"—where was Jim Craig from?—"Philadelphia and all his friends came out to see him."

"Jim Craig," Go-Go says, every word, every step, a concentrated effort, "is from Massachusetts. Like Father Andrew."

"Massachusetts, Pennsylvania. I always get them confused."

Tim has Doris fill an old thermos with ice water, reluctantly trades it for his beer, then falls in behind Go-Go. Still, they're losing ground with every labored step. Pretty soon, they can barely see the little girls with their baby carriages.

"You know, Jim Craig was a big hero in that game."

"I *know*," Go-Go says.

"And sometimes, when someone is a big hero, people carry him on their shoulders."

Go-Go doesn't break stride. If you could call those tiny, painful steps strides. "Did they do that with Jim Craig, though?"

"They did, I think, when he went home. To Massachusetts. I'm pretty sure when he went back to his hometown, that's exactly what they did."

He hoists his son to his shoulders. He's ten and wearing all that gear. It's no small thing. And it's so damn hot. Still, Tim makes better time than Go-Go ever could have. With each lumbering step, the skates bang his chest and Go-Go ends up hitting him on the head with the stick every time he tries to adjust himself. But they are narrowing the gap now. As they catch up to the parade and the spectators, Go-Go hands his hockey stick to his father. He then lifts his arms, hands clenched, clearly imitating some victory grip he's seen in a movie or TV show.

His brothers, who had been following the parade on their bikes, circle back, riding in slow, lazy circles around them.

"Let's take turns," Sean says. "We can go faster than you."

"He's too big for you to carry."

"Not for me and Tim together."

They leave their bikes by the side of the road—no need to fear them being taken here in Dickeyville, where everyone knows everyone, although some colored kids might come along. The brothers make a seat of their hands and carry Go-Go the next block. Tim then takes him back on his shoulder for a segment. And so they go, now part of the parade. But for the final stage, for the approach to the finish alongside the stream, Go-Go wants to get back on his father's shoulders and do his hand thing again. This time, Sean carries the hockey stick.

They're all dripping with sweat, smelly and disgusting. But the woman who frowned at Tim's can of Schaefer smiles at him now. He smiles for himself. Go-Go wins second prize—really, it should have been first, just for the sheer stamina involved—but he's pleased as hell with the ten-dollar gift certificate to G. C. Murphy's and the look on his face is more than enough reward for Tim. Even with Tim back at work, things are still lean for the family.

Go-Go must understand this because later that night, after running through a list of all the things a boy can do with ten dollars at G. C. Murphy's, he offers to put it toward school supplies.

"That's okay, buddy," his father says, tucking him in, something he seldom does in the summer, when the boys are allowed to stay up as late as they wish. Something he seldom does, period. "It was your costume, you get the prize, spend it on whatever you want. Where'd you get the idea?"

"I found a hockey mask."

"Where did you find a hockey mask?"

"In the woods."

"In the woods. I thought we agreed you weren't going to go into the woods alone."

"At the end, in the vacant lot on Tucker Lane. Not in the *woods-woods*."

"OK. So you found a hockey mask, just lying there?"

"Yeah. At first I was going to be the killer in *Friday the 13th*. I didn't get to see it, but Sean and Tim told me about it."

"That wouldn't have been a very nice thing to be on the Fourth of July, buddy. It's your country's birthday."

"I know. Besides, that would mean I was a girl because in the movie, it's a lady who wears the hockey mask so people don't recognize her when she's killing them. I don't want to be a lady."

"Of course you don't. You're a boy. You're all boy. And what you did, that was better. Jim Craig—that's in the right spirit." A pause. "Where'd you get all the other gear, buddy? The stick and the pads?"

"Oh, some boys lent it to me."

"Really? What boys?"

"I have to give it back. Not the skates. I wore my own skates. Do you remember when you taught me how to skate?"

Go-Go's memory is generous. Tim didn't exactly teach him how to skate. He left that to the older boys. He does remember the rink at Memorial Stadium, a bone-cold frustrating day of Go-Go walking on his ankles. Tim hated every second of it and kept retreating to the car to "get warm" and listen to the Colts playing out of town. Turns out that all that walking on his ankles had prepared Go-Go well for today. "Yeah, I remember."

"That was a good day."

"If that was a good day, then I guess today is a fantastic day."

"Yeah." Go-Go frowns. "It is, but it doesn't feel quite the same. Things aren't as good as when I was little."

That fuckin' freak in the woods. For all Tim knows, that monster gave Go-Go the hockey mask last summer, that's how he lured him into his house. That man took his boy's childhood and there's not a damn thing Tim can do about it. Talking makes the least sense, he doesn't care what anyone says. Nothing can undo what happened. He and Doris are united on this front at least. No psychiatrists, no talking about it. She prays and he does his best to set a good example of what a man is. OK, he wasn't doing a very good job there for a while. But he's back at work, he's earning again, *providing*. He will take care of his family. He just lost his way there for a little while. Go-Go showed him he needed to get it together.

"Things are as good as they were when you were little," Tim says. "It's only that all memories get better the further you get away from them."

"Really?"

"Really," he says. "Good memories get better and bad memories just disappear."

"Really?" Go-Go's voice scales up, awed, as if this has never occurred to him.

"Really." *One day you won't think about it. I promise, I promise, I promise.*

"I wish we could go to the ocean this summer."

"Me, too. Maybe we will for a day."

"Can we have saltwater taffy?"

"Sure."

"And Grotto Pizza?"

"Definitely."

"Thrasher's fries?"

"And funnel cake. I bet you're tall enough to go on the bumper cars this year."

He is. It's mid-August before they make it to Ocean City for a day trip and the drive is miserable, even though it's a weekday. But the traffic and the sticky hot car are worth the headache to see Go-Go in a bumper car. His smile is tight but real, jamming his car into his brothers' less-fleet vehicles. He's nimble behind the wheel, eluding them when they try to exact their revenge. He does get in a little trouble for going against the flow and creating a few head-on collisions, but hell, that's Go-Go.

That night, driving home, boys and mother dozing as Tim listens to the final inning of the Orioles game, Go-Go suddenly says from the backseat, almost as if talking to himself: "Today is a good memory already."

It takes all Tim's strength to keep his car heading straight in the westward-bound lane on the Bay Bridge. Oh, if only he could, he would make the old Buick rise in the sky, truly Shitty Shitty Bang Bang, farting black smoke all the way home. Anything—anything—to make Go-Go laugh again.

Autumn 1980

CHAPTER TWENTY-TWO

Tally is surprised how hard the news hits her, although she supposes one is never prepared for this. Her mother, after all, had to cope with the same situation when she was much younger. Implacable time, the one thing that never stops, that's the real certainty behind death, if not taxes. Time is relentless in its forward drive. She grips the phone, the cherry red wall unit in the kitchen, one of the few notes of color allowed in her all-white oasis, seeing details she stopped noticing long ago—the paper disk in the center of the dial, the tendons in her hand, the large squash blossom ring she wears on her right hand, scuff marks on the wall. Most rings like this are turquoise, but Tally's stone is coral. It clashes terribly with the red of the phone—

"April," Miller says. "I hope you don't mind that we waited."

"Of course not," she says. She thinks of an old phrase—*butter wouldn't melt in her mouth*. To her, it has never connoted anything but coldness, and she has never understood why others think it indicates charm and good manners. But she gets it now. Her mouth is like a covered butter dish, cool and contained and proper, presenting what is expected of her. She calls over her shoulder. "Clem? Clem?" The acoustics in the house are so odd. He could be steps away and oblivious. He could be upstairs and hear every word.

"What?" he calls back. It sounds as if he's on the second floor.

"Pick up the extension. Miller has news."

She stays on the line while Miller repeats his big announcement, makes the proper happy noises, then excuses herself, insisting that father and son should have a father-to-*father* talk. In hanging up the phone, she misses the hook and the receiver clatters to the floor on its long curlicue of a cord. She stoops to pick it up and slides it onto the cherry red base. She's going to be a grandmother. This is what happens to women who have children at nineteen. They become grandmothers at forty-three.

Nothing has changed. She looks as young as she did two minutes ago, when Miller called, taking advantage of the Sunday rates, as he always does, thrifty boy. It is only 3 P.M. out in Denver. Here, it is the end of a perfect autumn weekend, which Gwen has wasted by spending it indoors at a roller-skating rink. Tally is skeptical of Gwen's enthusiasm for such a wholesome activity. She worries it might be used as a cover for something else, something done out in the parking lot, assuming they really go to the rink at all. But what's the worst thing that could happen? Gwen will get pregnant. So what? Tally's already going to be a grandmother.

She knows her reaction makes no sense. If she had anticipated this development, prepared herself, she would be elated or at least somewhat enthusiastic. But it feels messy, being a grandmother when one child is still in high school. It makes her feel old and young at the same time—a grandmother at forty-three, but still a mother to a high school freshman. Clem, she knows, will have no ambivalence, and she steels herself for his arrival in the kitchen, his eagerness to celebrate.

Sure enough, he comes in and kisses her with an excitement he has not shown in—well, let's not add up all those weeks, months, she thinks. A year, at least.

"What are you looking for?" she asks, for Clem has released her and is rummaging through the small collection of wine they keep in a stackable Formica holder on the counter.

"Something worthy of the news."

"What news?" Gwen says, clattering up from the basement. Her cheeks are ruddy, her hair mussed. A completely normal by-product of roller skating, but also of other activities. And why did she enter through the basement?

"Your brother's going to have a baby."

"How advanced of him," Gwen says, going to the refrigerator and staring into it, a habit that makes Tally wild because she never takes anything, only studies the food with an almost voyeuristic delight. "I would have thought that Sylvia would have the baby, but I guess Miller is superevolved. *Kramer vs. Kramer* must have hit him pretty hard."

Tally knows that Clem hates this new tone of Gwen's, a flip sarcasm honed over the summer, but he ignores it today, determined to have his moment of joy. "If you like, you can have a glass with us to celebrate."

"A glass of what?" She's interested, Tally can tell. Gwen likes being treated like a grown-up. Tally was the same way at this age. Still, it makes her nervous, the way Gwen brightens at the thought of drinking something with alcohol. Don't move so fast, she wants to tell her daughter. Or next thing you know, you'll be on the verge of being a grandmother.

"This white Burgundy, I think. I've been saving it for a special occasion."

"It won't be cold in time," Tally says. "Dinner's at seven."

"I'll put it in an ice bucket. That will be good enough. Does it go with what you're fixing?"

It will, actually. She's making poached salmon, a light green salad for dinner. A summer dish, but it is technically summer for one more day, although the seasons also seem to be rushing impatient as Gwen. The light is pulling away. The days are darker at both ends. Tally hates to feel the ebbing of the light, even though she made very little progress over the summer when there were daylight hours galore. The new painting, which began with so much promise, is torturing her, has been torturing her for almost a year. But for once she's not going to give up.

While Tally wishes she could stop time, she understands Gwen is eager for the calendar to move forward. She is wearing fall colors today—a plaid skirt with burgundy knee socks, a navy sweater. This is Gwen's "new look," straight from *The Official Preppy Handbook,* and Tally objects to it on every front. It is expensive, first and foremost, and materialistic. She hates Gwen's sudden attachment to labels, the insistence on branding herself with tiny alligators, polo players, a socialite's signature.

But Tally also finds it confounding that her daughter wants to dress in this conservative, rigid style. If Tally had been a high school girl today, she would be listening to punk bands, embracing the most outrageous clothes possible. Why does Gwen want to look like a Junior Leaguer? Clem loves the new Gwen, but Tally suspects that the clothes are a cover, that the boys in plaid pants and crewnecks are much wilder than the scruffy hippies that Gwen brought home last year. She is dating a Gilman boy now and seems to attach a lot of importance to that. Her goal, Tally understands, is to get a bid to as many private school proms as possible. She has turned into a horrible flirt.

"You are turning into a horrible flirt," Tally told her just that morning, after listening to Gwen's end of a phone call. She wasn't eavesdropping. Tally was in the kitchen, cleaning up from breakfast, and Gwen chose to take the call here rather than run up to her bedroom. She wrapped the extension cord around herself, then uncoiled, all the while talking about her various conquests.

"Like mother, like daughter," Gwen said.

"I'm not a flirt."

"You don't flirt often," Gwen conceded. "Maybe that's why you make such an ass out of yourself when you do."

"Gwendolyn Eleanor Robison." She is named for the poet Gwendolyn Brooks. And a maiden aunt of Clem's, but Tally prefers to credit only the poet.

"Remember that time with Mickey's stepdad?"

She doesn't. She can't even remember his name. Then she does.

"I wasn't flirting with him."

"That's not how Mickey's mother saw it."

"That's not what happened—"

"Oh, don't spazz out about it," Gwen said with a flippant wave. "It's not important."

Then why bring it up? Probably because she knows Tally will brood on it for the rest of the day.

Tally must have seen Rick here or there—at the Exxon, sitting in Rita's car when they dropped Mickey off—but she first spoke to him at the end of Mickey's eleventh birthday, a Friday-into-Saturday sleepover. Gwen was not a whiny or demanding child, but she had lobbied relentlessly to attend this party for her new friend. Clem didn't want her to go. He was dubious about Mickey's home situation. But Clem didn't have the heart to tell Gwen his true objections, and she easily batted down the straw men he tried to put up—*you won't get enough sleep, you'll eat junk, what about homework?* All Tally could think was that Rita was a stronger woman than she was, having a sleepover for eleven-year-old girls.

Tally wanted to think she was better than her neighbors—and Clem—when it came to such snobbery. Mickey's house called her bluff. From the moment she crossed the threshold that Saturday afternoon, she was in distress. The smells—onion, bacon, a never-quite-clean diaper pail somewhere. The noise—there was clearly no quiet corner in the house. And the house, although newish, was showing its seams. Then again, so was Clement's dream house. Whatever the modern world had wrought, it did not include better-built structures. Old houses got scuffed and dirtied, true, but new houses gapped and sagged and peeled. Gwen seemed oblivious to it all. But Tally noticed, and Mickey's mother, Rita, noticed her noticing.

"We were living up in Wakefield, but there were only two bedrooms," she said. "After I got pregnant with Joey, we needed three bedrooms, but I didn't want Mickey to leave the school district. We didn't have a lot of options."

"Oh, that's good. That you were able to maintain that stability for Mickey. She's a very special little girl."

Rita squinted at Tally, as if suspecting she was being ridiculed. "We like her. Although I wish she would help more with the baby."

"I just turned eleven," Mickey said. "And he weighs, like, ninety pounds."

"Try twenty," put in Rick, the baby's father, although this dark, good-looking man didn't resemble his son, a white, doughy blob. Most babies were white doughy blobs, in Tally's opinion. Why did people pretend to find them fascinating? Tally hadn't even found her own children mesmerizing. She loved them, of course. But it had been hard, being a twenty-one-year-old girl with two children under the age of three. Hard and, well, boring.

"He's adorable," she said, flicking a finger under his chin. Chins. His mother shifted him on her hip. Rita was a pretty woman, despite being a little hard and faded. If Rick left her, she could still find another man. But after that? She wasn't going to have much of a shelf life.

Tally automatically made this calculation upon meeting another attractive woman: How many more men were in her future? It was like assessing another person's bank account. *What are you worth? Do you have more than me or less than me?* Most women had decidedly less. Rita was harder to judge. She was earthy, practically reeking of sex. Clem was a bigger prize than Rick, but Rick was a *catch. He can probably fix things,* Tally thought. He didn't bother with this place because it was a rental. But if he owned his own home, everything would work, always. His dream house would function, no corners would be cut, no mistakes would be made.

"Would you like a beer?" Rick asked. She said she would. Gwen shot her a look. The look said many things. Such as: *You never drink beer! If there's no rush to get home, why are you here already? What are you doing?* But Tally was just being polite.

Later, on the short trip home, Gwen said: "You acted sappy."

"Sappy? What do you mean?"

"Weird. Drinking beer. Staying late, when you always say that good manners mean not hanging on and on."

"I thought you wanted to spend more time with Mickey. She is your best friend."

"Mickey said—" Gwen paused. "Mickey said you were flirting with her dad. She said women do that all the time, right in front of her mother."

"I thought he was her stepdad and not even that, not really."

"What do you mean?"

"They're not married, right?"

Gwen's face clouded with hard thought. Oh dear, what was so obvious to an adult could fly over a child's head. Gwen honestly didn't know that people could live together and have babies without being married. Tally remembered her playing Barbies with a friend back in the old neighborhood, Gwen informing the friend solemnly: "They can't have babies if they're not married. It's a law." Her daughter was naive in a way Tally had never been.

"I didn't mean they're not married, darling. Just that they didn't have a big wedding. But that's typical of second marriages. Forget I said anything."

Talk about naive: children never forget what they are asked to forget. Within a week, Gwen had hurled this accusation at Mickey, after some silly argument, and Mickey reported the insult to her mother, who had, lord help them, driven to the Robisons' house to confront Tally. Tally claimed a migraine and asked Clem to take charge of the mess, but he insisted that she at least be present while he defended her.

Rita was headed to work, her hair in a messy upsweep, sort of a deflated beehive. Her fury was so palpable that one could almost imagine real bees buzzing furiously around her head.

"It was a misunderstanding," Clem said. "Tally never meant to say anything to Gwen."

"Misunderstanding? More like wishful thinking, if you ask me. I'm used to women throwing themselves at Rick. I'm not used to them using little girls to carry their ugly gossip. Maybe Mickey shouldn't be coming over here, if you have problems with my lifestyle."

"Mickey and Gwen love each other," Clem said. "They shouldn't be punished because an adult made a mistake."

"What do you mean, *love*? My girl's not queer."

"Not that kind of love." Tally could tell that Clem was working hard to keep his emotions in check, that he was repulsed by Rita's quickness in projecting romantic love on the friendship of two innocent little girls, and her knee-jerk disgust at homosexuality. Perhaps Clem suspected, even then, that Fee was gay. At any rate, he talked Rita down, apologizing for Tally's misstatement. (Which it really was; she had done everything to mitigate her slip.) He charmed her. Clem could charm. He had charmed Tally into giving her life away.

Now, almost four years later, watching her slim-hipped daughter switch about the kitchen in a way that seems designed to make the pleats on her skirt swing just so, Tally wonders if Mickey *had* loved Gwen in that way, if Rita's instincts had been better than theirs. It would explain so much—Mickey's abrupt disappearance from Gwen's life as she plunged into the world of boys, boys, boys, Gwen's fierce determination never to speak of her. What had they done, up in those hills, all those afternoons? A few Sapphic kisses, perhaps some show-and-tell? Then the Halloran boys had become part of their dyad, and Gwen had switched her affections to Sean. That ended, too. Everything ends.

"How do you feel about being an aunt?" she asks Gwen, hopeful that she will turn the question back to Tally, show a smidgen of empathy for her mother, or at least acknowledge that Tally is human, that she did not come into existence solely to produce Gwen, feed her, and clothe her.

"We never see them," Gwen says. "So it's hard to see how it will change much of anything around here. Why is that? Why don't they visit? Even when they were dating, he never came home."

"Well, he lives so far away—"

Her daughter can call bullshit with a glance.

"It's how things are, Gwen. Sons tend to be absorbed by their wives' families."

"They only got married three months ago." Tally remembers it well. Outdoors, in the Boulder backyard of the in-laws, Miller's studious little wife wearing a wreath of flowers in her hair, Gwen staring raptly at the young couple exchanging their vows. Too raptly, for Tally's taste. Gwen was seeing only the dress, the crown of flowers, the attention riveted on the bride.

"You'll see. Miller's just doing what most boys do, disappearing into his wife's family. But daughters are for life."

"What about Fee?"

"She's still in college. I don't expect Fee to partner off for a long time. Miller's the odd duck, marrying young, having a baby right away." But Tally wonders if Gwen is challenging her to gossip about Fee, to include her in the confidential discussions she and Clem have had about their oldest daughter.

"Huh."

"But when you marry—"

"I'm *never* going to marry." The viciousness of Gwen's tone almost literally knocks Tally off balance. This is sincere revulsion, not the cool mockery she has been practicing. Tally finds herself placing her right palm on the edge of the stainless steel sink, steadying herself. She hates this sink, cold and industrial. Sinks should be porcelain, like the one in her parents' home. Her parents' home, with its pantry and maid's room off the kitchen, a life she wanted no part of. Why? Why had she traded it for something even lesser? What was she thinking?

Perhaps Gwen realizes she has crossed a line because she softens her tone slightly. "I mean, I'm not going to marry young, or at least not have children young, not until I'm at least thirty. I want to have a career first."

Her attempt at tact is only more hurtful. Gwen's words hang in the kitchen, an utterly polite fuck-you to her mother. Why not just say: *Upon pain of death, I am not going to be you.* Tally wouldn't mind. Tally doesn't want to be Tally most days.

But if Tally hadn't been Tally, then there would be no Miller, no Fee, no Gwen, no in utero grandchild. *You can't hate me for the crime of having you,* Tally yearns to tell her daughter. Only it's not hate, it's disdain and pity, so much harder to stomach. Gwen, her plaid skirt twitching on her hips, is like some beautiful alien in a science fiction film, briefly looking back in disgust at the primordial ooze from which she has emerged. She wants to believe that she is the author of her own life, that she can take whatever form she chooses and it will have nothing to do with Tally. She needs to believe this, at least for a while. Tally understands, absolutely. She felt exactly the same way at Gwen's age. *I'll be anyone but you.*

Why does understanding only make it feel worse? Forgetting Clem's plans, she takes the Burgundy from the ice bucket, opens it, and pours herself a healthy slug of wine. Let the celebration begin.

CHAPTER TWENTY-THREE

Father Andrew is coming to tea. The invitation occurs to Doris just like that, when she stops by his office after altar guild to ask how Go-Go—Gordon, Father Andrew does not approve of nicknames—has been doing since school started.

"We should talk," he says. "Not now I'm afraid—I'm due at a meeting—but we should make time to speak privately."

She knows her heart should sink at those words. No mother—no good mother—wants to hear those words: *We should talk.* And, somewhere inside her, there is a horrible, pricking worry, something plummeting with the sound of a long, sad cartoon slide whistle. *I knew it. Things aren't getting better.* But that pathetic naysayer can barely be heard over the *Love, American Style* fireworks shooting into the air. They have to talk! Privately!

"The thing is, you are so in demand when you're here," she says.

"People always seem to be tugging at you. And my husband and I still have only the one car, and he uses it most days. Perhaps you could come to the house. For tea?" Yes, for tea, on an afternoon when Sean has band practice and Tim Junior. is at the library and Go-Go is outside, doing whatever Go-Go does. Doris has never served an actual tea, but how hard can it be? That is, she has drunk tea, but never set the table for tea. She has a proper teapot somewhere and a cozy and a trivet. She can bake cookies if she puts her mind to it, or at least buy fancier ones, Pepperidge Farm, although she bets Father Andrew likes something with more heft—banana nut bread, pound cake?

Father Andrew considers her proposal, probably sifting through his schedule in his head, nothing more, yet Doris can't help wishing more complicated calculations are going through his head. "That would be nice," he says at last. "Today?"

"Tomorrow," she parries, nervous that she will be punished for not accepting immediately what he offered, that it's wrong to ask Father Andrew to work around her schedule. But she can't ready the house by this afternoon.

"Tomorrow," he agrees.

The next morning, she can't wait for Tim Senior to leave for work. But once the house is empty, she is overwhelmed by the enormity of the task. When did the house get this dirty? How? Why can't Tim Senior ever put his own coffee cup in the dishwasher?

She decides to start on the first floor and work up, as if it were a mountain to climb, pushing the mess in front of her, like a child rolling the base of a snowman. If she doesn't finish the second floor, it's not dire. She scrubs out pots that have been soaking for days, separates the boys' laundry and folds it, putting it on their respective bureaus instead of leaving it in a heap on the hallway bench. She vacuums, she mops, she cleans the venetian blinds, wondering as she does so why they are called *venetian*. That could be a nice conversational gambit with Father Andrew. He seems to know such things.

She gets out a cookbook and realizes she has the ingredients to make a pound cake, although it will wipe out the butter and there will be hell to pay when Tim Senior has breakfast tomorrow. She can run up to the corner grocery later. Oh, she should have read ahead: the eggs have to be separated and beaten with a hand mixer. Where is her hand mixer? She finds it in Go-Go's room, under his bed. She is forever finding things under Go-Go's bed. She has to wash it, of course, grimed with dust as it is, and she screws up separating the first egg, which means she has none to spare, but she is perfect on the others. The house, neat for the first time in months, soon fills with the smells of vanilla and butter and sugar.

Can Doris work the same transformative magic on Doris? She goes into the master bathroom. Fluorescent light is unkind to everyone, but this is downright cruel. When did her face become gray and sunken, her hair thin and pink? She was one of the prettiest girls in her parish, second only to Sally McCafferty. Doris was like a rose, everybody said so, although her Aunt Ginny always added: "A plucked rose fades fast." People laughed when Aunt Ginny said that, and Doris, innocent as she was, assumed it had something to do with virginity. Or perhaps it was pregnancy? Or merely marriage? At any rate, she is good and truly plucked, but there must be something she can do. She gives her face a once-over with cold cream, then applies a thin coat to wear the rest of the afternoon. She takes her curlers out and runs a wet comb through her hair. Tally Robison wears her hair loose and smooth. Why shouldn't Doris? Hmmm, it doesn't look quite right. Maybe she can tweak the ends into a pageboy. Her nails are a mess, especially after today's work, but she cleans them, then files and buffs until they are presentable if not notable.

She goes to her closet. What to wear? Father Andrew has seen her mainly in skirts and blouses. Wouldn't it seem odd if she dresses up for his visit? But there is a wraparound skirt, green with white piping, which pairs nicely with a green-and-white-checked shirt. That works, although it's a little summery for November.

The timer pings. She brings the loaves out to cool, making

a mental note to hide them later. Tim and the boys would go through these like locusts. She feels a twinge of guilt: What kind of woman bakes a delicious dessert and then hides it from her loved ones? But in her mind's eye, there must be two perfect, uncut loaves on the serving plate. She wants her table to look like a picture out of *Better Homes and Gardens*. She needs a tablecloth and fresh napkins. She rummages through the dining room's built-in breakfront and finds a white tablecloth. Stained, of course. She tosses it into the wash with some bleach, hoping for the best.

When she was a newlywed, she didn't even have a washer-dryer. Also no dishwasher, no venetian blinds, only hand-me-down lace curtains at the windows. All their things were hand-me-downs, with the exception of their bedroom suite, which was a wedding gift from her father. They lived in a simple brick rowhouse off Ingleside, and she kept it spotless. Tim returned from work to home-cooked meals. She washed the dishes by hand while he sat on the back steps, listening to the Orioles game. She was happy. The women's libbers said she shouldn't have been, but she was. What happened?

Children. No one wants to say that out loud, but between the children she gave birth to and the ones she didn't, Doris was done in. They moved up to a bigger house, not that this place was that big, but it's that much more to clean. If she had to wash her dishes by hand now, it would take all nine innings to get through them, and that's despite trying to simplify meals, serving things like Hamburger Helper and Kraft Macaroni & Cheese, which the boys prefer to homemade anyway. Look at how many bowls and utensils went into creating a pound cake. Come to think of it, she better wash and dry those now, hide the evidence. She laughs at herself, thinking of a pound cake as a crime. But she is contemplating a crime, isn't she? Well, not a crime, but a sin, one of the biggest. To be sure, she's only thinking about it, but even the fantasy is wrong.

Four years ago, everyone laughed when the current president confessed to committing adultery in his heart. Tim Senior certainly had. For some reason, people thought that the president's admission made him even more of a—what did the boys call it—a *wimp*. But Doris dug out Tim Senior's *Playboy*—she had known the location of his secret cache for years—determined to read the article for herself. She flipped to the interview, trying not to see the naked women along the way—not because she was a prude, but because they made her feel so *bumpy*. It was natural for them to be young, with big bosoms and tiny waists, but the honeyed, creamy look of their skin taunted Doris. She never looked like that, even when she was the second prettiest girl in the parish. She found her way to the interview, and as she had suspected, there was more to it than people were saying. The president not only said that God forgave his lust, but he said that he, the president, also could not judge men who gave in to it, that he should not think he was better than a man who left his wife.

Well, Protestants, Doris had thought at the time. What do you expect? Yet those words lodged into her, granting her permission to have her own fantasies. She would never do anything, of course. But if she does—she might be forgiven. Only how would God feel about her taking a priest with her? Doesn't that make it a much, much bigger sin? Also, she knows she will be disappointed in Father Andrew if he proves capable of being seduced. *Not that she's going to seduce him.* She wonders how good the sex could even be if he has never had it before. All she has is her experience with Tim. Still, that pent-up energy should count for something, although it hadn't worked that way for her and Tim in the early years. Yes, she sometimes felt things. Okay, orgasms. She had them, thank you very much. Eventually. But they fell short of what the world had led her to expect. Not *Love, American Style* fireworks, obviously, she's not that silly, but something—transforming. Something worth all the fuss, not to mention the pregnancies, full-term and lost, those mounds of underwear on the hallway bench, the kitchen that's never clean. Her husband's anger, although she supposes that isn't a direct consequence of sex, or even the lack of sex. She wonders if Tim has ever cheated on her. She wonders if she cares. Caring requires a lot of energy, and she's pretty tired. Caring takes so much—she takes a breath and allows herself the curse word, if only in her head—so much *goddamn* effort.

By 5 P.M., the house looks almost as she had imagined it, although she doesn't dare set the dining room table. That would provoke curiosity. They eat dinner in the kitchen, and Tim doesn't even ask why. Tim never asks her anything. It is six-thirty by the time he stomps through the front door, knowing full well that they eat at six, but he says it's important for him to go out for drinks with his coworkers. He doesn't like the job at Tuerkes as much as he did at first, and Doris worries he won't last long there. He trudges through the clean house, noticing nothing, although he had no problem seeing the mess when it was there and criticizing it for advantage. Tim sees only what is wrong and blames her for everything, even the things that are clearly his fault, like his dinner being cold tonight. Some things just don't reheat well.

"Some things just don't reheat well," she tells him.

"I'm the head of this household," he says. "Dinner should be ready when I'm ready."

"The Pollacks have a microwave," Sean says.

"They give you radiation poisoning," Doris says, although she yearns for one. But it's better to have a reason for not wanting the thing you want than to admit to yourself that you want something you can never have.

Over the next two hours, Tim and the boys undo much of what she has accomplished today, and Doris is reminded why she stopped trying to stay on top of the housework. Quietly, trying not to draw too much attention to her actions, she goes behind them and puts the house back to rights. She is dying to set the dining room table, to see if it will measure up to the picture in her mind. Her anticipation over the scene is almost as great as the event. Should she find flowers? It's late in the season, there are only mums and asters, and they have never been to her liking.

"Do you smell that?" Tim asks, coming into the kitchen from the living room, where he has been watching *Quincy, M.E.* For a moment, she worries he has picked up the scent of vanilla and butter. She blushes like a thief, trying not to let her eyes drift to the cabinet where the wrapped pound cakes are hidden.

"What?"

"I don't know. Something bad."

She is almost startled into saying, *My pound cakes do not smell bad*, but then she notices what has caught Tim's attention. She has been too wreathed in Comet and Pine-Sol to pick up the scent, but there is a bad smell like—

"I swear, if that pipe has backed up again, I will"—Tim throws open the door to the basement and clatters down the stairs. "What the fuck are you doing?"

The next thing Doris hears is Go-Go crying—horrible, un-natural cries—as his father yells and, judging from the scuffling sounds, tries to land blows on him.

"Tim!"

He has Go-Go by the wrist, his belt half out of the loops.

"The little shit has shit himself. He was down here trying to rinse his underwear out in the laundry sink, but he left all his turds behind." He grabs Go-Go by the shoulders, shaking him. "What's wrong with you? What kind of ten-year-old boy craps himself? How were you going to get all that shit out of the sink?"

"I let him have a hamburger at the drugstore today," Doris lies, pushing between them, letting Go-Go grab her hips, even though his hands have traces of his own feces. "That probably gave him diarrhea. And he was trying to do the right thing by cleaning up after himself. He just didn't think about where . . . things would go if he used the laundry tub. It's not like he ever rinsed out a diaper, or saw someone do it."

"He's stupid," Tim rails. "Stupid, stupid, stupid."

"No, he's not. Stop saying that."

Another mess to clean up, then herself to clean up. It is late when she finishes, but she stops by Go-Go's room. He is lying in the dark, staring at the ceiling. He doesn't sleep well, her baby boy. He never has, though.

"I did have diarrhea," he says, his eyes fixed on the ceiling. "I mean, I didn't have a drugstore hamburger, but I did have diarrhea."

"Oh, Go-Go. What's wrong?"

"Nothing. I thought it was going to be a fart. I didn't know."

"Has it happened before?"

His silence tells her everything.

"At school, Go-Go? Has it happened at school?"

He turns toward the wall.

Doris knows now why Father Andrew is coming to tea. Her son has crapped himself at school. And now at home, within feet of a toilet. She isn't sure why this is so much more shameful than wetting the bed, yet it is. Something is terribly wrong with Go-Go. Is he crazy? Are all the little things that once made them laugh—the energy, the dancing—were those things they should have been worried about?

She sits on her son's bed and places a hand on his back. He's a strong boy, although short for his age, strength and energy almost pulsing through his body. He is, as always, warm to the touch, a furnace. She wants to remember the little boy that was put in her arms ten plus years ago, nine pounds, the biggest of her children, red-faced from his journey yet almost eerily calm. She wants to remember how sweet he was. She wants to believe he will be sweet again.

But all she can think is: *Father Andrew is coming to tea tomorrow.* And whatever else went wrong today, she has managed to save those perfect, perfect pound cakes for him.

Winter 1980

CHAPTER TWENTY-FOUR

The university starts its holidays by mid-December, and Clem is home, left to his own devices during the day as Gwen still has a week of school and Tally has her painting. Creativity doesn't take a Christmas break, she informed Clem loftily when he began enumerating the things they might do together. Loftily and a little desperately. "I have to make use of what godforsaken light there is this time of year," she said Sunday evening. She says that there are studies showing that some people need light, that she wasn't made to live in this climate. Clem pointed out—gently, he thinks, even comically—that her mother's people were Scandinavian. "And our furniture is Danish modern, so you should feel right at home. Perhaps you just need herring."

Tally doesn't find this funny. Tally finds very little funny as of late. She tells Clem that she hates their furniture, which she chose because it was the only style that worked in his house. *His* house. Clem isn't sure about the lack of light being the cause of Tally's moods, but the moods are undeniably real. She used to be more on an even keel, but now the happy—manic?—days are rare. For all the time she spends in her studio, she isn't getting much done, and he thinks this might be the real source of her depression. The big canvas that she started a year ago ground to a halt this summer. Clem knows because he sneaks into her studio. He shouldn't, of course. He should respect Tally's desire to show her work to him when she's ready. But he can't stop himself. He wants to see her work because he wants to know that this is really what she does, all day.

Until this latest project, most of Tally's canvases were the sort of thing that makes people say, "My kid could paint better than that." Tim Halloran said exactly that, adding: "And I mean Go-Go." When Tim teased his kids, it never sounded quite right. Not to apportion blame, but—if that man in the woods had shown the boy any kindness, then Clem could understand how it happened. Go-Go yearned to be held by someone, anyone. Clem remembers how he used to climb Tally, seizing her hair, as if she were Rapunzel.

Despite what philistines such as Tim may think, Tally has a gift for abstract painting. She owes a lot to Rothko and Mother-well, but those are good debts. She uses cool colors in shades so close to one another that it is necessary to stand back and study her paintings to understand how much variation there is. Completely self-taught, she's uncanny, and he's proud of her, wishes she believed in herself enough to push for a show or even enter an amateur competition.

The painting that has bogged her down is figurative, however. No one's child could paint this. It's huge, an oil of two entwined children—well, teenagers, Clem has decided, because otherwise it would be almost pornographic. They belong to some other era, based on the clothing strewn through the foreground, an ancient time. The girl has a wreath of white flowers in her hair. A lion watches them from a glade. Pyramus and Thisbe? But the classic couple did not have a chance to make love before the lion entered their story. The painting is disturbing, in a good way, not at all trendy. But the faces are giving Tally fits. She clearly has tried again and again, but they are never quite right. The boy looks as if he's in pain, not ecstasy, while the girl's face has never advanced enough to have any expression at all. He yearns to ask Tally about what has inspired her, but then he would have to reveal that he has been sneaking into her studio.

It is an hour before dusk. Tally has retreated to the kitchen, where she will drink tea and mutter while preparing dinner. Clem loves the light at this time of year. True, he's not a painter, but he can't imagine anything better than walking through these hills of denuded trees. The soft gray light suits his mood. He's not exactly upbeat himself these days. Ronald Reagan, president. A Republican-controlled Congress. It is scant comfort to live in one of the six states that Carter carried. If Tally's depression were situational, he could better understand it, but she's grown indifferent to politics. The only news that has affected her of late is John Lennon's murder, which she insists on calling an assassination. Clem cannot bear to have such an important word used for the murder of a musician, and he told Tally as much. The argument spiraled out of control, perhaps because they seldom argued and had little practice. She wheeled their large dictionary over to him, showing him that it was accurate to use the word for the murder of any public person. "But for political reasons!" Clem countered. "Mark David Chapman was crazy, pure and simple. The desire for fame is not a political stance." It was such a strange fight. Clearly, Lennon and Chapman were proxies for grudges they did not dare to address.

Now, striding across the hills in the fading light, it occurs to him that they were arguing over the fact that they were of different generations, that Tally had a stake in John Lennon's murder, while Clem did not. But she doesn't, not really. Although Tally is only four years older than Lennon, she is too old to be one of his true fans. By the time the Beatles came on the scene, she had opted out of her generation and joined Clem's.

But perhaps *that* was the underlying cause of the fight, Tally's lost youth—and the fact that she was the one who squandered it. He knows she doesn't regret their marriage or the children. But she can't stop wondering what might have been, a truly tragic affliction. Clem, born in 1923, had an old-fashioned education, the kind that involved lots of memorization and recitation. (How appalled he had been when Gwen had come home from her first day of high school and announced excitedly that her history teacher didn't believe in dates. As if this were progress, as if dates had no relevance. What next, a chemistry teacher who threw out the periodic table?) Clem knows not only the famous Whittier line *For of all sad words of tongue or pen / The saddest are these: "It might have been!"* but he also knows the whole poem, "Maud Muller," and finds the preceding lines far more chilling: *God pity them both! and pity us all / Who vainly the dreams of youth recall.*

What would his children regret? How could he keep them from having regrets? They are so different. Miller, always determined to do the right thing in the right way, marrying at twenty-four, now on his way to being a father. Fee, so shy and diffident, a mystery even to herself. Gwen, her mother all over again, which scares him more than anything. He wishes he could protect them from disappointment, but he lost that battle long ago. Once, when Miller was very young, Clem drove him to a railroad crossing in South Baltimore, near Stockholm Street. A freight train finally lumbered past, a long one with varied cars. Miller, not even four at the time, was thrilled. When the last car passed, the train's whistle blowing, he turned to his father and said: "Again." And when Clem could not make it happen, he cried bitterly, upset not only by the lack of another train but at his father's impotence.

Clem himself has no regrets. Well—he had no personal regrets until a little over a year ago, and he still can't see what he might have done differently, so is that truly regret? He crests another hill, sees the little house on the other side of the stream. Is there smoke coming from the chimney? Are there chickens in the yard? He speeds up, almost running, splashing through the creek without thinking about his shoes, much less the risk of tetanus. It was all a horrible dream, then. The night never happened, the man never died, that's why his body didn't show up at the morgue.

But when he reaches the house, there is no smoke, and the "chickens" are old newspapers, blowing lazily in the breeze. The house looks different, though. And Clem can be sure of this because his walks, over the past fourteen months, keep leading him back here, although he hasn't entered the yard for a month or two. Someone has been here recently. Probably kids. Only it looks neater, which makes no sense. Kids, even good kids, don't leave things neater.

How did the children ever find their way here? It's a question he has asked himself over and over again. The adults knew about the old man, of course, if not his predilections. In winter, the cabin's roof was visible from the road they all used as a shortcut. But to the grown-ups, the house was a blight, an embarrassment. Clem and Tally, in particular, felt odd, living down the street from a man whose life seemed little better than a sharecropper's. Meanwhile the Hallorans were appalled because the man was black, not that they were polite enough to use that term, or even Negro. Doris Halloran pronounced people "colored," as if it were the enlightened thing to say, and Tim Senior—well, he liked to mix up his epithets. He seemed to think his large stock of synonyms passed for wit. *Jungle bunny, coon, tar baby, spear chucker.* But never *nigger*, which only convinced Clem that Tim was dangerously racist beneath his I'm-just-having-fun-I-dare-you-to-say-otherwise gaze. Clem wonders if he still uses those words. He doesn't know, because he can't bear to be in the same room with the man, not that they had spent much time in each other's company before the night of the hurricane. Maybe at a potluck, or the progressive dinner Tally put together one time, inspired by a book she was reading to Gwen, but he wasn't sure.

He tries to tell himself that he objected to Sean as Gwen's first boyfriend because of Sean's father, his fear that any apple that dropped from the Halloran tree had to be poisoned. Oh, he liked Sean as much as any man could like a teen daughter's first boyfriend, but he was glad to see him go. In the early stages of Tally's stalled painting, he worried it was inspired by Sean and Gwen, that she knew something he didn't. But, no, it just can't be. He's a doctor. He understands, theoretically, that Baltimore is full of teenage girls having sex. But not his daughter. Not with Sean.

And then he realizes that thought is as bigoted and snobbish as anything Tim Halloran ever dared to say out loud. Every time Clem wants to think he is different from Tim, something reminds him that he is not blameless. He will never be blameless.

He starts walking back, crossing the stream, a relative trickle today, then heading up the hill. This is the steepest part of the terrain. He imagines this spot as it was in the storm, what someone would have seen from where he's standing now. Two men, hale and sure-footed, running down the slope, then kneeling in the rushing water, a slightly older one making his careful way toward them, flashlight strafing them with light. He sees the older man bending down—but he can't stay outside the scene any longer. He is there again, realizing that the inert object at Tim's and Rick's feet is a man, dark as coal except for odd patches of unpigmented skin. And dead.

• • •

"He was dead when we got here," Rick said.

"But Tim was ahead of you, going down the hill, he had at least twenty-five yards on you—"

"He was dead when we got here. Right, Tim?"

Tim Halloran nodded. He was shaking all over.

"The fall killed him," Rick said. "See? That rock, that's where he hit his head, and he's been lying in this stream ever since, his lungs filling up with water. Between that and the head injury, he never could have survived. It doesn't matter what the kids did. Leave him here."

Clem bent down, tested at the neck for a pulse, knowing there would be none. He had no obligation to the dead, had taken no oath on their part. Still, it seemed wrong to leave the man here.

"He lived in these woods. He has no family, no one looking out for him," Rick said. "It was an accident."

"Was it?" Tim and Rick had crested the hill before him. Clem had heard shouting, though, seen an arc of light moving wildly through the night. He wouldn't be surprised if there was flesh and blood clinging to Tim's flashlight, even in this driving rain.

"An accident," Rick repeated. "There's nothing to be done. He slipped and fell. Talking about how he came to fall, or why we were here looking for him—there's no point. We'll have to talk about . . . everything. And that's not going to be good for anyone."

They left him there. Clem later made an anonymous call to the police from a pay phone downtown. A week later, when Clem hiked back into the woods, the man was gone. Clem wanted to believe that his anonymous call had yielded results, that EMTs had somehow found his body. But wanting to believe it didn't make it true.

"Did you see his guitar?" Gwen asked one night, weeks later.

"Whose guitar?"

"The man in the woods. When you found him—did you see his guitar? It was steel, it was probably ruined in all that rain."

"Honey, there was no guitar."

To his amazement—and to his gratification, for Gwen had seemed cool and frivolous of late—she burst into tears. But it was the last time they ever spoke of the incident. Now, only a year later, she chatters away about dates and boys and, very occasionally, about school itself. The hurricane is forgotten. Her old friends appear to be forgotten. Mickey never comes to the house, although there's still a drawer filled with the sugary junk she loved. The Halloran boys have abandoned the woods, although Clem sometimes sees little Go-Go walking along the top of the hill, where there's a path.

It is the old who are supposed to have memory problems. Senility, Alzheimer's, dementia. But in Clem's experience, no one can forget the way a young person can. He specializes in the elderly, he is himself becoming elderly, but to be interested in old age also means thinking constantly about youth. That's the paradox. His daughter is now almost the age her mother was when Clem first glimpsed her, a beautiful, high-spirited girl. No one thought it was that outré. Yet if a thirty-two-year-old man were to regard Gwen with anything approximating lust, he would want to kill him.

Only he wouldn't. That's the difference between him and the Tim Hallorans of the world.

Dead when they got there. Sure, why not? Could be. The man was dead when Clem had gotten there, and wasn't that all that mattered? He hadn't done anything except agree to a reality that meant a little less pain for everyone. Go-Go would never have to speak to strangers about what happened to him. Tim would not be called into account for his actions, whatever they were. Clem and Rick would not be labeled accessories. And the women and the children were allowed to sleep the blissful sleep of the ignorant, protected by their men, which is what men are supposed to do, first and foremost.

He turns back, looks at the funny little cabin, comically small and lopsided from this distance. Funny, how they never connected it. The grown-ups drove past this cabin, saw something shameful, a man living like a sharecropper only a few miles from downtown Baltimore. The grown-ups saw the past, complicated and cruel. Their children saw a playhouse. The man who lived here saw a potential victim in Go-Go.

What if it were your child? Tim had asked Clem that night. To this day, Clem thinks: *It wouldn't be.* He knows that's wrong. He understands intellectually that anything can happen to anyone at any moment. Even in his world of medicine and science, there are no absolutes. People smoke their entire lives at no seeming physical cost, while someone who has never so much as held a cigarette can get lung cancer. But he has to believe that his own daughter is immune to such danger, that she never would have allowed herself to let a stranger touch her as this man touched Go-Go.

He probably was dead when Tim got there. He slipped, he fell, and his lungs filled with water when the children ran to get help. Who can fault them for not staying with him on that dark rainy night? Who would ask them to administer first aid to that monster, lying in the creek? Yes, there was the strange arc of the flashlight going up and down, instead of side to side—*Stop,* he tells himself. Believe what's easiest to believe. There's no harm in it.

He is home now, or almost there, at the peak above his house. *Your* dream house, as Tally always says. It is. He built a house to his taste on a site that he loved, assuming his wife and children would love it, too, but only Gwen shared his affection for the place. Now even she wouldn't object to moving, as long as she could continue to be the queen bee of her social set at Park School.

Someone—Clem has no idea who—called children and wives hostages to fortunes. He will never see it that way. His wife and his children are his real contributions to the world. He isn't demeaning what he has accomplished professionally. He's good at what he does and enjoys it, the best of all possible combinations. But there is always someone to take one's place in any profession, no matter how singular or vital. There's no shortage of men who want to be president or discover vaccines or explore the Amazon. Only Clem can be Tally's husband, father to Miller, Fee, and Gwen. Only he can love them as he loves them.

As he descends the hill, he realizes that as much as he hates Tim Halloran, he envies him, too. Because Halloran proved he would do anything for his children, whereas Clem couldn't even give up this jury-rigged, imperfect house. What Halloran did was savage. But it was also love, immutable, enormous love. He killed the man who touched his boy. If a police officer ever shows up on Clem's doorstep, Clem will sell the others out in a heartbeat, cut a deal for himself. But their silence, their pact, was not simply about avoiding discovery. When they agreed that night to say nothing to anyone else about the man's death, they condoned what Tim did. He avenged his son. He was a real man.

Something wraps around his ankle, and he starts. It felt like a bird. But it's only a scrap of paper, a piece of trash blowing through his beloved woods, scampering down the hill toward his house.

PITY THEM

CHAPTER TWENTY-FIVE

Gwen lives in the future. All magazine editors do. Here it is, the last night of March, and she is already focusing on September, which brings the annual "best of" issue, exhaustive and exhausting. When that's done by midsummer, Christmas will be bearing down on her. Her daughter is dreaming about the Easter bunny, whose arrival is less than a month away, and Gwen is trying to think about "hot gifts for cold nights!" She hopes her copy editors can do better than that.

So she has agreed to her publisher's pressure to attend the opening reception for the big craft fair, the kind of work duty that she loathes and is usually spared. Her boss once adored attending all these things, but even he is burning out on the endless plastic cups of bad wine and prosciutto-wrapped bits of melon and mini crab cakes. Or perhaps his social interactions are less enjoyable since the magazine has started silting bits of real journalism among the themed guides (best doctors, best neighborhoods, best schools, best restaurants, maybe Tim was on-target with the best prostitutes issue) and shopping-friendly features. Gwen is particularly proud of a recent piece on one of Maryland's most famous cold homicide cases, the 1980 murder of a nun. The article managed to upset everyone—the nun's family, the diocese, the newspaper journalists who wrote about the case a decade earlier. Margery, her star reporter, took a measured approach toward the crime, and that seems to have inflamed everyone. The family is desperate to believe that a priest killed the young nun, but Margery's dispassionate analysis makes a good case that the more likely suspect was a serial sex offender who later died in prison. Meanwhile, the diocese is displeased at the implicit criticism that its knee-jerk circle-the-wagon response to the initial police inquiries probably impeded the investigation in the first place. Gwen thinks it's a good sign that everyone is unhappy. Her publisher does not see it the same way, but at least no major advertisers were offended.

Yes, maybe it would be a good time to go to the craft fair and start scouting new artisans they could feature. She asks Margery to go with her.

"Am I being punished or rewarded?"

"A little of both. I'll buy you dinner after."

At least they don't have to contend with the crowds that flock to this show once it is officially open to the public, and there are some beautiful things to see. Gwen's real complaint is that it cuts into her evening with Annabelle, a situation made more problematic by the fact that Karl is out of town again, leaving Annabelle in the care of a babysitter. Annabelle cried on the phone when she called to tell her of the plan. Stoic Annabelle, who seldom cries, her girly-girly tomboy who combines tiaras with cowboy boots. "I ha-a-a-a-a-a-a-ate Kristen," she gulped out in heart-wrenching sobs, and Kristen is her favorite babysitter. When Annabelle was a baby, she cried so seldom that when the tears did come, they were almost a source of marvel to Gwen and Karl. They would stand, transfixed—only for a moment—watching tears roll down their daughter's face. She was cute when she cried.

But perhaps that was because they were sure they could end her tears easily, something of which Gwen is now less and less sure. She caused her daughter's tears tonight. She may cause her more. How can she do this to her daughter?

"So you're still staying at your dad's and driving over there every morning and night?" Margery asks as they move through the endless aisles of handcrafted goods, their eyes quickly growing numb to all the stimulation. Their goal is to spot things that are local, original, and, if possible, eco-friendly, as their Christmas issue will be built around a green theme.

"It's barely been a month," Gwen says. "It's not so bad." Actually, it's awful, just as her father and Karl predicted, but she can't back down now. Besides, her father needs her, even if he won't admit it. The daytime aide does the bare minimum. Gwen couldn't sleep if she had to leave her father in another aide's care at night.

"When did everyone become a purse designer?" Margery's voice isn't loud, but it's clear and it carries. "Or jewelry designer? When did these become the default professions? You think that between Monica Lewinsky and all those reality-show types who run around with BeDazzlers and glue guns, people would have too much pride to make this crap."

The woman at the nearest booth shoots Gwen a glance that is at once puzzled and wounded. Gwen shrugs, hoping the gesture serves as a blanket apology for her opinionated friend. To further make amends, she stops, examining this particular crop of purses. They are clutches woven from recycled materials, candy and gum wrappers and newspapers. Not original—she has seen bags like this in other stores and catalogs for the past several years—but well executed. Besides, being of-the-moment is not important in Baltimore.

"Are you from here? Do you have a card?" she asks the woman, who points to a little stand with embossed business cards: LH DE-SIGNS.

"I've only been at this for a few months, but I've managed to place my bags in some local stores," she says. "Are you—"

"Just an editor, not a buyer. Gwen Robison of *Baltimore* magazine."

"You looked familiar, but I guess that's why. I've probably seen your picture in it."

"Not mine." That bit of vanity is reserved for her publisher, the moneyman. He pays the bills, which entitles him to a monthly column, rambling on about some safe, boosterish profundity that never angers anyone. Except, perhaps, people who dislike exclamation marks and chamber-of-commerce boosterish crap.

"Still, I feel I have seen you somewhere."

"You look familiar, too."

She holds out her hand: "Lori Halloran."

"Oh my god—the funeral. I'm so sorry."

Margery has kept moving all this time and is far, far down the aisle. She turns around, makes an impatient hurry-up gesture. But there's no way to walk away now. Lori Halloran is young, early thirties at most. She was Go-Go's second wife, Gwen recalls. Estranged at the time of the accident, although she and her daughters were down front in the church, sitting with Tim Junior's wife and girls, while the brothers flanked their mother. They were the little girls who wouldn't go up to the casket.

"I'm really sorry," Gwen repeats. "I've known him since he was a little boy, although we had fallen out of touch—"

"He talked about you a lot."

"Me?" *A lot?*

"All of you. His brothers, you, a girl named Mickey, although it was a while before I even realized Mickey was a girl. He said that was the best time in his life, playing in the woods."

"Really?" Before, perhaps. Before Chicken George did whatever he did. Why does Gwen still feel that twinge of guilt she always feels when that memory returns, unbidden? *We shouldn't have left him there. He was hurt. Whatever he did, it wasn't right to leave him there to die alone.*

"I admit, that's not saying a lot. He wasn't a very happy guy."
How much do you know? What did Go-Go tell you?

Gwen chooses her words with care. "We had a lot of freedom. Sometimes I think we were the last generation to live that way. These days, we live near a state park, very pretty and bucolic, and I would never dream of letting my daughter play there, unsupervised."

The "we" is a lie, used for convenience's sake but it gives her a pang.

"Gordon was real paranoid about our girls, too. He didn't even like them to be in our fenced backyard by themselves."

"I saw them at the funeral. They're beautiful little girls." Gwen is not being polite. The girls are beautiful, as is their mother—blue eyes, blond hair, fair skin. Go-Go, for all his rough-and-tumble ways, always liked beauty, respected it. He had high standards, too. He clearly thought Tally Robison exquisite, he loved to look at her, grab her. Gwen, even after her transformation, did not impress him.

"My mother-in-law blames me for his death," Lori says. Her tone is matter-of-fact, as if commenting on the weather, but she has to know this is a shocking thing to say. Neither Tim nor Sean mentioned it to Gwen. But then—Tim and Sean are a long way past the time when they felt obligated to tell Gwen things.

"Oh, people say all sorts of things when grieving—"

"She's not entirely wrong."

An older woman jostles Gwen to get to Lori's bags, but that is the point of the craft fair, after all. She paws the little bags, snaps them open, runs the zippers up and down, fingers the lining. The bags deserve kinder hands, but if the woman is a buyer, Gwen doesn't want to come between Lori and a sale. Lord knows if Go-Go had a life insurance policy, or if it paid off, given the uncertain circumstances of his death. Gwen digs through her own shoulder bag and finds her card, adds her cell and the landline for her father's house.

"If you want to talk," she says. "About anything."

She assumes, hopes, Lori won't follow up. Go-Go's secrets are, in part, Gwen's, although she likes to think she is the least guilty of the five, the sole bystander. All Gwen did was agree to go along, to let Sean be the spokesman and not insist on including the troubling details that might complicate their story when they told their parents. No, Lori will think better of it, decide she doesn't want to talk, not to a virtual stranger. But if Lori does confide in Gwen, is Gwen obligated to tell her there are all sorts of reasons why Go-Go might have driven into that concrete barrier, none of which have anything to do with his second wife kicking him out? No need to worry. Lori won't call. Even if she does, Gwen owes her nothing.

Yet several hours later, when Gwen places her cell phone by her girlhood bed, there is a text from Lori staring up at her.

I REALLY WOULD LIKE TO TALK TO YOU. SOON?

It's the question mark—unsure, pleading—that makes the request impossible to ignore.

Chapter Twenty-six

It has taken several days, many promises, and a few threats, but Tim has finally corralled all three daughters and taken them to his mother's house for Sunday lunch. "What about Mass?" his mother asked when told of the plan. He couldn't bear to let her know her oldest two granddaughters are basically heathens, so he made up a story about the SATs and a sleepover and sent Arlene to Mass with his mother as the family's sacrificial lamb. In old age, which seems to have fallen on Doris suddenly and even a little precociously—she's barely in her sixties—she is as distractible as a baby.

The house on Sekots Lane was a desired destination when the girls were younger, a place they clamored to visit. It had a doll's house feel to them—smaller in scale than the houses in their Stoneleigh neighborhood, and full of wonders. The carpet sweeper, a waist-high freezer in the basement stocked with Good

Humor bars, Grandma's "goodie jar," the dogs. But the house and its inhabitants long ago ceased to entertain the girls. Lunch finished, the three sisters slump on the sofa in the downstairs rec room, watching the flat-screen television, a gift from Tim and Sean, connected to cable, a bill that Tim pays monthly, dismissing Doris's protestations that she doesn't need it. If not for cable television, the girls would never come here, but he doesn't want to spell that out for his mother.

Yet even the television barely holds their interest. The older two are bent over their phones, texting, texting, texting, while the baby, as he still thinks of eight-year-old Karen, twirls her hair and watches them covetously. She has been told she can have a phone at age twelve, a decision she challenges daily, sometimes with fresh arguments, more often with mere petulance. Yesterday she told Tim she should have a phone because it would keep her safe from child molesters.

Only if you see them coming from a long way off, sweetheart.

What could the older girls be texting about on a Sunday afternoon? And to whom? Only last week, Lisa left her phone unattended and Tim seized the chance to read every text still in it, rationalizing that he was right to violate her privacy because of the Dani/joint incident. Yet the conversation, such as it was, revealed almost nothing. The only topics were location (at mall/at McDonald's/at skate park) and mood. Everything is lame. Everyone is lame. Parents, friends, school, any activity. The jokes of the other texter are lame. Lord, is it any wonder that zombies are enjoying a resurgence in pop culture? This generation is the new walking dead, except they lumber *away* from brains, disdainful of anything that requires thought, passion, participation. He imagines his daughters vacant-eyed, arms stretched in front of them, tottering down the street moaning: *"No brains, no brains."* But still texting, all the while.

"Some help with the dishes?" He tries to make it sound like a suggestion, yet one that cannot be ignored.

"Sure," Michelle says.

"In a minute," Lisa says.

Nothing moves except their thumbs. He thinks of the heroine of Tom Robbins's *Even Cowgirls Get the Blues*, imagines a generation of girls with giant thumbs, hypertrophied from overuse. What he can't imagine is his daughters hitchhiking. Not because it's forbidden, but because that's way too much effort.

"Leave the girls alone," his mother calls down the stairs. "There's not that much to do. And it's easier to clean up when there aren't so many bodies in the kitchen. Do the girls want some more cookies or chocolates?"

They look up, dazed. Certain words, such as *cookie,* can penetrate the force field around them. "OK," Michelle says, as if conferring a favor. All three continue to sit.

"Well, you can at least go upstairs and get them yourselves," Tim says.

A pause. "That's all right," Michelle says. "I'm not really that hungry." But Doris is already bustling downstairs with her "goodie" jar, a huge Tupperware container that holds opened bags of cookies and a selection of miniature candy bars. The goodie jar is a long-standing tradition in her household, but Tim has noticed on recent visits that sometimes the items are quite stale. This was true even before Go-Go died, but it troubles him. He asked the girls not to mention it. They said they hadn't noticed.

Doris spoils all her grandchildren this way. To be fair, she spoiled her sons almost as much. They had few responsibilities in the house and only marginal ones in the yard because their father loved his lawn mower and did not want to entrust it to them. They were savages. Or so Arlene said in the early years of their marriage, when she discovered that Tim did not know how to do anything domestic—wash his clothes, sew a button, scour a pan, run the vacuum.

He did not think Arlene should have been surprised. She had

seen his apartment, after all, even pretended affection for his bachelor ways. But Arlene, like a lot of women, had one set of standards for her boyfriend, another for her husband. The difference was that Arlene really did manage to change him. Everyone said that people couldn't be changed and perhaps it was all semantics, perhaps Tim had chosen to change. Still, he believed that Arlene transformed him by the simple act of loving him. Despite being raised in a household where nothing was expected of the males and everything was given, he learned to shoulder household tasks and, when the time came, child care. If anything, he did more than Arlene around the house because she left all traditional masculine chores to him. He was, after all, the only man in the house.

He often wonders now if his mother felt similarly isolated as the sole female in a house of men. In the years since his father's death, Tim has put in a lot of time helping his mother create the pretty, well-maintained house she never really had. The basement rec room was one such project—white paint brightened the inevitable knotty pine paneling, his father's beloved bar was replaced with a craft table, the crappy old sofa was tossed. He also helped her wallpaper the dining room and do some modest updates in the kitchen. Mother and son paid lip service to the idea that these renovations were geared toward an eventual sale. Yet Tim knew his mother would never move. Because if Doris moved, where would Go-Go go when he boomeranged, as he did every few years or so? That was one room they never touched, Go-Go's little bedroom at the head of the stairs. Through high school, college, and two marriages, Go-Go's room remained the same, waiting for him to fail again.

Yet although Go-Go's intermittent homecomings should have been disappointing to their mother, she never quite saw it that way. Doris was thrilled to have him back, and Go-Go, whatever his faults, was good company for their mother after their father died. So Tim did the work, standing in for the father who had died too young, and Go-Go made their mother laugh, the perpetual baby of the family. Yet it is Sean, far away, who still gets to be the good son, the perfect son, the pride and joy. How does that figure? Maybe being perfect can be achieved only at a distance.

Tim wipes down the counters, letting Arlene carry the conversation with his mother. It's mindless, maddening chatter—analyzing various mutual acquaintances, discussing that morning's Mass. Tim may not have standing as the best son, but there's no doubt that Arlene's the best daughter-in-law, steady and reliable. Doris likes Lori, too, or did before she threw Go-Go out. Doris can't take the side of anyone who has hurt one of her sons, no matter how justified it might have been. Sean's wife, Vivian, is on Doris's permanent shit list because Doris thinks it was her idea to move to Florida. Funny, because Sean was for it. So why does Doris blame Vivian? Probably because Sean told her as much. A lot of lying goes into being perfect.

As a prosecutor, Tim feels he has a particular insight into lying. People lie to him all the time. Perps, of course, but also cops who don't want him to know about corners cut, rights violated. Even colleagues lie. Tim lies, too. Everyone lies. It's a cardinal rule of homicide investigation, but he feels this maxim has broader applications. He lies to Arlene—harmless things, not for advantage, just to keep the peace. He lied to her, for example, about "loaning" Go-Go money a year or so ago. They do OK, with her back to teaching school, but they don't have money to throw around. Loaning—OK, giving—money to Go-Go was, by definition, throwing money around, out, away. But Go-Go was never more sincere than when he promised to pay back a loan, and Tim couldn't bear not to reward Go-Go's belief in himself, wan and flickering as it was. Had Go-Go ever been truly confident? He was loud and brash, yes, but that's not confidence. When Tim tries to talk to his daughters about the dangers of the world, they roll their eyes, wholly convinced that they know everything.

Go-Go was never like that. He was bold, but not fearless. He knew the world could hurt him. He just didn't know how.

Doris and Tim Senior made it clear that Tim and Sean were never to speak of what happened the night of the hurricane. They led by example. If someone mentioned Hurricane David, his parents would pretend to need to be prompted on the date. Eventually it didn't even seem a pretense. "Oh, that storm," Doris might say. "That was the night that we went to the Robisons' house and stayed because the power was out and the street in front of their house filled with water." Tim and Sean were more than happy to leave it at that. If Go-Go was never molested, then Chicken George never died. It was almost as if Chicken George never existed at all.

In law school and later, preparing for the bar, Tim sometimes laid out the facts of that night as if it were a case he might one day prosecute. A man who had been sexually assaulting a child chased him and another child through the woods. He slipped and fell, injuring himself fatally. The children dutifully reported this to their fathers, who trekked back into the woods and found his body. There was no crime in this. Well, Mickey pushed Chicken George. She admitted as much. But she was acting in self-defense. She was not even fourteen, a child by the standard of the law at the time. No, they committed no crime that night. Still, as an adult, as a father, Tim has often longed to speak of it. Not to Go-Go, never to Go-Go. That would have been unfair to him.

He can't tell Arlene either because they have been together too long now, the time for such secrets is past. There's Sean, but Sean is even more adamant than their parents that they must not speak about the night of the hurricane. Tim thinks it's because it doesn't jibe with Sean's version of Sean. Gwen, Mickey-now-McKey?

Gwen. Despite his habit of teasing her, he likes and respects her. As a kid, he was even a little into her, and not just out of envy for whatever sexual favors his brother was being granted. Tim liked

Gwen before, when she was a plump little girl. She was smart beneath all her girly mannerisms. He doesn't have any present-day yearnings for her. Arlene is the love of his life, and he is grateful for the clarity with which he sees that, accepts the compromises required by monogamy. He's a man. He thinks frequently about other women, wonders what it would be like to fuck this one or that one. There are things, extreme things to be sure, that he has never done, and it now seems unlikely that he will. It's okay. He has a good imagination, which serves him well when he's alone. Still, he would like to talk to Gwen, just talk.

Tim carries the clean platter, one of his mother's "good pieces," to the built-in corner cupboard. It goes on the highest shelf, which is not quite within his reach. "Ma, where's the stepladder?"

"Oh, I put that out in the garage, years ago. Just stand on a chair."

He does, although he's nervous about his weight, and he doesn't like the idea that his mother gets up and down from a chair when she needs something from the upper reaches of the breakfront. He really should get that stepladder out of the garage, have it closer to hand.

His father always complained that the house wasn't well built, but it appears more solid to Tim than the overpriced town house Go-Go bought for his family last year. Tim couldn't begin to help with that purchase. One thing to hide a thousand or so from Arlene, quite another to come up with fifty thousand. His mother mortgaged this house without consulting him or Sean. He probably should be grateful that the housing market had already imploded, even if the stock market crash did ding the hell out of his girls' college funds. Otherwise, his mother would have taken out even more and ended up underwater in her mortgage in a house that had been hers in full before his father died.

Both Tim and Sean were outraged when they heard about the loan, but it was too late to do anything. Doris claimed she didn't understand why they were angry with her. "I bought a house for my grandbabies, and that's who all my money is for anyway, the grandchildren." Tim didn't want to explain to her that she had taken her primary asset and given it in full to two of her six grandchildren. The whole subject made him feel small and mercenary. But Sean had no problem expressing his fury. He told Doris she should rewrite her will to make up for this inequity, reflect the fact that the $50,000 loan was an advance against what the girls might have inherited and they would be entitled to nothing else. A disproportionate advance, he added, with surprising bitterness. Of the three boys, Sean is the best fixed. Only one kid, the kind of kid sure to score a financial aid package to college because of his cross-country stuff. Plus, Sean's father-in-law is loaded. "It's not about the money," Sean said heatedly when Tim called him on this.

In Tim's experience, *everything* is about the money, especially whenever people say it's not about the money. Granted, the money stood for something in Sean's eyes, but what? Attention, love? Sean never lacked for either. And he still gets to be the good son, even though it's Tim standing in their mother's kitchen, drying the things that are too precious or too large to go in the dishwasher.

Arlene catches his eye and gives him a smile, one in which there is a world, a history of understanding. She is both insider and outsider in the Halloran family and her perspective, more dispassionate, yet also more forgiving, keeps him on an even keel. Go-Go got the beauties. Sean's Vivian has a wealthy, privileged family. But there's no doubt in Tim's mind that he, of all the Halloran boys, made the best match. How did he do this? How did he find the right woman when he was a sophomore in college, only a few years older than Michelle is right now? Let Sean be the favorite. Tim's the lucky one, and he'll take lucky every time.

CHAPTER TWENTY-SEVEN

The problem with Florida, Sean thinks, is that the weather means more yard work. Sure, its partisans would reply, but there's no snow to shovel. Ah, but snow shoveling ends, eventually. Yard work never does, especially here in St. Petersburg, even with Duncan's reluctant help. Duncan despises working in the yard even more than Sean does, but Sean is adamant that Duncan must have some household responsibilities. He rejected Vivian's suggestion that Duncan do laundry or help with meals, two things he genuinely enjoys and might execute without protracted nagging. "Life isn't just about having fun, doing what one likes to do," Sean told Vivian yesterday. Even as he said it, he heard his father's voice in his head, but it was too late to back down. Plus, the old man had a point.

What would Tim Senior have done with a son like Duncan? Not that Tim Senior would have had a son named Duncan to begin with. Like so many things in Sean's life, this was Vivian's decision. "Duncan" was mapped out years ago, back in Vivian's college dorm room, or possibly in doodled daydreams in high school or even junior high. It was a plan of such long standing that Sean couldn't begin to counter it when she laid it out after they became engaged. They would wait exactly two years into their marriage to start trying to have a child. They would have only one child. Sean was OK with both those decisions. If the child was a girl, she would be named Madeline; if a boy, Duncan. Sean did not approve of Duncan, but Vivian claimed it was a family name. Later, her mother admitted it was merely a name she loved and wanted to use, only she never had a son. Sean should have started a betting pool on how old Duncan would be before some kid at school started calling him Donut. That clocked in on the first day of third grade here in St. Petersburg, when they were new to the town.

What was less predictable, at least to Sean, was Duncan's ability to roll with such teasing, deflect and thereby neuter it. Even at eight, he was a confident kid. "Just like you," his mother said, and Sean would have liked to claim Duncan's poise as his own. But he knew, even then, that it was different, that his own so-called confidence is all bravado. Duncan is genuinely comfortable in his own skin, which may explain why Sean feels this need to make him uncomfortable from time to time. It's not that he's competitive with his son, not at all. The kid just takes so much for granted. He wins races, he's first chair in all-county orchestra, he gets the lead in all the school plays. Not the musicals, because he can't sing well enough, but the straight plays. Anything he wants to do well, he does.

So it's infuriating to watch him half-ass it around the backyard, acting as if he can't quite understand what is required to prepare the garden for the hot months ahead. Sean doesn't understand, either, but at least he listened to Vivian when she gave them their marching orders after lunch. She was very clear. Vivian is always clear about all her expectations. For example, if Sean decides he doesn't want to do yard work at all, that's fine: Vivian will hire someone to do it. Not some guy with a lawn mower and a truck, though. Vivian will hire the full Magilla Gorilla, a landscaping service, guys in uniforms, with mulch that costs about the same per pound as caviar, not that Sean has eaten much caviar in his life. Vivian's family isn't *that* fancy.

The full Magilla Gorilla. That was a Go-Go-ism, a mangling of the cartoon and the arch phrase, which he probably picked up from one of the gangster films shown on *Picture for a Sunday Afternoon.*

Vivian's family doesn't describe themselves as rich, if only because it would be vulgar to do so. But they are undeniably well-off, and when Sean married her, her father let it be known that marrying his beloved daughter meant supporting her in the style to which she was accustomed. It was like buying a sports car. *Sure, you've got the cash now, but do you realize how much the maintenance will be?* Her parents are on the young side, and they plan to retire early and enjoy their money. These things are never put into words, yet there is no doubt about their expectations. Vivian is the same way. She somehow makes everything clear without being blunt or even raising her voice. After she presented Sean, for example, with her timeline for having their one (and only) child, she added: "And, of course, I will be staying home."

"Of course," he replied, although he had assumed she wanted to work. She had seemed so gung-ho ambitious when they met.

"I could go back to work, but almost all my income would go to child care, so what's the point of that?"

"Of course," he repeated.

"Which means you'll probably want to leave the newspaper and go into a corporate position."

"Of—what?"

They had been living in Charlotte then. It was a hot newspaper, coming off a Pulitzer win for its coverage of Jim and Tammy

Faye Bakker, part of a much-respected chain. Sean, who used his aborted premed education to position himself as a medical reporter, had planned to go as far as he could there, then move on to one of the big dogs, the *Washington Post* or the *New York Times*. It was not an unreasonable dream in 1989. It would not have been an unreasonable dream even ten years later. Twenty years later—the chain that owned the paper doesn't even exist anymore. If he had followed his heart, he might have been one of the lucky ones, safe and sound at a big national newspaper when all the other papers started to shrink. But he was long gone from journalism by then, exiled to corporate communications, first in Charlotte's banking industry, now for Blue Cross and Blue Shield of Florida. He makes good money, and he earns that salary in income-tax-free Florida. It was enough—just—to buy Vivian the house she expected in a neighborhood she deemed worthy, Old Northeast, although without a water view. It's a good life. Really.

Together more than twenty years, they never fight or raise their voices. They disagree. They often disagree. Then Sean explains his side and Vivian explains hers and they end up doing what Vivian wants. Or so it seems. Sean knows, realistically, that he can't be losing every disagreement, but it sure feels that way. When he starts to feel sorry for himself, he thinks about his son, who really is a delight, and maybe that's because of all the attention Vivian has lavished on him. Straight-A student, good enough at track to be certain of a scholarship, sweet, yet popular at school.

And almost certainly gay.

He and Vivian have not spoken about this yet. That's Sean's decision, for once. If they speak of it, then it will be true, and he's not ready for it to be true. Let Duncan bring it up. Isn't that how it works? It's up to Duncan to come out to them. When he does, if he does, Sean will be OK with it, he really will. But he's in no hurry to hear this particular revelation. He could be wrong. He's known some effeminate guys who were amazing pussy hounds, although Duncan isn't effeminate. At any rate, Sean doesn't bring it up to Vivian, doesn't ask Duncan awkward leading questions. (*I see Ricky Martin came out. Not that surprising, huh. What do you think about "don't ask, don't tell"? Gay marriage?*) Instead, he talks to Duncan about the Tampa teams, the Bucs and the Rays, or his inclinations about college, which are kept as close as his sexual preference. Duncan never admits to liking any college, turning all questions back on his parents. "What do *you* think about Bard?" "How bad do you think the winters in Ann Arbor are?" He is vague, too, about what he plans to study or whether he is committed to the idea of continuing to run cross-country, fearful that he may have peaked, that he's fighting his body type. The other day, Sean caught him pinching a nonexistent slice of flab at his waist, making a face in the mirror. Would a straight kid do that?

Duncan also watches the strangest mix of television shows—*American Idol*, another singing show, some dancing shows, a lot of reality television—part of a standing date at a girl's house. Not a date-date, and not a girlfriend, just a girl who's a friend. This is how Duncan says it, word for word, in a high singsong voice, followed by a sigh. *Not a date-date, not a girlfriend, just a girl who's a friend, DAD.*

Really, it's almost a relief to have him here in the yard, grumbling about a chore and doing it poorly. It seems more normal, more boylike.

"You have to be careful pruning," Sean says, taking the massive trimmers from Duncan and demonstrating the technique, the proper place to cut. Duncan sighs and imitates Sean's motions with arch lassitude.

"Mom says you want to go to Baltimore for spring break." They usually shoot for a special trip for the spring break, something splashy, often underwritten by Vivian's parents.

"I'm not sure about *want*. But I think we need to check in with your grandmother over Easter. It will be hard for her, being alone."

"She's not alone. Uncle Tim and his family live twenty minutes away."

"Still, we should go."

Duncan focuses on the branch in front of him. "Some kids from school are going to New Orleans to work with one of the house-building programs there."

"That's still going on?"

"Of course it is. You don't rebuild a city overnight."

Sean knows New Orleans wasn't rebuilt overnight. His surprise is that school and church groups are still going, that the attention-deficit-disordered world hasn't moved on to a new tragedy. Events move into the rearview mirror quickly these days. Earthquakes, tsunamis—it seems like every month, celebrities are back on television, running some phone bank.

"I thought I would go," Duncan says. "It will look good on my college applications. I'm light on volunteering and community service."

"Can't you do something similar in the summer?"

"I'm going back to Stage Door, then doing an intensive cross-country camp, one that attracts scouts."

Scouts mean scholarships, and Sean is no enemy of financial assistance for Sean's college education, although he knows that's the sort of bill that Vivian's family will pick up if he really finds himself on the ropes. And if the school is impressive enough. Sean isn't sure which schools will make the cut, but he knows his alma mater, Washington University, isn't among them, although it's no safety school. But no one in Vivian's family is familiar with it, and what they don't know can't possibly be worth knowing. Vivian went to Duke, and Sean's room has been filled with blue-and-white devils almost since the day he was born.

"You haven't seen your grandmother in a while. You didn't even make it to the funeral."

"Dad, I had that competition in Orlando. If I hadn't gone, the chamber quartet would have been penalized."

"You're the only grandson—and the only one who doesn't live there."

"That's not my fault," Duncan says in his factual, even-keeled way, so much like Vivian. "And being the only grandson shouldn't matter. Are you saying boys are more important than girls to Grandma Dee?"

"It would make her really happy if you came with us. That's all."

"But we've already bought our plane tickets."

"We?"

"Mom and me. She's planning on being one of the chaperones on the New Orleans trip."

Duncan's face is turned away from Sean's. Sean has never been sure how much Duncan picks up on his parents' dynamic. Sean's father, if he were still alive, would probably say Vivian wears the pants in the family, but that's not exactly right. She's not a ball-buster. Her manner is unfailingly polite, reasonable. She simply cannot see Sean's side of things. When they clash, her attitude is almost pitying. *Poor silly Sean, thinking that's a viable idea.* She humors him, hearing him out.

He thinks of another thing his father liked to say: *Don't marry above yourself or you'll never get out from under.* He chose Vivian because she was a prize, something bright and shiny on a shelf barely within reach. The problem is, she sees herself the same way.

He waits to talk to her until he has showered and dressed, picking a collared shirt, one he knows she likes on him. She is in the family room, sewing something. Vivian is seldom at rest and she expects Sean and Duncan to follow suit. To be productive, almost every waking hour, is her goal. But Sean has earned his beer, the right to have the television on mute, baseball scores scrolling by. He still thinks of the Orioles as his team. They still break his heart on a regular basis.

"Duncan says he's planning to go to New Orleans over school break."

"Yes," she says, biting a piece of thread. "With a group from church. I think it's a great idea."

"The thing is, my mom is pretty fragile right now and I think it's important for all of us to go see her."

"Certainly you should go. I understand."

This is how she does it, he thinks. She doesn't even acknowledge there's another side to the issue. She's seizing the high ground, being magnanimous for allowing him to go see his mother.

"She loves Duncan, dotes on him. It would be great if he were there, too."

"I'm sure she'll understand when you explain how important this is to his college applications."

"But how do I explain you not being there?"

"Oh, honey—it's New Orleans. I wouldn't feel comfortable if I wasn't one of the chaperones. It's a very dangerous city. I'll make you miserable, worrying about Duncan, so I might as well go."

He wants to argue on principle, then thinks *Fuck it.* He'll go back to Baltimore, stay with his mom, something Vivian abhors, although she never admits it. But when forced to spend even a night in his boyhood home, she goes through the day murmuring, murmuring, murmuring, keeping up a running litany of disapproval that pretends to be disinterested commentary, as she ticks off everything that bothers her about the house, about Dickeyville, about Baltimore. It's been years since they've stayed under his mother's roof as a family.

Sean will go home, spend the long Easter weekend, look up some old friends. Maybe even check in with McKey, if only to assure himself that what didn't happen between them definitely didn't happen between them. And if it did—if he's already cheated—then doesn't he deserve to remember it?

Chapter Twenty-eight

Doris sits in the chair where her husband died, reading a mystery novel.
She goes through two or three a week. As she tried to tell Tim
Junior when he bought her that ridiculous plasma thing, she has
little use for television these days. It makes her jumpy, and the
more channels and control she allegedly has over it, the more she
feels in its control. She was happy with the five local channels and
rabbit ears.

But she can read when and wherever she wants. Her favorites
are the modern American versions of the old-fashioned English
mysteries, with a dash of humor. She likes series because she likes
the details that repeat—the beloved restaurants, the irascible but
adorable landlords, the kooky families, the on-again, gone-again
boyfriends.

She reads in Tim's old chair because it has the best light and is also the most comfortable. It has been reupholstered, but only because Arlene insisted. It's not as if it were stained or marred in any way. Thoughtful girl that she is, Arlene wrapped the chair project inside the larger job of redoing the living room, but Doris knew that she thought the chair bothered her. It's funny about Arlene—as much time as they spend analyzing other people, it never seems to occur to her that Doris parses her motives as well. Luckily, Arlene is unfailingly well intentioned. The fact is, if the chair harbored bad memories, no mere slipcover could redeem it.

But Doris no longer imbues objects with any kind of significance or meaning. She did that for a long time, too long. In a house of rowdy boys, it was hard to have nice things, so she cherished the ones she managed to protect from their roughhousing. Then one day Go-Go broke a pitcher that Father Andrew had given her. Waterford crystal, brought back from his summer vacation in Ireland. She caught Go-Go holding it one afternoon and yelled at him to put it away. Startled, he dropped it.

He was thirteen, too large to paddle, yet she paddled him anyway. *And he slapped her.* It was the most shocking thing that ever happened to Doris. Even Go-Go was appalled, bursting into tears. Doris sobbed, too, hugging him fiercely, something else for which he was too large, too old. He begged her not to tell his father, or even his brothers, about the slap. She had no desire to tell anyone. In Doris's opinion, Go-Go was right to slap her. Yes, he had dropped the pitcher, but only because she yelled at him. No, he shouldn't have picked it up in the first place, but it was a beautiful thing in a house with very few beautiful things. She couldn't blame him for wanting to touch it, even if he had been explicitly forbidden to do so.

And Go-Go, unlike the other men in the house, noticed beautiful things, beautiful people. As he got older, he cared about his clothes, dressing better than either brother. He chose beautiful wives. Merely beautiful, unfortunately, with little else to offer, especially that first one. Terrible, terrible girl, and Doris blames herself for that choice, too. Lori wasn't much better, in Doris's estimation, but she didn't pummel Go-Go, and she was the mother of two of Doris's grandchildren. Lori has power over Doris, and she knows it. Vivian plays the same game. Just this afternoon, Sean, in his regular weekly call, admitted that he would be visiting alone for Easter because Duncan has other plans. He tried to disguise it as positive news—*such a good cause, very valuable for his college application, who could be a better chaperone than Vivian.* There's a name for what her son is, and it isn't very polite.

What Sean didn't realize was that Doris considered it a case of good news/bad news. It is bad news that she won't see Duncan, but very good news that she doesn't have to see Vivian, who always enters the house on Sekots Lane as if it smells. True, sometimes the odor of cabbage lingers—everyone else in the family loves her cabbage rolls—but the house is pin neat these days, a perfect case of be-careful-what-you-wish-for. It is neat because there is no one to clean up after except herself. It takes Doris three days to fill the dishwasher, almost a week to have a load of clothes to run through the wash. If it weren't for the dogs, she'd probably never have to sweep the floors. She remembers—not quite wistfully, but with a little more perspective—the days when she thought she would be found dead under a mound of boys' underwear.

Yet there also is solace in being alone because her loneliness makes sense now: she is lonely because she is alone. Why was she lonely when the boys were here, when Tim Senior was still alive? Part of it was being the only female, the butt of every joke. Tim grew disenchanted with her for a time, and he let the boys see that. Doris Halloran, the enemy of fun. Now Doris believes she was born lonely. Lonely is who she is. If she had been born a man, she would have been a good priest, yet she didn't think she was cut out to be a nun. Nuns were meant to function in groups. Priests got to run the show.

She had enjoyed the final years with Tim Senior, when it was just the two of them, with occasional rebounds, as they called them, from Go-Go. There is something to be said for lowered expectations. Tim mellowed a lot as he aged, especially when he saw how the boys turned out. It gave him a thrill when one of Tim Junior's cases ended up in the news, and he endorsed Sean's idea—really Vivian's scheme, in Doris's view—to leave journalism for a more lucrative field.

Go-Go's fitful path through life was hard on them both, but Tim Senior himself had been in his midforties when he found the right professional fit, running a small handyman company. Funny, because he wasn't particularly handy, but then he wasn't the handyman. He was the guy who sat in an office and dispatched his workers to the women who needed them, the guy who kept the books, filed the paperwork. The idea had come to him in the mid-1980s, when he saw that cartoon on the cover of a newsweekly, the one that announced the era of the yuppies, a new word at the time. Tim told Doris: "If both people are working, then there's no time for doing stuff, but extra income to pay others to do things that we always did for ourselves." The business was steady, if not spectacular, and he sold it two years before he died for a tidy sum that left them comfortable. Not go-to-Florida-for-the-winters comfortable, but he paid off the house, a big deal. They celebrated with dinner at Haussner's.

For Tim Senior, the big secondhand revelation of running Mr. Handy was how—he blushed when he used the word in front of Doris—*horny* the women were, how often his guys were propositioned. They never said yes. Or at least they told their boss they never said yes. But here was the kicker: These women, in their power suits, married to men pulling down six figures, were gaga for guys with tool belts.

Doris and Tim could talk about sex because they were actually having it again. While her early menopause had seemed tragic at first, the end of her monthlies made it possible for her to have sanctioned sex with her husband with no more fear of creating life—or death. Doris began to take better care of herself and even used Rogaine for her hair loss. They found they could talk about all sorts of things that had once been taboo—the miscarriages, which Tim admitted he blamed on Doris, how cowed she had been by his temper. They could talk about almost anything. Except Go-Go. Any discussion of their youngest son either escalated into an argument or ended abruptly, as if they had run into something hard and unyielding.

So when Tim Senior, sitting in this chair, clutched his chest and fell to the floor and said "Go-Go," Doris knew he believed himself to be dying. There is no other way he would have gasped out those two syllables. She hoped he was wrong, even as she tried to remember CPR, assuming she had ever learned it. But when she started to run to the kitchen phone to call 911, he grabbed her wrist, desperate for her to stay with him, to have someone there for his last few minutes of life.

And then he was dead. The story has become a legend in the family because it happened on October 9, 1996, during the Orioles' play-off game with the Yankees, the one where a boy interfered with play and the Yankees won. It's a good story, one that appears to make her sons feel better, and isn't that what stories are for? Doris has no intention of telling them that the game had ended an hour earlier and that Tim Senior accepted the Orioles' bad luck philosophically. There was a time when he would have broken something over a bad call, but those times were long behind them. In middle-verging-on-old age, Tim and Doris had found a rhythm together, contentment if not true happiness. And contentment is pretty good if you've never been particularly happy.

Only it turned out that Tim Senior wasn't even content. That was the sad part, learning in those final moments what lay beneath the muted, restrained temperament of Tim's last years. Doris thought his mild success had made life easier for him, but Tim had kept a secret all these years: "I killed that man. For Go-Go. I killed him." Why did he tell her? Why should she have to know such a terrible thing, and what should she do with it? It made her wonder if the years she thought of as contented had felt different to Tim Senior, if he held his temper and treated her nicely because he considered it his penance.

For fifteen years, Doris guarded Tim's secret, and she assumes the other men did the same, although she has her moments of wondering. She tries to remember her encounters with Tally Robison over the years, if she dropped any hints about knowing something, but the woman always acted superior to her, so her conceited manner was no clue. She never saw Rita again, although her daughter was around sometimes. She considered tracking down Father Andrew—long gone from the parish, out west somewhere—and talking to him about the situation, albeit in a hypothetical way. If a man killed a man who touched his child, would God forgive that? Is that murder? But Doris doesn't want to know the answer. She thinks Tim did the right thing.

Which is why she told Go-Go, when he came back this time, the last time. Always given to moping, he had fallen down a very deep hole after being kicked out by Lori. He said she had no cause, but Doris assumed her daughter-in-law had *some* complaint. She worried it had to do with other women. She's not sure why, it's just a feeling she has. Go-Go has a problem with women, did all during his first marriage, which is part of the reason why Claudia got violent, started attacking him. The alcohol was merely a substitute for the thing he really wanted. So when Go-Go was drifting around the house, feeling sorry for himself, she finally told him: Your father did this for you. Your father loved you.

Within a week, Go-Go was dead.

She puts down her book, although she is only twenty pages from the end. Doris hates to go to bed with a book finished. She can't say why. Certainly it's not because she fears dying in the night and never knowing the ending. Maybe it's because it's a little less lonely, knowing she has a group of people waiting for her in the morning, people who can't go on unless she opens the book. *Hello, Meg! Hello, Josie! What's up with you?* For a while, her favorite series was about two Alabama sisters, and then the writer died, which felt almost like a betrayal. Then Doris discovered she can still reread those books and derive almost as much pleasure from them. The books never change, the characters never disappoint.

Whereas with Go-Go, all she can do is wonder how many secrets she's required to keep, and for how long.

CHAPTER TWENTY-NINE

It is no small thing for two mothers of young children to arrange a coffee date, and it takes several days for Gwen and Lori to find a convenient time and place to meet. They end up agreeing to late morning, at a Starbucks in the Columbia Mall, which is only a few miles from Lori's town house. The suburb of Columbia came into being as a planned community, and although that plan included abundant green space and man-made lakes, Gwen feels that the seams show. She wonders how Go-Go felt about nature in such an orderly state, if he compared it to the untamed landscape they had known. Whenever she reads *Where the Wild Things Are* to Annabelle, she thinks about Go-Go, how he, too, would have liked to wear a wolf suit and sail to a place where he was king, commanding all the beasts to follow him in a wild rumpus. In a sense, they had, although only Go-Go danced.

"How did you happen to move out here?" she asks Lori, making conversation as they settle in with their drinks. The Starbucks is opposite an enormous carousel and train, which seem old-fashioned and a little out of place in this cookie-cutter mall.

"For the schools," Lori says. "And the yards. I loved the city— we had a great apartment in Brewers Hill—but it didn't make sense when our second one came along."

"How old are the girls—"

Lori silences her with a hand. "You don't need to make conversation for conversation's sake. I know you're busy, and I am, too. Let me say what I have to say: Yes, I threw Go-Go out. But it wasn't for drinking, like it was the last time. He was sober and had been doing pretty well, too."

"What was the reason?"

"That's the thing. I don't know."

"You threw your husband out for reasons not even you know?" It sounds ludicrous. Then again, Gwen is no less ridiculous, using her father's accident as a way to attempt a trial separation from Karl for reasons she still can't articulate.

"He was up to something, but he wouldn't tell me what it was. So I told him to leave."

As a journalist, Gwen is used to hearing people's life stories in choppy, nonsequential bursts, with much presumption of context on the listener. She will have to guide Lori through this if Lori really wants their meeting to go quickly.

"Back up. When did you ask Go-Go to leave?"

"Right after the holidays. The calls started before then, but I wanted to get through Christmas for the girls' sake."

Ah yes, the timetable of the failing marriage. *After Christmas, after his birthday, after Valentine's Day.* Gwen is familiar with how it works

"Calls?"

"A woman telephoned the house, looking for Gordon. Very

polite, said he knew the reason she was calling and she was hoping to hear back from him. When I gave him the message, he acted weird. Jumpy. He said it was a scam and he wasn't going to call her back. But then the same number began showing up on his cell phone, several times."

"And you know this because—"

"Because I check my husband's cell phone log. And his e-mail. If he had a Facebook page, I'd check that, too." She gives Gwen a can-you-blame-me look, and Gwen, who continues to monitor her husband's Facebook page, understands.

"Did Go-Go—Gordon—give you a reason to"—Gwen thinks it best to choose her next words with great care—"keep close tabs on him?"

Lori stares down into her drink, backing away from eye contact for the first time.

"Not really. I don't think he ever cheated on me, although I know that was an issue during his first marriage. I mean, he looked at porn on the Internet, but so what? I didn't care as long as he cleaned out the cache and the children couldn't stumble on those sites. But something was . . . missing, always."

Something in Gwen—her stomach, her heart, her throat, it's too quick to pinpoint—clutches. This is how she feels. Something is missing. But her fear is that it's in her.

"What do you mean by 'missing'?"

"It's like—this is going to sound weird, but I can't think of a better way to put it. When I was younger, living on my own, I got this video center from Ikea, and one of the parts was missing, or I couldn't find it in the packaging. But it didn't seem essential, because I put the thing together and it held. Then one day, without warning, the whole thing came down with a crash. I feel that's how it was with Gordon. There was some little piece missing, something no one could see, and he finally fell apart."

What had Go-Go told Lori, if anything? What happened to

him was his story to share. But what happened to Chicken George belonged to the others as well. Could he have told Lori the first part without the second? Again, Gwen chooses her words carefully: "Did Go-Go—Gordon, I'm sorry, he'll forever be Go-Go to me—acknowledge this? Did he see it, too?"

"He wasn't a talker that way. And, for a long time, there was the drinking. He was an alcoholic, and that explained everything. Then, this latest time with AA, it seemed to take, and yet he was still kind of mysterious, closed off. It was like he was holding a piece of himself back. From me and even the girls, although he doted on them. But he was never fully present."

Gwen thinks of the boy she knew. His one gift was to be startlingly, insistently there. The boy who ran for the ball, fearless of a truck bearing down on him, while the others stood frozen, debating. The boy who did the wild dance. He was never self-conscious, not then. Then the rumors started, disturbing stories about putting cats in milk boxes, shoplifting, acting out in school. However wild and frantic Go-Go was when they roamed the woods together, it was only after the night of the hurricane that he became wild in a frightening, disturbing way. But Gwen had broken up with Sean by then. Go-Go wasn't her problem.

"Like, here's a classic Gordon story," Lori says. "We had a neighbor, Mrs. Payne, back in the city. And she *was* a pain. Strange, paranoid. She was the last holdout on the block, everyone else was young, like us, and she hated us all, but Gordon was the only one who cared. She yelled at us for not cleaning up after our dog, and we didn't even have a dog. Thought we stole her mail, thought we stole her newspaper. And Gordon couldn't stand it. He had to make her like him. When it rained or the weather was bad, he started carrying her paper up to her door, putting it inside the storm door. With a note! So she would know it was him. One day he came home from the store with our oldest, Mia, in her car seat. She would have been eighteen months or so. And he saw Mrs.

Payne dragging her little grocery cart down the street, and nothing would do but he had to get out and carry her groceries and put away the cold things—leaving Mia in the car! He completely forgot about Mia. I happened to come home from the gym and found her sleeping in the car. She was fine, but what if something had happened while he was carrying in groceries for a woman who didn't give a shit about him?"

Gwen can imagine the scene too well—the sleeping baby, slumped over in the seat, unharmed, while the mother runs through every nightmare that might have happened. In some ways, tragedies averted are even more terrifying than the things that actually occur.

"Jesus," she says.

"I know," Lori says. "And all because he's sucking up to some woman who still didn't like him. He shoveled her walks during snowstorms, too, put out ice melt crystals, and all she did was complain that it left pockmarks on her steps."

"It is human nature to chase after those who don't like us." *Although*, Gwen thinks, *not Karl's nature.* He's done very little to encourage her to return home. He has spoken his piece, said he loves her and wants to continue to be married to her, but he sees no reason to repeat himself. He thinks she is acting like a child. She thinks she's acting like a human being. They both could be right. "I bet Go-Go chased you hard during your courtship."

"No." Lori shakes her head, smiling at some private memory. "I pursued him. Everybody said he was no good, but I didn't see that. I thought he was sweet and funny and a really good time. I converted for him."

"He was still a practicing Catholic?"

"It was more about his mother, I think. I didn't care. I loved Go-Go. Doris was part of the package."

"But wasn't he married before?"

"Yes."

"So Go-Go got an annulment?"

"Apparently. Again, I think his mother pressed for it. She called in a favor, that's how I heard it."

"It's just hard to imagine he would have had grounds. Or, frankly, the kind of drag one needs with the church."

Lori shrugs. Everything she does is pretty, dainty, adorable. "All I know is Gordon's first wife was bat-shit crazy. Violent, even, although Go-Go didn't like to talk about that. She hit him, I mean, she whaled on him. At any rate, he got whatever he needed, and we married in the church. It was really important to Doris."

"How's Mrs. Halloran doing since he died?"

"I don't know and I don't care. She's all but put Go-Go's death on my doorstep, said it was my fault for throwing him out. But I couldn't go on. Whatever he was doing, he was definitely lying to me about something. I'd had enough. I wasn't going to be made a fool of."

"Did you ever call the number on his cell, try to find out who the mystery woman was?"

"Oh, yeah. I was on the verge of my own private *Jerry Springer Show*. I called the number, ready to throw down. Only the woman who answered said I had the wrong idea, she was a private investigator and really had been paid to find Gordon, although she couldn't tell me why. When she found out I was his wife, she urged me to get him to call, said it was really important, that someone from Gordon's past needed him."

Someone from his past. Gwen's stomach lurches, even as she tries to remind herself that Go-Go had forty years of life, only a scant part of which intersected hers. It could be anyone, anything. Go-Go was a mess. He must have left a lot of messes behind.

"Did you call her after Go-Go died?"

"What would be the point? If she couldn't tell me why she was trying to find him when he was alive, she wasn't going to tell me anything after he died." Lori makes a sound that is supposed to be a laugh, but it is strangled, mirthless. "Someone from his past needed him. Who cares? It's like Mrs. Payne all over again. Could anyone from his past need him as much as his girls do, as much as I did? I know it's a stereotype, Catholics being guilt-ridden, but I have never known anyone as guilty as Gordon. He was up to something. I just never figured out what it was."

Gwen wonders if Lori can pick up on how guilty Gwen feels at the moment. About Go-Go, but also about Chicken George. She is remembering how Chicken George came and went without ex-planation, how he had been missing much of that summer—and how she and Sean had used his little cabin for their own furtive means. As children, they had accepted the mystery of his life as a given. There was much about adults that didn't make sense to them. They were incurious. The cabin was there, if not the steel guitar, which always went with Chicken George. Who cared why he wasn't there? Who could possibly notice the boy and girl who visited there?

Now, as someone with experience in the world, it occurs to her to wonder where he went during those absences. Jail? A hospi-tal? A mental hospital? What if Chicken George had a family, who intervened, forced him to get treatment and had to sit back when he signed himself out of the hospitals, never crazy enough to be declared incompetent? And what if those family members lived on and still wonder about their relative's death? Because, after all, who ventures out on a night of a hurricane, steel guitar in hand?

"Do you still have the private investigator's number?" she asks.

CHAPTER THIRTY

Annabelle sits on Clem's bed, telling him a story. He can't begin to follow it, and for a moment, he feels anxious. It is finally happening. His mind is slipping. Clem knows too much about aging to worry about the occasional grope for a word, the inability to dredge up some name that should be on the tip of one's tongue. He understands these lapses are "normal" from a relatively young age on. But the inability to follow a complicated story—that's qualitatively different. He has no idea what Annabelle is talking about, which is worrisome until he remembers—she's five. *She* doesn't have any idea what she's talking about. She strings together names and events willy-nilly, expecting her listeners to be up-to-date on all the personalities and politics of her preschool, neighborhood, and toy box.

"—and then Mr. Gray put Fred in a time-out but it wasn't a real time-out because—"

The effect is akin to dealing with Tally when she was excited about something. The one-sided conversation went on and on, but Clem indulged them, because the fast, intense talking days were preferable to the silences. Tally had especially bad postpartum slumps after Miller and Fee, something he has come to understand in hindsight. Then there was a long grace period, until Gwen went to college. Tally, of all people, struggled with having an empty nest. The ups, the downs. Most people would compare it to a roller coaster, he supposes. But on a roller coaster, one has a clear sense of the duration of the ups and downs. The entire trip is telegraphed, the tracks are visible, the safe landing is guaranteed.

But then, everything is understood in hindsight. Hindsight, in Clem's experience, gets a bad rap. Foresight is the fraud. No one has the ability to predict the future. People have hunches that they remember as wisdom because they happened to be right. They conveniently forget all the times they were wrong. Just as rare is the ability to understand, in the moment, exactly what is happening and how a moment that has already passed will affect one's entire future. A swinging arc of light, a man's lifeless body, an angry man, snorting like a bull in strong emotion—how could anyone process that moment and its multiple futures, how that moment would determine the next minute, hour, day, week, month, year, decade of life?

"—then Noah got to take the hamster home, which wasn't fair because he already had a turn and some people haven't had any." Annabelle looks wistful. "I haven't had a turn. Daddy forgot to sign the slip."

It takes Clem a second to grasp this, too. *Sign the slip*—why would someone have to sign an undergarment? Oh, slip of paper, permission slip.

"Can't your mommy sign it?"

Annabelle looks at him pityingly. "She could if it was real. I was telling you a story. My class doesn't even have a hamster. I wish it did, but Seth has allergies." Annabelle's disdainful tone makes Clem feel sorry for Seth, whom he imagines as a snuffling, unhealthy-looking boy, saddled with the onus of denying his entire class the pleasure of a hamster. "Now it's your turn."

"Do you have a book you'd like me to read? Did you bring some books for the weekend?" She is staying here through Sunday, as she does every other week. Clem still disapproves of Gwen's separation from Karl, but he enjoys the visits from Annabelle. "Or we could read this book, *A Tree Grows in Brooklyn*, which I read to your mother."

"I want a made-up-for-real story." Again, her syntax confuses him so much that he questions his mental competency. How can something be made up for real? Ah, Annabelle wants an improvised story, conjured on the spot, just for her. She wants to be present for the moment of its creation.

Clem looks out the window. His bed is set up in the sunroom at the rear of the house, so it feels as if he's surrounded by trees. Spare and spindly at this time of year, but if one looks closely, the leaves and buds are there. Spring is coming. Right now, he can glimpse the edge of Tally's old shed, its prefab walls badly weathered but still standing. Soon it will be hidden by the foliage, which has been allowed to grow wild around it, the need for light long gone.

"Once there was a little girl who lived at the edge of a forest," he begins.

"And was her name Annabelle?"

"Why, it was," he says, and Annabelle bounces with approval, which sends a painful wiggle through the mattress, essentially his cosmos these days. He has not been as faithful as he should about physical therapy, skipping days here and there. Why? It is one of the most mystifying questions in medicine and human nature. Why don't people do the things they should? He's not thinking of the hard things, changes required by genuine addictions. He

252 / LAURA LIPPMAN

understands how difficult it is to quit smoking and change one's diet, even when the consequences of inaction are dire. It's the neglect that otherwise rational people allow—skipping annual exams, declining exercise, refusing to eliminate foods that cause them actual distress.

Tally was casual about her health, not that it would have mattered. No diet, no regimen, no amount of vigilance, no regular checkup would have yielded a different result in her case. She was stage IV at the time of diagnosis. It turned out that she had been experiencing abdominal pain for years and never mentioned it. And that she sneaked cigarettes in her studio. With the paint fumes and the little space heater—he's surprised it didn't go up in a ball of fire years ago.

Sometimes he wishes it had. Without her, of course. He considered the shed, Tally's studio, his romantic rival in some ways.

"And Annabelle had a little house in the woods."

Clem asked Gwen a few months ago if they should try to make the shed, which stands empty, a playhouse for Annabelle. "A little house in the woods," he said. "A little house in the woods," Gwen echoed, her face troubled. A little house . . . maybe it wasn't the best idea. Or maybe it was. Maybe if one had a little house on the edge of the woods, children wouldn't press farther into the real woods.

Not that Annabelle would ever think of walking through the woods, even with another child. Gwen wouldn't allow it. Probably no modern parent would. Clem has always been skeptical of any pronouncement about how times change. Very few things about people have changed in his lifetime. Machines change, people don't. Yet childhood—technology can't change it, but technology has been used to plug all those beautiful, empty hours that children once had to fill on their own. What else can children do but stare at screens when the outdoors is denied to them, except in scheduled doses of sports practice and supervised playdates?

Do mores change? Attitudes about profanity and behavior have changed, but the real change is that people speak of that which was once kept covert. Addictions, affairs, perversions. So much confession, yet America's collective soul doesn't seem to benefit from it. Peter De Vries, a writer that during his forties Clem particularly liked, once said that confession was good for the soul in the same way that a tweed coat was good for dandruff. A *palliative*, De Vries noted, not a cure, and Clem admired a layperson's use of that distinction. Clem should read De Vries's work again. He wonders if it holds up. The conventional wisdom is that such humor, dependent upon knowledge of an era's social customs, has an expiration date. Yet Dawn Powell has come back and even Patrick Dennis, whose work Clem discovered because it nestled next to De Vries on the library shelves. He will ask Gwen to pick them up from the library, assuming they're still *in* the library.

"What did the little girl do in her house, Poppa?"

"She lived there with a dog, a goat, and a horse named Charley."

"Boo," Annabelle says.

"Are you haunting me?" he asks, startled.

"No," she says with a giggle. "The horse is named Boo."

"Ah, of course, a horse named Boo. And she likes to—" He pauses, knowing Annabelle will direct the story where she wants it to go.

"*Cook.*"

"Cook. Your grandmother liked to cook."

"I didn't know her," Annabelle says. "She died a long, long time ago."

True, yet harsh, a reminder that twenty-five years ago, when Tally died, Clem was very much alone in his own house in the woods, without even so much as a horse named Boo. Gwen returned to school, after much melodramatic agonizing and self-exploration. It didn't seem to occur to her that her father had lost his wife, much less that Miller and Fee had lost a mother, too. But

Miller and Fee were adults. Young to lose a parent, but still adults. Miller was born an adult, and Fee became one more or less on schedule, upon college graduation, whereas Gwen—sometimes he feels he is still waiting for Gwen to become an adult. Anyway, Miller and Fee went back to their households, their respective partners and lives, while Gwen pursued and married a man so inappropriate that Clem felt as though he were watching a Restoration comedy that forgot to guide its lovers toward the proper partners at curtain. And now she is separated from Karl. Clem always thought Fee would be the one with a rocky romantic life.

Fee had come out just before Tally's diagnosis, surprising no one, and she still lived with her first love, an instructor at Mills College. The match had overtones of Clem and Tally: Fee's lover was significantly older, an academic. They were still together, although they had weathered a tough time, quarreling bitterly about having children. Interestingly, it was Fee's lover, almost sixty at the time, who thought they should adopt a child. Chinese adoption was fairly new when this came up. But Fee thought it was wrong to become parents to a child if one didn't have a reasonable belief of being there for all a child's milestones. *Oh, Fee,* he tried to tell her. *You can't control that, no matter when you have children.* Tally, a bride at eighteen, missed so much. Gwen's wedding. Both Gwen's weddings. Fee and her partner's marriage in that first, brief window of legality. Annabelle.

Who has taken over the story, as he knew she would, allowing his mind to wander. "And they made pudding and soup and cake and doughnuts and chocolate jelly—"

Clem was fearful when Gwen informed him of her plans to adopt overseas. Could he love a child who was not his biological heir? What about developmental delays? Then Annabelle arrived, he looked at her—and all his fears vanished, just like that. He was heartened to discover that his heart had room for someone new to love. Because in the twenty-five years since Tally's death, no adult woman has found a way there. Many have tried. When his two older children speak of him moving to a senior community, as they always call it, their selling points include "company." This was exactly what kept Clem in his house. He didn't want to deal with all those widows looking for companionship. He is happy as he is. Still women call, drop by. Since his accident, there has been a second wave.

Last week even Doris Halloran showed up on his doorstep, casserole in hand. Unsure of the etiquette, he had his daytime aide invite her in to share it with him, which she did with an almost frightening alacrity. Silly Clem. Doris wasn't looking for a mate. She wanted absolution. She unburdened herself to him and left, seemingly happy. The casserole, whatever it was, might as well be called the misery dish, for once he ate of it, he could never be happy again. What he had always feared, what he knew but did not have to admit, had been thrust on him: Tim killed the man in the woods. He told Doris so before he died. She defended her husband's actions to Clem, said she believed it was the right thing. "Think of the other children he might have hurt, that man."

Clem has thought of them. He thinks about them constantly. Yet he still cannot persuade himself that these potential crimes entitled Tim Halloran to murder the man. And it makes him nervous that Doris knows. She was not there; her husband is dead. Clem has long lost track of Rick. Doris has little to lose by telling others what happened. Clem's entire life could be taken from him retroactively. Everything he has done and accomplished— the career, the children, the grandchildren—would be wiped out by the fact that a man was murdered in front of him and he kept his silence for sheer convenience's sake. Why? Because he knew the man in the woods didn't count, that no one would miss him. It was the coldest, most inhumane calculation of his life. He can never make it right.

"And then I got on Boo and he ran and ran and ran—"

"Galloped," he corrects gently. "Horses gallop. Or canter. But you can say *run*, too."

"I want to ride horses. Daddy says it's too dangerous." Annabelle curls into his side, looking up through her lashes. That is Gwen's look, Gwen's wheedling tone, Gwen's feminine confidence.

"Well, daddies get to decide such things. Daddies know a lot about danger."

Father knows best. If they're telling stories, he might as well go whole hog.

Chapter Thirty-one

Tim is surprised and pleased when Gwen calls out of the blue and asks to meet him for lunch. It's as if she has picked up on his own desire to talk about the past, about Go-Go. He asks her to meet him at the Towson Diner, in part because he likes it, but also because it's bright and shiny, the kind of place where friends meet. He is sensitive to appearances, especially since he has begun toying with the idea of vying for state's attorney in the next election, or maybe positioning himself for a judgeship. Gwen is a good-looking woman, and if Baltimore is a small town masquerading as a city, then Towson, the county seat, is smaller still. He never goes out for lunch or runs an errand without seeing someone from the courthouse or the police department.

Here in the Towson Diner today, he spots two homicide cops, good guys, not like the lunkheads who have handed him his latest loser of a case. Although, of course, it's his boss who deter-mines the assignments. He wonders if his ambition is showing. He would not run against the sitting county attorney, not unless there was a major fuck-up to exploit. That would be idiotic. Un-fortunately, the time to run was probably four years ago, when his previous boss stepped down. Why didn't he go for it then? But Tim's late-blooming ambition has been fueled by watching some-one no smarter than he is do the job. Now he knows he can do it. He doubted himself before.

Tim has often doubted himself, and although he hates the whole blame-your-parents school of thought, especially since he is now a parent, he can't help thinking it would have been nice if his father and mother had been a little more rah-rah on his behalf. He was once doing something idiotic, and his father called him stupid. Doris, parroting advice gleaned from a woman's magazine or daytime talk show, said: "They say you should never call children stupid, but say that their actions are stupid." Tim Senior took his oldest son's full measure with his eyes and said: "This is a stupid child."

Of course, Tim was tough-skinned, a good foil. Go-Go was so crazed that a statement like that wouldn't land as a joke. And Tim has never doubted it was a joke. His old man had his moments, dry and inappropriate as his humor might have been. If his father had been around for the Twitter generation, he definitely could have been the hero of Shit My Dad Says. He was anti-PC before there was PC.

Sean, for all his confidence, was a sensitive little shit, could not stand for the joke to be on him. So it fell to Tim to be the butt of most family punch lines. Tim and Doris, to be fair. They all ganged up on her. She was the odd woman out, the spokes-woman for cleanliness and sanity and don't-play-ball-in-the-house. Tim loves his daughters, but he wouldn't have minded one son, if only so that there would be someone in the household he actually understood on a regular basis.

Gwen breezes through the door and catches almost everyone's gaze, especially the younger homicide cop, a total hound of a guy. Tim has logged a lot of hours in courthouse corridors, passing time by listening to this guy's exploits, as his sergeant likes to call the guy's one-night stands. "Tell us about your latest *exploit*."

The stories were funnier before Tim's daughters started growing up.

There is a moment of awkwardness when Tim and Gwen greet each other. At Go-Go's funeral, an embrace had been the proper thing, but here—she starts to shake his hand, then almost kisses his cheek, only to pull back, lets him kiss *her* cheek.

"Not a very diet-friendly menu," she says, studying the laminated place mats.

"You don't have to worry about that," Tim says. If anything, he thinks that she should put on a few pounds. Her slenderness looks a little rough, the result of stress. He doesn't think Gwen was really meant to be thin.

"I've been worrying about my weight for most of my life. If I stop, I won't know what to do with myself. Cottage cheese and a pear! I love that. Did I enter a time machine?"

Tim knows she's making fun of the diner, not him, yet he feels a little mocked. So it's not tapas or sushi, or whatever the fuck she eats most days. It's good, honest food.

"What the hell, I'll have an open-face turkey sandwich with mashed potatoes, gravy, and a fountain Coke. What's the point of coming to a diner if one doesn't eat diner food? Seize the day. One never knows—" Her voice trails off, and Tim doesn't have to ask where her train of thought is headed.

"What's the point?" he echoes. "And what's the point of this meeting? You promised it wasn't work related. You know my office doesn't do the glory hog thing. I'm not going to talk about my current case."

"No, although if you did want to talk—" She gives him a

mischievous smile. "It is awfully interesting. If you ever do decide to spill the beans, I expect you to honor your old friend with the story."

"Are we old friends, or once-upon-a-time friends? We haven't really stayed in touch."

Gwen shrugs. "When you're friends as kids, it never really ends, does it?"

"Sure it does. Childhood friendships end all the time. I see it with my girls. Friendships end, romances end, half of all marriages end. Family's the only thing that's forever, and I'm not even sure about that sometimes."

"I'm here about family, actually. Your family." She studies the photo of the open-face sandwich on the menu, as if she might not recognize it when it arrives. "Did you know that a private investigator tried to get in touch with Go-Go earlier this year?"

Tim, by dint of his profession, is used to treating conversations as poker games. Surprised by Gwen's information, he automatically reverts to state's attorney's mode, guarding his emotions. "Where did you hear that?" It's a calculated phrase. He's not admitting that Gwen knows something he doesn't and he wants to find out more before he commits himself.

"I ran into his ex-wife, and she told me. It's why she threw him out. A PI kept calling, saying she needed to talk to him, that someone from his past needed him. But he wouldn't talk to the PI and he wouldn't tell Lori what was going on. She decided he must be cheating on her and threw him out."

"That's her story."

"Well—yes."

Tim has enough information now to stake out his territory. Some would say he's being the devil's advocate, but as he sees it, he's standing up for his brother, who isn't here to defend himself. "Did it ever occur to you that Lori wants to revise their history?

She threw him out, he started drinking again, he ended up dead. She doesn't want to be responsible."

"Yes, but why confide in me?"

"Because here you are, sharing it with his brother. She saw you at the funeral, she knows there's some connection. She's trying to get back on my mother's good side."

"Why?"

"What?"

"Why does she need to be on your mother's good side?"

"For one thing, my mother essentially owns the house she lives in. She loaned Go-Go the money to buy it. She could call in the note."

"Grandmothers don't do that to their grandchildren, no matter how they feel about their daughters-in-law. Lori is the one who has the power in this situation. She could sell the house and move away. She can keep your mom from seeing the girls. Anyway, I assume you know your sister-in-law better than I do, but that strikes me as way too devious for her. She's pretty direct."

Tim is ready to counter—to say he does, in fact, know Lori better than Gwen, to ask who she is to presume to tell him about his family, his sister-in-law—but he starts to laugh instead.

"What?"

"It's like we're kids again. This is how we argued then."

Gwen laughs, too. "So maybe we are still friends."

"Maybe." He can't go that far. As Gwen said, it's like entering a time machine. They went into the past there for a moment. But they can't stay there. He doesn't want to stay there.

"Look, Tim, the reason I called you is because—this private detective. What if she was hired by his family?"

He is confused by the pronoun. "Go-Go's? My mom, you mean?"

"No." She lowers her voice and leans toward him. He wishes

she wouldn't. Her posture is a secret personified. He leans back, crosses his arms. "*His*. Him. From the woods."

It takes another second to process. "He didn't have any family."

"That we know of. But he would disappear, remember? Why did he disappear? I never really thought about it, but chances are that a family member would intervene from time to time, if his health was jeopardized. They'd get a judge to put him in a hospital for his own good, but then he would sign himself out. I know it was easier to institutionalize people then, but if he was considered sane, he couldn't be kept anywhere against his will."

"OK, so maybe he had family. So what? He fell down in the woods, he hit his head, and bled out or drowned. It *was* an accident. Mickey didn't mean to—well, you know. It was just easier not to explain that part, or to tell our parents how well we knew him, how we created the circumstances that ended up with Go-Go being assaulted. Those omissions don't change the basic facts."

"I know. I was there. And if we had told the full story at the time, it wouldn't have made a difference. But if it were your relative, if he was found in the woods without his guitar, his single most precious object, a day or so after a horrible hurricane, based on an anonymous call—would you think it was an accident?"

"He had the guitar."

"When we saw him. My father told me he hiked back to make sure if the EMTs had found him and there was no body—and no guitar."

"Paramedics probably stole it. Besides, why wait thirty years to pursue it? Why now?"

"I don't know. But who else from Go-Go's childhood would think he could do him a favor?"

"You said 'need,' not a favor."

"Yeah, well a smart private investigator isn't going to say, 'Hey, I'm looking into a suspicious death of which you might have knowledge.' She's going to set you up to think it's something good, then lower the boom."

Their food arrives, but the gyro, which Tim had been looking forward to with almost pathetic anticipation, is tasteless. If the guy does have family, if there are suspicions—well, there goes any chance of political office. He'll be lucky to keep the job he has. But how would anyone know to look for Go-Go? Someone else would have blabbed. Not him. Not Sean. Not McKey. Gwen? She's a journalist, and they're a little too free with information in Tim's experience. It's their currency, they can't help it.

Then he thinks of Go-Go, on a bender. Not the most recent one, but a year or so ago, the next-to-last time he fell off the wagon. Go-Go was not good with secrets, and his feelings about Chicken George would have been understandably confused. No one had shown him greater kindness. No one had betrayed him more thoroughly. Go-Go drunk was capable of saying anything to anyone. And now he's dead.

"So what do we do?" he asks Gwen.

"That's why I called you. You're a prosecutor. Can't you make the PI talk to you? I mean, I have no standing, but you're his brother and an officer of the court—"

He shakes his head. "Gwen, that would be a horrible violation of my office. And, by the way, PIs, if retained through legal counsel, can't be forced to give up information about their clients. They enjoy almost the same privileges as lawyers. I mean, yeah, if you subpoena someone, but—no, no way. Even if this PI would talk to me, I don't want to put us in play. Does he still call Lori? Has he called you?"

"She," Gwen says. "The PI is a she. And, no, there's no evidence she's tried to get in touch with anyone else."

"So drop it."

"But—"

"Drop it, Gwen. You're overthinking this. I understand the impulse. I'm on intimate terms with it. You're worried that something's going on, something you can't control. You want to get out in front of it. You can't. Leave it alone. Let me tell you this much: Among the three of us, the brothers? We never spoke of it. Neither did my parents. They thought it was for the best. It probably wasn't, and maybe Go-Go ended up telling someone he shouldn't. But there's nothing we can do about it, and the minute you start poking around, you're more apt to stir things up."

Gwen sips her Coke. For all her big talk about seizing the day with an open-face turkey sandwich, she's barely touched her food, only moved it around on her plate, a trick he knows from his daughters.

"It's not just this. My father—"

"How is he?"

"He's doing okay, all things considered. Breaking a hip at his age is no small thing. Anyway, the day he fell? He claimed it was because he saw a chicken on the stairs."

Tim can't help himself. He laughs, an all-out guffaw. Gwen looks genuinely hurt.

"I'm sorry, Gwen, but—what do you think this is, some horror movie, where a relative bent on revenge stalks us and our parents? Hires a PI to pressure Go-Go, then surreptitiously places a chicken on your father's steps? Forces Go-Go to drive into the barricade? What about you, Gwen, do you hear steel guitars in the night? I mean, come on."

She tries to act as if she's in on the joke, but he can tell she's not entirely persuaded. "OK, I'm a little paranoid. Go-Go's accident, then my father's accident—"

"Gwen, it's fucking middle age. Parents die. *People* die. I lost my dad fifteen years ago, you lost your mother before that."

"She wasn't even fifty, and I was in college. There was nothing middle-aged about that."

"My dad went young, too. I'm just saying—we're in our forties, and this is when the bullshit begins to mount. Just when you think you've got things figured out—boom, boom, boom. We start losing our parents, then we start losing our friends. Your father fell down the steps? He's in his eighties. I'm even less surprised that Go-Go's gone. The shocker there was that he made forty. Look, my brother broke my heart. You don't think I haven't asked myself again and again if a more open, touchy-feely family would have been better equipped to deal with what happened to him? You don't think I suggested psychiatrists, even offered to pay if that's what it took? I found that AA meeting for him. Sean tried, too. So sure, I'm racked with guilt, but about that. Not about that monster dying in an accident."

Gwen stares out the window at York Road, and Tim follows her gaze. It's one of those places that seem to have changed very little over the years. It's ugly now, but it was always ugly.

"I'm going to go talk to her."

"Her?"

"The PI."

Tim shakes his head. "Don't. This is about my family, not yours, Gwen."

"It's about all of us. There's no hierarchy."

"Really? Were you sexually molested in the woods? I mean, nonconsensually?"

She blushes. "That's a little crude, Tim. Even for you."

"Sorry, I don't mean to take the bloom off your first love, the tender memories of dry-humping and second base."

He has been too specific. She shoots him a look. "I always thought you watched us."

"Only once," he admits. "And not out there. In the basement."

She looks down at her plate. "That summer, when Chicken—when he—disappeared that last time, Sean and I started using the cabin. Only a few times. It smelled so bad. I felt dirty there."

"And not in the good way."

"*Tim.*"

God, they are their young selves again, him teasing Gwen because he's so insanely jealous of his brother, having a willing girlfriend when Tim can't find one. It's not that he wants her, or ever really wanted her. It's that his brother leapfrogged ahead of him. Later, Go-Go got more pussy than the two of them combined. You don't have to be Sigmund Freud to figure that one out.

"Did you ever go back?" she asks. "After?"

She doesn't have to specify back to where. "No."

"My dad did. He went back again and again. He doesn't know I know this. He would set out for these long walks on weekends and he wouldn't invite me, the way he used to. I'm sure that's where he went."

"He probably thought you had no interest. You were a teenager by then. Trust me, teenage girls have very little use for their fathers. Their fathers' wallets, but not their fathers."

"My dad and I got along well. Then and now. Yet we can't talk about this."

"Gwen, let it go. This isn't about you."

Gwen glances around the table, in search of something. She grabs a napkin, rummages in her purse, finds a pen. A much-chewed pen, Tim observes, the one thing about Gwen that is not put together, polished. She draws a star in the way that grade-schoolers are taught, with five slashing lines.

"This was us. The five points of a star," she says. "Remember? Mickey said we were like a starfish."

"A starfish regenerates its limbs. My brother isn't coming back. *My* brother, Gwen." He is trying to underline to her that he gets to decide this. He and Sean, if it comes to that, but not Gwen.

"Now look at the center. When you draw a star this way, it forms a pentagon at the center. That was Chicken George. Not just him, but the woods, and our adventures there. When he molested Go-Go, when he died—we were all cut off from each other. I suddenly couldn't stand to be around Sean. I didn't know why, I just know it was so. And I think he was relieved that I didn't want to go with him anymore. Mickey went to a new school, and we didn't see her anymore, but we had always gone to different schools, so that wasn't it. You think it's dangerous to look closer at this. I think it's dangerous to look away."

Their appointment had been for twelve forty-five, late for lunch in this part of town, and the diner has emptied, entered the afternoon lull. He sees the homicide detectives up at the cashier, paying their separate checks, shaking toothpicks free from the dispenser. A lawyer he knows, a formidable defense attorney, is finishing her coffee at the counter, reading the paper. She catches his gaze, arches an eyebrow at him. That old bag doesn't miss a trick.

"I've got to get back to work." In his mind, he is running through the chain of events if this were ever to become public. What if Gwen decides to write about this, for God's sake? Writers have so few boundaries. Didn't she publish an article about her own daughter's adoption a few years back, complete with details no one needed to know about her fertility problems? Maybe he should tell his boss, confidentially and preemptively. Hell, forget his boss, how does he tell Arlene, someone from whom he has no other secrets? *When I was a kid* . . . But even now, even with Go-Go dead, it feels like a betrayal. *They are not supposed to talk about this.* Even with his mother, in the weeks since Go-Go's death, they have strenuously avoided the topic. "You don't think—" his mother said the weekend after the funeral, when everyone else's lives were going back to normal and they were left alone in their new normal, this territory of grief, whose boundaries lie far beyond their range of vision, making it impossible to know how long they will be here, if they will ever leave. "No," he said. He didn't think it was a suicide. He didn't think it had anything to do with what happened when Go-Go was nine because why now? It made no sense. He got drunk. He cracked up his car. End of story.

His conversation with Gwen has nowhere to go, but they make a stab at it. They talk idly about their children, schools, whether they fit the definition of helicopter parents, although they're both pretty sure they don't. Gwen wraps a strand of hair around her finger, a habit he remembers from childhood. She's going to do whatever she wants. She always has. A moment ago, when she mentioned breaking up with Sean, Tim almost blurted out what he has always known about his brother: Sean was relieved that Gwen broke up with him because he was terrified of her, of sex. Oh, Sean wanted to have sex. But not with Gwen, because she was too scary-good at getting what she wanted, and what if she wanted to be his only girl, ever? As a newly pretty girl, Gwen was rough with her power, as reckless in her own way as Go-Go. She was like a child discovering a loaded gun in Daddy's nightstand. Even if nothing happens, the sight is terror enough, the weapon juggling in those small hands, so many possible outcomes, almost all bad.

As a woman, she is smoother, but still not as smooth as she thinks she is. She will do whatever she wants, with no regard for anyone's feelings. She always has.

CHAPTER THIRTY-TWO

Rita can tell it's going to be a bad day even before she opens her eyes. She feels it in her bones. Well, technically, she feels it in her *joints,* which are not the same thing as bones, as she now knows, thanks to all those smarty-pants doctors, men younger than her, who could be the very residents who used to undertip her at Connolly's. In spite of herself, Rita has learned a lot about the body, her body. She could probably pass whatever test people have to take for medical school from all the tedious blah, blah, blah about her joints, tendons, lining, inflammation. Her situation boils down to this: She hurts. A lot.

Besides, Rita has no desire to go to medical school, so having all this information at her fingertips—her swollen, clumsy, useless fingertips—is like being asked to familiarize yourself with the life story of a person who ran you down with a car. What's the point of understanding a disease when the disease can't be cured? Rita has to settle for *managing* her rheumatoid arthritis. Her doctor keeps trying various drugs in new combinations. *A little more of this, a little less of this. Wait, this is interacting badly with that.* He reminds her of Mickey as a child, busily arranging spindly wild-flowers in a jar, the stems wilting, the blossoms drooping from all her handling. Meanwhile, Rita can't find a sleep drug that works. Even with Ambien, her sleep is thin, barely sleep at all.

She bets her doctor sleeps beautifully. Probably has one of those special beds—the one designed for astronauts, or the one with the individual controls. There's not a bed in the world that could help Rita sleep better. Rita, who could sleep sitting up, in a car, even on her feet once upon a time. She tried a water bed after she was diagnosed, thinking the heat would help, but it was a bust. She gave it to Joey, who gave it to Mickey, which pissed her off a little. "If I want your sister to have something, I'll give it to her," she told Joey. "But you never want her to have anything," he pointed out. Not exactly true. It's just that anything Rita has to give, she always offers Joey first.

And why shouldn't she? Mickey—Rita's not about to use that stupid name she's conferred on herself, kids don't get to pick their own names, that's a parent's right—doesn't do anything for her. Never visits, even though she almost certainly gets to fly for free, deadheading or whatever they call it. Won't send money when she knows Rita is perpetually short. Says she doesn't have any, but Rita doubts it. That girl is a squirrel, putting away anything she can. As a child, Mickey had drawers full of things she had found, stupid, nasty things. Nests, rocks, birds' eggs. She yowled when Rita threw them out, but you can't have things like that in the dresser drawers. Dirt attracts dirt.

Rita brings her legs over the side of the bed. Stiff, but not awful. Then again, her legs never bother her that much. The pain lives in her upper body, in her hands, wrists, elbows, shoulders.

She makes her way to the kitchen, bumping the corner of the old-fashioned bureau. The slight movement almost knocks off the scarf she has draped over the mirror. Rita has covered up all but one of the mirrors in the house, a small makeup mirror in the bathroom, the one she uses when brushing her hair and applying lipstick. She's OK with seeing herself, but she doesn't like to be surprised by her image, doesn't want that moon face sneaking up on her. She has to be prepared. It's a tough thing, trying to get rid of one's image. Her bungalow, it turns out, is full of reflective surfaces—the windows at night, the microwave door, even the faucet. The world keeps throwing her face in her face.

In the kitchen, she puts the water on to boil, shakes a cigarette out of the pack, which she leaves here at night so she won't be tempted to smoke in bed. When rheumatoid arthritis was finally diagnosed—after three years of chasing so many other demons and diagnoses—she was advised that smoking was a risk factor and she should quit. "But I've got it already," she told the doctor. "Can't unring the bell, can I?" Her fingers are knobby and stiff; lighting the cigarette off the burner and getting it to her lips requires effort. But it's worth it. Smoking's one of those pleasures that never dims. Smoking and orgasms, and Rita's resigned to the fact that the only orgasms in her future will be thanks to her Medicaid-subsidized massage tool, applied to one of the few places where she feels no pain.

The aches started about eight years ago, moody and intermittent. Rita assumed they were occupational, as did most doctors. She had spent decades carrying trays, scrubbing down tables. Something was bound to give, and she'd have chosen tendinitis over varicose veins any day. Rita took good care of her legs. She would come home from work, prop them up on the coffee table, coax her guy into rubbing them, applying cream, promising there would be rubbing in his future, a promise she always kept. Rita was no tease. Funny, Rick did the best job, bone tired as he was after a day at the garage. Larry had him beat in bed, but Rick—well, Rick knew what it felt like to put in a hard day's work, while Larry didn't have a clue. Yeah, Rick was the better man all around. But she didn't love him, and it would have been wrong, staying with him only because he treated her well. If you don't love a man and you stick it out with him, you're little better than a whore in Rita's book, whether it's his paycheck or his love or a roof that's keeping you with him. Even if Larry hadn't resurfaced, she would have ended up cheating on Rick.

Not that she counts Larry as cheating. She wishes she could have done it more gracefully, not let things get so nasty between her and Rick. But she doesn't regret doing it. Rita doesn't regret anything.

The water boils as she finishes her cigarette. Her hands cushioned in oven mitts, she manages to pour most of the water in her cup, splashing only a little on the counter. But the jar of Folgers mocks her, its lid unbudgeable. She thinks about the ease with which she opened those huge jars back in Connolly's, how she was the one who could get any top off. Where's her gripper? Joey has given her an assortment of tools and devices, but she constantly misplaces them. She'll catch herself in the act time and again, putting something down and thinking, *Oh, I shouldn't put that there, I'll never remember,* even as another part of her brain chimes in: *But you can't forget this spot, it's such an unlikely place.* Sure enough, when she goes looking for something, she remembers she put it in an unlikely spot, just not what that spot was. She's got to have a jolt of caffeine. She will have to search her bungalow for the gripper, and small as the place is, her water will probably be cold by the time she finds it.

Rita moved to Florida, real Florida as she thought of it, shortly after Larry turned out to be Larry. Unreliable, incapable of holding down a real job, no interest in being a father to his son. She had no one but herself to blame—and no interest in doing so. She tried to make a go of it with her kid's real father, a man she loved. How can that be wrong? She relocated to Boca Raton with Joey and a guy who seemed steady. She was trying to be pragmatic again, but the guy didn't last, as it turned out. Other men came and went in the little bungalow. One stayed five years, the rest were more short-term. Joey never minded, although he liked it better when it was just the two of them. No, Rick was the one who raised a fuss, back when she first left. He challenged her for custody, and she pulled out her ace in the hole, said he wasn't Joey's father anyway. A judge laid it out for Rick: He could act like Joey's parent, keep paying support, have a relationship with him. Or he could walk away, scot free. Either way, he couldn't have custody and he couldn't force Rita to stay in Baltimore. So what did that sap do? He decided to keep paying, so she would at least send Joey up there for a couple of visits a year.

Maybe Rick deserves a little credit for how Joey turned out. Her son stayed in Florida, although he lives down in Fort Lauderdale, married a nice girl, who looks a little like Rita in her prime, has three kids. He visits every weekend, fights her battles for her—got her on SSI disability, arranged for cheaper drugs, found whatever agencies to assist her. Now here's a kid who has every right to hate her, and he rocks steady. It's Mickey who barely picks up a phone. What ails the girl? She doesn't call her brother, either, and has never even seen her nieces and nephew, except in pictures. Joey shrugs it off. "We're just not that close, Ma. I'm ten years younger, and we moved away when I was eight, leaving her in Baltimore."

"So why did you give her the bed?" Man, that bugs her.

"I had to drive a rental truck up there anyway, to bring back stuff from Dad's house. And we couldn't give that thing away on Craigslist. Why not give it to Mickey? It was nice to see her, even if it was for Dad's funeral."

Rick died at the age of seventy last year. A stroke, out of nowhere, and no way to prepare for it. A weakness somewhere, maybe lurking there for years and then—*kaboom*. Dudley Do-Right to the end, he included Joey in his will, despite having two kids with the namby-pamby he married. Maybe it's because they're both girls and Rick was very specific about the things he wanted Joey to have—tools, a Jet Ski. He left him a little money, too. Rita's emotions were all over the place when she heard about Rick's death. Sad, mocking, resentful. Joey decided to drive a U-Haul up there and bring back the things his not-father had left him, despite having little use for them. He's not particularly handy, can't fix anything for shit. He is Larry's son.

Rita's sixty-three now, but crabbed and wrecked as her body is, she never doubts she's going to live a long time, even with the smoking. "There's nothing wrong with you," her doctor always says. "I mean, other than the rheumatoid arthritis. Your cholesterol's good, your blood pressure is good." He says it grudgingly, as if Rita doesn't deserve any good health. That's the thing about doctors. They secretly want to call the shots, decide who gets the good life, and it pisses them off when someone like Rita isn't crushed by illness.

Rita walks through her house, checking surfaces low and high. It's a tiny house, two bedrooms off an open area that contains the kitchen, dining nook, and living room. The Strawberry Hill apartment was bigger. Where did her grabber go? Again, all she remembers is the very thought—*Well, this is a weird place to leave it*. Ah, she spies it through the sliding glass doors that lead to a tiny patio, sitting on a wrought-iron table. That's right. It was a pretty evening last night, warm but not hot, probably one of the last decent nights before full-on summer lands. Rita sat on the patio, eating an entire jar of cashews, rationalizing that she needed a treat. Her days of watching her figure are long gone, and although she's not fat—Rita's genes keep her lean, another thing that probably pisses her doctor off—she's got a few rolls on her.

The patio door's lock is sticky, hard to maneuver on her best days. It's easier to slip out the front door and circle around, grab the grabber, and come back to the front door—which has locked behind her. *Fuck.* Her bones, her joints, whatever, didn't begin to tell the story of how bad today was going to be. Given the nature of her relationships with the neighbors—she hates the one to the east, the one to the west hates her—she can't see knocking on their doors at 7 A.M., asking to use the phone to call Joey. Who, bless him, would be here as fast as he can with her spare keys, no questions asked. She could walk to the Circle K and use the pay phone, but it would take her forever to shuffle that dusty mile. Plus, while her loose flowery nightgown and slippers pass muster for sitting on her front steps, it's not an outfit that a sane woman wears walking down a busy street. She'd get picked up and taken in for a psych exam.

She sits on the steps, picks up the paper, which they won't stop delivering no matter how often she cancels it. She gets all the news she wants from television, and the last thing she needs is something that comes in the house only to pile up and have to be discarded. Her grandchildren lecture her on recycling. On re-cycling and smoking and voting. When did children get so *moral*? Weren't the parents and grandparents supposed to be instructing them? She has asked them as much, and they say: "But, Grandma, it's going to be our world."

She doesn't have the heart to tell them that you get the world on loan, on terms you don't dictate and can't control. It's about as good a deal as those furniture leases with all the hidden inter-est rates. Rita figures she had the world for about twenty years, from age twenty to forty. Then it was Joey's turn to step up, take his bite out of it. Being Joey, he took a small, polite bite, sort of like: *Oh, thank you for my job as a probation officer and my nice wife and my three children, but really, I couldn't eat another bite.* He was born good, that's all there is to it, and Mickey was born—not bad,

276 / LAURA LIPPMAN

but angry and fretful, always discontent, so concerned with the fairness of things that she ended up with nothing. Best Rita can tell, Mickey's never had a happy day in her life, and it breaks her heart, truly. Because for all she has to mourn—the breakdown of her body, being alone, all the daily demon worries about money and bills—she had a lot of fun, when there was fun to be had. A lot. She scratches her ankles, one part of her body that hasn't succumbed to the pain or the steroids, smiling at her memories.

A patrol car idles by and she flags it down, thinking the cops can help her break into her own house. She's pretty sure the bathroom window is unlocked and someone could wiggle through it. Someone whose body is reliable, that is. The officers are Latino, very handsome, but Rita's not deluded enough to flirt with them, although she's happy when one sees a photograph of her in the front hall and asks: "Is that you?" She nods and he says, respectful-like: "You must have had to beat them off with a stick." He adds quickly: "I bet you still do."

"No," Rita says. "Now I have to beat them *with* a stick and drag them in here." She brandishes her grabber at them, and they laugh. Rita doesn't need the pretense that she hasn't aged. The idea of aging bothers her less than it might have, perhaps because she has a specific reason to look as she does. She can tell herself she'd look good if it weren't for the steroids. "I got a daughter, though, who looks exactly like that now. Better, if you want to know the truth."

That's not exactly true. But she suddenly feels generous toward Mickey, wants to balance the scales of her own mind, where she's been running her daughter down.

"You'll have to introduce us when she comes to visit."

That'll be the day, Rita thinks, going back to her teakettle, the jar of Folgers, restarting her morning. *What did I do, Mickey? I know I wasn't perfect, not by a mile, but if Joey can forgive me, why can't you?* The difference, she thinks, is that Joey is a parent. He gets it, he knows how high one's hopes and aspirations are—and how awful it is to confront the gap between the parent you want to be and the parent you are. Maybe she shouldn't have had kids, but where would Mickey be then? Would she rather not exist at all? Rita, for all her aches and pains, for all her mistakes, thinks life is a hoot. She'd do it all over again, and the exact same way, knowing full well where she's headed.

Coffee in one cramped, crabbed hand, she shuffles to the living room to watch the news, smoke another cigarette.

Chapter Thirty-three

Gwen has met many people who hate journalists—they announce it happily, proudly, often at cocktail parties where she has just been introduced—but none quite as vociferously as the private detective who tried to contact Go-Go in the weeks before his death. Tess Monaghan has refused to return Gwen's calls and didn't even acknowledge e-mails sent to the bare-bones Web site she maintains. After several days, she finally sent back a terse note:

I don't talk to reporters.

Gwen wrote back, under her personal e-mail:

I'm not approaching you as a journalist, but as a friend of Gordon Halloran, who died in what may well be a suicide commit-

ted after **you** tried to contact him, wreaking not a little havoc in
his life.

Another day went by before she received this e-mail:

My office, 2 p.m.

The office is in Butchers Hill, less than a mile from the magazine's headquarters, yet worlds away in a sense. While Butchers
Hill caught a whiff of the go-go real estate boom of the century's
first decade, it is nothing like the glass canyon where Gwen's office
is located. It has retained its human scale, tucking new restaurants
and shops into old rowhouses. Tess Monaghan's office, which was
virtually unmarked, sits two blocks from Patterson Park.

"It's open," a woman's voice calls out. Working behind an
unlocked door seems a little casual for this neighborhood, even
during the daytime. But as Gwen enters, she is immediately in-
spected by two large dogs, a greyhound and a Doberman, and
a jumpier, miniature version of the greyhound. They circle and
sniff her, apparently with satisfactory results, as they then return
to the sofa, where they arrange themselves in an overlapping
lump. Tess Monaghan, sitting behind her desk, doesn't rise at all,
but she has good reason: she is holding a baby, who is spitting up
on her shoulder.

"Way to miss the burp cloth, Scout," she says, clearly unper-
turbed by the fountain of curdy white liquid that trails down her
sleeve.

"He's adorable," Gwen says, making conversation. She can't
really see much but the dark hair. She doesn't have any real experience with infants. Annabelle was eight months when they met
her in a Beijing hotel.

"She."

"I thought you said scout?"

"That's her name. Her middle name." Tess Monaghan has a manner of speaking that makes questions seem not only unnecessary but also rude. The things that Gwen might normally ask—from *To Kill a Mockingbird*? Why do you use her middle name? How old?—die on her tongue.

"I don't normally bring her to the office," Tess says. "We had a child care crisis today and I didn't want to cancel on you."

"No one has to explain child care crises to me. Most of my employees are working moms. She's so tiny, but—" Gwen stops, not wanting to comment on a stranger's appearance, but this woman looks pretty fit for having had a baby recently.

"She was really early. She's technically almost five months old, but if she had been on time, she'd be barely three months." Again, it is somehow clear there are to be no follow-up questions. "So, Gordon Halloran. Just to be sure we are on the same page—I am speaking to you off-the-record and this is not for anything you might write, ever, on any subject."

"Right."

"And by off-the-record, we both agree that means nothing I say is to appear in print, attached to my name or to an unnamed source?"

"I'm not here as a journalist."

"Would you be willing to sign something to that effect?"

"Sure," Gwen says. "After it was reviewed by my attorney."

Tess smiles. "Fair enough. I just have to be super careful."

"Were you burned by a journalist?"

"Worse. I was one. Your magazine did once put me in your hot singles issue, when I was neither single nor really all that hot. Although now when I see photos of myself from back then—only a few years ago—I think I look magnificent."

"I'm pretty sure that was before my time," Gwen says, then blushes. She was trying to reference the magazine, not the issue of Tess Monaghan's looks, which merit the not-quite-compliment of handsome. Strong features, hair pulled back in a ponytail, a fresh-scrubbed face. "We still do the singles issue—it sells very well, and we make a bucketload on the advertising—but I've tried to add some serious journalism to the mix."

"I've noticed. That's why I don't want to talk to you about Gordon Halloran in any kind of professional capacity. Besides, there's not much I can tell you. I've spoken to my client. My client prefers to remain anonymous."

Shit. That doesn't assuage Gwen's conscience in the least.

"Could I have any nonidentifying information about your client?"

"Such as?"

"Age, gender, place of residence. Race." If the client isn't African American, there's little chance that one of Chicken George's relatives has hired Tess Monaghan.

"I can ask. But my client is pretty paranoid. And unnerved by Gordon Halloran's death. As am I, since you told me it might be a suicide. The news reports last month didn't say that. At my discretion, I haven't passed that information along to my client yet, but I will. It—" She pauses. "It complicates things for us, and I'm afraid it will make my client, who is a very nice person, feel quite bad. Are you sure?"

"It's unclear," Gwen says truthfully, not wanting to admit that she guilted the PI into this meeting. "It will probably always be unclear. He had been drinking after several months of sobriety. He drove into the concrete barrier at the foot of I-70, where it dead-ends into the park-and-ride. He was speeding, but he was always a reckless, fearless person. He could have been playing some silly game, misjudged the end of the highway."

Tess Monaghan shifted the baby on her shoulder. Annabelle had been tiny, too, for her age. Still was. But Gwen had forgotten how alien young babies look, with their comically smushed faces and toothless smiles.

The detective says: "But he was a regular at AA."

"Was. He didn't go to the meeting that night."

"Right."

"Right—wait, how do you know that? I said only that he was sober."

"One of my employees was attending those meetings."

"That's *horrible*." Heedless of the lie she had told to gain this audience, Gwen is genuinely appalled. "The whole point of twelve-step programs is to provide people with a safe place to unburden their hearts. It's a—desecration to send a spy there."

Tess surprises her by nodding. "I wasn't wild about it. I'm not wild about a lot of the things I do. But my client—well, my client is an honorable person who has a right to set the record straight on a matter that goes to the heart of my client's very being. There was a possibility that Gordon Halloran was someone who could help do that. I sent someone into the meeting to see if he ever spoke about certain events in his past, if he contradicted what my client was telling me."

"And—?" Gwen is shocked at how nervous she feels and hopes that Tess Monaghan can't tell. It's like driving down the road, glimpsing a cop in one's rearview mirror and starting to shake despite being within the speed limit. No, it's not like that, because Gwen is not without blame.

"He never spoke at all, not during the meetings. He was a little more open during smoke breaks." Tess Monaghan laughs. "My poor partner, who hates cigarettes, took to smoking clove cigarettes and now has a bit of a penchant for them. Still, he talked only of his family, his wife and his daughters, how he was doing this for them."

"It's your messages to him that got him kicked out of the house," Gwen says, eager to shift blame, to make someone else feel as twitchy and uncomfortable as she feels. "Which is probably why he started drinking again. And died."

Tess Monaghan studies her intently. "Do you believe that? That's not a rhetorical question."

"Not exactly," Gwen admits.

"You were attempting leverage, to guilt me into telling you things I just can't tell you. I might do the same thing in your position. But please understand, I am working with an attorney—a very high-powered one, not my usual kind of gig. I have to respect the client's wishes or I'm in violation of the agreement I signed, and this lawyer will come down on me like a ton of bricks if I do that. He's a prick that way."

"So why are you in business with him?"

The baby emits a comically large burp, delighting her mother. "The client's a sweetheart. And the circumstances—I almost wish I could speak of them because it's darn fascinating." She laughs again, this time at herself. "Darn! As if this lump in my arm would be shocked by my old vocabulary, but I really have trouble cursing in front of her. Let's just say my client is that rare person who's interested in justice."

Again Gwen is feeling far from comforted.

"Can you tell me anything?"

Tess thinks for a moment. "The client lives quite far away. New Mexico. I'm willing to tell you that one detail so you'll understand it's not someone you can find."

"At what time in his life did Go-Go know this person?"

Tess gazes at the ceiling, absentmindedly places her lips against her daughter's temple. "I don't think I've ever said that Gordon *did* know this person. Or that he didn't. When I finally spoke to Gordon—"

"You spoke to him? His wife thought—"

"I didn't stop trying to speak to Gordon after he moved out, although I didn't realize my calls had anything to do with that. And he affirmed what I believed and what my client believes. But now he's dead and all I have are my notes from that brief conversation, and my notes—they're not enough."

"Enough?"

"They're not proof of anything. I will say this much: I think my client was right in assessing Gordon's character."

"Meaning?"

"He's essentially an honest person and has a hard time carrying secrets. He very much wanted to do the right thing. Look, my investigation is ongoing." Gwen feels another flush of panic. "That's why I have to be reserved about it. And any media attention, the barest whiff, would have horrible repercussions. You can't imagine."

Gwen can, though.

Tess Monaghan walks her to the door. It's cool for April, and she cups a hand protectively over the baby's scalp. "I worry about her immune system because she was a preemie. I make her wear hats to guard from cold, no matter how balmy it is, overdress her. Like all women, I have become my mother."

Only Gwen hasn't. Her mother never would have left her, under any pretext, not when she was Annabelle's age. Her mother waited until Gwen was a teenager before she even dared to stake out a life of her own, through her painting. And by then Tally had so little time left. Would she approve or disapprove of Gwen as a parent? Could Gwen ever have lived up to her example—the well-kept house, the perfect meals? No, she runs a magazine for those who aspire, as she does, to be like her mother—effortlessly stylish, abreast of things. Gwen does a fair imitation of Tally, but it requires mountains of effort. Perhaps her mother put in just as much effort. Perhaps beneath the sweet, serene surface she also roiled with self-imprecations and disappointments. Still, she never let Gwen see that, whereas Gwen already has exposed her much younger daughter to a world of doubt.

Gwen's thoughts are derailed by the squeal of brakes, a small but undeniable crash: an MTA bus has managed to stop before hitting the van that is blocking the street, but a Toyota Corolla behind the bus hasn't been as fortunate, plowing into it. And now people are filing out into the street, but only one or two people are peering at the Toyota's driver, who appears unhurt if dazed. No, most of the people are trying to get *on* the bus, prying open the doors, while the bus driver shouts at them to stop. Tess Monaghan laughs so hard that her baby daughter wobbles on her shoulder.

"This is why MTA buses have cameras," she tells a mystified Gwen. "Whenever there's an accident, people try to say they were on the bus in order to file a claim. And it's why," she says over her shoulder, retreating back into the tiled vestibule, "that I have a thriving business. People are always looking for an angle, another pocket to pick."

Walking to her car, Gwen is briefly entranced by the insight that Tess has just handed her, wonders if there's a feature in it for the magazine. But then she thinks about the larger meaning of Tess's words. *Another pocket to pick.* If Chicken George's relatives wanted to file a wrongful death suit against someone, then Gwen's pockets—actually Karl's—would be the deepest. Can she be sued under such circumstances? Could any of them? What if she goes ahead and divorces Karl? Does that make her more vulnerable or less?

Yet it would be a relief if money is all that someone wants from them. Money always can be found, some way, somehow. If someone bears a grudge toward them, if someone knows that they left a man to die—money will be the least of their problems.

CHAPTER THIRTY-FOUR

It was never McKey's intention to continue attending the AA meetings at the old St. Lawrence, and no one was too alarmed when she skipped the first few sessions after Go-Go's death. She uses the cover of her work schedule, tells her sponsor that she's attending meetings in Minneapolis, where she has frequent layovers. Luckily, the sponsor knows nothing about a flight attendant's life and has no idea how little time she has on such trips, the airlines turning them around as fast as the regulations allow. At the same time, the sponsor is worried about her. A death in the group is a dangerous thing, especially when it involves someone falling off the wagon. He keeps checking in, and McKey decides it would be easier to show up than to endure Dan's achingly sincere phone calls. Guy wants to bang her so bad, it's pathetic.

She doesn't share at the meetings. Go-Go didn't either, at least not after she started showing up. But McKey's work has made her good at appearing to be an empathetic, interested listener, and those who do speak seek out her gaze, especially the men. She is the best-looking woman here, there's no use being modest about it. And the ban on relationships gives male-female interactions a kind of buzz that McKey hasn't experienced since grade school, if even then. Men want her, or think they do because she meets their eyes and nods, encouraging them.

"We were worried about you," Dan says when the others step outside to smoke, one vice McKey has never known.

"Because I wasn't here?"

"And because of Gordon."

She measures her words. "That was shocking."

"You knew him, right? Outside of AA."

Never lie until cornered. Counter first. "What makes you think that?"

"You two talked about how this place used to be a Catholic parish, back in the day."

She remembers now, how Go-Go reacted the first time she came here, his inability to disguise his feelings at seeing her. She let him—them—off the hook with some inane chatter about St. Lawrence, showed him how to play it off. Just like when they were kids.

"My little brother went here, but he was much younger than Go-Go."

"Go-Go?"

Shit. "What?"

"I thought you said—"

"One of those things. Gordon. I meant to say Gordon. I barely know my own name, after working eighteen hours yesterday. Mouth not connected to brain." She smiles, lets him contemplate the mouth in question, full and wide under a fresh coat of lipstick. "Gordon. Duh."

Joey had gone to St. Lawrence, at Rick's insistence. Rita hadn't even known that he was Catholic when they were together, but when he realized how close Rita's apartment was to the school, he insisted that Rita enroll Joey there and he paid the tuition. McKey went to public school, not that she cared. She didn't want to wear a uniform every day. Now that she wears one for work, she finds she enjoys it. One less decision to make. Joey went to St. Lawrence through third grade, the year that McKey graduated from high school. Her mother, by then on the outs with Larry—big surprise, *that* not working out—decided she wanted to move back to Florida, make a new start. Rick objected, and that's when she dropped the bomb: Joey's not your kid. Nowadays, there are talk shows essentially dedicated to paternity testing and baby-daddy-dom, but twenty-plus years ago, this was considerably more novel, the kind of judicial issue that all but required a Solomon. Rick was lucky enough to land a progressive judge, someone who said it was basically his choice: He could continue to pay child support and inhabit the role of Joey's father, although he still couldn't stop Rita from taking him to Florida. Or he could suspend ties altogether.

McKey thought it should be a no-brainer: if he couldn't prevent Rita from moving away with the kid, he should definitely end support. But Rick didn't see it that way. After the breakup with Rita, he became almost insufferably proper. Rita cheated on him, played him for a fool, but Rick acted as if he were the one who had to make amends. He started going to church, enrolled Joey in the parish school, married a young goody-goody, ended up adopting two kids when it turned out she couldn't have any of her own. He stayed in touch with McKey through college. "I'm here for you," he would say, and she always wanted to say back: No, you're not. Because Rick, for all his goodness and niceness, could never quite treat her like a daughter. She was his girlfriend's daughter, his son's sister, but not his daughter. It obviously wasn't a blood thing because the lack of a blood connection to Joey didn't keep him from wanting to be Joey's dad. Eventually she stopped worrying about it.

What did she know from fathers and daughters, anyway? The only example she had close to hand was Gwen and her dad, and that wasn't anything to emulate. For one thing, he was old and he looked it, even back in the day. And he was always—what was Tally Robison's term for it?—*holding forth*. On the occasions that Mickey ate dinner with the Robisons, the meal was like another class, with quizzes on current events and science and history and vocabulary. She didn't even try to participate, except when it came to plants and trees. Even as a girl, Mickey knew as much about those subjects as Dr. Robison. She didn't have all the right words, but she understood the natural world in a way that Gwen didn't. She was aware of the seasons and the smells. It was Mickey who taught Go-Go how to catch salamanders, Mickey who lured crawfish from the old storm drain at the bend in the creek, Mickey who found the tiny little fossil, which Rita threw away.

"You should study botany," a bored high school adviser told her. But that wasn't right for her. No job was. Park ranger, gardening—there was no paying gig that could return her to the way she felt when she roamed the hills of Leakin Park as a child. Maybe there is no job that can make a person feel as she felt at ten, eleven. That do-what-you-love bullshit—it's another scam, as far as McKey is concerned, another way people set you up for disappointment. She loves having a job she doesn't love because she's always clear on why she's there: to pay the bills.

The AA meeting gets under way and she assumes her attentive posture, listening and nodding, capable of taking in the stories, even while following her own thoughts. There really are only so many variations to addiction stories. Names change, but bottoming out, based on what she hears here, appears to be a largely universal experience. How much longer must she attend? Perhaps she'll tell Dan she's moving to Minneapolis. Always tricky to tell such a lie in a small-town city like Baltimore, where people's paths are forever crossing, but if that day should come, she'll find a plausible reason to be back here, no? Dan is a pain in the ass and too chummy for her. Maybe all his concern really is part of his role as her sponsor, but she's dubious.

Take tonight, his insistence on walking her out to her car, as if there's any danger in this church parking lot.

"I'm glad you're back," he says. "Now we just have to worry about Daisy."

"Daisy?"

"The older woman who used to bring knitting to the meetings. Very Madame Defarge."

She stares at him blankly, realizing she should recognize the reference, but not caring if he sees it has gone past her. Just like dinner with the Robisons, all those years ago, all that talk, talk, talk flying around the air. Mickey stared into space, defiantly bored by the Robisons, who thought they were so interesting.

"Big woman," Dan says. "Wore flowery dresses. Smoked clove cigarettes."

"Oh, yeah." McKey doesn't pay much attention to women because they are seldom of use to her.

"Her sponsor tried to call her, but she's not answering, doesn't even have voice mail."

"Maybe she died."

"*McKey!*" Dan acts as if she's making a dark joke, but she was being merely factual. Daisy's an old lady, probably alone. She could have fallen in her apartment. She could be lying there right now, dead or dying. Does Dan think all the tragedy of the world is linked to drinking? He probably does. He's built his life around it.

"Be safe," he says as she gets behind the wheel.

"I always am."

It's a haul, getting back to her apartment. It's a haul getting almost anywhere from this corner of Baltimore, and she wonders, as she has often wondered, how her mother ended up there. Because of Rick, of course. She met Rick, he worked at the Exxon station, and there you have it. Or was it the man before Rick? Rita followed men wherever they led her, yet now she is living manless in Florida. This must explain her sudden interest in McKey, the messages on her answering machine. *Call me, call me, call me.* No thanks. *Not my problem you're alone and bored. I'm alone and never bored.*

McKey lets herself into her apartment and goes straight to the refrigerator, pours herself a glass of white wine. Nothing like pretending to be an alcoholic to give one a craving for drink. Liquor is like porn to those people, and after listening to them talk about it nonstop, she can't wait to have a drink, although normally she can take it or leave it. Wrangling drunks at 30,000 feet puts one off alcohol. It was stupid, telling Sean she was in AA with Go-Go. And he probably blabbed to Tim—boys are the worst gossips—maybe even Gwen. Should they meet again, she won't be able to drink in front of him. And she wants to see him again. Although it would be nice this time if he weren't so blotto. He was useless.

She examines herself in the mirror, pleased by what she sees. Her body, like her mother's, is naturally hard, at least for now. Hard is good. Hard is what she strives for across the board. Hard of body, hard of heart, hard of mind. McKey is a warrior, a survivor. She's ready—for the plane to go down, for a terrorist to pull a knife, for the world to end, for whatever comes. And, increasingly, it feels like something is coming for her, but she's sidestepped it for now. She's pretty sure she's sidestepped it.

But at night, alone in her water bed—her mother's old bed, a gift McKey accepted from her half brother because she thought

it ironic, although she has lost track of what the irony was supposed to be—at night, on the edge of sleep, it's hard to stay hard.
She ends up crying as she has cried every night since Go-Go died.
Even the night Sean was passed out in her bed, when she was
finally so close to having the one thing she'd always wanted, she
found herself weeping for the little brother of the man lying next
to her.

PITY US ALL

CHAPTER THIRTY-FIVE

When Sean's plane touches down at Baltimore/Washington International on Good Friday morning, he is thinking about the first time he landed at this airport, which happened to come at the end of his first plane trip. He was in college, heading home for a surprise Thanksgiving visit after signing up to courier a package, a not uncommon arrangement then. Twenty years old! Duncan has been on a plane at least twenty times, possibly more. He's on yet another one right now, en route to New Orleans, a place where Sean has never been. "It's just not on my list," Vivian had said when he proposed it as a romantic getaway for the two of them a few years ago. "The food is so heavy."

The airport where Sean landed in the mid-1980s had already switched its name to Baltimore/Washington International from Friendship, an unlikely moniker for any airport in these hostile days. Sean travels enough for work that he is a low-maintenance passenger—shoes off, laptop unsheathed, liquids in the right volume, stowed in a plastic bag of the dictated size. He has little patience for the petulant fliers who treat everything as an affront, who have decided that the security line is the place to throw down for their dignity, to argue for the *five*-ounce bottle of hand cream, which is apparently made from ground diamonds if it's really a hundred dollars an ounce, as the woman at the Tampa airport kept insisting. For Christ's sake, even if you seldom fly, is it so darn hard to get on the Internet and do a little homework? The only people who don't annoy him are the very old travelers, often infirm, who seem genuinely overwhelmed by the experience. He does the math—people in their late eighties were born before the Depression, knew a childhood in which cars were far from the norm. He thinks people have a right to be spooked by anything invented after they were twenty-one. Commercial air travel is a relatively recent phenomenon. His own mother can't manage the trip to Florida on her own. Or so she says.

Twenty-seven years ago, when Sean made his first flight, he tried to play it cool. But between the novelty of the plane—a little disappointing, except on landing, not at all what he thought flying would be like—and the responsibility of being a courier and the coiled surprise of showing up unexpectedly for Thanksgiving— oh, how happy he was going to make his mother—it was hard not to be giddy. He checked his bag, a boxy suitcase without wheels, and held the package on his lap throughout the flight, although it was only a stack of legal files that needed to be in Washington, D.C., the day before Thanksgiving.

He handed these papers to a local courier who met him at the airport, then realized he had no idea how to get into Baltimore without ponying up for a cab, which probably cost twelve, fifteen bucks at the time. He was Timothy Halloran's son and couldn't bear to pay that much for something so simple. He wandered the terminal, found a free hotel shuttle to a place over on Security Boulevard, then caught the bus from there to Dickeyville. Two buses because he couldn't walk the final mile with that heavy suitcase. In the end, it took almost three hours to get from the airport to the house, while the flight itself had been barely ninety minutes. That was okay. It just heightened the pleasure of the surprise, of the anticipation of walking through the door and saying jauntily, "I'm home!"

But the house on Sekots Lane was empty that day. Empty, yet with a sense of things having been interrupted very suddenly—his mother had clearly been in the early stages of preparing the Thanksgiving sauerkraut, one of those Baltimore customs that Sean didn't think to question until he ventured out in the world. Cabbage sat on the cutting board, a knife was in the sink. Hours later, the family car, yet another one of his father's Buicks, pulled into the driveway, and Sean, peeking through the curtains, saw his parents get out, Go-Go between them, almost as if he needed to be propped up.

"Oh—Sean," his mother said. "I didn't know you were coming in."

"I wasn't," he said, his happy secret shriveling, dying within him, displaced by whatever accident, tragedy, fuck-up had befallen Go-Go. "What's wrong with him?"

"A little woozy from loss of blood," his mother said.

"Loss of blood?"

"An accident," his father said. "Very common this time of year, according to the ER doctor over at St. Agnes. That place is a sea of sliced thumbs and fingers."

The bandage was on Go-Go's wrist. Sean looked at it, looked at his father, and decided not to say anything.

While his parents led their youngest son upstairs, Sean went back to the kitchen, examining the knife in the sink. It was clean. The cabbage may have been left behind, but there was time to wash the knife. Or maybe the knife was innocent. Maybe Go-Go had raked something disingenuous across his wrists just to get attention.

Go-Go wore long sleeves to Thanksgiving dinner. Sean thought of taking Tim aside and saying something, but Tim had brought his girl, Arlene, and was too wrapped up in her, wouldn't leave her alone for more than a minute or two with either parent, although both seemed to like her. And suddenly it was Sunday and it was time for Sean to fly back to St. Louis, and there was never a time, really, to ask anyone—his mother, his father, Go-Go—what had happened the day before Thanksgiving. To this day, he has never told Tim about the incident. What would he tell? He knows nothing. He supposes that he should be the one arguing that Go-Go's car accident was a suicide, given what he knows. But he believes it was like the Thanksgiving Day incident—not serious, an attempt at an attempt that caught Go-Go off guard by being successful. He was always trying to get attention.

At least, Sean thinks, getting into a cab that would probably cost forty-some dollars, *I learned not to try to surprise my parents.* What was the point, really? That was Go-Go's role in the family.

He arrives to a shining house, a cake on the sideboard, the table set for tea. "You didn't have to do this for me, Ma," he says, kissing her papery cheek. He likes being reminded that he's her favorite, even though he knows he's no longer deserving of the post. How did he and Tim end up switching places in life? How did Tim become the reliable one? And does that make Sean the loudmouth? Sean thinks it's the difference between Arlene and Vivian. One wife pushes her husband toward his family, the other drags him away. He wonders how Vivian will feel if Duncan falls in with a girl as relentlessly out for her family as Vivian is, as sure that her family does everything right and Duncan's does everything wrong.

And if it's not a girl—but Sean's mind balks, again. He simply has no idea how that works.

"Oh," his mother flutters, embarrassed. "It's not for you. I mean, of course I hope you'll join us, but an old friend is stopping by. Do you remember Father Andrew from St. Lawrence?"

"Not really. He came after I was already at Cardinal Gibbons, remember? I remember you talking about him, though. He gave you that Waterford pitcher, the one that Go-Go dropped, and he used to come to the house."

"Once," his mother says. "Just the once. For tea."

"Mom—" Suddenly he wants to ask her about that long-ago Thanksgiving. He wants to ask her about everything, all the things that they weren't supposed to ask. Why was his father so angry all the time? Why is she sad? Was she always sad and he didn't notice, or is the sadness new? Is he still her favorite? Does he deserve to be her favorite? What would she think if her only grandson—?

He says: "I'll clear out, after I've had a shower, let you two talk over old times."

Within an hour, he's sitting at Monaghan's Tavern, enjoying a beer, watching ESPN. He feels totally outlaw—a beer at 3 P.M. Sitting in the bar where his father used to go, which probably hasn't changed much in all that time. He takes out his phone, checks e-mail—a note from Vivian, saying that they've landed, all is well, although she's appalled by the hotel the church group has chosen and is trying to rebook; a few odds and ends from work, even though it's a holiday on the calendar. He calls up a number that he has left on his log yet never stored in his contacts. He summons it up, puts it down, summons it up, hits the wrong button, finds himself making the call that he honestly wasn't sure he was going to make until this moment.

McKey doesn't even have an outgoing message. It seems odd

at first, this complete void. He could be speaking to anyone's phone, even though he's pressing the number that her phone sent his phone last month, almost as if the technology was calling the shots. He decides the lack of a message is reassuring. McKey, unlike, say, Gwen, doesn't need to put everything in words. You can't imagine her with a Facebook page or a blog or a Twitter account. He speaks into the space she has left: "I'm in town. We should get together to talk. All of us—Tim, Gwen, me—or just you and me, whichever you prefer."

He's pretty sure which she's going to prefer.

CHAPTER THIRTY-SIX

Good Friday reminds Gwen of how deeply Catholic Baltimore still is. Although it's not an official holiday for businesses, many companies offer it as a flex day. And if schools are not already on spring vacation, students are guaranteed the day off. So she has brought Annabelle to her office, never really a good idea. The place fascinates Annabelle—for about forty-five minutes. Then the whining begins. Gwen has parked her in a conference room with a DVD player, a stack of Disney movies, a stapler, and some scratch paper and asked her to "work" on the paper. Like many children, Annabelle yearns to be useful. She quickly abandons the project, curls up in a chair, and begins sucking her thumb as she watches princesses cavort.

"There will be something," another parent in Gwen's group told her when she entered the China adoption program. This woman was going back for her second child, and Gwen initially appreciated her advice and expertise. "What do you mean by something?" she asked. They had met—it seems silly now—in a Chinese restaurant up in Towson.

"Well, in our first group, one of the girls was a hoarder. She hoarded immense amounts of food, trash. She was older, almost two. Another child clearly had medical problems. The question was how serious they were. The family had to take a leap of faith to bring her home."

"And?" Gwen could not believe how nervous she was about the answer to her question, how invested she had become, in the space of a sentence, in a family about which she knew nothing.

"She was fine."

"Did your daughter—"

"Lily."

"Yes, Lily. Did she—?"

The woman stared off into space, but that didn't keep her eyes from welling with tears. "There was a bonding issue. She was very attached to my husband, but she had nothing for me for a long time. It was hard." She swallowed, blinked, smiled. "But it turned out great. These are such great kids."

Inevitably, Gwen started trolling the Internet. She lasted about a week on a forum for prospective parents. It was too much, an aggregation of nightmares and dreams.

In the end, she didn't really have *something* with Annabelle, other than the expected developmental delays. She had been warned that Annabelle would think her new parents smelled funny and looked funny, that she would stare at the ceiling when overwhelmed. But her daughter had an indomitable spirit. It was a strange thing to think, but Gwen sometimes finds herself wondering how Annabelle would have fared if she hadn't been adopted. She believes she would have thrived. She believes her daughter would have thrived anywhere. Though Gwen and Karl are important to her, beloved by her, they're not shaping her in any way. She is who she is. All Gwen can do is stand by, rather helplessly, and love her to pieces.

This year Annabelle will spend Easter weekend with Karl, by his request, which surprised Gwen. Karl has never been religious and had no desire to see Annabelle brought up in his faith, Catholicism. They have been taking Annabelle to the little Presbyterian church in Dickeyville, a place that Gwen attended until she announced, at age twelve, that she didn't want to go anymore, and her parents didn't object. Gwen isn't sure what Annabelle is taking away from it, but it's a nice ritual, going to church, then stopping by her father's house for Sunday lunch.

But this year, Karl's sister has arrived from Guatemala, and he is putting on a bit of a show for her, taking her to services at the cathedral, making reservations for brunch at one of the downtown hotels. Gwen will be alone. Well, with her father, but alone. She has entrusted Annabelle's Easter basket to Karl, with careful instructions about where to put it this year. It kills her, not being there, but Annabelle will be out of bed by seven, maybe even six. For a moment, Gwen was tempted to tell her there was no Easter bunny, just so Gwen would have a reason to bring the basket the day before. But Annabelle is only five. She deserves several more years of believing in impossible, lovely lies.

The office, never a loud place, is still today, with most of Gwen's employees opting for the flex day. If she could drag her thoughts away from Annabelle, she could get a lot of work done. But what she really wants to do is go to the conference room and curl up with her, watch whatever Disney princess is enchanting her. Feminist that she believes herself to be, Gwen has no problem with little girls wanting to be princesses. Want to find the damaged women among you? Look to the ones who had their femininity thwarted at every turn, the poor hulking girls who were asked to play the boys' parts at their all-girl summer camps or schools.

Margery, her most aggressive, ruthless reporter, loves bags and shoes and wouldn't step out of the house without makeup. It's not an either-or world. It's possible to be a feminine feminist.

Becca, her assistant, pops her head around the door, and Gwen is instantly on alert. "Annabelle OK?"

"Oh, yeah. She's in heaven. She can't wait until noon, when I've told her we can go to the vending machines and pick two items each, as long as one of them doesn't have chocolate. No, you've got a call that came through the main switchboard. A woman, doesn't want to give her full name, very cloak and dagger, but she says she's been calling and calling your cell and you don't answer and she does, in fact, know the number to your cell. Clearly, she thinks this is somewhat urgent."

Gwen glances down, realizes her phone has been on silent. When Annabelle is with her, there's no reason to be vigilant about the cell. She touches the screen and sees a series of three calls over the morning, each from a number with the caller ID function blocked. But it's a number she recognizes, kind of. Local. A number she has dialed recently. She touches it, the phone on speaker, and is amazed how quickly the call goes through, how a voice jumps out of the line like a coiled snake.

"Jesus, about time," says the voice, which she recognizes as Tess Monaghan's. "You were on the verge of missing an opportunity."

Gwen turns off the speaker function and picks up the phone, which only piques Becca's interest, but so it goes. "An opportunity?"

A pause, a sigh. "My client is in town. And despite the fact that I have advised him strongly not to do this, he wants to meet with you. But the window is very small. He came here to meet with his lawyer. He has to go back home tomorrow, so the only window is early evening."

"He—so I'm allowed to know the gender now."

She is teasing, but Tess Monaghan doesn't seem to enjoy being teased. No one does. "You're going to know everything soon. Look, there's a movie theater out on Nursery Road. Meet him in the lobby there."

"Why there?"

"He can walk there from his hotel. He's already turned in his rental car, so he's kind of limited in his mobility."

"How will I know—"

"He'll find you. Frankly, I am hoping against hope that he stands you up or backs out at the last minute. I don't think there's anything to be gained by him talking to you—and much to lose."

Gwen is quite familiar with the movie theater on Nursery Road, which is barely five miles from her house in Relay. It is never crowded for some reason, possibly because of the larger multiplex a few more miles down the highway, which is part of an enormous mall. She, Karl, and Annabelle have come here for virtually every talking animal movie and Pixar film made over the last two years. It is a ridiculous place to try to have a conversation, she thinks, especially as the ticket takers begin to eye her skeptically. Is it so unusual for a woman to wait in the lobby of a movie theater?

An African American man comes through the door, sixty or so, and her stomach lurches. *This is it.* This is the moment she will be called into account, told that the man they left in the woods to die was someone's father, grandfather, cousin. She will counter, of course, share the horrible truth about what he did to Go-Go, but it doesn't balance out, not quite. Unless Go-Go's death balances it out. Chicken George died in a night. Go-Go spent years dying.

The man walks by, gets in the ticket line. She glances at her watch. The mystery client is going to stand her up after all. She feels relieved for some reason. He doesn't want to see her. He

306 / LAURA LIPPMAN

has nothing to say to her. This has nothing to do with Chicken George.

She checks her e-mail on her phone, checks her messages. Nothing. Now she's angry. She could have had this hour with Annabelle at the house. They could be sitting in the kitchen, dyeing eggs, baking. She's getting irritated at this phantom client whose on-again, off-again decisions have affected her. She begins playing a game of Angry Birds, feeling like a very angry bird herself.

"Mrs. Robison?" a man's voice inquires.

She looks up into the face of a white-haired man, broad shouldered, quite handsome. He is wearing a turtleneck beneath a well-tailored camel's hair coat.

"Yes." She doesn't even bother to correct him, say it's Ms.

"I'm sorry I'm late. It's farther than I realized, the walk here. It looked so close on a map. And I felt I was taking my life in my hands, walking along the shoulder. I thought there would be a sidewalk."

"There often aren't," she says, feeling stupid. "I mean—in the newer developments." She cannot imagine what this immaculately groomed man has to do with Go-Go. Perhaps he senses her confusion, for he extends his hand. He is the kind of man who takes another person's hand in both of his, holds it, making eye contact.

"I am Andrew Burke," he says. "Gordon Halloran knew me as Father Andrew, but I left the church several years ago. Last fall I asked Tess Monaghan to find him so he could do me a favor of sorts. He said he would. Then he changed his mind, and now he's dead. A possible suicide. I feel horrible about that."

Perhaps because he's a man who seems skilled at giving comfort, Gwen also wants to comfort him. "No one knows, for sure. If it was a suicide."

"But you think it is."

She wants to tell the truth. "Sometimes you can't know."

He shakes his head. "True enough. But I feel that I inadvertently pressured him. You see—we spoke, after Tess found him. I wasn't supposed to call, but I couldn't help myself. I'm afraid I frustrate her, with my inability to follow her instructions. But I wanted to hear from him—what I needed to hear. He ended up telling me things, things I think I should tell someone close to him. I considered his mother, but I don't think Doris could bear it. When I heard about you from Tess, I realized that's who I needed. A friend, someone who cared enough about Go-Go to ask questions after he died. Besides, you're a part of the story, aren't you?"

Gwen wants to run, dash out to her car in the parking lot and drive back home. Drive back in time. But how far back will she have to go? How far must she go to escape what has happened? *You're a part of the story*—well, she is. But so is Sean, so is Tim, and McKey. Why is she being singled out?

Because she wouldn't leave it alone. Because she had to go to the private detective, had to pry. Tim warned her not to do this. But how could she know that Tim would grow up to be not only smart but wise? When did that happen?

"Is there somewhere we can go? Somewhere private?"

"There's actually an airport bar outside security in terminal A," says Gwen, who has always wondered who drinks *outside* the security gates in an airport. Now she has one answer. People who can afford to sit while others rush by, people who want to be as anonymous as possible. "Let's go there."

"A drink would be nice," says Father Andrew—no, just Andrew Burke, not a priest, not anymore, which Gwen finds bizarrely comforting. He puts a gentle hand between her shoulders. It's as if he has had some experience with people who need help moving toward something unpleasant and inevitable.

Chapter Thirty-seven

As McKey's flight begins to make its descent into Baltimore, she hears the passengers start the usual patter about what they can identify on the ground below. "There's Big Lots. Is that Ritchie Highway?" "I see the Applebee's. The one on Route 175." The Chesapeake Bay should make it easy for people to orient themselves, yet much of what she overhears is off-kilter, people mixing up east and west. McKey finds the whole ritual strange. Who needs to orient themselves from the sky? By the time you identify where you are, you're no longer there.

She makes the final pass through the cabin. There's always at least one person who doesn't put electronic equipment away after the announcement. This time, it's a Kindle user, who maintains that the prohibition doesn't apply to e-readers. *Yes, it does, sir.* She's firm but not bossy.

It is almost eleven. The airport will be a ghost town, with all the newsstands and food places closed for the evening. She won't even be able to grab McDonald's on the way out. She'll end up eating canned tuna and whatever she can scrounge from her own fridge. She should shop tomorrow, make it special. No. That will spook him. She'll have beer and wine—shit, she told him she was in AA. Fuck it, she'll tell him she realized she didn't really have a problem. But isn't that what everyone says? Maybe she'll tell him the truth, that she was there to watch over Go-Go. But then he'll ask why. As always, the less said the better.

She picked up Sean's message in the shuttle on the way to Detroit Metro. "What are you smiling about?" one of her coworkers asked. McKey hadn't realized she was smiling. She knew he would call her. It has taken more than thirty years, but Sean finally wants to be bad, and he has chosen her. Not Gwen, *her*. There are some women who would say that's because Gwen is a nice girl while McKey is not, but McKey doesn't see it that way. For one thing, she doesn't think Gwen is all that nice. She cultivates the appearance, as many women do, but Gwen has lots of bad in her. Everyone does. Goodness isn't natural. All other living creatures put themselves first. Only people try to pretend they're different, that they have any goals beyond survival.

Sean probably wants a one-off, no complications. That's what she wants, too. She thinks. She's pretty sure. God, if he fell in love with her, imagine the headaches. He might get a divorce, which he probably can't afford, and then there would be his kid and all that shit. McKey is not angling for *that*. Although it would be cool if he fell in love with her short-term, if he got a little crazy for a while, then sobered up and went home. A prolonged fling would be perfect.

It's funny to McKey how men think they're in charge, making these decisions. They never are. If a man leaves his wife, it's because another woman has finagled him into asking for a divorce.

Or he gets kicked out, which wasn't what he wanted, even if he was having affairs and the like. Rita always engineered the end of her relationships. Shed Rick for Larry, shrugged Larry off to follow that big-talking loser down to Florida. She may not have made the best choices, but they were hers.

McKey could end it here. It's enough that Sean has called, that he wants to see her. To *talk*, he said in his message. Right, sure, uh-huh. I bet your wife doesn't understand you. I bet you've grown apart. She's very cold. She never pays you any attention, never has a kind word for you. McKey has heard all those things over the years. Not long ago she heard them from her ex, who came sniffing around her door, and OK, she let him in one night. No one got hurt. No one ever gets hurt if people are quiet and discreet and mind their own business. It's the talkers of the world who make trouble.

Tally Robison was a gossip, although she didn't have any awareness of this, proclaimed to be the opposite. When Mickey sat in her kitchen, waiting for Gwen to return from school on the cute little half-bus that kids took to private school—even her bus is better, she remembers thinking—Tally talked on and on, and all her stories were about how wonderful she was and how awful everyone else was. The drab clothes worn by so-and-so, the awful casseroles the other mothers brought to the church potluck. The wonder of her taste, her style, her knowledge, her wit. She would flip through magazines, sighing. *It's criminal to have the taste without the pocketbook*. McKey now thinks Tally overrated herself, but she was mesmerized at the time, nodding raptly over her miniature packets of Smarties and Twizzlers. Oh, the pain of being so beautiful, so bright, so stylish. How do you stand being you, Mrs. Robison?

She always thought it came down to the mothers. That's why Sean chose Gwen. Because he bought into those fables, the specialness of the Robisons. True, there was that dramatic rescue, the day he saved Gwen from the stream. But it was merely the climax to a story already written. He was going to choose Gwen no matter what. Mickey saw it coming a long way off, well before anyone else knew. Which was good. It gave her time to practice the art of not caring. An art that, three decades later, she has almost perfected. Being with Sean will obliterate everything else somehow.

Won't it?

There's the baseball field. There's the little park. There are the lights of the runway. Why do people need to narrate their lives? What is the point of all this talk, talk, talk? Words don't make things more real. *Quite the opposite,* McKey thinks. The more you talk about a thing, the less real it is. That's what she was trying to get Go-Go to understand before he died. Shut up, shut up, shut up, shut up, SHUT UP.

He finally did.

Chapter Thirty-eight

Tim hangs up the phone, looks at Arlene, and lies to her face with an ease that breaks his heart.

"Work," he says. "I need to go in to the office."

She says: "On a Saturday? Poor you," and rubs his shoulders. This is the payoff for being a relatively honest husband all these years. He can lie to his wife without her suspecting a thing. Interesting how scrupulously honest people and pathological liars end up sharing the same advantages. Those who never lie have so much credit stored up. Those who lie all the time get very good at it. It's the poor schmucks in the middle, the sometime liars, who suck at it.

He always had Go-Go pegged as one of the poor schmucks in the middle. But if Gwen is right—he shakes his head. She can't be right.

"I might as well go in now, get it over with," he says, grabbing the car keys, ignoring his daughters' wrathful looks.

"Is it the jewelry store murder?" Arlene asks.

"Sure," he says. He almost wishes she would call him on his shit, ask what could possibly require him to go to the office on a Saturday, short of a cop killing. But she doesn't pick up on it, only smiles and pats his shoulder again.

Behind the wheel of his car, he tries to concentrate on the roads even as he keeps reviewing the time line. If Gwen is right— if Father Andrew is telling the truth—

If. There is another way of looking at this. The old priest is a liar. And with Go-Go dead, he can spin the story however he wants. But why spin a story at all? What does he have to gain? With Go-Go dead, he's in the clear, assuming he's the one who molested him. Only he says he's not, that he's never touched a kid, and that he was counting on Go-Go to tell people that.

He also says that Chicken George never touched a kid. At least—he didn't touch Go-Go.

The priest was quite firm, Gwen told Tim. *Go-Go said he was molested by two high school boys in 1980. The night of the hurricane—*

Was in 1979, not 1980. People get those details wrong all the time. Trust me, Gwen.

But Go-Go said it was two high school boys, Tim. Not Chicken George. Why would he tell Father Andrew that?

Maybe he didn't. Maybe the priest is using Go-Go's death.

Father Andrew, it turns out, is essentially being blackmailed. A former student is threatening to go public with lurid tales of sex abuse in the parish. With the statute of limitations long past, he can't bring a civil or criminal suit, but he can ruin Father Andrew's life. The claim is baseless—Father Andrew says—but as an ex-priest and one who is now living openly as a gay man, he feels vulnerable. So many people don't understand the difference between homosexuality and pedophilia. Yet he refuses on principle to pay this amoral opportunist. His lawyer started assembling character witnesses, students who would testify as to his behavior. Go-Go was one of those students, and he had agreed to give a deposition.

Go-Go was making a clean breast of things. He wanted to know if he had to talk about other sexual experiences, in his deposition, and Father Andrew promised him that it wouldn't come up. He was only going to be asked about his relationship with Father Andrew, if he ever saw anything untoward. Go-Go said he was happy to do it. But then he changed his mind, refused to talk to the private investigator or Father Andrew.

Did he tell him—

About Chicken George's death? No. But he insisted he was molested by two boys, then blamed this older man.

Tim arrives at his mother's house. She has a book in hand, holding her place with her finger, and she looks surprised—really, almost a little annoyed—at her son's unannounced visit. It never occurred to Tim that his mother would prefer anything to seeing one of her sons.

"Sean's meeting you there," she says.

"Where?"

"The golf course. He said you were playing golf this afternoon, but he had some errands to run first."

Interesting. Why has Sean created such an elaborate lie to get away from their mother? But Tim instinctively takes his brother's back.

"Our tee time isn't for another couple of hours. Mom, where did you say you keep the stepladder now?"

"Why do you need the stepladder?"

"I just do."

She has to think—or pretend that she's thinking. "In the garage. I so seldom use it."

It is the stepladder from his childhood, the one that used to be kept in the upstairs hall closet, the one that he needed last month to put away things on the high shelf of the china cupboard. In the event of a fire, they were to drag the stepladder to Go-Go's room, lift the rectangular board that led to the attic crawl space, then proceed to throw a rope ladder out the attic window and clamber to the ground. The only problem was that their father never anchored the rope ladder to the sill, which meant it was useless. If the house ever caught fire, they would have been safer jumping out the second-story windows than clambering down an unsecured rope from the third. Still, the stepladder belonged in that upstairs closet. It's the only way to get to the attic. He was surprised that his mother had moved it to the garage. Now he has a hunch why.

It clearly has been years since anyone has pushed open the door, leading to the storage space under the eaves. Someone— Go-Go, his father, his mother?—has tried to nail it shut, but it's a piss-poor job. Tim pushes it with his shoulder and the nails slide from the thin, splintery wood.

Tim isn't particularly tall, but once in the attic he has to stay hunched to keep his head from grazing the ceiling. He pulls the chain on the single-watt bulb only to watch it die with a pop. There's enough light from the window for him to make things out, though. He begins taking inventory. On a set of low shelves, he finds the hockey gear that Go-Go wore in the Fourth of July parade. Hadn't he said he borrowed it? That was the summer of 1980. It never made sense, Go-Go showing up with that gear. Tim always assumed he stole it. But if Father Andrew is right—it could fit. Someone could have given Go-Go the mask, the stick, the padded glove to ensure his silence. Interesting, but is this reason enough to seal up the crawl space? He pokes and prods the various cardboard boxes, filled with the most incredible debris, stained clothes, and broken toys. Tim sees a pile of old sheets in the corner, yellow with age, wrapped around something, and he moves toward it, keeping his head low, almost crawling.

A steel guitar.

He rocks back on his haunches, tells himself that there is more than one steel guitar in the world, that the guitar's presence here means nothing. But it is Chicken George's guitar. Go-Go went back for it, went back to where Chicken George fell and took the guitar. Why?

Because Chicken George never touched him. Because it was all a lie. And Go-Go wanted to be caught in the lie, wanted someone to ask him about it.

When he comes downstairs, his mother is in her chair, but no longer wrapped up in her book.

"You knew it was up there," he says, not bothering with his professional techniques, not setting up a careful path of questions to which she must answer yes, so she can't deny the established facts. His father might not have been handy, but he would have done a better job at nailing that door in place. Go-Go, too, for that matter. His mother hid the guitar, his mother nailed the attic up and moved the stepladder, hoping that it would deter anyone who decided to go up there. How long has she kept Go-Go's secret?

"Yes," she says.

"Why?"

"Because I knew it meant something."

"What? What did you think it meant?"

"Something bad."

CHAPTER THIRTY-NINE

Clem hears the front doorbell, a conversation between Gwen and a man.
Karl? Has Karl relented and decided to let Annabelle spend Easter
weekend here? He feels Annabelle's absence keenly. As much as
he wants Gwen to stop being an idiot and go back to Karl, he likes
the fact that Annabelle has been here almost every weekend. He
has started reading *A Tree Grows in Brooklyn* to her, over Gwen's
protestations. Gwen says Annabelle's too young, which is probably true. But Clem thinks that Gwen's real problem is that she
wants to read the book to Annabelle and he is usurping her. He is.
Given his age, there is so much he will never do with this grandchild. He will never run alongside her two-wheeler. He couldn't
carry her even before he broke his hip. He feels as if he has missed
out twice-over on being a real grandfather. Miller's children lived
too far away, and now Annabelle has arrived when he's too old.

He might not even see her through grade school. *Gwen might have a little more empathy,* he thinks.

In general, Gwen might have a little more empathy. The problem is, she thinks she does. But Gwen's idea of empathy is that she knows how she would feel in any given situation. If she fell down and broke something, she would throw herself into physical therapy, do everything right, so why won't Clem? If she were Karl, she would pursue her runaway spouse, do whatever was necessary to woo her back. Gwen has a good heart, but a person can have a good heart and be self-involved to the point of blindness.

Yet it is Clem who does not register, not right away, how much distress his youngest daughter is in when she enters his room with a lunch tray.

"I thought I heard someone at the door," he says.

"You did. Tim Halloran stopped by."

"What did the lummox want?"

"He's not."

"What?"

"He's not a lummox, actually. Not really. He can be crude and coarse, and he was kind of a bully as a boy, but he's smart and surprisingly . . . " She does not find the word she's looking for. "We have to go out later. Tim and I. We need to . . ." Another sentence left unfinished, and Clem finally realizes his daughter is agitated, pale and drawn.

"Gwen, I feel you haven't been telling me everything."

"Everything?"

"About Karl. Why did you leave?"

The question catches her off guard. Her thoughts are far from her husband, her domestic situation. She seems almost relieved by the change of subject. She sinks on the chair next to his bed.

"There was infidelity," she says.

"You said Karl was insistent nothing happened, that he didn't even realize what that woman on the Facething was trying to do."

"No, not Karl. I cheated. Just once—no, that's a lie. I still can't tell the truth about it. More than once, but it wasn't what you would call an affair. It was something really stupid I did, but something I can't take back. Last summer, with someone at the office. Someone much younger. I don't know what I was thinking. I could be fired over it."

"And Karl threw you out?"

"No. He doesn't know, doesn't even suspect."

"So why did you leave?"

"Because I don't want to tell him, but I don't know how to go forward if I don't tell him. Yet if I do tell him—"

"He will throw you out."

Gwen shakes her head. "Worse. He'll forgive me. If only for Annabelle's sake. But I'll be in his debt forever, then. It will be official: I'm the bad one and he's the saint."

"Husbands and wives aren't working off a balance sheet, Gwen. Look, I think it would be OK not to tell him. I really do. This mania for honesty—"

She catches her breath, almost as if she has been hit unexpectedly.

"I'm just saying that people don't have to tell each other everything."

"Easy for you to say, with your perfect marriage."

He takes her hand. "Really? That's what you saw? A perfect marriage?"

"Yes. You never quarreled. You adored her. You *saw* her, encouraged her, praised her. My husband can't even pretend to be interested in what I do. And perhaps by the standards of what he does, it is shallow and trivial, and perhaps people shouldn't have to pretend . . ." Her voice trails off, her point lost even to her.

"Gwen, I'm not even sure your mother truly loved me."

"How can you say that?"

"We got married because she believed she was pregnant."

"That makes no sense. Miller was born more than a year after you married."

"I didn't say she was pregnant. She believed she was pregnant, but she was terrified of going to a doctor anywhere in Boston, assumed there was no way she could keep the secret from her parents. She all but asked me to marry her."

"Well, of course you did the right thing."

"No, you don't get it. She didn't tell me she was pregnant. She was proud. She didn't want anyone to think she made a mistake, that she wasn't in absolute control of her own destiny. So we married—and she lived with her mistake the rest of her life."

"She loved you."

"To the best of her ability, yes. And she stayed with me after she realized she was wrong. We never spoke of it. She had no idea that I knew. But I did, and there was always that seed of doubt there. I had to wonder if she loved me as I loved her."

"She was so young," Gwen murmurs. Excuses, always excuses. Tally trained everyone to make excuses for her. "Karl is older than I am, allegedly a grown-up. But he never thinks about anyone but himself."

"Gwen—most people don't think about anyone but themselves and maybe their children. Your mother would have walked through fire for you." A pause. "As would I. But we don't ask that of our spouses. Oh, we can ask, but we're sure to be disappointed."

Gwen shakes her head. "I've lived my whole life believing my mother to be happy, someone who struck a perfect balance before anyone even worried about such things. And now you're telling me it was a lie."

"Not a lie, exactly. But I don't think she ever stopped thinking about the life she might have—what might have been. If she had gone to Wellesley, as she planned, if she had studied painting seriously—well, she couldn't know who she might have been. The generation of women who came up behind her, girls barely a decade younger, were encouraged to do whatever they wanted. She ended up abandoning the painting she thought would be her masterpiece."

"The painting of the young couple in the woods. What happened to that?"

"She painted over it, gave up."

"I sometimes wonder about those paints, their toxicity, that poorly ventilated shed. And then there was all that diet soda she drank. Do you think either one could have caused her cancer?"

"I don't know. I don't care, Gwen. Knowing the cause means nothing. She was the love of my life, and I never regretted how our marriage came to be. But I'll never know if she would say the same thing."

"What should I do? About Karl? Go home and tell him everything? Go home and tell him nothing? For all the time we've been together, I've had the small comfort of being the good spouse, the one who made everything work. If I tell him about the affair, I won't even have that anymore. I'll just be the one who cheated."

"I've had only one marriage, Gwen. You've had two. Perhaps you should be advising me."

"I felt old," she says. "And unattractive."

"Dearest Gwen, there are only so many details I can handle."

She looks down at her hands, and Clem's eyes follow. They are shaking. The veins stand out in sharp relief, the skin is dry. He thinks about Gwen's baby hands, cupping his face. Annabelle's hands. Tally's hands, dry and a little coarse from being denuded of paint every day, how she hated to leave a speck behind. His daughter's hands make him feel so old.

"It's easier to talk about Karl, what I've done, than the thing that's really bothering me. Daddy—do you remember the night of the hurricane?"

It's a double blow—the use of "Daddy," the mention of that night.

"I wouldn't be likely to forget that."

"Tim and I—we've learned some things since Go-Go died."

Blabbermouth Doris. Who hasn't she told by this point?

"It wasn't true," Gwen says. "It didn't happen."

"Go-Go didn't die?" He is honestly confused, and that one moment of confusion scares him, as it always does. The inability to follow a conversation—that's a far more serious indicator of a failing mind than mere memory lapses.

"He wasn't molested. Not by the man in the woods. He lied, he and McKey."

"Who?" He decides it's the sheer anxiety that he feels at the mention of the hurricane that is making it hard for him to focus.

"Mickey."

"But why—"

"We're not sure. We—Tim and I—are going over to McKey's apartment and talk to her. Maybe Go-Go lied to her, too, and she was caught up in it. She was the one who pushed the man—we never told you that part, McKey begged us not to, she was terrified, and it was an accident. That's when he hit his head. That's why he died. But we thought—Tim and Sean and I—we really did think he had hurt Go-Go. It was easier to tell only that part. You see—we knew him. We visited his house all the time."

He looks at *A Tree Grows in Brooklyn* on his bedside table, a handsome special edition with illustrations of which he doesn't quite approve. That's not *his* Francie Nolan. He and Annabelle haven't gotten very far, but they have already read the scene in the first chapter, the one about the old man in the bakery, who is gross and unappealing to Francie. Then she realizes that he was once a baby, that a mother loved him, welcomed him into the world with joy. It is just what Clem used to think, walking up Eutaw to Lexington Market, seeing the city's saddest souls. Everyone was loved once. Everyone was a baby. He knows that not all children are loved, that many come into the world without provoking joy. But most do.

And now the moment has come. He must let his daughter know of his mistakes, his cowardice. No wonder Go-Go drove into a wall. His well-meaning mother had to tell him that his father killed a man, just for him, not knowing that the man was innocent, that she was inadvertently putting the murder on her son.

The chickens have come home to roost.

"Gwen," he begins. "I can tell you almost definitively that McKey was not responsible for the death of the man in the woods."

He starts, much as he gingerly made his way down the steep pitch of the hill, watching the swinging arc of light, knowing, yet not wanting to admit, that he is watching a man kill another man. It happened. And only by admitting it can he take the sin off his daughter, the other children. It's too late for Go-Go, but at least he can spare the others, assume the mantle of guilt that is his, his alone. He will walk through fire for his daughter, at last. *What if it was your child?* Tim Halloran asked him all those years ago. It is.

Chapter Forty

Doris watches Tim come and go until it is almost 2 P.M. He does not tell her what he is doing. He barely speaks to her at all. Why? Why is he mad at her? She did what a mother should do, tried to protect her son. It was no different from washing his sheets.

She found the guitar under his bed a week or so after the night of the hurricane. She knew there was no way that Go-Go could have come honestly by such a possession. She didn't know what to do. He had been through so much. It seemed wrong to ask him about the guitar. She took it away, put it in the attic. And over the years she was the one who made sure they had no reason to go up there. She moved the stepladder to the garage, put the Christmas ornaments in the basement. By the time she was done, the only things up in the crawl space were the guitar, the hockey costume, some old boxes, and the rope ladder. As far as she knew, Go-Go didn't even remember it was there.

Something bad, she told Tim. She has always known that the guitar stood for something very bad. But how bad could a little boy be, especially Go-Go, who didn't have a mean bone in his body? Yet it wasn't long after the discovery of the guitar that the bed-wetting started. Then he showed up with that hockey stuff, also expensive. She pretended to Tim Senior that she bought it, told him she used money from a birthday check from one of her aunts, withstood his criticism for being wasteful when the household needed every dime.

Something bad. The truly bad thing was when Doris told Go-Go about his father, what he had done for him. Her intention wasn't only to raise Tim Senior up in his son's memory. She also— oh, what parent feels like this?—yearned to tear Go-Go down a little, let him know of the sacrifices made for him. She was tired of his brooding, his "poor me, poor me, poor me" routine. He had a house nicer than any Doris had ever known, two beautiful little girls, and a good-enough wife.

All she wanted him to say was thank you, or words to that effect. To say that Tim and Doris did right by him, the best they could. To tell her that it wasn't her fault that he couldn't get his life together. Was that wrong? She tried to explain herself to Father Andrew yesterday, without telling him all the details. But Father Andrew isn't as satisfactory a confidant, now that he's not a priest. She isn't sure why that should be, and maybe it's just her own prejudice, but he seems less wise to her now, and much less sympathetic. He's of the world now. He has lost his perspective. He wears a turquoise ring.

Tim goes out to his car, carrying the guitar. Good. She should have gotten rid of it long ago.

"Are you going to throw it in Leakin Park?" she asks him.

"Throw it—?" He shakes his head. "Sure. Why not? It's where all Baltimore's best dead bodies go."

"Will you be here for lunch tomorrow?"

"It's Easter. We're always here for Easter lunch."

"So you don't hate me?"

He could be a little quicker in his reply, but when he does answer, he seems sincere. "No, Mom. I don't hate you. I know you always had Go-Go's best interests at heart."

"When I told him about your father—I thought it would make him happy. Well, not happy, but proud. Loved."

"I know, Mom." He kisses her on the forehead. "You meant well. You always meant well."

"You called me the enemy of fun."

"What?"

Even Doris is surprised by how this old grievance bubbles up. "Your father, but all of you agreed, behind my back. You didn't know that I knew, but I knew. You thought I wasn't fun."

"Being fun isn't the most important thing in the world."

"We'll have fun tomorrow," she says. "With the girls and Easter lunch. I have all the usual things. Ham and sweet pota-toes."

"We'll have fun tomorrow." Although he's only echoing her words, and with less conviction than she would like, it has the weight of a promise. They'll have fun tomorrow. Whatever is happening is happening only now, and it will be forgotten by to-morrow. A person can forget a lot, if she's willing to try. Doris has always been willing.

CHAPTER FORTY-ONE

Gwen finds herself almost laughing—almost—when Tim tells her the guitar is in the trunk of his car.

"Exhibit A, prosecutor?"

"I know," he says. "It's ridiculous. But I wanted it out of my mother's house. She thinks I should throw it into Leakin Park, and maybe I will."

"So why bring it?"

"Because it's concrete. Real. Nothing else is. Real, that is. We have our memories, but Mickey is the only person left who can tell us what really happened that night, why she covered for Go-Go."

"And my father." She has to ask. "Tim—can he be prosecuted?"

"Legally? Yes. Your father says he witnessed a homicide and didn't report it. At the same time, he also says he didn't believe it, not until my mother visited him a few weeks ago. He managed to persuade himself that he couldn't know, in fact, that my father killed Chicken George. But my dad's dying declaration changed that."

"As an officer of the court—are you obligated to tell someone? Someone official?"

"Yes."

She wants to cry, she wants to pummel him, she wants to throw herself out of the car. It's unfair, this mess that his father has left behind for hers. Before she can do any of these things, Tim says: "But I'm not going to. *We* didn't do anything, Gwen. You, me, and Sean. We agreed not to tell the grown-ups that Mickey pushed Chicken George, or that we had an ongoing relationship with him. But we believed everything we said. My father believed us. Your father, too."

"What about Rick? He was there as well."

"He died a year ago. I found his obituary online. I think this is a case where all the lucky ones are dead."

"You can't call Go-Go lucky."

"No—no, that's true."

"I wish we could find Sean," Gwen says. They have both tried him repeatedly, but his cell phone goes straight to voice mail, and they have been reluctant to leave any message beyond "Call me." Gwen is actually a little hurt by Sean's inattention.

Tim gives a laugh that's a good imitation of the sound she made when she heard about the guitar. "I have a hunch he'll meet us there."

McKey's apartment has a security system that requires visitors to call up. But when Gwen reaches for the receiver, Tim grabs her and sweeps her up in an embrace, pressing her against the wall and pretending to kiss her, although he has his hand over her mouth.

Frightened by his odd behavior, Gwen is getting ready to kick him in the shins, then stops when she realizes his intent. He is counting on the person entering the vestibule to be embarrassed and not protest when Tim grabs the open door and hustles in behind them.

"It's not much of a security system, especially if the apartment number is next to the name," he says. "They should use random codes, so people can't find someone if they sneak in as we did."

"It was a neat trick."

"Thanks. I stole it from a movie."

He pounds on McKey's door even as he presses a button on his phone, sighing when he hears a distinctive ring tone from the other side, a burst of classical music.

"You have McKey's number in your phone?" Gwen asks, mystified.

"No," Tim says. He pounds again, speaks in a firm voice. "It's Gwen and Tim. You have to let us in." There is no sound on the other side of the door. Tim presses a button on his phone again, the same ring tone sounds from the other side of the door. But what does this prove, Gwen thinks. McKey clearly is not here. She just happened to leave her phone behind.

Tim speaks into the door. "I've got Vivian's number in my phone, too. I'm dialing that one next."

Vivian?

"It's a three-one-seven number, right? Is that the cell or the home phone?"

McKey answers the door, wearing a floor-length robe, a bit of floaty lavender far too pretty to be useful. Gwen cannot begin to read the look on her face. Triumphant? Smug? Angry?

"Why did you bring Gwen? Do you think it makes you look less pathetic?"

"I don't think I'm the pathetic one in this situation. I mean, I'm not the one who had to make up a lie about a golf date so I could cheat on my wife." He walks over to her coffee table. Gwen sees a bottle of wine, two glasses, both with some dregs.

"I thought you were in AA," Gwen says stupidly. It's easier to focus on this small detail than the larger one, the buzz of words from Tim, the details that don't track. Two glasses. Cheat. Golf date. That robe.

"I was," McKey says. "Then I realized I'm not an alcoholic, that I was just a little unnerved by some episodes before the holidays. I can drink in moderation."

"Yeah, two glasses is really moderate," Tim says. "Look, let's not drag this out. His phone is here. We heard it ring."

"He stopped by earlier today. I didn't realize he left it here. This is awkward. I'm entertaining."

"I bet you are," Tim says, holding his phone out at arm's length. Gwen understands. He can't read the screen close up without reading glasses. "Here's Vivian's number—I wonder if I can set up a conference call among our three phones."

Sean comes into the living room, fully dressed. Gwen wants to laugh at the silliness of it, this odd little moment straight out of a bedroom farce. Sean proper and composed, as if the fact of his clothing, his combed hair, proves he's innocent. Yet she's sad for him, too. *Oh, Sean. I wish you had told me what you were thinking. Because I would have talked you out of it.* Not out of jealousy, although she admits to herself that she is jealous, that she does feel as if McKey has seized something that was hers. But mainly she's sad because he's done something he can never take back. And she knows he'll want to take it back, whatever the outcome, even if there is no outcome. Her father may be right about people being too honest. But the problem with cheating is that you can never be spared that knowledge about yourself, whether you tell or not.

"We forgot our prop," she says to Tim, not wanting to think about what's happening here and now.

"That's okay. We won't need it. We might all need alcohol,

though." McKey has no intention of playing the hostess, so Gwen goes to the kitchen, finds it stocked with wine and beer and a healthy array of whiskey, although no food. She brings a selection to the table, with a choice of glasses. She herself selects bourbon. She's not driving in any sense of the word. Let Tim take the wheel.

"Over the past twenty-four hours, Gwen and I, separately and together, have learned a lot of things that change everything about what we thought we knew about the night of the hurricane." Tim is in his professional mode. "First—and this is going to be hard to hear, Sean—Gwen's father says that Chicken George was probably alive when they got to him, but our father killed him, beat him to death with a flashlight. And our father told Mom as much the night he died."

Sean shakes his head. "If that's so, it would have been reported at the time. There weren't so many bodies dumped in Leakin Park that such a thing would have gone overlooked."

"It didn't. But the body was out there for a very long time, much longer than anyone could have guessed, washed into a culvert. It was months before it was found, but it happens that there is an open case from the winter of 1980." Tim looks at McKey. "Was it hard, going back and seeing him there, or had the stream already washed him away?"

Gwen understands that Tim is testing McKey. There's no reason to believe that she took the guitar, but the accusation might shake something loose.

"I didn't go back."

"Someone did. I found the guitar in my family's attic today. And it's hard for me to imagine Go-Go going back by himself, to see the body of the man who allegedly molested him."

Gwen sees Sean's head snap up at the adverb *allegedly*. McKey has no reaction, and that's reaction enough.

But all she says is: "I don't know why Go-Go did what he did. He's dead, so I'll guess we'll never know."

"Want to know something interesting about Go-Go's death, Mickey? A few months ago, an old priest from our parish asked Go-Go to be a character witness for him. A former student had come forward, said he had recovered memories of sexual abuse, seemed to be interested in shaking cash out of the archdiocese or even the priest himself, who comes from a well-to-do family and has pockets deep enough to be attractive to someone angling for a quickie settlement. Go-Go agreed to be his character witness. Then he abruptly backed out, wouldn't even answer phone calls from the person trying to set up the deposition. Why would he do that?"

"Why do you keep asking me about Go-Go, what he did? He's not *my* brother."

Gwen realizes that McKey is even smarter than she ever knew, careful not to say anything. She has not made a single assertion so far, other than insisting that she didn't take the guitar, and she may be telling the truth. But she knows Go-Go wasn't molested by Chicken George.

"Go-Go did tell Father Andrew that he wanted to do this for him because years ago he was molested by two high school boys, but he lied and blamed it on someone else. The weird thing is, based on what he told Father Andrew, he was molested by the older kids in 1980. So what really happened the night of the hurricane? What did you see? Why was Chicken George chasing you, trying to grab you? You, Mickey, not Go-Go. He tried to grab you—and you pushed him."

"Only because I was closer to him. Go-Go was faster. I went to the cabin. I saw Chicken George touching Go-Go. He chased us."

"I think you took the guitar that night and that's why he chased you. It never made sense for him to run after you with it, as you said."

McKey smiles. Why is she smiling? "Suit yourself. But, as you recall, your brother and I agreed on what happened. What little boy would tell such a story if it wasn't true? As for the high school boys—I don't know what that's about. Maybe Go-Go thought that was more credible. Maybe Go-Go liked sex with men."

Sean has been listening intently, trying to catch up. He is uncomfortable, Gwen knows, with having the least information of anyone in the group, and now he breaks in. "That's ridiculous. Go-Go wasn't gay."

"I'm not saying he was." McKey's tone, when talking to Sean, is earnest, sweet. She's trying to create teams. With only four of them, they can go two-on-two. "I'm just playing Tim's game. He's making stuff up. I'm making stuff up, to show him how ridiculous it is. Look, I'm truly sorry about your dads. It can't be fun, finding out your fathers are killers. It was easier on everyone when we thought this was an accident."

"Rick was there, too," Tim says, even as Gwen tries to parse McKey's grammar, her tenses. *It was easier on everyone*— She already knew this part. She knows about what Tim Senior did. Yet Go-Go didn't even tell his brothers. Why would he confide in McKey? Because she's as responsible as he is for whatever happened.

"Yes. Well, Rick wasn't my father. It's different. Still, they did what they did. Don't make this about me."

"Go-Go told Father Andrew—"

"According to Father Andrew. And who knows what Go-Go would say on any given day?"

Something tugs at Gwen's memory. Tim said something about picking pockets. She hears a squeal of brakes, a woman's laugh. She is standing on the steps of the private detective's office. No, it's not that moment. It was something from earlier in their conversation, something about her methods, which even she found deplorable.

"You went to AA to spy on Go-Go, just like the private detective's operative did. No, not spy, because obviously he saw you and knew you were there. You wanted him to see you, wanted him to know you were watching him. You wanted to make sure that he didn't talk in AA, the way he did to Father Andrew. Why did you care, McKey? What secret did you need Go-Go to keep? Chicken George's death? Something else?"

McKey drops her eyes to her lap and picks at the embroidery on her robe. It's pretty, feminine, the kind of thing that Tally used to wear. In fact, it's a dead ringer for an old robe of Tally's that was in Gwen's dress-up box. They played dress-up on the rare days they spent indoors, and McKey, who lived in overalls and cutoffs, always chose the frilly, girly items.

Gwen thinks about the cabin, the night of the storm. Why would McKey and Go-Go have gone there together? It has never made sense, McKey stumbling on him there, two of them winding up there independently. No one went there alone—except Sean and Gwen, and she didn't want to go anymore because she thought someone was watching them. Tim said straight out that he tried to watch them only once, in the Halloran basement. So if someone was watching—

"Did you spy on us, in the woods. You and Go-Go? Did you watch us?"

McKey's posture is defiant, but she won't meet Gwen's eyes. "It was an accident. We went there to play and you were . . . already playing. Anyone would do what we did."

"But it wasn't just the one time, was it? You went back. You went back again and again. You went back the night of the storm, but we weren't there." No, she and Sean were in her bedroom, trying to figure out how much they could do without arousing Tally's suspicions. And Gwen, as always, was the bolder one. Sean was scared to death of being caught.

"You went to watch us, but we weren't there. We hadn't been there for a while. What did you do, Mickey?" There is no doubt in Gwen's mind that Mickey is the person to whom she needs to talk, the one who has the answers. "What did Chicken George see?"

"Nothing."

"Mickey—"

"A game. Just a game."

"A sexual game?"

Mickey's eyes skate, looking for a safe place to land. She decides on Sean. "I guess you could call it that."

"He was nine. You were almost fourteen."

"There was no law against it."

"There is now." Gwen has no idea if this is true, and she looks to Tim for confirmation. But he and Sean seem mainly bewildered, unsure of how to react. "You had to know it was wrong, otherwise you would have admitted it. Chicken George knew it was wrong. Even Go-Go must have known. That's why he followed your lead, when you lied and said Chicken George molested him."

"*He* pushed Chicken George. Go-Go. From behind. All these years, I was protecting him."

But not even Mickey sounds convinced of what she's saying, and Tim comes back to life. "Oh, come on."

"He did. I was covering for him. That's why he was willing to lie, because he was the one who hurt him. We weren't doing anything bad. We made each other feel good. What's the big deal?"

"He was nine," Gwen repeats.

"Most nine-year-old boys would be thrilled to have a girl touch them." She appeals to the two men in the room. "Am I right?"

Sean starts to stammer something, then stops. "Don't ask him," Tim says. "He'd pay a crack whore to initiate his son into sex if it could keep him from being gay."

"Fuck off, Tim. Duncan's not—"

"*Out,* Sean. Not out. But everyone knows he's gay. His cousins get it, even our littlest. Mom has figured it out. Everyone but you. Has it ever occurred to you that Duncan hasn't come out because he can sense you're less than thrilled, that he's being solicitous of your feelings?"

Gwen sees Mickey's eyes gleaming. She has distracted them, divided them. She's winning.

"What about the boys?" Gwen asks her.

"What boys?"

"The high school boys. The ones that Go-Go told Father Andrew about."

"As I said, maybe he liked sex with boys." She tries to give a blithe shrug but can't pull it off.

"Did it appear that he liked it?"

"What do you mean?"

"I think you were there. You made it happen. If it was just you and Go-Go, that one time, then he might figure out one day that he really hadn't done anything wrong, but you had. So you made sure that he had other things to be confused and ashamed about. You came up with more *games,* knowing that Go-Go would always want to do whatever the big kids were doing."

Mickey curls into herself. She crosses her arms, brings her feet beneath her. She's like the turtles she used to torture, poking them with sticks so they withdrew all their limbs, even the snapping turtles. Gwen can tell that she's not going to talk, not to her. And not to Tim. Gwen looks to Sean, who is flushed and angry. Over the comments about his son or his brother?

Gwen asks: "Why? Why did you do it?"

Although it is Gwen who is pressing her, she addresses herself to Sean. "I didn't think it was wrong. I wanted to be with you, but you chose Gwen. So I chose Go-Go."

Tim says: "If you had wanted to fool around with one of Sean's brothers, I would have been glad to oblige."

If he meant the joke to distill the tension in the room, he has failed. Not even Tim seems amused by this brief return of his lummox self.

Sean asks: "Is Gwen right, Mickey? About the boys? Did you do that to Go-Go?"

"Hockey mask," Tim says. "It's in the attic, too." Sean nods. Gwen has no idea what they're talking about.

Mickey shakes her head. "I gave him that. I got the money out of my stepdad, telling him it was for school stuff." She looks small, sitting on her sofa. Gwen remembers the girl she met almost thirty-five years ago. So pretty, so scruffy, so lacking in things that the others, even the Halloran boys, took for granted. A girl who would be your best friend for a drawer full of candy.

"You know something?" Gwen is speaking to the Halloran brothers. "Go-Go never said anything about Mickey. Even to Father Andrew, whom he told about the high school boys. He lied about Chicken George to protect her. All these years, he's protected Mickey, for whatever reason."

"Because they're responsible for a man's death," Sean says.

Mickey—and she is undeniably Mickey again to all of them, so young and vulnerable she reminds Gwen of Annabelle after being caught at something, miserable not at being caught but about being bad, which no one ever really wants to be—picks at the lush, embroidered flora of her gown, which is riotous with green tendrils and scarlet blossoms. *Pretty,* Gwen thinks again of the silk robe. Not the gown of a femme fatale, but of someone who wants love and romance. She is repelled by what Mickey did but can't disavow her.

Yet it is Tim, the father of three girls, who goes to sit next to her. "Talk to us, Mickey. Tell us everything that happened. We won't turn our backs on you."

"But you did," she says. "You all did. Except Go-Go. You left me."

"We're here now."

She takes a sip of bourbon—from Gwen's glass. "For all these years—for all these years—we felt responsible. Chicken George grabbed me, and I pushed him to get away. He fell. It was our fault, even if we didn't mean to do it. Then this priest comes along and Go-Go wants to tell everything. *Everything.* For his own sake, not caring what will happen to me. I told him it was too risky to talk at all. We were responsible for Chicken George's death and that's something that never goes away."

"Not legally," Tim says.

"Not in any way," McKey says.

"What about the high school boys?" asks Tim. "The ones that Go-Go told Father Andrew about?"

"I met some guys when I went to the new school. Seniors. They wanted to mess around, and I was cool with it. Go-Go wanted to play, too. You know how he was. He always wanted to do what we were doing. So he wanted to do this, too."

"No," Sean says. "That I don't believe. You forced him."

"He didn't know enough to know he shouldn't like it," Mickey says. "And, yeah, they gave him money sometimes. Gifts. Bribed him, I guess, so no one would tell. But they were more interested in watching Go-Go and me do things together than in doing things to him. They laughed at us."

"But they did do things." Not a question on Tim's part.

"Nothing—nothing invasive. I mean, you can probably guess. Then they got bored. It was no more than three, four times. And, okay, it fucked Go-Go up a little. But he managed. He kept going, more or less—until your mom told him what your dad did. That's when he went off the rails. Yes, I went to AA to watch him, make sure he didn't break down and confess. Mr. Halloran was dead and had nothing to lose. If Go-Go started telling people about what happened—I wasn't sure where it would lead. I didn't know what to do."

"Here," Gwen says. "We ended up here."

Tim puts an arm around Mickey, tender and careful. Gwen sees in that moment something she will tell Tim later: *She didn't choose you because she looked up to you, because you were more of a father to her than any of the men who passed through Rita's life. She needed someone she could control, and that was Go-Go. She was trying to hurt all of us through Go-Go. She did—herself included.*

Gwen will tell Sean things, too, when the time is right. That he shouldn't confess to Vivian what happened here today because, in a way, it didn't happen today. It happened a long time ago. Today was simply the resolution, a bill that came due. Her father might be right about this modern mania for honesty. It isn't that we talk too much or talk too little, Gwen decides. It's that most people choose an all-or-nothing approach. They speak of everything, or they speak of nothing. When we confess, it's because we need to be absolved, and we don't care how that affects others.

Yet Gwen decides she will unburden herself to Karl. She will tell him what she's done, the stupid affair—and forever forgo her role as the perfect, put-upon spouse. She has wronged him in a way that obliterates every slight, every moment of inattention and neglect. Because he's Karl, he won't hold it over her head. He will forgive her eventually. He will forgive her, but he won't ever forget. Sadness will move into their house, an invisible sibling for Annabelle, a quiet, sneaky child who will on occasion misbehave outrageously, if only to remind Gwen that she's there. It will be hard. It will be worth it. Allowing one's self to be forgiven is just as hard as forgiving. Harder in some ways. Because to be forgiven, one first has to admit to being at fault.

Mickey needs them. They need Mickey. They will never be five again. They won't even be four. But there's no doubt in Gwen's mind that Go-Go would want them to take care of Mickey, that he wishes her no harm. Go-Go was the most generous of all of them.

Gwen goes to Mickey's kitchen, pokes around, knowing she will find a stash somewhere. Yes, here are circus peanuts, candy Boston baked beans, and in honor of Easter, Peeps. She puts them on a plate and sets them in front of Mickey, urges her to eat, joins her. Tim and Sean also join in, although without much enthusiasm. It all goes down surprisingly well with bourbon.

Chapter Forty-two

Gwen went home.

We all went home. Gwen to Karl. Sean to Vivian. Tim to Arlene, although there was never any suspense about that. It's not clear who told what to whom. We no longer share everything. But then—we haven't shared everything for a long time. It's possible we never shared everything.

Doris stays in the house on Sekots Lane, where she continues to entertain—or not entertain, depending on one's perspective—all her grandchildren, including Go-Go's daughters. There are even visits from Duncan, at Sean's insistence, three-day weekends carved out of his crammed schedule. That is Sean's newfound talent, being insistent with Vivian. Duncan has yet to reveal his college preference or his sexual preference, but Sean is trying to find a way to convey that he is comfortable with anything Duncan wants, or is.

Clem left his dream house and has taken up residence at an assisted-living facility in the D.C. suburbs, a mere thirty-five-minute drive from Gwen's home, as close as many of the retirement communities Clem might have chosen on Baltimore's north side. He has made a full recovery, although his hip aches on cold, sharp days. The Robison house has not yet sold, and Gwen agrees with Karl that it is wildly impractical for them. It is a unique property, to use the real estate parlance, waiting for a special buyer, someone who values trees, if not light, and a sense of isolation. A new Clem Robison.

We try to stay in touch. Of course Tim and Sean were always in touch, but now Gwen checks in with them from time to time, which is more than she used to do. They talk about their kids and their parents. These are dutiful conversations, full of pauses. If the subject of Go-Go comes up, it's only in the safest of memories. *Remember how he chased the ball into the street that time? Remember how he danced?* It's hard to say how much longer this will go on.

McKey has made it clear that she does not care for speaking on the phone. But a few months after we saw one another last—and that night, in her apartment, was the last time we were together, probably the last time we will ever be together—she sent everyone a note, announcing her marriage to a man she met on one of her flights. A botanist, she wrote, underlining the word three times. The other three talked among themselves about the meaning of that underline. Sean thinks she is excited to have met someone who has made a profession out of the thing she loved most. Tim thinks she just likes to underline things.

Gwen believes that McKey wants us to know that she has been rewarded, which is proof that she never did anything wrong. And who knows, maybe she didn't. Maybe they were just two children, playing a game, as children always have and always will. Maybe she was as much a victim as Go-Go of the high school boys. Maybe. It is hard not to judge things from where we stand now, by the standards of the present, but we try not to. A girl and a boy played at being grown-ups. Another girl and a boy imitated them. Was anyone right? Was anyone wrong?

We take a step farther back, consider our parents. Clem Robison marrying Tally when she was barely out of high school. Imagine how Tim would feel if a thirty-two-year-old man dated his high school daughter. Rita, flitting from one man to another as if they were cheap furniture, things you acquired with no intent of keeping. Was she liberated or merely pathetic? Doris and Tim Senior, left on the sidelines by a quirk of timing, too old to join the fun, too young not to miss it. At least Tim got to march in one parade.

Chicken George remains in the pauper's grave where he was buried more than thirty years ago, the usual arrangement for a man who dies as a John Doe, with no family to identify him. We are his family. We would come forward to claim him if we knew his real name, but we never even thought to ask his real name. That's how incurious we were. Our parents allowed us to roam the thickly wooded hillside of Leakin Park, while warning us about its dangers, large and small—hair-matting burrs, the polluted stream, the poisonous red berries on those spiky shrubs, rusty nails, broken glass, the possibility of rabid animals and, after the fact, the alleged pervert in the ramshackle house. They tried, they really tried, to anticipate everything that could bring us harm. But it was us, in our naïveté and heedlessness, who were to be feared. We were the most dangerous thing in the woods.

ACKNOWLEDGMENTS

*This is the most autobiographical novel I have written in strict geographi-*cal terms. For many years now, I have been circling the unusual neighborhood in which I grew up, determined to write about it, but wanting to wait for the right time and story. Very careful readers—one might even say obsessive—will realize that several of my previous books have gotten close to this territory. The cabin in the woods, the crafts store near High's Dairy, Monaghan's Tavern, the dead-end highway, Leakin Park, the cops and the attorney sitting in Towson Diner—they've all shown up before.

But because Dickeyville and Leakin Park are real, it's important to say what's not true in the preceding pages. There is not and never has been a house such as Clem Robison's in what would be the 4700 block of Wetheredsville Road. The Hallorans' house on Sekots is also wholly an invention of mine. St. Lawrence, the

Catholic parish school near Dickeyville, has indeed closed, but I know of no allegations against any priest who worked there in the 1980s. All the families in this book are drawn from my imagination.

Perhaps because this book was intensely personal, I asked for less help than I usually do. Still, I am grateful for the daily support of: Carrie Feron (and everyone at William Morrow/HarperCollins); Vicky Bijur; David Simon; Ethan Simon; Theo and Madeline Lippman; Susan Seegar (my favorite bookseller); Dorothy Simon. I have stolen jokes from my brother-in-law, Gary Simon, often enough to give him credit here. And while Dana Rashidi technically doesn't work for me, she's awfully good-natured about the way my life bleeds into hers. Alison Chaplin has become a vital part of my writing process. Alison has called my attention to factual errors in the text; to the extent that any remain, it is because I do think novelists have some leeway. I also am grateful to my two "offices"—Spoons in Baltimore, Starbucks in New Orleans—and the people who work there. A special shout-out to Niki Hannan.

But nothing would have gotten done this past year without the help of several wonderful young women, especially Sara Kiehne. A woman is only as good as the people taking care of her children. A man, too, probably. Like Tally Robison, I am keenly aware that I have only a limited amount of time to work every day now, that I must put my work away before the sun goes down. Unlike Tally, I am happier for it.